SHIPWRECKED ON AN UNKNOWN SHORE

There was a cluster of coconut palms nearby. Ridge was determined to shimmy up one of them, and did so, despite the impossible grip and the sting of broken flesh. He scraped his chest through his dress shirt and roughed the insides of his arms. His bare feet were of little use, owing, in part, to the gash on the sole of his right foot. He wrapped his legs around the tree and gradually pulled himself to the top. With his face pressed against the bark, he let go of the palm with his right hand and swung at a couple of coconuts. They tumbled to the ground.

Ridge lowered himself a few feet and jumped the remaining six to the ground. A splintery pain shot from his injured foot through his leg. He tumbled to the sand and stared at the coconuts until he recovered his grit. He gathered up his prizes and took them to a cluster of rocks along the surf. He held one over his head and smashed it with two-handed force. The sharp crack echoed through the bush and up the foothills.

The soft gritty coconut hardly satisfied Ridge's cravings but the simple act of eating bolstered his confidence. "I can make it," he said to himself, gazing across the inexorable waves. He grinned at the thought of looking like a mountaintop sage when he and the others were rescued.

He got to his feet and tucked the remaining coconut under his arm. His eyes lingered on the distant atoll where Mira was doubtless worrying about him. The coral rise was an indistinct disk. He started up the beach again, pushing against the sand with his toes, stretching. His wound was an aggravating throb. Then he stopped.

Where the beach mingled with the bush, a half-dozen aborigines stared down at him from the shafts of their throwing sticks.

Other Works in the Nightscape Series

Main Series Books
Cynopolis
The Dreams of Devils

Double Feature Books
No. 1: The Thousand-Eyed Fear | The Q for Damnation

Short Fiction
Spawn of Cloud & Sword

Comic Books
Entombed

Plays
The Barren Cross

Films
Nightscape (or, Road without End)

Albums
Project Nightscape, *To Sin Against Our Mercies*

NIGHTSCAPE
EARLY DARKNESS

David W. Edwards

IMPERIAD
ENTERTAINMENT

Portland, Oregon USA

Imperiad Entertainment
Portland, Oregon USA

First Imperiad Entertainment trade paperback edition August 2017.

For information about special discounts for bulk purchases, please contact Imperiad Entertainment at info@imperiad.com.

Cover art by Santiago Caruso (www.santiagocaruso.com.ar)
Designed by Ryan Peinhardt

Manufactured in the United States of America

ISBN 978-0-9897487-4-2

For more on the Nightscape universe, visit www.nightscapeseries.com

For my wife, Michelle, and my sons, Devin and Brant

NIGHTSCAPE
EARLY DARKNESS

David W. Edwards

Acknowledgements

Once again I've had the privilege of working with editor extraordinaire, Sarah Cannon. Her clarifying notes and creative suggestions helped improve this manuscript in every respect. Thanks also to Michael Malone for his encouragement and insights throughout the drafting process.

Contents

Etymology

gold (n.)

Old English *gold*, from Proto-Germanic **ghl-to-* (source also of Old
Saxon, Old Frisian, Old High German *gold*, German *Gold*, Middle
Dutch *gout*, Dutch *goud*, Old Norse *gull*, Danish *guld*, Gothic *gulþ*),
from PIE root **ghel-* (2) "to shine," with derivatives referring to bright
materials, yellow colors, bile, and gold (compare Old Church Slavonic
zlato, Russian *zoloto*, Sanskrit *hiranyam*, Old Persian *daraniya-*, Aves-
tan *zaranya-* "gold;" see glass (n.)). Finnish *kulta* is from German;
Hungarian *izlot* is from Slavic.

gold (adj.)
c. 1200, from gold (n.). In reference to the color of the metal, it is recorded from c. 1400. *Gold rush* is attested from 1859, originally in an
Australian context.

—*Online Etymology Dictionary*

Extracts

Here, in this desert, there live amid the sand great ants, in size somewhat less than dogs, but bigger than foxes. The Persian king has a number of them, which have been caught by the hunters in the land whereof we are speaking. Those ants make their dwellings underground, and like the Greek ants, which they very much resemble in shape, throw up sand heaps as they burrow. Now the sand which they throw up is full of gold…

—Herodotus

One came to the war all over gold, like a girl. Poor fool! it did not save him from cruel death.

—Homer

If it were possible to cure evils by lamentation and to raise the dead with tears, then gold would be a less valuable thing than weeping.

—Sophocles

You are, all of you in this community, brothers. But when god fashioned you, he added gold in the composition of those of you who are qualified to be Rulers (which is why their prestige is greatest); he put silver in the Auxiliaries, and iron and bronze in the farmers and other workers.

—Plato

O accursed hunger of gold, to what dost thou not compel human hearts!

—*Virgil*

By gold all good faith has been banished; by gold our rights are abused; the law itself is influenced by gold, and soon there will be an end of every modest restraint.

—*Sextus Propertius*

And a river went out of Eden to water the garden; and from thence it was parted, and became into four heads.

The name of the first is Pison: that is it which compasseth the whole land of Havilah, where there is gold;

And the gold of that land is good: there is bdellium and the onyx stone.

—*Genesis 2:10 – 2:12*

The fear of the Lord is clean, enduring for ever: the judgments of the Lord are true and righteous altogether.

More to be desired *are they* than gold, yea, than much fine gold: sweeter also than honey and the honeycomb.

—*Psalms 19:9 – 19:10*

Their idols *are* silver and gold, the work of men's hands.

—*Psalms 115:4*

How much better *is it* to get wisdom than gold! and to get understanding rather to be chosen than silver!

—*Proverbs 16:16*

There is gold, and a multitude of rubies: but the lips of knowledge *are* a precious jewel.

—*Proverbs 20:15*

Thou hast been in Eden the garden of God; every precious stone *was* thy covering, the sardius, topaz, and the diamond, the beryl, the onyx, and the jasper, the sapphire, the emerald, and the carbuncle, and gold: the workmanship of thy tabrets and of thy pipes was prepared in thee in the day that thou wast created.

—*Ezekiel 28:13*

And the building of the wall of it was *of* jasper: and the city *was* pure gold, like unto clear glass.

—*Revelation 21:18*

Hunger for gold is made greater as more gold is acquired.
—*Aurelius Prudentius Clemens*

Take, saith he, crude leaf gold, or calcined with mercury, and put it into our vinegar, made of saturnine antimony, mercurial, and sal ammoniac, in a broad glass vessel, and four inches high or more; put it into a gentle heat, and in a short time you will see elevated a liquor, as it were oil swimming atop, much like a scum. Gather this with a spoon or feather dipping it in; and in doing so often times a day until nothing more arises; evaporate the water with a gentle heat, i.e., the superfluous humidity of the vinegar, and there will remain the quintessence, potestates or powers of gold in the form of a white oil incombustible. In this oil the philosophers have placed their greatest secrets; it is exceeding sweet, and of great virtue for easing the pains of wounds.

—*Artephius*

Nature also forges man, now a gold man, now a silver man, now a fig man, now a bean man.

—*Theophrastus Paracelsus*

You are an alchemist; make gold of that.

—*William Shakespeare*

But in truth, should I meet with gold or spices in great quantity, I shall remain till I collect as much as possible, and for this purpose I am proceeding solely in quest of them.

—*Christopher Columbus*

But the true medicine of metals is referred to Malkuth, for many reasons; because it represents the rest of the natures under the metamorphoses of Gold and Silver, right and left, judgment and mercy...

—*Aesch-Mezareph*

Indian Gold, Heart of the Sun, Shade of the Sun, Heart and Shade of Gold—for it is stronger than Gold; it holds the gold in its heart, and is itself Gold.

—Martin Ruland the Younger, a.k.a., Martinus Rulandus

In Gold the seeds of Gold do lie, / Though buried in Obscurity.

—Jean d'Espagnet

Gold hath these Natures: Greatness of Weight; Closeness of Parts; Fixation; Pliantness, or softness; Immunity from Rust; Color or Tincture of Yellow. Therefore the Sure Way, (though most about) to make Gold, is to know the Causes of the Several Natures before rehearsed, and the Axioms concerning the same. For if a man can make a Metal that hath all these Properties, let men dispute, whether it be Gold, or no?

—Francis Bacon

I took the calcined gold and poured on it the secret spirit of vitriol. It dissolved the gold within twenty-four hours and extracted an essence like a ruby, leaving a white Body like fixed silver. Thus I could obtain the whole preparation and perfection within eight days, because the real spirit of vitriol has the power of attacking, decomposing, and liquefying gold without violence. No other menstruum can easily do this … Anyone in possession of it could produce the quintessence of gold—but not everything is revealed to us, nor would it always be good to do so.

—Joannes Agricola

Our science encloses the whole Magistery in one root ... This root contains two substances, which have only one essence however, and these substances, which are initially only Gold and Silver in power, become eventually Gold and Silver in act, provided we can well equalize their weights.

—*Francesco Maria Santinelli, a.k.a., Marc-Antonio Crassaleme*

This is the end of the Work; you have made the Elixir
    Making all the miracles which you have seen.
You have the golden Key, potable Gold,
    The Medicine of all things and perpetual Treasure.

—*AlexFoucher Toussaint de Limojon, Sieur de Saint-Didier*

The possession of wealth leads almost inevitably to its abuse. It is the chief, if not the only, cause of evils which desolate this world below. The thirst for gold is responsible for the most regrettable lapses into sin.

—*Jules Verne*

The Alem-Rahul sees as Adam did on the first day. The holy crystal is evident in everything and the divine in us shines through, spangling the earth and animal alike in airy gold.

—*Psalms of the Black Sun, Gnostic Wisdoms 8:21*

CHAPTER 1
Catastrophe

In the early morning darkness, the vintage pleasure boat juddered to a stop, startling Ridge awake. He wiped the sleep from his eyes and sat upright in bed. His fiancée Mira eyed him lazily. He screwed up his angular face into a look of great concentration, waiting... Christ almighty. A resounding shriek of fiberglass confirmed his suspicions. Something had definitely struck the boat, or more likely, the boat—no longer secured—had run into something, caroming around the South Pacific like a pinball among the sandbars, coral reefs and atolls. He slid off the bed and hastily pulled on the gray slacks he'd worn the night before.

Brushing her straight black hair from her face, Mira whispered, "Did something run into us?"

"I don't know," Ridge said. "Maybe we're drifting. I'll be right back." On the way out of the room, he tried the lights. Nothing. *Great.* "Just stay here," he cautioned Mira before slipping into the hallway.

On the stairway off the main salon, Ridge spotted Aaron about to enter the engine room. The two of them, sons of southern privilege, were the only ones aboard with yachting experience. They were old boarding school buddies, both Princeton Class of 1989. Aaron carried a flashlight and a diving mask. He was a stout bear of a man with squinty eyes too small for his round head. The soft moonlight streaming through the salon gave him a dim supernatural glow. "Aaron," Ridge called. There was a barely discernible Georgia lilt to his voice. Schooling in the north had stifled his accent.

Aaron paused in the foyer leading to the engine compartment, pointing the flashlight's beam at the carpet. "I'd say this is a red alert, Ridge." He stamped the damp loop pile carpet like a drum corps leader.

Oh, no. Oh, Christ. We're taking on water! Ridge rushed down the stairs.

Aaron put a big doughy hand on the door to the engine room.

"Ready?" he asked, and without waiting for an answer, pushed it open, releasing a gush of cold seawater into the foyer. He swore under his breath as the water rushed over his bare feet. Then he stepped into the engine room in his navy silk boxers. The water was almost knee-deep. The twin diesel Caterpillar engines were flooding with the silent alacrity of a bathtub filled with a garden hose.

Ridge looked at Aaron in open-mouthed disbelief then rushed into the room after him. *Un-goddamn-believable. One night on the open water and... blam! Total disaster.*

"Check the bilge pump," Aaron suggested.

"I am," Ridge said. His mind riffled through the possibilities. "The non-return valve's shut. All this water, it has to be a breach in the hull." He splashed his way back to the foyer. *Just what the hell happened? The anchor must have come loose.* He recalled a vague warning about those old fisherman anchors. He should have known better. *If only things hadn't gotten so out of hand the night before, earlier this morning—whenever it was they'd finally settled in—this would never have happened.*

"Yep," Aaron said, holding up a long pointed shard of fiberglass. "This looks promising."

Aaron may as well have plunged the fragment into Ridge's heart. What was he going to tell the Senator? Ridge had assured him and everyone else that he could handle the boat, secure it for the night. He could already picture the Senator listening patiently to his excuses: a slow nod of the head, a sage pitying look. The Senator wouldn't rebuke him; no, he'd only blame himself, say how sorry he was that he'd disappointed everyone. But the others would know who he really meant. "Check around. Look at the hull fittings and the intake hose on the cooling system and whatever else you can think of. I'm going to run to the pilot house and see where the hell we are."

Mira followed him, tying a cotton robe around her waist. A stiff ocean breeze scarcely diminished the tropical humidity. "What's going on?"

"I don't know yet," Ridge said, looking at the blanked radar. "Is everyone up?"

"I heard Kenny and Paige talking. I don't know about the Senator."

Ridge hurriedly manipulated the radar's trackball to change its scanning range. *C'mon, c'mon. Where are we?* Since the 58-foot cruising yacht had been anchored in open water, he'd left the radar on long-range scanning overnight. The radar worked by sending out short-duration radio bursts then calculating the boat's distance from surrounding land masses based on the time it took for the signals to return. Sometimes in long-range mode, however, the pulses were too long for the radar to calculate accurately. In those cases, the returning pulses interfered with the ones being sent out, rendering targets invisible. Ridge controlled for the duration of the pulse by re-setting the radar's range. Within seconds, an extensive array of green dots appeared on-screen.

"Looks like a barrier reef," Ridge announced. "Either that or a shallow." With the flip of a switch, he laid a navigational chart over the current image and studied the results. "No. It's a reef."

"But we were anchored, right?" Mira asked.

Was she questioning his abilities? Didn't she know he'd done everything he could? "It must have slipped loose." He tried again to recall the warning about fisherman anchors … Something about the way they're shaped … He would just have to embellish. "These old fisherman anchors—sometimes if the yacht swings with the tide or the wind, well, you know that both arms don't hook in, right? Sometimes then the line gets wrapped around the unburied arm and yanks the whole thing out." He wasn't sure that was the design flaw exactly, but it sounded reasonable. He pounded the air with his fist. "Goddamn it."

Ridge rushed down to the engine room to confer with Aaron. The water came to mid-thigh now.

"There's water in the engine, Ridge," Aaron said in a voice made nasally by a diving mask. His curly auburn hair was wet, matted to his head. "Just look at the crankcase."

"Have you found the leak?"

"Oh, yeah." Aaron handed him the diving mask and an underwater flashlight and pointed to an area behind the engines. "Bigger than a tractor tire."

Ridge slid the mask over his head, crouched down and eased his face into the water. The flashlight revealed a low jagged cavity along the wall. The sea beyond was Bible black. He felt so exposed. There was nothing between him and the endless sea. Nothing. Ridge assumed his full height, stripped the mask away. "Christ, are we in trouble."

"Yeah, I'd say this is *Salem Express* serious." Aware his natural tone had a mocking inflection, Aaron scowled to emphasize the sincerity behind the sentiment. The *Salem Express* was a Saudi ferry involved in a horrific accident two years earlier. The vessel had struck a reef in the Red Sea and sunk within ten minutes. Almost one-third of its 1,600 passengers were lost, most of them pilgrims returning from Mecca.

"We need to radio the nearest port right now."

"Where's the closest one?"

"I don't know," Ridge said. Why hadn't he checked earlier? Reflexively, he started spewing what he did know: "There's an atoll about a half-mile away. What about the bilge pump?"

"No good."

Ridge's heart felt increasingly heavy. There was no easy solution. "This is unbelievable. We're out here one day and … Christ."

"You think we should get in the life raft?"

"Abandon a half-million-dollar yacht? And the Senator … One of his high muckety-muck supporters owned it for Chrissake. But what else could they do? The radar indicated there wasn't even a sandbar or coral promontory where he could safely run the boat aground. "Guess I don't see a choice, do you? If we can't get the engine started, the boat's a lost cause."

"What the fuck?" shouted Kenny, the Senator's chief of staff, as he barreled down the stairs, stopping short of the bottommost steps already underwater. "Hey, Ridge, are you in there?" With his thick South Georgia drawl, the words came out: *you in theah.*

Ridge and Aaron exchanged exasperated looks. Ridge said, "Yeah, I'm here."

"What happened?" Kenny demanded.

Ridge stepped into the foyer, followed by Aaron. "I don't know exactly, but somehow the boat got loose and we hit a reef."

"We can repair this, right?" Kenny asked, standing on the stairwell in his Armani slacks and tuxedo jacket.

The question was meant to be an order. Kenny was an accomplished order-giver. He had a pinched face, mottled-pink skin and in his own words "an old soul" by which Ridge figured he meant wisdom beyond his years. What he exhibited most often, though, was an indomitable cunning. Politics was bloodsport for Kenny. Ridge sighed. "Look, it's complicated and right now we've got to radio for help."

"I'll do it," Aaron volunteered and started to squeeze past Kenny.

"Oh, no," Kenny said, holding up his hand. "This is Philip Loudon's boat. You know how much he's contributed to the Senator over the years? Just imagine the Senator telling him he lost the guy's prized yacht. I mean, y'all gotta do something to save the situation."

Ridge locked eyes with him. "Kenny, the engine's down, the bilge pump's down, the boat's powerless and who knows how far we are from the nearest port. The only thing we can do is radio for help, get in the life raft and wait for someone to pick us up. If the engines were working, I could run it aground somewhere, but the way things are … There's just no other way."

The eerie tap-tap-tap of the boat against the reef momentarily drowned out the conversation. The noise echoed menacingly in the still air below decks.

"You don't think anyone can get here in time?" Kenny pulled his charcoal blue jacket tighter across his naked chest.

"We screwed up, all right?" Ridge said. There, he admitted it. "We shouldn't have been out here in the first place. All of us got carried away celebrating and we just got stuck. Navigating these reefs and shallows at night would've been suicidal. Once it got dark, there's nothing we could've done but wait. I feel responsible, I really do. But right now, we don't have time for this. We've got to get everybody ready and get out of here."

Aaron asked, "How much time do you think we have? An hour? Less?"

"I don't know," Ridge said. "But we should plan for less."

"Once I get off the radio, I'll get some gear together in plastic bags or whatever we have." Aaron disappeared up the stairs.

"Just how did this happen?" Kenny demanded again.

Ridge brushed by him on his way out. "Why don't you get the Senator packed up? If we're lucky, we can indulge in recriminations later."

CHAPTER 2

The Rescue Plan

The six passengers assembled in the flybridge helm around the teak table, some sitting on the beige leather L-shaped settee, others standing. Since no one had anticipated a night at sea, everyone was still wearing formal evening attire from the night before. They looked like disheveled and bleary-eyed stragglers at an apocalyptic party for the *beau monde*. Ridge, wearing a dove-gray Italian suit without shoes, gestured to Aaron, who stood around the table with two large diving bags at his feet. "What did you grab?" He hoped this would be a tactical discussion—no finger-pointing, no blame-laying.

"Everything I could think of: first aid kit, metal match, knives, flares, flashlights, a hatchet from the fire extinguisher kit, a few blankets…rope, bottled water…uh…I found a clock radio, but no batteries." Aaron used a flashlight to peer inside one of the two drybags. He'd opted to go without a shirt, exposing his hairy chest and stomach. When he bent over, his gut oozed over his belt. He rooted around in the bag with his free hand. The tubular black bag—about the size of a gym bag—opened from only one end. An elongated flap clipped to the rim ensured a water-tight seal. He shook his head. "Nothing else."

"I got the food," Paige said, grimacing. "There wasn't much in the fridge or the pantry. Mostly snack stuff." Her Boston accent sounded a discordant note among the mellifluous southern inflections around her.

"I have to tell everyone, though," Aaron said with uncharacteristic gravity. "I was inflating the life raft—you know, how it automatically inflates—and it just got away from me. I mean, I shouldn't have done it on deck anyway, but that's where it was—under the helm seat."

"What do you mean?" Kenny snapped. "It just got away from you? The fucking raft went overboard?" His country accent gave the phrase an enfolding roundedness: *Tha fawking rahft want ovuhbawd?*

Looking at Ridge instead of Kenny, Aaron said, "I'm sorry. I don't know what else to say except I'm sorry."

There was an audible intake of breath. Senator Bryant Neeland rose from the settee, gesturing with his thin arms. His decade-old silk tuxedo hung loosely on him. When he raised his arms, he took on the appearance of a starved crow. He was the host of this affair, Georgia's tall patrician senior senator. Since his tour of duty in World War II fighting in the treacherous waters of Iron Bottom Sound, he'd often retreated to the primitive grandeur of the Solomons. A long-time campaign contributor, real estate magnate Philip Louden, regularly loaned him the use of a weathered condo on Santa Isabel. This time, the Senator had brought along what he hoped would comprise the nucleus of his campaign staff in an upcoming bid for governor. The group had flown into the ramshackle capital of Honiara three days ago and taken a chartered vessel to the condo which Louden shared with a Chinese businessman. The Senator had arranged for a cruise and formal dinner aboard Louden's Bell Marine yacht to consolidate his plans for the race.

The group had hardly begun discussing the campaign, however, when Kenny casually mentioned it was Paige's 27th birthday. Paige was a recent flirtation for Kenny, a New England liberal whose occasional hippie rhetoric belied her crystalline intelligence. While Paige had met the Senator briefly in the course of lobbying for universal health care, she was introduced to the others for the first time on this excursion. Petite, with close-cropped red hair, she sported waifish good looks and a sometimes misplaced sarcasm. Much to Kenny's chagrin, she'd referred to religious evangelism as "a jackbooted Babysitter's Club" in conversation with the Senator, a firm, albeit moderate, Southern Baptist.

The Senator, genuinely hurt that Kenny hadn't mentioned Paige's birthday beforehand, decided the crew should make an evening of it. He promptly broke out bottles of Glenlivet and Bombay Sapphire Gin as well as his own trademark bourbon; Aaron warmed Courvoisier VSOP over hot water; Mira put the infectious swing of Glenn Miller on the CD player; and Ridge arranged the furniture in the wide salon to allow for dancing.

Although Paige was the acknowledged *cause celeb*, the Senator had dominated the proceedings with his enthusiastic storytelling. His voice deepened by drink, he'd regaled them with tales from the Old South of Jim Crow and white primaries, how, for instance, a rival for his old House seat had played the race card by distributing a photo of the Senator with several black members of the Atlanta Hawks at a post-game champagne dousing. The story about racial politics that got to everyone, however, had nothing to do with electoral politics as such.

"Most of you know my daddy owned a large farm—wheat, cotton, corn, sweet potatoes, even did some beekeeping—so we had a good number of black farm hands," the Senator had begun, his lips wet with bourbon. "Some of 'em worked in the store, too. We had a little merchant store there on the farm. Anyways, when I was a senior in high school, everyone got all worked up about the Joe Louis-Max Schmeling fight. You folks are prob'ly too young to know that Louis was something of a symbol to blacks, like Jackie Robinson. So naturally, the black farm hands are all for Louis as the fight comes up and my daddy, he's for Schmeling all the way.

"You gotta understand something 'bout my daddy here. You know how they call people the pillar of the community? Well, daddy was like the Roman Colosseum of the community and, this was a while before civil rights you understand, he was a moderate on race. He called blacks 'nigras'—kind of a blend of 'negro' and, well …

"As the fight got closer and there was more and more talk 'bout it on the farm, I decided to get under my daddy's skin a little by making a bet. But I didn't just make any bet. I didn't even use my own money. Instead, there was this wholesaler's son, a college boy name of Hank who was goin' to school up north, University of Chicago or something. When Hank came home on vacation or whatever, he'd stop by sometimes to visit with my mama, who liked to hear the news from that part of the country, bein' from Wisconsin and all. Hank used to make daddy madder'n a wet hen by coming to the front door instead of the back, which was the accepted etiquette for blacks at the time. Daddy was a real stickler for form."

"That's what no one understands about the 60s," Paige interjected.

The Senator smiled indulgently and gestured for her to continue.

Paige had traded her usual bohemian attire for a slinky slip-dress. The dress's dirty neutral color and intricate lace neckline gave her a captivating vintage quality. "It wasn't about 'free love' or self-indulgence or anything," she said. "It was a rejection of outmoded social norms like that—ways of doing things that put down blacks and women and minorities in general, kept them in their place."

"Well, that became a motivating force for me—bringing the South out of that thinking, countering the Wallace vote."

Laying a hand on Paige's arm, Kenny said, "That was a big part of the Senator's farewell speech to the Senate—his record on civil rights and everything. Now, the plan's for him to emphasize a vision for the New South, beginning with a commitment to civil order, stopping crime, generally getting people to be better citizens. As Edmund Burke, one of the few good conservatives said, 'Good order is the foundation of all good things.'"

"And here I always thought it was the Good Lord or maybe the Great Pumpkin," Aaron said.

"No," Kenny said, "the Great Pumpkin's gotta be a liberal, what with sharing out candy and gifts."

Aaron countered: "I don't know. Charlie Brown got that rock. That's some Moral Majority shit right there."

"But that wasn't—"

"How did we get to talking about Charlie Brown?" Mira asked.

Kenny said, "Now you know what our meetings are really like."

"They just keep me around to referee, haw," the Senator said, punctuating his own joke with a honking exclamation. "Anyway, what was I saying? It was about Hank, yeah. Hank happened to be in town a week or so before the fight and even though he was a couple a years older'n me, he seemed to respect me and not just because I was white. And we got to talking and Hank brought up the fight, assuming I was for Schmeling and I told him, no, I thought Louis was the better fighter. In fact, I said I'd be happy to bet his money against daddy on the fight. He agreed right away. It was a five dollar bet, which was pretty respectable in those days.

"So on the night of the match, daddy hooked up an old radio to a car battery on the front lawn for the farm hands to listen to and we listened to the fight on the Zenith tombstone set in the livingroom. Daddy thought I'd made the bet as a lark. He refused to believe I was really rooting for Louis. Said I was 'smart as bait' to make that bet. As it turned out, Louis was in the pink of condition and took Schmeling in the first round by knockout. Of course, the guys out front let out a tremendous whoop and started carryin' on and daddy couldn't stand it. Sometimes he had a thumpin' gizzard for a heart. He went out there right away and told 'em to go on home, kinda shooshin' 'em like you would a whinin' child.

"And I shouldn't have told my daddy then, but I was so swelled up with emotion I couldn't hold it in. I told 'em the bet wasn't really mine but Hank's. He got really quiet and I thought for sure he was gonna bust me in the head. When we were in trouble—my younger brother or me—he used to say, 'I'm gonna wear you out 'til your hide won't hold shucks.' But he didn't. He pulled a five dollar bill out of his wallet and put it on the coffee table. Wouldn't even hand it to me. And I knew then there was a deeper divide between whites and blacks than I figured 'cause my daddy wasn't racist the way it was defined back then. But he thought I'd betrayed something, some notion of the country. I know he did and I knew even then that his idea of America was wrong."

"So that's why you ran for ... Congress, was it?" Paige asked.

"No, not exactly," the Senator said. "My passion on that issue came later. But that's how ingrained it was, that kind of thinking." He downed the last of his bourbon and said, "Anybody ready for another?"

The evening had worn on, with everyone drinking more than they should, and when they'd figured it was too late to head back to port, they'd dropped anchor and spent the night on the boat.

"Lord knows, we don't have time to start blaming each other," the Senator said, still feeling a little rummy. "In the full light a day, after all, I'm prob'ly more at fault than the rest of you. Right now, we need to concentrate on what's going to save us, what we'll need to survive."

"I did send the distress call," said Aaron.

"Channel sixteen? The international channel?" Ridge asked.

"No, I decided to go with the country music channel," Aaron said. His face was flushed pink.

"Just making sure." Ridge couldn't let anything to chance now.

"Well, stop, okay? We still have the two horseshoe buoys or lifesavers or whatever you call 'em. I think we should tie the bags—one on each lifesaver—and drag 'em. Other than that, we have to put on life jackets and swim for it."

"Pardon me, Senator, after your plea for sanity here," Kenny said, cutting his eyes at Ridge, "but this is fuckin' crazy. I bet a duck's ass-feathers that not even everyone can swim. There has to be another way to do this." His throat tightened in anger.

"Yeah, there is Kenny," Aaron said. "You know all those diving tours of sunken ships? You can be a regular attraction on one of 'em."

"Hey, it wasn't me whose Richie Rich sailing expertise got us into this fuckin' nightmare in the first place. Y'all just won't admit you fucked up."

The Senator intervened, waving his hands to signal an end to the arguing. "Kenny, this is my responsibility and you are beginning to waste precious time."

"Well, is there anyone who can't swim?"

There was a queasy silence.

Oh, this was the worst, what Ridge dreaded most—the moment when the guilty are singled out and publicly excoriated. Ridge looked at the floor. *Please, no one say anything. Please.*

The prolonged silence forced Kenny to recover his cool. "Where the hell are we going, anyway?"

"The radar shows an atoll less than a mile away," Ridge said. "I have a compass on my watch. Everyone will just have to try to stick close to me."

"Is that the plan then? Swimming for it?" Kenny sounded contemptuous, as if swimming were somehow beneath him.

"I'll drag one of the lifesavers," Aaron volunteered. "Kenny, you can swim, can't you? Why don't you take the other one?"

"Fuck you, Aaron."

"Oh, yeah. The first one to say that wins."

Paige stepped forward, embarrassed by Kenny's lack of civility. "I'll take it. I'm a pretty good swimmer. At least that's what the guys at the Cape used to tell me." The moonlight silhouetted the appealing curves beneath her gossamer summer dress. The outfit hung loosely on her slim frame. That, combined with her boyish cut, gave her the appearance of an Irish pixie.

"Why don't you take it, Ridge?" Kenny asked.

"Because I'm going to have to help the Senator," Ridge said. "You know with his arthritis he can barely swim. And he's never been comfortable in the water." He turned to the Senator. "You're not going to like it, but you're going to take my help."

CHAPTER 3

The Disclosure

Amid the hurried preparations, Mira put a hand on Ridge's arm and drew him from the salon into their cabin. Ridge followed reluctantly, preoccupied with finding a way to repair the breach in the boat's hull or safely run the yacht aground. There had to be something he could do to avoid the inevitable but what? His options dwindled with each passing moment.

"Ridge," Mira sighed. "I don't mean to add to your worries, but … I don't feel good about this—swimming to shore. There isn't any way we can get instructions over the radio?"

Scattered starlight provided the room's illumination. Ridge could barely make out Mira's face. He desperately wanted to see her expression. How could she ask that? The question amplified the shrill accusatory voices in his head. He was convinced some elegant solution lay just beyond his grasp, some forgotten trick he would remember too late. "Not that I can see."

She took his hands in hers. Her heft was a comfort to Ridge. She wasn't one of those privileged diet-trim girls who'd hung decorously around him at college. He'd tired quickly of that starched Main Line ideal. A pleasing warmth was more important to him than Rococo slenderness. Not that Mira was awkward-looking. On the contrary, she carried her classical figure with ease, the head held gingerly and fastidiously high, the dark gray eyes softened by polite reserve. "I'm not like Paige," she said. "I'm not a good swimmer. Being in a pool has always made me feel heavier. Probably from seeing my mom at water exercise class." She smiled at her little joke. "I just don't know if I can do it."

"With the life jacket on, you'll be fine. You can do a breaststroke kick. That's all you need to do—just move your legs and stay close." Even though Ridge believed in what he was saying, he knew his voice sounded too weak to be persuasive. The notion that he had put his fiancée in real danger, if only through inattention, had taken the wind out of him.

"I'm sorry, Ridge. I shouldn't have said anything. *Eppes*, I just feel nervous," she said, leaning into him. He drew her close. The back of her wool crepe gown gathered around her neck and shoulders.

He gave her a languorous squeeze. It was only a matter of confidence. He could handle that. "It's all right, honey. I know. We're all scared. But we'll make it. Just stay close."

Mira nodded, her mulberry-colored lips in a tense smile.

CHAPTER 4

The Main Chance

The Senator stood on the foredeck looking across the expanse of sea. The water glistened as though papered with fish scales. The large waning moon and wealth of stars were brighter than he'd ever seen. He tried to determine where the sea ended and the sky began. "My mother always told us to stay away from water," he explained to Ridge, who was busy fastening his life jacket. "You know, I grew up in a time when drowning was a real danger. You'd see stories in the paper all the time 'bout kids drownin' in the crick or the lake or even the little run-down well out back of the house. Swimming just wasn't encouraged." He looked uneasily down the length of the yacht which had begun listing to port. Inside, the chilling black seawater crept past the double doors aft of the salon.

Ridge wasn't listening. Even now, he thought he might formulate a better plan. "It's not like a personal failure or anything if I help you," he said, securing the last of the straps. "I was a lifeguard after all. And I know you try to downplay your arthritis, but the water's going to be rough and a half-mile in it is going to seem like forever."

"Oh, I know, Ridge. It's … It just makes me look helpless, like a burden."

All right, just pile on the guilt. "Now you're talking crazy. Without your generous invitation, we wouldn't be here to enjoy the islands in the first place."

The Senator offered a weak smile.

Ridge went over to Aaron and Paige, who were fast securing the drybags to the lifesavers with duct tape. He couldn't believe they were going to jump into the ocean. "Y'all just about ready?"

"Yep," Aaron replied without looking up.

Paige had stripped down to her sepia-colored silk slip. She seemed unconcerned that her panties and plunge drop bra were clearly visible. Ridge could see clear to Christmas. He tried to focus on her honey-colored eyes. "You're going to get awfully cold," he said.

"I'll be all right," Paige said. "The dress would never have made it and I figure once I get moving, I'll warm up." She glared at Kenny, who stood several yards away.

Kenny pretended to find something interesting in the singular blackness.

Paige had reluctantly accepted his invitation to take this trip after having known him for less than two months. She'd been uncertain of her feelings for him and felt awkward at the prospect of celebrating her birthday among strangers. She'd agreed to come partly on the condition that Kenny keep her birthday a secret. She felt Kenny had a lot to answer for given that his broken promise had led to the current situation.

Mira put an arm around Ridge's neck. "Not me," she said, pointing at Paige. "Don't expect me to do that."

"You won't hardly be able to move in that dress. You should at least cut it so it's above your knees." Ridge retrieved the scissors Aaron was using to cut lengths of duct tape and sliced Mira's dress from the hem to mid-thigh. Her legs were a creamy white, fleshy around the knees and ankles.

"Uh, uh, uh," Mira warned. "That's as far as you go, *neshomeleh*."

Ridge kissed her on the cheek then called to Paige. "Can you shine the flashlight over here for a second?"

"Like this?" Paige aimed the beam square at his chest.

Positioning his watch to catch the trifling ray of light, Ridge said, "I want to check the compass. Just keep it on me. I want to face the right direction from the deck." He negotiated the deck until the tiny pointer on the compass indicated he faced northeast. The compass was so small. How would he ever see it in the dark on the ocean? "Thanks." He nodded to Paige to aim the flashlight elsewhere.

"Should we throw the lifesavers in first?" Aaron asked nobody in particular. With a slip-knot, he'd looped the rope tied to the lifesaver over his right shoulder and under his left arm. There was about eight feet of slack between him and the lifesaver.

"I'll give you some help," Mira said. She bent down to push the lifesaver and its tied-on supplies toward the edge of the deck.

"Wait," Aaron said. "I don't want to go over first. If I'm pulling the lifesaver with all my weight, I'm afraid all our supplies'll shake loose and then where would we be? Here, let me take this off first and I'll get in after." Aaron removed the rope connecting him to the lifesaver and dropped it to the deck. "Okay, go ahead."

Mira edged the lifesaver under the stainless steel rails and into space. The supplies made a soft splash and bounded a few yards from the boat.

"Guess I'm next," Aaron said, stepping over the rails. "Here goes." He leaped from the deck feet first and disappeared for a moment in the liquid black. When he bobbed back to the surface, pulled by his life jacket, he jerked his head to one side to clear the hair out of his eyes. "The water's not so bad, Kenny. I told you."

Ridge leaned over the side. *At least we've got that in our favor.*

"What are we going to do with the flashlights?" Paige asked. "It's not like I can swim with it, you know, holding it in my hand. I guess I can use a little rope and tie it around my neck, but I'm not sure how much good it's going to do."

"I'm not carrying anything, Paige," said Mira. "Why don't I take it?"

"And Kenny can take the other one," Ridge said. "The more we can do to keep track of each other, the better. We don't know how the ocean's going to be—if we'll be able to keep from getting separated."

Kenny and Paige were next to jump overboard. "Go ahead," Kenny urged his girlfriend.

"Women and children first, is it?"

"Whichever fits."

"You're the one acting juvenile."

"Me? You've been complaining ever since Honiara."

"Can I help it if I dislike vacationing in other people's grief?" Paige turned to the Senator. "I don't mean to be ungrateful."

"Hey, no one liked Honiara," said Kenny, appealing to the group. "But you didn't have to be such a guilty Boston brahmin about it. No one likes an American apologist."

"That's right, ridicule me for caring about this trash planet. But I guess going negative's what you're best at, isn't it?"

Without another word, Paige turned her back on Kenny and shoved the second lifesaver's worth of supplies overboard. She climbed over the railing, her face reddened with anger and embarrassment. Then she slipped into the ocean with scarcely a splash. The water issued a soft gurgle as though it had claimed an empty milk carton.

Ridge stifled the impulse to applaud.

Kenny gave the Senator an apologetic look before he followed his girlfriend into the roiling water.

Paige maneuvered wonderfully in the Stygian sea, stretching her arms with short powerful butterfly arcs. Kenny, however, appeared tentative. Perhaps it was the ghoulish cast of the flashlight dangling from his neck, but he seemed to have taken on a dispirited pallor. The flashlight, rising and falling with the movement of the sea, was going to be a poor defense against the overwhelming night.

Mira's heart beat uncontrollably as she gave Ridge a hurried kiss. "I'm okay," she said. "I'm okay." Slowly, she climbed the railing and turned to face the darkness. Her shoulders heaved with her labored breathing. She glanced back at Ridge and before he could nod in encouragement, she jumped feet first, hands tense against her thighs to prevent her dress from billowing up around her waist. The tropical water rushed over her head with surprising force. For a moment, she felt weightless, suspended somehow above infinite space. Then she broke the dimly lit surface, anxious.

As she tread water, she felt constrained, her arms slack and useless against hostile immensities. Her doubts were a watery roar in her head. But seeing Ridge's eye on her through the flashlight glow, she smiled in a way she meant to be reassuring.

The deck was nearly pitch-black, the night and the ocean, absolute. The Senator found the handrail and cautiously stepped over it. Holding on, he turned to face Ridge then looked back over his shoulder to ensure he wouldn't land on anyone. For the first time in a long while he felt his age down to the nub. "All y'all out of the way? The old man's coming down." He pushed off, swinging his legs into oblivion. Though he was submerged for only a moment, he came up for air clawing at the emptiness.

Ridge was the last to leave the sinking hulk. From his perspective, high above the water, his friends appeared the hapless victims of some vast Manichean struggle. When he jumped, he imagined, he would shrink and shrink until—like them—he became a mere speck in a sea meant for giants. This was it. He was actually going to jump overboard. There was nothing left to try. Nothing he could think of anyway. He edged away from the boat and into emptiness, still disbelieving... When he burbled to the surface, he blinked hard to clear his vision. *The dark, Christ almighty.* The bleary moon and stars accorded mere gradations of black. Approaching waves assumed a pale mercurial aura as they lifted him up then darkened in the giddy down-going rush. But the other waves—the ones beyond and beyond—were impossible to make out.

His experience as a lifeguard seemed hopelessly trivial and remote. As part of his Red Cross training nine years ago, he'd hauled a classmate around a pool for 20 minutes with considerable effort, but he'd never been in a real lifesaving situation. *This isn't going to work.*

With a few broad arm motions, Ridge sidled up to the Senator. "Mira, I'm going to need the light." The feeble beam caught the Senator doing a shivery dog paddle. "Thanks," Ridge said. He told the Senator where to place his hands and legs. "This is going to seem funny, but it's the best way I know how."

"Yeah, well, don't expect no marriage proposal, haw," the Senator said as he leaned back. An unexpected wavelet washed over his head. The Senator straightened for a moment, choking. Big stress tears trickled down his bony cheeks. Then he leaned back again, placed his hands on Ridge's shoulders and wrapped his legs around Ridge's waist. Entwined with the Senator in this way, Ridge trialed an abbreviated breaststroke. It seemed a paltry gesture against the awful pull of events. "This will work fine," he assured the Senator. His charge nodded, eyes darting in fear of the ocean's next capricious affront.

Louder, to the others, Ridge asked, "Okay, is everyone ready?" He glanced at the small compass on his watch and kicked himself and the Senator into position. In a few minutes, he knew Mira would either be too distant or the flashlight too difficult to aim in the worrying sea to allow him to consult the compass again. "I'm going to go slow at first," he shouted as he saw Kenny slide inexorably over a swell and, temporarily, out of view. "We don't want to get tired early on."

Before starting out, Ridge looked at Mira, the curve of her neck, the intermittent view of her arms as she tread water. Christ. To die like this, together—so young and unfulfilled—as if they'd fallen into space. Ridge knew Mira believed that "all is in God; all lives and moves in God." But how could she justify His silence in this? The sea eased Ridge into a swirling gully. The salt-spray was sharp in his nose. The Senator searched Ridge for assurance as the ocean spun them around. His leonine head jutted forward and the cords on his neck strained against uncertainty. Ridge adjusted their direction with a few forceful strokes. His slacks chafed his upper-thighs. The trough shallowed out. The stars along the horizon vanished amid pitched shadows. Ridge braced for the next black wave. Sea blurred into circumscribing sky. He hoped for more life with Mira but refused to pray. To his mind, silence was consent.

CHAPTER 5

Castaways

Ridge lay on the white sand in a motionless sprawl. The afternoon sun warmed his face. The ocean lapping ashore sounded like the dull throb of an earache. He could make out a conversation nearby but the words were unintelligible, lost to the wind. Mira? Kenny? Definitely Mira, thank God. He sat upright with a solemn effort. His head pounded. Shielding his face from the luminous sky, he slowly opened his eyes. A blinding light. The beach stretched for a mile or so, disappearing into a hazy white nothingness. Ah, the goddamn ocean ... "Ridge, you okay?" Mira asked. Her voice resounded in his ears. She crouched to kiss him lightly on the temple. "You've been asleep a long time, *meshugana*. You scared me to death at first. I felt you breathing but thought maybe you were knocked unconscious."

Ridge turned to Mira, blinking up at her deep-set eyes. Her thick black hair curled down around her exposed shoulders and under her chin. There was a spirited blush to her cheeks. He brushed his lips against hers and leaned into her hair to breathe in the reality of her. She felt so good. Solid and warm. Mira pressed him close for several minutes until, at last, Ridge had shaken off the fears of the night before. With his hands on her shoulders, he gave her another soft kiss.

Kenny came up behind Mira in the remains of his tuxedo. He wore his customary expression of complaint. The dark lines at the corners of his mouth were drawn tight. His dress shirt was now sleeveless, his pants reduced to expensive cut-offs. A day's growth of beard gave him a mildly rakish appearance.

"We were wondering when you'd wake up," he said. "Sorry you missed breakfast with our *Gilligan's Island* crew. It's pathetic, but that's the first thing I thought of when I got up this morning—that stupid TV show." Kenny gave a halting laugh. "What a miracle, huh? Fuckin' crazy."

Kenny's voice aggravated the pounding in Ridge's head. "Is everyone all right?" He pushed himself unsteadily to his feet. "Where are the others?" He looked down for balance. His bare feet were crusted with sand.

"Paige's over there." Kenny gestured toward a cluster of palm trees at the water's edge. "She's gathering coconuts and whatever else we're supposed to eat on this rock."

Ridge rolled up the sleeves of his soiled dress shirt. *Okay, what to do now?* "What about the supplies?"

Mira glanced at Kenny, biting her lower lip. "Paige's are here … But *neshomeleh*, I'm sorry, but … No one's seen Aaron." The words tumbled forward too quickly.

It couldn't be true. He'd seen Aaron all the way through, right? He distinctly remembered … What? When was the last time he'd seen Aaron? There was the sight of him, soon after they'd abandoned the yacht, gripping his life jacket, kicking against the current … Beyond that, only the cold and the blackness, the incessant surging and swirling … Kenny looked from Ridge to the surf and back again. The sun flashed off his Christian Dior glasses. "You couldn't have helped him, Ridge. You had the Senator to carry. Everyone knew he was in trouble. He put on a good act, joking around like normal, but everyone could tell he was scared stiff."

What the hell do you know? Ridge trembled with sudden anger at Kenny's tone. He averted his gaze, looked at the ground. Aaron flashed across his mind's eye as a puckish classmate at Choate, dressed in an oversized pin-striped suit. *Aaron. Goddamn it.* Ridge was seized by a creeping guilt. His throat tightened. He managed to ask Mira, "Water?"

She handed him a half-full sports bottle.

Kenny droned on: "On deck, he had that blank look like he was already lost."

"I'm sorry, *neshomeleh*," Mira repeated.

Ridge took a draught of water. A hollowness had spread from his chest to his extremities. He was having trouble focusing. The haunting white landscape appeared cockeyed now. For a time at boarding school, Aaron had been the only thing that made life bearable. They'd shared juvenile insecurities about their families, about girls and sex, about their futures. They'd served as counterparts, equal and opposite in temperament: Aaron, wayward and jovial; Ridge, disciplined and intense. There was no sense of balance now, no rightness to things. *Christ. Why Aaron?*

Mira gave him her hand and drew him into a tight, comforting embrace. She counted on him to put Aaron's death to rest for everyone, to show hurt, anger, even guilt, just so they wouldn't have to be cautious around him, waiting for a breakdown.

Ridge closed his eyes and tried to screen out the world. Impressions of Aaron's last moments came to him unbidden: the ache in his vitiated lungs, the waves closing over the night ... Kenny cleared his throat, looking toward Paige. "We'll have some coconut milk if we can break them open." He turned back to Ridge. "Somebody ought to be looking for us. The mayday signal or whatever it was that got sent before we went down, right? And anyway, the Navy or whatever will be out looking for the Senator—once they figure we're gone."

Just go away, will you? "Right," Ridge said without opening his eyes. "Where is he?" His voice scarcely seemed his own. The paralyzing mixture of guilt and gloom which had first emptied him out began to solidify, to make a hardness in his chest. This was his mistake. He had to own it for the others. If only to relieve his effusive guilt, he needed to be strong.

"Exploring the rest of the atoll," Mira said, shading Ridge's face from the sun with her hand.

Drawing in a deep breath, Ridge sat up to study the coastline. "Have you seen any boats?"

"No, not yet." Kenny gave Ridge a quick hopeful smile. "But it looks like there's another atoll—a larger one—two-three miles away." He pointed across the phosphorescent green lagoon. "It looks large enough to have a port, even an old naval base from World War II. Who knows?"

Mira put her hands on Ridge's broad shoulders as he gazed across the ocean. The land or *motu* of the atoll appeared to be substantially above sea level. Ridge could make out a range of dense green foothills. A small island? He turned to Mira. Her high, round cheeks were pink from the hot sun. "I'm going to try for it." It would be the easiest way to move on—to get clear of the others, take charge of things. "I'm the best swimmer and the longer we're out here without sustenance, the weaker I'll get. We just have to hope that once I get there, I can find a fisherman or a village of some kind. Hell, for all we know, there could be a resort hotel." He attempted a smile. See? He could put Aaron behind him for the moment.

"Why don't you wait?" Mira asked. "There's no reason to go now when we don't know if we've been here long enough to spot anything or for anyone to find us. Besides that, the Senator hasn't come back. Maybe he's found something."

Why did she keep questioning him? First on the boat, now this... "I won't drown," Ridge said. "Look at how calm it is." The lagoon was deceptively placid. Borne by a mild breeze, the water ruffled gently to shore.

Ridge knew the sea beyond the atoll's barrier reef would be much swifter. He was grasping for reasons to take action. The thought of waiting for rescue, thinking of what he would tell the authorities, his father and invariably, the press, replaying scenes from the night before again and again, urged him on.

"Ridge, please," Mira said. "Don't do this. I know what you're trying for and drowning yourself won't help."

He was stunned by the way she'd gone straight at him. His voice cracked. "I can't just sit here. I can't—" Unwelcome tears came to his eyes, smearing the horizon. Goddamn it.

With a compassionate glance at Mira, Kenny started back toward his girlfriend.

"C'mere." Mira held out her arms for Ridge.

His strength gone, Ridge accepted Mira's embrace. He sobbed quietly, warm tears coursing down his cheeks. As soon as Aaron had slipped from the center of his vision, his defenses had collapsed. It was the talk about rescue that had done it, the mundane logistics which had nothing to do with his friend. He gave in to the levelling emotion, let himself cry a while to clear his head. He felt Mira's shoulders relax. She comforted him in silence. She knew to do that—to hold him and not say anything.

Gradually, the pressure in his chest abated and he became numb again if only through fatigue. The horizon assumed its proper clarity. He wiped away the last of his tears with the back of his hand and looked out over the galling-blue Pacific. *I have to do it. The sea is just a body of water. I don't need to fight it. This is a contest with myself.*

CHAPTER 6

Back to the Open Sea

After a late-afternoon meal of coconut water, saltines and smoky cheddar cheese, Ridge slipped on his bright orange life jacket and waded into the ocean. He pushed forward even though his arms and legs felt stiff and unresponsive. The waves splashed against his thighs. He turned around to see Mira, Kenny and Paige staring glumly back at him. Mira waved to him. Her gray eyes were rimmed with red. "Be back soon. *Hazak*," she called, repeating God's admonition to Joshua at Jericho: "strengthen thyself." She knew smatterings of Hebrew, Yiddish and German. She believed these phrases to be sacred—the language of personal revelation—and used them as linguistic charms to ward off danger.

Ridge returned her lazy wave then dove into the resplendent surf. The plunge quenched the heat of shame warming his skin but not its effects. He swam vigorously through the bright smooth sea for a few hundred yards. The effort felt surprisingly good, almost relaxing. With his face in the water and his eyes closed, he narrowed the sea to the thin strip of rippling foam that emanated from the tips of his fingers as they entered the water. Just inch forward… Yes, a strong pull now, smooth over the top… Okay… By concentrating on that small action, he avoided confronting the sea's austere depths.

His arms tired quickly, however, and his lips and tongue soon felt swollen with the salty brine. Keep calm… slow down. From shore, the water had looked dead calm, as easy to swim in as bathe. The invisible drifts which had plagued him last night had returned with equal, if not greater, intensity. He remembered the tugs and pulls of the ocean like fits in a dream.

Ridge paused to check his progress, treading water. The sudden flow of unrestricted air made him feel lighter, more buoyant. It also made him more conscious of the feebleness of his steady kicks against the sea. *Goddamn it.* Though it seemed he'd swum a good distance, the coral atoll behind him looked as radiantly close as ever. The clumps of mangroves and coconut palms along the shore caught the purled light from the water. His friends continued to stand on the shore looking after him.

The majesty of the sea and the sky dominated the sorry humanity on the beach. Ridge felt smaller and weaker than ever. He'd tried to live a principled life, to do right by others and what had all his efforts come to? One instance of misjudgment or perhaps, mere hard fortune, had reordered his life. Deep in his heart, he knew his future would now consist of endless assays at redemption. He would grow old before his time, always looking backward, waiting for the moment he could make things right.

Surveying the neighboring island, Ridge saw a twisted column of coral shining above the water, part of a fringe reef curving around the shoreline. He set his sights on that slender break in the drift. His initial pace was too exhausting. He resumed swimming, this time using a deliberate breaststroke. Pull, kick, all right, pull, kick... Ridge's life jacket bunched up around his throat. Crashing against the jacket, the sea intermittently lapped his face, filling his mouth and momentarily blinding him. Ridge could see flashes of the expansive ocean between dowsings, which inspired a wearying sense of awe. In a strange way, he thought, the ocean honored him with its constant threats, encouraging him to push harder, faster.

Scrambling from crest to crest, Ridge' breath grew ragged. He paused again to collect himself. Ah, ah, ah... The ocean swallowed him in greedy valleys then spit him out on fleeting promontories. He was alone, at risk against the wind and cold and continuous swells, far from any help, nothing to spirit him on but shame and animal fear. His lifeless body would cast the merest shadow under the sea.

Recollections from the night before came in flashes. Ridge estimated the grueling swim to the atoll had taken an hour or so. During that period, Ridge had considered everyone lost at one time or another. He'd noticed Aaron's hands tight around the top of his life jacket, riding the vigorous current. He'd yelled at him to kick toward shore. The sea had persisted in separating them with forceful, irregular motions. The coral reefs beneath them had created unexpected flows. His focus had been the Senator; he'd needed to make sure he wasn't taking in too much water. The Senator was so frail, his neck veins ropy with effort, his mouth twisted into a fearful O.

When Ridge had finally reached shore, he recalled putting his life jacket aside and checking on the Senator, Mira … *At least* the Senator and Mira. He thought he'd seen Aaron, though, as everyone collapsed on the sand. Had he imagined it? No other lucid images came to mind. Just the sensation of a headachy blackout sleep.

Aaron. What a friend he'd been, an outsider at Choate like himself but fearless in his isolation. He remembered that prank with the geese … He pictured Aaron chasing a half-dozen agitated geese down the hall of Choate's West Wing dormitory, throwing up his arms in a vain attempt to force the birds out the window leading to the fire escape and freedom. As a prank early that morning, Aaron had lured several geese from the nearby pond up to the second floor with a trail of bread crumbs. His intention, as he explained it to Ridge later, was to leave them for their headmaster to discover.

As soon as Aaron had exhausted his supply of bread, however, the geese had unexpectedly flown into a panic. They fluttered against the walls, honking hysterically and sending up small bursts of gray feathers. Fear of enclosure weakened their bowels and what started as a trifling joke turned into a literal shitstorm.

The commotion awakened everyone on the floor. Ridge and some of the other boys ventured into the hall, scrambling to the safety of their rooms whenever a bird skimmed overhead. The balding headmaster, spittle gathering at the corners of his mouth, chastised Aaron from inside his room. Aaron could scarcely breathe he was laughing so hard. Amidst a riot of feathers, his bathrobe thoroughly soiled, he clutched his knees for support. What was it Kierkegaard had said about being trampled by geese?

Aaron would have been expelled had it not been for Ridge's father. Not only was Aaron a notorious discipline problem, but his semester tuition was three months past due. His father had recently lost most of his inherited wealth in another failed entrepreneurial venture, and what remained went to medical expenses for Henry, Aaron's younger brother, who suffered from childhood leukemia. Whether Aaron's father was too embarrassed to talk about it or simply figured he'd find a way to make the payment, he hadn't told Aaron about the outstanding bill. Aaron found out from the headmaster the day before his hearing in front of the school's directors.

Aaron had been more worried about losing his friendship with Ridge than anything else. He'd confessed to his family's financial problems in a sort of invitation for Ridge to snub him. It would have made it easier to leave if he knew Ridge had rejected him because of money.

Instead, Ridge had persuaded his father to support Aaron's tenure at Choate and later, Princeton. With the exception of Aaron, he'd been nearly friendless at Choate. Aaron had encouraged him to take risks where he was once timid. The thought of boarding school without his one reliable companion was intolerable. Ridge would get himself expelled, too, if it came down to it. They were like brothers after that. Ridge's father had even served as Aaron's informal advisor, recommending his course of study and arranging jobs for him, most recently his stint doing logistics and fundraising legwork for the Senator.

It was near dusk now and the horizon assumed a menacing darkness. Ridge's brief respite had unexpectedly become a bleak holding action. He almost felt as though he could tread water in his sleep, the repetitive motions were so reassuring. The nearly stationary trade clouds threw ponderous shadows on the ocean. The face of the water bled from livid blue to black as if a storm were gathering in hell.

The westering sun exacerbated Ridge's growing insecurity about being on the open water. The coming blackness threatened to join everything below the stars in a horrifying limbo. There would be no warnings of attack.

Ridge stiffened momentarily at the thought of sand sharks. When he was in grade school, the Senator, then a member of the House, had told him an apocryphal story about a World War II pilot shot down over the Pacific. The pilot spent several hours in a life raft without food or water, unsure if anyone had spotted his bail-out. He soon made himself delirious with the thought of drowning.

Although the pilot knew he shouldn't drink from the ocean, he'd already convinced himself that his situation was hopeless. He leaned over the side to dip his cupped hands into the water when a sand shark surged out of the deep and took him under. As the Senator told the story, the rescue crew of the PT-boat found the raft empty.

Like many of the Senator's stories, this one was clearly fictitious (the crew of the PT-boat couldn't possibly have determined how the pilot died). Nevertheless, Ridge's recollection of it induced a welcome anxiety—an anxiety which pierced the dreamy temptation to give up. The unfamiliar horizon, the hypnotic rhythm of the wind-whipped waves, the deepening blue of the ocean: these things threatened to lull him to sleep. What kept him awake and moving was the reptilian instinct to flee or struggle.

The island gradually appeared in detail. Ah, at last . . . the shore. Ridge could make out some bushes and discrete groups of coconut palms. A ring of white sand gave way to a thick forest. The verdant foothills sloped to the west. The coral he'd spotted earlier was tantalizingly near. Just a little farther . . . The sun limned the horizon line with its waning glamor. Almost there . . . pull, goddamn it, pull . . . okay . . . switch . . . He resumed swimming breaststroke in hopes of relaxing his tight arm muscles.

The hook-shaped ridge of coral, framed by the spangled sea and the darkening sky, taunted him with romantic images of a castaway life. If only he and Mira could live that life, so sweetly primitive and free . . . Trees topped with large green fronds bursting with pomegranates and mangos . . . Papayas and frangipani, and some nameless golden fruit, polished and perfectly round . . . Three small streams providing them with clear fresh water. He imagined Mira laughing as she tried to balance a cornucopia of fruit in the folds of her gown.

The fantasy obscured the living dangers of the stark portentous deep. Below him, he knew, the ocean teemed with life: plankton in all its dazzling forms fed on shads, sardines, herring and menhaden; he was aware how these fish despaired of yellow tuna, barracuda and sharks. Further up the hierarchy of marine life, pelagic squids and sperm whales vied for mastery. Deep in the icy darkness, there were no comforting prejudices.

He swam breaststroke then tread water, flipped on his back and took up freestyle. The drift pressured him toward the lagoon, but he fought against it.

The tide was low when Ridge approached the fringe reef. He felt for it with his right foot, touched something solid. Finally. He pushed himself up. His arms were finished. He took a gulp of warm air and started toward shore ... *Christ, his foot.* Blood oozed up from between his toes, his right foot slashed by the coral. The delayed sting of salt water relieved the numbness. He stepped gingerly from one rock to another along the reef until he reached the thin stretch of beach. The sand was a dulling comfort.

Stupid with exhaustion, Ridge collapsed on his back and wriggled out of his life jacket. His arms were so tight with fatigue he could barely lift them above his head. The sun had descended faster than he'd anticipated. It was a ghostly aura behind the gathering mist. There was nothing more he could do today. He would lay in a clutch of grass higher up on the beach and sleep. The atoll where the others were making camp had been reduced to bare outlines. In the dusk, it seemed impossibly small and far away.

CHAPTER 7

The Senator's Story

Senator Bryant Neeland ranged aimlessly through the bushes toward the beach. He just wanted to be alone with his thoughts. Stunted Buka trees and desert magnolia vines dotted the landscape. He picked a heart-shaped leaf from a magnolia at his feet, twisted it idly between his thumb and forefinger. His gray hair was in wild disarray. The lines around his mouth, what his late girlfriend Sarah had called his "frown wrinkles," ran deep. He looked down at his sand-specked feet. Lord knows, he wasn't anxious to be rescued. He knew his political career was over. Last night's accident had finished it. There would be nothing left, no governorship, that's for sure, not even the chance for redemption as an elder statesman. He could write the truest, wisest memoirs and nay, nay, nothing but dust and ashes.

He walked on, permanently hunched from sitting for endless meetings, hearings and caucuses. Forty-three years. He'd spent more than four decades of his life—well over half—doing the public's business in Washington—first in the House then in the Senate. Now, what a way to go out ... He'd always hoped to retire on his own terms, his reputation for good judgment and plain-dealing unquestioned. He'd worked tirelessly for that reputation. He'd earned it, goddamn it. The press was sure to bury him now. Once the accident made the news, they'd be all over him about the owner of the sunken boat, Philip Louden. Great God. What kind of end was that? To go down with Louden ...

He'd first met Louden when he was making $30,000 a year as a young Congressman with a new wife. Competing with wealthier colleagues was tough when it came to delivering on lavish gifts and glamorous dinner parties. Neeland sat on the Banking and Finance Committee, a locus of attention for special interests seeking federal subsidies. Louden was the son of a prosperous Atlanta builder with an exquisite Japanese wife and a self-professed obsession with all things Asian. What a salesman—that shock of blonde hair, that full rich voice ... He seemed so worldly and important. Louden anticipated the advent of Japanese imports years before the first Toyopet Crown hit the US car market and knew where to find the best yum cha in Hong Kong. And he cared. Neeland was convinced he cared ... The sympathy, no, the pity, in Louden's voice at Neeland's financial straits ... He couldn't just ignore it, right?

At first, he resisted Louden's solicitations for monetary support. Yes, at first he'd puffed himself up, congratulating himself on his moral discipline. During that time, if he felt discouraged in his work, the thought of resisting Louden gave him renewed confidence. But soon enough, his confidence waned. What kind of advantage was moral superiority—unrecognized by the public—compared to a level playing field? That's all he wanted—an equal chance to make good on his promises. It was only a few "shrewd investments." So, a few months after his introduction to Louden, after his envy had grown stronger and his ambitions demanded richer tokens of success, he made the call. "If something comes along," Neeland told the businessman, "I'd be willing to look it over." Louden cut him in on a suburban apartment complex on the same terms as the rest of the Louden family. Neeland chipped in just $2,000 for an eventual return of $260,000 and change. Though Neeland had reported this investment as required by law, he'd significantly underestimated its value. He told himself he would have voted for those housing subsidies anyway, and besides, he'd refused every similar deal since.

The Senator cleared the bushes and walked along the beach. The coconut palms with their roots in the brackish sea made postcard-worthy silhouettes against the setting sun. The Senator took long loping strides. He didn't want to worry the others by staying out past dusk. He walked as though he'd never grown accustomed to his gangly body. He slumped his shoulders and lowered his head. The moist sand collected around the hem of his ruined silk trousers.

He considered his options for extricating himself from his anticipated problems. The lack of possibilities compelled him to stop for a moment. The idea of lying about his relationship with Louden to his friends and subsequently carrying out a prolonged deception made him tired. He couldn't *perform* like that, not in close, intimate settings.

Besides, he didn't know how he could suppress the truth. Perhaps it was time for him to finally rest. He could even settle down, learn to appreciate gardening or spectator sports, maybe write his memoirs, for history, though, discretion be damned. He'd lived alone in his 19th century home—full of baronial spaces and fluted pilasters—for almost thirty years. He was divorced and childless. His girlfriend, Sarah had died of breast cancer almost seven years ago and taken a good piece of him with her. His only legacy was the laws he would leave behind—scatterings of changeable, anonymous policy.

Oh, it was stupid to pretend. How could he rest with his reputation ruined? What kind of rest was that for a man with his sense of historic mission? He'd done wrong with Louden, sure, but only from a need to give him and his constituents a fair chance in Washington. "I don't know," he sighed. "I just don't know anymore."

As he started walking up the beach again, the evening mist sent a chill up his spine.

CHAPTER 8

The Island

By the following afternoon, the coastal mist had dissipated and the sky was an intense blue. Ridge walked the length of the beach with the lifejacket loose around his neck, looking for boats or some sign of civilization on shore. Hunger and thirst had hollowed him inside and his strength was drained. He'd torn the collar from his dress shirt and tied it around the wound on his foot. The clotted blood shown through in spots as a coppery brown. The unclouded sun intensified his light-headedness and it was hard to see. One time, he thought he spotted a sailboat, but it turned out to be a promontory a few hundred yards from the island. He found an old radio antenna half-buried in the sand. He threw it in the surf.

The wonders of modern life plagued Ridge like an undeveloped talent. On a typical day, he worked with dozens of technological marvels, all pulsing with resonant codes and meanings: automobiles, radios, telephones, fax machines, televisions, computers, microwaves, automated teller machines... Together, these devices comprised a casual defense against nature. They bent time and space to his needs, shielded him from the burdens of mere existence. But what did he really know about them? What could he make with his bare hands and the sparse resources around him to further his survival? What kind of progress is it when the ancient Melanesians prospered in places like this and all he could do was hope for rescue? He couldn't even make a fire.

Ridge was a thoroughly modern man, a purveyor of ideas rather than a maker of things. His Princeton education in international business had prepared him for a high place in the great chain of industrial types. He'd been tutored in the intricacies of the burgeoning global economy: balance of payments, eligible paper, price controls, wage-fund theory, inflationary and deflationary pressures, the Macmillan Gap, transmission mechanisms, the European currency snake, rational expectations... A business education hadn't been his first choice. No, in the spirit of intellectual adventure, he'd wanted to throw his lot in with the rest of the freshman undecideds. But his father had persuaded him that, as the inheritor of the family fortune (current estimate: $236.8 million), the ultra-Darwinism of the global economy should demand his full attention. His father was the founder, president and CEO of the prestigious Atlanta-based venture capital firm, Dantley and Associates. A sixties idealist in another, rarely mentioned life, he was popularly known among the south's *hoi polloi* as the King of Capital. Wealth, however, hadn't imbued him with charisma. He cut a spectacularly unimposing figure. He had a large bulbous head, soft glassy blue eyes and a weak chin. When he broke out into a retiring smile (as he often did), he looked like a reluctant medalist. He owed everything to a charming persistence.

Though Ridge had dutifully received his business degree (as well as joined the oldest, most expensive eating club at his mother's behest), he found the very language of high-finance—the drab heaviness of it— repulsive. The Orwellian meaningless of corporate-speak ... the dismal alphabet soup (*IPO, M&A, LBO, ROI*) ... the short-cut metaphors (*thinking outside the box*) ... the buzzwords (*win-win situation*) ... the euphemisms (*rightsizing, anyone?*) ... God, how could you preserve your faculties reading one-page, bulleted memos replete with that junk? Ridge needed an authentic language of ideas.

He'd taken up journalism his sophomore year, writing for the university's student paper as a pleasant way to find his own voice. But he'd never considered journalism a viable profession until he'd begun taking advantage of his mother's involvement in The Nineteenth Century Club, a coterie of progressive female activists who could trace their lineage to some exemplar of democratic virtue. He slowly allowed his mother to open up a broad, fascinating circle of public figures to him. Not only was he wary of using his family's social connections for professional gain, he'd always suspected her obsessive *noblesse oblige* as the motivating reason for his exile to Choate.

Although his mother came from a decidedly middle-class South Georgia family, she was a born aristocrat. A petite, immaculately dressed blonde with full red lips, Ava was a whirling dervish of progressive activism, a generous supporter of the Carter Center and a constant organizer. She was the proud descendent of John Overton, a Tennessee lawyer and personal friend and business partner of President Andrew Jackson. Overton, who became a superior court judge when Jackson left the bench, belonged to a group of Nashville supporters who helped secure Jackson's Senate seat and promote his presidential bid.

Ava was the Nineteenth Century Club's richest and most celebrated member. She'd hosted virtually all of the club's meetings for nearly thirty years and regularly threw elaborate Democratic *soirees* in their tony Alpharetta home. At these lively gatherings of the so-called "natural aristocracy," the news came to Ridge in unforced relationships and exclusive intimate settings. He merely reported what he saw and heard. He'd always been a keen observer of people and that ability, combined with his love of history and privileged connections, made him a natural journalist.

Now, after four years at the *Atlanta Journal-Constitution* on the political beat, he'd begun to consider getting into the arena himself—not as a career, of course, but ... who knew? Serving as the Senator's press secretary in the 1994 gubernatorial campaign would be a notable first step. At least in politics, he felt he could really earn respect—respect for his ideas, for what he'd done rather than who he was. Christ almighty. What a way to grow up ... Wave after wave of embarrassment on behalf of other people ... The incessant deference paid to him by maids, butlers, chauffeurs ... Friendly little gestures from his father's otherwise harried portfolio managers ... The indulgences of powerful family friends like Senator Neeland ... And the spectacles in public, oh, better not to think about those ... He'd been a regular prince in his youth, the Heir Apparent to his father's reign. But the inheritance had unsettled him. Who but an unthinking egotist would have accepted this—this conflation of riches and virtue—without question? The whole coddling environment had turned him inward, made him prematurely serious. He wanted desperately to burst the bubble of his rarefied past and be worthy of everyone's esteem.

So what was he going to do now? Politics ... God, how could he even think of a future in politics after the accident? After *Aaron*? What a scandal the Christian Right would make of that. The Senator must be dying inside with anticipation ... All he could do was try to redeem himself a little bit at a time... The island then gave Ridge no comfort. He was unfit for simple survival. The natural world didn't respect, much less reward, a mastery of words. What use were they against the violence of the elements? Unsettled nature had its own order of rank. Culture and class meant nothing within its borders. Nature's secrets weren't laid out on a picnic blanket for the welfare of everyone. Those secrets were reserved for those who overcame their complacency, for those whom danger made alert.

Based on what he'd seen from the open sea, Ridge estimated the island stretched for about ten miles. He would have to eat before exploring it. He suspected there were edible nuts and berries deeper in the bush but was reluctant to stray far from the beach for fear of missing a passing boat.

There was a cluster of coconut palms nearby. Ridge was determined to shimmy up one of them and did so, despite the impossible grip and the sting of broken flesh. He scraped his chest through his dress shirt and roughed the insides of his arms. His bare feet were of little use, owing, in part, to the gash on the sole of his right foot. He wrapped his legs around the tree and gradually pulled himself to the top. With his face pressed against the bark, he let go of the palm with his right hand and swung at a couple of coconuts. They tumbled to the ground.

Ridge lowered himself a few feet and jumped the remaining six to the ground. A splintery pain shot from his injured foot through his leg. He tumbled to the sand and stared at the coconuts until he recovered his grit. He gathered up his prizes and took them to a cluster of rocks along the surf. He held one over his head and smashed it with two-handed force. The sharp crack echoed through the bush and up the foothills. The husk shattered. Ridge grabbed the largest fragment before it fell into the sand then retrieved the rest and moved down the beach to eat.

The water near the shoreline glistened in hues of blue. Deep stretches of fractured coral broke the water into crystalline tiles. Sapphire abutted against cobalt, azure bordered on indigo. A murky blue tangle bound the darkest blues together but none of the colors mixed. They were beautifully separate. Where had he read that, as evinced by Homer's "wine-dark sea," the ancient Greeks lacked a word for blue?

Speckled in silver pulses, the Pacific Ocean beyond was the whole horizon. Its vastness concealed the force of its currents. The sea moved as a single mighty river encircling the earth. Everything else was debris.

The soft gritty coconut hardly satisfied Ridge's cravings but the simple act of eating bolstered his confidence. "I can make it," he said to himself, gazing across the inexorable waves. He grinned at the thought of looking like a mountaintop sage when he and the others were rescued.

He got to his feet and tucked the remaining coconut under his arm. His eyes lingered on the distant atoll where Mira was doubtless worrying about him. The coral rise was an indistinct disk. He started up the beach again, pushing against the sand with his toes, stretching. His wound was an aggravating throb. Then he stopped.

Where the beach mingled with the bush, a half-dozen aborigines stared down at him from the shafts of their throwing sticks.

CHAPTER 9

The Navel of the Earth

Mira wished she were bold enough to walk around in her slip like Paige. If only she could be so blithely natural. She thought Paige was beautiful in the same way as the mussed boyish models in designer perfume ads. She watched Paige brave the bullying sun with gusto. Paige was piling driftwood and tree fern fronds to make a signal fire, bending and lifting with a ballerina's strength.

Flushed from the dispiriting heat, Mira sat on the beach cooling her swollen legs in the surf. Her black shift dress clung awkwardly around her bosom and upper-thighs. She tossed bits of coral into the sea. The island across the channel could be seen in greater detail today than before. She could make out the contours of the foothills that split the island in two. *Maybe Ridge is getting help right now. It looks like a big enough island—like there would be somebody around.*

The shocking fact of the accident was beginning to wear on her. She'd gone to sleep last night half-expecting to wake up in the Atlanta apartment she shared with Ridge. She associated shipwrecks with television images of floods, hurricanes, tornadoes, wildfires and earthquakes. These were disasters seen but not felt—disasters rendered in unreal statistics.

Kenny dropped to the sand beside her. Mira coyly smoothed her gown over her lap. Why couldn't he leave her in peace? The Senator's confession last night had upset him, compounding his already fraught relationship with Paige. She'd half-listened to the couple bicker for the better part of the day, pretending to be preoccupied with her own thoughts.

"Ridge'll be all right," Kenny assured her.

"I know," she said. "But I can't help it. Anxiety's part of my heritage." She smiled unevenly.

They sat there in strained silence for a while, gazing across the silvered ocean. Its vastness gave Mira an uneasy sense of distance, desolation, Biblical time. She said, "Water has a special meaning to Jewish mystics, the Kabbalists. There aren't many of them anymore—pure ones, that is—but a lot of their beliefs are pretty mainstream now. Madonna, you know ..."

"They aren't the austere, all-in-black orthodox ones, are they?"

"If you mean the Chasidim, yes, they're the most fundamentalist."

"They always remind me of the Amish. They seem to have the same kind of Luddite outlook."

"Little *boychik*, they're mystics, they don't care so much about material things. Anyway, I was telling you about The Book of Creation, what water means in it, because ..." *Because I don't have anything else to say to you.* "I don't know, because we're surrounded by it now." Her voice sounded strange refracting on the water.

Kenny laughed into his chest.

"They think, like in Genesis, that the waters of the sea are everything, the whole universe, and God created heaven and earth out of them. Water is the source of life and all that, but they also think water symbolizes the way wisdom is passed down from teacher to student, you know, like how water flows from a higher place to a lower one. That's because of this myth that the water of heaven flows down and the water of the earth rises to the surface. And the only thing that keeps the two from joining is the foundation stone in the floor of the temple, which was a jewel from the throne of God hurled into the water to form the navel of the earth."

"Now, if only that jewel were here someplace, we could pull it out and drain the ocean and just walk home." Kenny rested his arms on bent knees. "Who knows? Maybe the Senator's better off here." *Muhbee tha Senatuh's bettuh ahf heyeah.*

Mira crossed her plump legs. Though she was comfortable with the fact her body fit Renaissance ideals, her thick ankles were a source of embarrassment. "What do you think of the Senator's story?" She looked Kenny squarely in the eye. "No, forget for a moment that you work for him. I don't want the official answer. I want *your* answer."

"I don't know what to think," he lied. Besides rescue, he'd thought of little else since the Senator had explained the nature of his relationship with Philip Louden and the likely consequences of the shipwreck on his political future. Kenny fingered his glasses for a moment. He wasn't about to surrender his confidence in the man who'd first recognized his promise. He'd been an undergraduate at Emory, busting stock at a ladies shoe store when the store's owner introduced him to someone from the Senator's campaign staff. He'd volunteered immediately. He canvassed, phonebanked, stuffed envelopes—lowly tasks which enabled him to earn higher positions with other campaigns and edge ever closer to the center of American power.

Six years later, when the Senator was up for re-election for a third term, Kenny was ready to play a prominent role. After the campaign, the Senator, remarking on the similarity of their humble origins, chose Kenny as his deputy chief of staff. Kenny remembered that moment with religious clarity. Finally, he thought, he'd arrived at a station in life which suited his intellectual gifts.

"No politician's 100% pure," Kenny said. "But using Southern politics as the standard, the Senator's deal with Louden is—I mean, how much did he really make? Less than three hundred thousand? In, say, Louisiana, he'd be considered either a saint or a fool for goin' so cheap. There's a term there—lagniappe." He pronounced the word deliberately: 'lan-yap.' "It's like a tip, 'a little something extra' is what it means literally. That's all the Senator got compared to the larger corruptions he never gave in to."

"But the way he rationalized it as his younger self—like he was a different person altogether—that really bothered me. Do you really think it's worth it for him to run for governor?"

"The odds are against him anyway. Hell, the country just ousted the last World War II president for someone who coulda been his son. But you never know. If he approached it the right way, conceded some wrongdoing up front before the press jumped all over him … I don't know. He's got a solid record of helping ordinary people. On Medicaid and taxes and job training, he's been a strong dependable voice for the middle-class. I would just hate to see Georgia lose out because of some personal indiscretion when his public life is so … so immaculate, really."

"But Kenny, he used his office for personal gain."

"I guess I'm more cynical or more realistic about politics, depending on your point of view. And some of this goes back to growing up in South Georgia like the Senator, but I always measured political success in terms of gains on behalf of the little guy against the monied interests. Ethics got their place, don't get me wrong. But in the scheme of things, if the Senator can do good for common people while makin' the rich think he's on their side for takin' a few bills, that's pure brass-ball genius there. See, Machiavelli gave pragmatism a bad name but for a hardscrabble guy like me that's what it all comes down to—whatever works," Kenny said. "I just assume they're all crooks 'cept some have the heart to steal for the rest of us."

"I guess I expect more. Or, I just have more romantic illusions about it all." She tried to strike a tone of finality.

Kenny nodded, looking at the hard-packed sand. "He's out there again, wandering around. Maybe he won't even come back."

"I guess the whole thing's not worth worrying about until we get off this rock." Mira smiled wistfully to take the edge off her voice then flicked another pinch of coral into the water and watched the ripples dissipate against the incoming surf.

CHAPTER 10

The Hunting Band

Ridge approached the aborigines with his hands outstretched in what he hoped they'd recognize as an expression of surrender. The Melanesians were darker than any people he'd ever met, almost blue-black. Their blunt features and face paint gave them a wicked-looking mien. They tracked his movements with their smoothed throwing sticks. The decorative carvings around the endpoints resembled fish scales.

"See? No weapons," Ridge said, shaping his words carefully.

The aborigines stared in silence. They had low broad foreheads, flat noses and wavy black hair. Glistening red and black shapes covered their faces. Their limbs were thin and sinewy. A piece of bark doubled over a band of coarse string served to cover their manhood.

A man with a monkey tail wrapped around his head stepped forward, his spear held at his hip. A crimson design stretched from the bridge of his nose to his right cheek like an uncoiled eel. He screeched something unintelligible, leaving a thread of black saliva dangling from his chin.

Ridge shook off his grip. "I'm—I don't understand."

The monkey tail man pursed his lips and concentrated on enunciating. "Me tek you," he said. More tobacco spittle escaped from the corners of his mouth.

Another aborigine lurched forward and pulled Ridge by the arm. He reeked of acrid body oil and primordial mud.

Ridge shook his hands off. "I'll go," he said and walked into the bush unaccompanied. He kept his hands up, afraid of upsetting the natives by making any sudden movements. He could only hope they'd lead him to a nearby port or village frequented by English speakers.

The natives walked in single file—three ahead of Ridge and three behind—toward the nearest of the rugged foothills. They tread a familiar path, scattering the bush with their throwing sticks. Ridge toddled forward, swinging his right foot out at an awkward angle so the unscathed heel bore the brunt of his weight. He considered asking some questions of the monkey tail man but then thought better of it. The leader's command of English appeared severely limited. Ridge could only hope that help wasn't too far.

CHAPTER 11
The Duel

The high coral limestone island was a stinking mass of vegetation: crooked tea trees and yellow pines and broad ironwood trees; spidery vines the texture of rotten flesh; ferns and other broad-leafed bushes; and clusters of thick green bamboo. Kunai grass, edged like a bandsaw, grew up to seven feet in places. Early in the ascent up the razorback foothill, close to the shore, Ridge had spotted some torch ginger—sparkling red flowers with long leafless stems—but now only clusters of white orchids broke up the oppressive blur of dark green.

Ridge couldn't detect a trail. The Melanesians cut a steady swath through the dense bush with their curved machetes. Ridge followed. His coral-slashed foot smarted on the brambles and limestone rocks littering the ground. Only the tantalizing chance of rescue kept him going. With each agonizing step, he said to himself, yes, yes, yes as if the next would end in swift relief. The air was still and stiflingly hot, humming with flies and mosquitoes.

About midway up the steep foothill, the pandanus and other trees grew closer together, the underbrush thicker. The sun scarcely penetrated the upper canopy. Confined to shade, the savannah grasses were stunted, pale.

Ridge had turned to the native behind him several times to ask how far they were going. The answers were unintelligible. The aborigines habitually chewed wads of rank tobacco. Slimy black strings of it trailed from their mouths.

As the sky turned a violent wash of red and gold, the island came alive with sound. There was a vivid cacophony of birdsong—twitters and wails, hoots and cackles. He spied a bird of paradise with dark metallic wings flitting across a break in the trees. Several times, the bushes rustled with activity. He knew from his travelogue reading that bush mice and skinks flourished here. But none materialized.

The foothill sloped more acutely near the summit. The balls of

Ridge's feet barely touched the ground. His legs flared in pain. He reached for a nearby tree to steady himself and came away with a handful of bark and a metropolitan swarm of biting ants. Ridge hugged his shoulders, slapped his arms, his sides, the back of his neck. *Christ.* His neck erupted with blotchy red welts. The natives hurried him along with light nudges. Their red shell and bamboo necklaces beat time against their chests.

Ridge was impressed with the natives' resilience in the harsh environment. Despite himself, his first impulse was to romanticize them, to make them into living exemplars of Rousseau's noble savage. What it must be like to live that way … A purifying, physical existence free from the distractions of the outside world, settled into tradition. For all the apparent integrity of their lives, however, the natives seemed curiously grim. They scarcely spoke to each other during the trek through the foothills, much less laughed or sang. Ridge had yet to see one of them smile.

Sweat rolled down Ridge's face and stung his eyes. He tore at his shirt to wipe away his perspiration. The natives didn't let the pace flag. Aaahhh … His chest heaved with effort. He swung his arms more freely and at last, reached another summit, his legs shaking from fatigue. Ridge estimated they'd gone about five miles up and down the foothills. The natives led him through a clearing of foxtail and other bush-like grasses. An elongated trade cloud hovering directly overhead threw a deep shadow over the landscape.

The kunai grass undulating in the wind reminded Ridge of the Peachtree Golf Club's lush fairways where he'd spent considerable time with Aaron. Soon after graduating from Princeton with an impressive record in amateur golf, Aaron had taken a junior sales position with Sonnenfeld Medical. The medical imaging equipment company had given him ample opportunity to entertain clients at the club's scenic course. He'd taken up golf as a form of self-discipline at Choate and developed a bold style of play. He was known for the hard win, the bravura gesture. In a game which generally favored position over power, Aaron had wielded his driver like a club, overwhelming opponents off the tee.

Ridge had seen him power a ball out of the rough and, by applying just the right amount of backspin, drop it precisely onto the green. "You just need to play to win," Aaron had teased on several occasions. "You get your ass kicked when you play just to keep from getting beaten."

The likelihood of Aaron's death changed the way Ridge framed his memories of his old friend. Every connection, no matter how trivial, felt poignant. It was a vain attempt, he realized, to make sense of things. All he could do now, still silently repeating his mantra of yes, yes, yes, was to hold out hope that Aaron had somehow survived.

On the far side of the summit, the trail narrowed to a steep zigzag. The hillside had been clearcut, leaving a wide natural scar of gray rock and tree stumps. Several black pits were scattered over the flattened earth. A jumble of pine and ironwood logs littered the bottom of the trail. The sun embellished the abandoned timber with the last of its light. The rest of the wooded valley was hidden in darkness. The swollen trade cloud shone purple.

It was closing on sunset now. Ridge breathed in the humid air and started down the hill. As he descended the path of hard packed earth, he heard the dreamy murmur of a stream. Between tentative steps, he looked for the source, but no moonlight penetrated the arrow-shaped cirrus cloud, which, along with its lesser neighbors, kept essentially the same shape throughout the year. A consistent trade wind pushing against the foothills sent a warm current of air into the sky, producing the ominous shape. The cloud seemed more substantial at dusk than during the day.

The journey down the foothill gave Ridge no relief. The increased pressure on his injured foot left it bloody. Resisting the urges of gravity worked forgotten muscles. He didn't hike down the hill so much as simply keep himself from falling. Discouraged, he began to question his decision to go with the natives without a struggle. He even formulated an angry speech for them in case they didn't lead him to help. *Regardless of whether they understand me, they'll know I'm mad.*

Ridge had the sense there was no connection between events. Only two days before, he'd been lounging on a yacht with his friends; now, Aaron was probably-definitely dead and he was slogging through the forest with men out of time and as black as night. He pondered how Mira would explain the turn of events in terms of God's will. Part of her charm was the ease with which she carried the history of Jewish persecution. She wasn't weighed down with pious fatalism. Though outwardly she might appear nervous, even exasperated, she tended to brave misfortune with a bright determined faith.

The core of her beliefs bordered on the auspicious pantheism of Spinoza. She was a fleshy great-souled woman who saw the natural world as the ultimate proof of His existence. To her, God was the supreme artist and the Earth and everything on it, wondrous evidence of His infinitely creative love. She complemented her Jewish observances with New Age flourishes. Fascinated with the life of angels, she read *The Celestial Hierarchy*, studied the Talmudic and Midrashic literature, as well as the more fanciful writings of the Hasidim, bought popular books on the afterlife. She rejected American materialism in her very being. That's why Ridge loved her so much and relied on her for warm sleepy comfort: she half-lived in the heavens already. Ridge's notion of God was dry, Aristotelian, unfit for passionate devotion. But at Mira's best, when she was funny and spirited and gracious, he believed people had undying souls.

What must Mira be thinking? Ridge wondered if he'd only made the rescue more difficult than it would've been had he stayed with the others. Perhaps everyone had already been rescued and the local authorities were scouring the island for him. What if his whole attempt, however well-intentioned, turned out to be a costly mistake? The possibility gnawed at him.

The lilting sound of water grew louder as Ridge neared the bottom of the hill. It was a captivating melody below the forest din. The path the Melanesians cut through the forest widened and leveled off at the bank of the unseen creek. Ridge wanted to stop and rest, but the natives pushed him on. They bounded over the uneven terrain, leading him downstream. The forest was pitch-black. Ridge tripped several times over the roots of the sago palms along the bank. Hands stretched out of the dark to help him recover his footing.

Ridge searched the sky in vain for the guiding light of the moon or the stars. The forest appeared to have closed in on him. Every flutter, squawk and hiss was amplified by apprehension. He perceived a savagery greater than the forest and its denizens. There was a palpable mysteriousness, a constant threat of the unknown.

Night rendered the world irrational. Ridge's childhood fears assumed an ominous logic. Images culled from dimestore novels and B-movies flashed through his head: sleek jaguars on the hunt; fierce pygmies, poisoned arrows notched in their bows; cargo cults eager to make him their next human sacrifice; giant, irradiated tarantulas; cannibalism... He glanced at the wiry Melanesian behind him. Some of the aborigines wore bones in their noses and a few sported indistinguishable pelts around their waist. Maybe these items were souvenirs from hapless castaways and not the rewards of the hunt as he'd first assumed. Were there still cannibals around? He vaguely recalled a discussion in his college anthropology class about cannibalism. What was it the professor had said? Something about it being a justification for imperialist zeal. Did that mean it was a *mistaken* stereotype? He couldn't remember.

Familiar with the uneven ground, the natives tramped into the valley without difficulty. Ridge cracked his left ankle on a spidery sago root. He swore under his breath, more determined than ever to make his frustration known to the natives. They were really going to hear from him. Leading him who the hell knows where while Mira and the others were waiting, worrying...

Through the inky tendrils of the forest, Ridge made out a series of thatched pandanus leaf huts. Wood smoke filtered through their roofs and into the veiled sky. He inhaled the pungent odor, anxious to get the lay of the village. He heard voices... Spanish or Portuguese... English... Americans! Thank God. He'd done it. He'd taken a gamble and it had paid off... Christ. It was about time, the swim, tramping through the forest... Everyone had doubted him, yes, even Mira, and now... Now he'd cruise into the lagoon, standing on the deck of an old steamer or stern trawler... *Take that, Kenny!* The voices were largely indistinguishable. He caught every third or fourth word: *still... bastard... on surface...* an argument, maybe. But a singular bellow—strong and clipped—stood out from the chorus.

When Ridge's escorts heard the commotion, they abruptly abandoned him and raced ahead into the village square. Ridge stumbled after them. The central clearing was crowded with people under harsh lamplight. The mass of bodies screened the center of attention from view. Ridge moved around the perimeter of the crowd. There—in the inner circle—he could see a number of non-natives. It was a sampling of the world's laboring classes: white, brown, black, yellow and red—every one dusted to a spectral pallor, alternately haunting and haunted-looking. Most of the aborigines confined themselves to the shadowy margins. A few reclined in the trees. The whites of their eyes gleamed in the kerosene glare. What the hell was going on? A fight?

The distinctive voice Ridge heard earlier emerged from the well of dusty souls: "You see, Maslen? I'm cutting you loose. I want to settle this fairly, the Marokatu way." Ridge shifted position to catch sight of the speaker—a white man of superior build. The man's black hair, streaked with gray, ranged around his sculpted face and broad shoulders. He had sun-bronzed skin and impenetrable, deep-set eyes. "No farther than the edge of the clearing now," he ordered his opponent.

Through a narrow gap in the crowd, Ridge caught a glimpse of Maslen shaking his hands free of rope. Then Ridge lost him in the surge of bodies as the throng cleared an alley for the combatants. A long line of spectators arranged themselves in front of the four rough ironwood shacks which circumscribed the far side of the central clearing. Ridge eased his way forward, apparently unnoticed by the people around him. What was this place? The way the natives had treated him, this coming brawl … *Christ almighty.* He was probably a captive, just momentarily forgotten, rather than a guest. But where could he go? Even if he fled, there was no way he could find his way back to the beach in the dark. Alone.

Standing in the back of the crowd, which was now three or four people deep, Ridge got a better view of the rivals. A suspended lamp behind Maslen highlighted his silhouette. He had fiery orange hair and a slender frame with slim rounded hips. He wore a dirty undershirt and chinos. A pair of dog tags dangled from a silver chain around his neck. He pulled nervously on his unkempt beard.

His rival, Tarrant, peeled off a gray button-down shirt to reveal a black tank top. He made a formidable figure: his heavily tattooed arms bulged with rigid brawn and his stomach was a latticework of muscle. He shouted commands to the natives in their own tongue. They gathered throwing sticks for each man.

Ridge's heart quickened at the distribution of spears. *No. Oh, Christ, no.* He remained at the edge of the crowd, scared and at once strangely fascinated.

A confluence of lamplight gave the men in front of Ridge unlikely halos. "Goddamn and done..." "¡*Qué chingados!*" "All bets are off, man..." "Bloody oath." "What'd he expect? Fuckin' Christmas tangerine?" "*Piiiiz'dets, blyaaaa.* In *Rodina,* duel for nobleman, you know, like Pushkin and d'Anthes."

His arms crossed in weak defiance, Maslen urged his fellows to turn on Tarrant. "How can you just stand there and watch?" His voice coarsened in desperation at the end of each phrase. "You can't think this won't happen to you 'cause it will, man. He didn't stop at Angus Biggs or Ol' Isra or any a the others and he won't stop with me. None a you are safe. So why don't we join together? He ain't so tough we can't take him."

The hard-faced men around Ridge turned to each other then looked askance in shame. A few muttered curses at the ground. The natives observed the scene indifferently. Perhaps their closeness to nature had inured them to this kind of cruelty.

"Valero," called Maslen, pointing out a stout man in overalls. "You were with me on this deal. You think I'm goin' down by myself? No way, man. No way."

Valero looked at the ground and shook his head. Shaggy windblown hair fell over his eyes.

Tarrant was content to let Maslen go on haranguing the others. "Oh, you talk tough, yeah. Every night, I gotta listen to you rattle on about how you gonna kill Tarrant in his sleep. To hear you say it, man, you fuckin' cutthroat," Maslen continued. "But when it comes down to it, when it comes to the dirty deed, you ain't got the guts, man. Motherfuckin' coward."

"Is that true?" Tarrant asked, grinning.

"I don't know what the fuck he talkin' 'bout," Valero said. "You know how it is—you hear some *vato* say crazy shit all the time, after a while you just nod your head, you know, like it's all right. I mean, I didn't plan nuthin' and I didn't agree to nuthin', Tarrant. You gotta believe me on that."

Tarrant nodded solemnly. Valero didn't seem comforted. Then Tarrant said, "Looks like it's just us, Maslen, *mano a mano*."

"Valero, man," spit Maslen. "I'm gonna haunt you. I'm gonna haunt you 'til you prayin' to die." A native handed him a rock-tipped spear. Maslen felt the weight of the bamboo weapon in his hand.

Tarrant picked up his spear and hefted it over his shoulder. The crowd instinctively retreated a couple of steps. The native women gathered their errant children, crouched down and shielded their naked young with their arms.

"See, though the Marokatu settle their grievances this way, they rarely get hurt," Tarrant explained. "Their leaders are usually so old and their aim so poor they can't hit each other. Or, say in the case of adultery, when you have two young natives, soon as somebody suffers a flesh wound, the contest's over. But for you and me," he said, pointing his spear at Maslen, "this is final."

The way Tarrant stalked Maslen, all the while daring the crowd with his eyes … He stood apart as if from a great height. In good conscience, Ridge couldn't watch one man kill another in this way. But how could he possibly interfere? For the past two days, he'd scarcely eaten and, in swimming to the island and hiking over the foothills, had taxed himself to his physical limit. If he were to challenge Tarrant, he wouldn't only perish with Maslen but forfeit any hope of rescuing his friends. Overwhelmed by the conflicting moral impulses, Ridge watched in silence.

The scene inspired a nervous frenzy among the two dozen or so non-natives. They were frightened and, at the same time, viciously expectant. Some shouted encouragement to the big man, who received their comments with a knowing smirk. A small bespectacled man in Tarrant's corner led this group with wild hoots and gestures. Perhaps due to the magnifying effect of his glasses, his eyes appeared as large and slow as those of a horse. His sandy hair was slicked back into a ponytail held together by an oversized rubber band. He bounded up and down the first row of spectators, barking at the crowd. The throng made a ferocious clamor pitched between enthusiasm and horror.

Appalled, Ridge retreated a few steps, wondering if the men here had been so deadened by their primitive conditions that murder meant nothing more than entertainment.

Tarrant roared above the crowd: "You have the first throw, Maslen. That's my one concession. Usually, the accused opens the contest."

"Don't do me no favors, Tarrant," Maslen snarled. Now that his fate had been decided, he bristled with melancholy courage. His eyes flashed defiance at his fellows. He hunched down, stretched his arms out and shifted his weight from one foot to the other.

Tarrant stopped smiling. He nodded to Maslen and turned around to take a few steps back to establish some running room. About twenty-five yards separated him from Maslen. The spear was bathed in sacred red and black paint. The point was a jagged green curve of limestone.

The shouting ceased. The dissonance of the forest inundated the crowd. Ridge moved forward as if to speak out. But his lips refused to part.

There was a near rush of wind. The spear pierced Maslen's left thigh. He gasped and collapsed to one knee and, at first, appeared more shocked than hurt. The bamboo shaft protruded from his leg just below the hip. Gritting his teeth, the red-headed Swede tore away the spear. His beige chinos darkened with blood. Maslen leaned on his spear to stand again then discarded it and was handed another.

Ridge winced. God, how could he stand it?

"What'd I say, man? Fuck me ..." "Jayzus, Mary and Joseph ..." "... not worth a Zack." "*¡Pinche idiota!*" "Had no choice after—" "Oh, that's bullshit. Only choice you ain't got is bein' born." "*Zakroy rot!*"

"My turn now," said Maslen shakily. He blinked through the pain, relying on his good leg for balance. He tried to steady his throwing hand. The spear felt slippery, insubstantial. In secret, the crowd dared to help him, to guide the spear in imagination and take fanciful vengeance. Apparently ready, Maslen tumbled forward.

The stick skounced across the dirt.

There were a few hushed groans amid the mocking laughter. Tarrant glared at the assembly of shadows. Some of the natives smiled at each other. The horse-eyed man pounded the butt of his spear on the ground in exultation.

Maslen pushed himself to his knees. His wound oozed a rust-col-

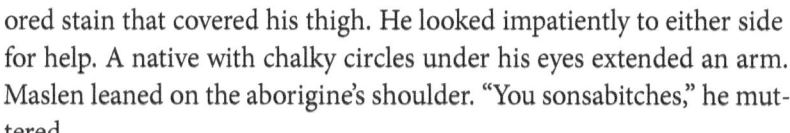

ored stain that covered his thigh. He looked impatiently to either side for help. A native with chalky circles under his eyes extended an arm. Maslen leaned on the aborigine's shoulder. "You sonsabitches," he muttered.

"Always thought he was an asshole." "This kinda life—you gotta be." "Ha, *kak auknetsya—tak i otkliknetsya*. How call to forest, it come back." "Whatever the fuck that means."

Ridge resolved to help Maslen. He couldn't continue standing there, mute with disgust. The horror of Tarrant's cruelty stirred his deepest sympathies. It was natural for him to accept these kinds of emotional obligations. But every visible sign—the crowd's acquiescence, the unmoved natives, the forbidding forest—cautioned him against it. He didn't want to die. And even though a consistent exercise of morality demanded it, not for a stranger. He cursed himself for his ignominy. But like the others, he didn't intervene.

Maslen was too exhausted to howl a last curse at Tarrant. He waited for death with a blank stare.

Tarrant regarded him with serene detachment. Like a hunter confronted with a wounded animal, he was without hate or regret. His eyes were black pits in the hard lamplight. He hurled his spear in a fluid lunge.

When the end came for Maslen, it was surprisingly quick.

CHAPTER 12

Self-Exile

Sitting alone on the beach, Senator Neeland watched a distant squall without really seeing it. He was preoccupied with the prospect of political exile. His confession of wrongdoing the night before last had pained him more than he'd expected. He'd told the truth at least. Haw. Like that made him a hero. Lord knows, he was no stranger to lies. But the public lies he'd told had been mere political distortions—evasions for a faceless television audience. He'd rationalized them without effort.

White lies were an accepted part of the job, the kind of niggling poker bluffs that covered his bets back home or, like his deals with Louden, the kind of trivial hedging that did no harm. But those lies hadn't required continuous deception among his closest friends. They hadn't required him to forfeit a piece of himself.

Against his will, Mira's stare of disappointment came back to him. The memory made him feel old and hollow inside. He recalled a reedy desperation in his voice. If he quit politics entirely, he could put an end to the lies. He hadn't announced his bid for governor yet, at least not formally. Many would perceive it as a step down, anyway. But what about his legacy? His reputation? Lord knows he just couldn't cross that damn river. His sense of mission wound all through him.

He lay flat on his back and took in the glazed blue sky. The sun appeared closer to the earth than what seemed natural and the sky was uncomfortably bright. He'd appreciated the night's rank humidity, though. He'd slept on the far side of the atoll, away from the others, curled up in the beach grass like a frightened child at the foot of his parents' bed.

The others would start looking for him soon. He should head back before they did. The last thing he wanted was to cause a scene. The wedge-shaped atoll was less than two miles long. He could walk its length in about a half-hour. Maybe if he lay on the beach long enough, the sun would blacken his flesh to a fine ash. Haw. To leave nothing more behind than an indistinct trace in the sand ... What pushed him onward was vanity, an unerring pride in his own capacity for greatness. He didn't recognize this creaturely instinct, of course. He obscured it with noble dreams of a New South ... He had to run. Just one uncompromising term. That's all he needed. With one term and no worries about re-election, he could do so much: force a legislative ethics bill through the General Assembly; reform the state's civil service system; take on the timber companies and regulated industries ... This election wasn't about him. Not even close. It was about saving the South from itself.

He could be the greatest reformer in Georgia history since Governor Ellis Arnall some 50-odd years ago. He even shared Arnall's boll weevil philosophy of frugal but compassionate government. Lord knows Arnall accomplished some lasting good in his time: abolished overly generous tax exemptions to large corporations, set up a merit system for government workers, forbid deficit spending, struck references to the white primary in the state constitution, improved prison conditions, spent twice as much on public education as his predecessor ... Haw. To join the likes of that record ...

This moment was the culmination of his generations-spanning career. He had Old South manners and a New South outlook. Young and old, black and white, urban and rural—everyone trusted him. He was the only one who could speed the transition from Old to New. If not him, who? There wasn't anyone left from his political class with the requisite gumption, and the up-and-comers, well, for many, especially rural voters, they just weren't credible. Too many Northern pretensions. They were like Ridge (who he knew harbored political ambitions): from the South but not *of* the South. Stage actors performing scenes from the Southern Renaissance without really understanding their parts, or the larger, often subtle, meanings of the plays. But the voters knew. Lord knows they could spot a fake. Sharp-witted comers like Ridge made a fine impression at a Chamber of Commerce luncheon, sure, but could they work a good ol' boy crowd at the International Raceway?

He took in the frothy tide and the expanse beyond. Oh, he had to run. Caught up in serving caucus leadership, he'd hoarded his political capital for years. As governor *for just one term*, he could—at last—expend it freely. He couldn't lose that opportunity because of some...accident. Great God, he had the sand to weather the inevitable attacks. The GOP's prosecutorial ratbags, the Moral Majority bullyboys, the tabloid TV news shows—he'd take 'em all on. No more platitudes and bullshit. No more dead-sour words in his mouth. He'd give them the hard truth. How both parties have allowed global capitalism and special-interest money to render moot the social contract between rich and poor. How liberals have devolved into center-left pragmatists loath to talk religion and faith. How conservatives have twisted up the Bible to dupe the middle-class into voting against its economic interests. How the last two decades of grievance-based populisms have made the common good out to be simple-minded nostalgia. How about that? Shock 'em with the truth...

Haw. Who was he kidding? In this era of partisan tribalism, who would even recognize the truth when they heard it? The mood of the South, especially, had turned parochial and defensive. Hard truth, what, like in Carter's 'malaise speech'—to be second-guessed, caricatured and abused past all recognition? No, he'd leave it for historians to suss out. Let his fellow politicians perpetuate the illusion that power flows upwards from the people (how flattering!). Let the people perpetuate the illusion they care about anything other than getting a leg up on their neighbors. The banal predictability of the scorn he'd accrue made him sick at heart. He'd just earn universal enmity for revealing the mirror tricks that keep the country afloat. Eventually, he thought with growing vehemence, as the American Dream passed from memory to myth, sheer lack of belief would bring it all crashing down anyway.

CHAPTER 13

The Proffered Gun

"Anybody know what part to read?" asked Gerrit, holding a ragged copy of the King James Bible over the open grave. His dim eyes scanned the men gathered around the pit. There was a scarcely restrained wildness to the stocky Southerner. His body seemed tight with anger. At the end of each spoken thought, he pursed his lips into a thin line.

The men in their muddied denim and t-shirts looked at each other uneasily. Tarrant had permitted a brief morning service for his wretched victim. But even though the men assembled here had judgment enough to bury Maslen, none had the knowledge that comes from regular church-going. These were con-men, thieves, ruffians, drug-runners, killers, adventurers, fugitives from society, denizens of a Hobbesian world. If they had any religion, it was only what had been folded into their animal DNA.

Ridge stood off to one side, wearing a castoff t-shirt and jeans, wondering what the hell he was going to do. There was no easy way out. He'd already written off help from Tarrant. Sure, he'd ask for it, but there was no way he could see Tarrant letting him go. The murder was only part of it. Last night Gerrit had told him the camp was an illegal gold mining operation. The pits he'd seen from the top of the hillside were preliminary diggings. Not counting a few Marokatu, there were twenty-six men breaking their backs in hopes of getting their share of a reputed motherlode. Some placer gold had been found in the nearby stream, but almost five months into the operation, no lode gold had been discovered on the hillside. According to Gerrit, the chief overseer, Tarrant was none-too-pleased with their limited progress.

Christ almighty, Ridge thought. What had he done to deserve this? First the yacht, now this craziness... If only he hadn't been so anxious to prove himself. The others had to have been rescued by now. He tried to wipe away the pain behind his eyes. His head ached. He looked at the men on either side. A few sat on the ground with their arms resting on their knees; others leaned against surrounding trees or stood at the foot of the grave, avoiding Maslen's dead stare. They were uniformly tired and dirty. The furtive search for gold had apparently blunted their features. They smelled of dried sweat and rich sweet earth.

Looking toward the lush foliage of the forest, Ridge suspected that to survive here, you had to be more violent than the next guy. They were all just stray dogs momentarily restrained by the lure of riches and Tarrant's wrath. Ridge had never been at ease among men defined by their physicality. He'd suffered a series of debilitating illnesses as a child (colic, mononucleosis, successive bouts of pneumonia) which had left him with chronic headaches. A mixing bowl for catching his vomit had been a permanent nightstand fixture. His parents had sent him to Choate after a particularly nasty episode of mono—four months spent mostly in bed, reading comic books and Edgar Rice Burroughs paperbacks. They'd counted on Choate to toughen him up as if it were a boot camp for children with poor immune systems.

Though he'd played lacrosse with creditable enthusiasm, he'd excelled only in swimming, a solitary sport which suited his exacting nature. The very medium of the sport had seemed a sure test of fitness. The water reinforced silent single-minded concentration. The bright air other athletes could take for granted was gone. Giving in to the maddening impulse to breathe could mean the difference between winning and losing. And to prove yourself better than a mere animal meant starving your muscles of oxygen. During one particularly tight 100-yard freestyle race in his third year of competition, Ridge had lost all feeling in his legs because he'd refused to breathe more than once per lap.

By his last year at Choate, rigorous year-round exercise had made him reasonably athletic but had added little bulk to his thin frame. The solid brawn he envied in others eluded him; instead, he had the same type of lean strength as the Melanesians—the musculature of a survivor rather than a conqueror.

"C'mon. Ain't nobody got any ideas?" Gerrit asked.

The men exchanged empty looks until Ridge, dreading an unfelt and unbecoming prayer, said, "If you can't find anything else, you could read Psalm 23: *Yea, though I walk through the valley of the shad-*

ow of death…" He wished he could fast-forward the proceedings like a home video. Mira and the others had to be fearing the worst by now.

A wiry Mestizo with a red bandana around his balding head asked, "Where in hell you come from, *ese*?"

"Don't go gittin' yer gussie up," Gerrit said. "He's done all right for a guy of a touristical nature." He held up a hairy-knuckled hand. "Some a the island niggers found him on the beach. Says he was shipwrecked. Black-ass terrible, ain't it?" This last comment elicited a chorus of laughter and ridicule.

A voice cried out, "Shoulda gone down with the ship, Tourist."

Ridge let the derisive remarks pass without comment. Though Gerrit was an unapologetic bigot, he was grateful for the man's rough kindness. Without him, he would've slept under a tree last night. Gerrit had even provided a change of clothes: a dingy green Gotcha t-shirt, some castoff jeans and a pair of oversized work boots. Ridge didn't want to betray his confidence by provoking an argument.

After Tarrant had disposed of Maslen, the camp had become a riot of hard drinking. Tarrant had demanded it, rolling out a 55 gallon drum of native pulque. The milkish brew of fermented coconut was his heady gift for loyalty. The men, aching to purge their anxieties, had taken to their reward like a baby to his mother's breast. The pulque had filled the camp with the odor of sour milk. Ridge had dipped a tin cup into one of the brimming drums and washed down the bile rising in his throat.

Gerrit had approached Ridge amid the bacchanalia and, after hearing his story, had cleared a corner in one of the ramshackle bunkhouses for him to sleep in. ("Jus' like porch-sleepin'—somethin' we Southerners is used to.") The parade of drunken men crashing through the bunkhouse at odd intervals had ruined any chance of restful sleep. Though Ridge had barely tasted the pulque, he felt as dull-witted as any of the men who had indulged in the native liquor with gusto.

Following the psalm word to word with his index finger, mistakenly pausing at the end of every line, Gerrit read: "*You prepare a table before me in the… presence of my enemies…*"

No one had cleaned up Maslen's corpse. It was a muddle of discolored rags stretched over ashen skin. One arm lay across his chest; the other arched crookedly over his head. The dried blood in his beard made for a devilish grimace.

The corpse conjured up images of Aaron on the night of the accident: the swirling waters; the stars aqueous and unsteady in their orbits; Aaron clinging to his life jacket, pallid with fear, pulled further and further into the black. The scene upset Ridge's sense of a just natural order. What had Aaron done to deserve dying like that? Was it fear itself that had doomed him?

These men here, thought Ridge, live willingly with death but they aren't free. *They act like sleepwalkers going through the motions. They're just waiting for their turn.* Ridge envied the men in one respect, however. They would know where Maslen was buried and, provided they cared, that knowledge would ease the pain.

In the dolorous silence between the end of the psalm and "Amen" the body was pummeled with a barrage of shoveled dirt. Every minute the men spent at the gravesite meant another of exacting labor in the stream or on the hillside.

"Is it sunk?"

Ridge turned around to face an older man with a bulky prosthetic for a left arm. "What?"

"Your boat. Is it sunk?" the bearded man asked.

"Yeah, it's gone."

The man nodded slowly then turned around and walked away.

"Ready?" Gerrit asked Ridge, kicking a final cloud of dirt over the lip of the grave.

"Yeah, as soon as I can see him, that would be fine," Ridge said. He'd played out the anticipated conversation with Tarrant in his head any number of times but now he couldn't recall any details other than his failure to imagine the man letting him go.

Gerrit led him across the smoke-filled central clearing to Tarrant's hut. The clearing was defined by an incomplete circle of four ironwood bunkers, a mess tent, a native lodge fronted by a figurative statue and a scattering of native huts. Made largely of thatched pandanus leaf, the huts were roughly rectangular with low-pitched roofs that came within a foot or two of the ground. There were several entrances to each shelter which required the natives to get on their hands and knees.

Ridge had noticed last night that the doorways had been covered with leaves and grass, presumably for privacy or protection. The huts were surrounded by small decorative gardens of shells and flowers.

The ground was still wet with dew and the morning air was brisk. To warm themselves, some aborigines gathered around small familial fires, the women either eating or feeding their children a pale plaintain mush; the men, chewing tobacco. Chickens and pigs milled around their feet. Several of the gray wild pigs sported tusks. Farther on, men could be seen taking their morning toilet or washing themselves in the stream with bracing splashes. On the hillside, Ridge could make out an elaborate series of long wooden troughs resembling a water ride at a broken-down amusement park. The linked troughs sloped from the hillside to a trench near the stream.

Ridge tried to shake off an emaciated tan dog. He could count the ribs on the rudely shaved animal. There seemed to be at least a dozen of them running around the square, all the same breed and in various stages of starvation.

"Poi dog. Just kick the damn thing if'n it bothers you," Gerrit advised. "The island niggers treat 'em worse'n that, believe you me."

Tarrant's two-room shack, which had served as a backdrop for last night's contest, leaned to one side as though its uneven ironwood boards had been permanently warped by the wind. The roof was a patchwork of salvage tin. A whip-like radio antenna arced the length of it, secured near the tip to the roof's edge by fishing line. Hardened splashes of black pitch ran down the sides of the hut, dangling between gaps in the sideboards.

Ridge approached the door with mounting trepidation. A sound conversational strategy eluded him.

Knocking gently on the door, Gerrit said, "Mr. Tarrant?" He listened for a response and, hearing none, knocked again. "Mr. Tarrant? We got us a visitor, sir—castaway."

The door flew open with unexpected force. Tarrant towered in the doorway, dappled sunlight glancing off him. The awe and dread with which Ridge had regarded him the night before returned doubly strong.

Gerrit said, "Some a the natives found him, sir. Yesterday on the beach. Got here last night in time for the challenge."

"Right, right." Tarrant grinned. "So you showed him how we bury the dead, did you, Mr. Gerrit?"

Gerrit was too solicitous to be sincere. "Yessir. He even picked out the part I read."

"Oh, ho. Well, if you know your Bible you'll find yourself a singular source of faith out here," Tarrant said. His sunken black eyes narrowed. "Ain't too many of these Sunday school outcasts got ears for the Good News, right Mr. Gerrit?"

"That's right, sir."

"Go about your duties now." Tarrant grabbed his Bible from Gerrit's hand and swept Ridge into the shack. "Come in, have a seat there on the stool. If I lived in a gentler place, I'd apologize for the scraps of wood that pass as chairs and shelter and things. But seeing as how I don't, you gotta be satisfied with whatever you get."

Ridge rubbed his eyes to adjust to the squalid darkness. Unlike the bunkhouses, Tarrant's shack had no windows made of empty fruit jars. A small Coleman lamp set on a long desk provided scant light. The desk was littered with disorderly piles of books and looseleaf paper. An unslung hammock dangled from a hook in the far corner of the ceiling like a spent balloon.

As Ridge began to make out finer, more distinct shapes, his curiosity was piqued by the shelves of books that lined the walls. A split of bark separated each book from its neighbor, likely to allow the tropical air to circulate. Even so, owing to the humidity, the salt air and a variety of nasty bugs, the volumes were in poor condition. The spines sagged like the flesh around an old man's waist and the yellowed pages between the covers looked as though they might flake away on first touch.

"Surprised at my library?" Tarrant asked, sitting on the edge of the desk.

From his place on the three-legged stool, Ridge scanned the titles. *The Genetical Theory of Natural Selection. Alchemy Rediscovered and Restored. Gnostic Apocrypha, Including the Acts of Thomas. Freedom from Known Moralities. Psalms of the Black Sun.* Several generations-old volumes lacked titles along the spine. Others were in an indecipherable script.

"Thought me a dumb savage, did you?" Tarrant's lips widened into an oblique smile.

Ridge took a deep breath. *Okay, here goes…* "I'd just as soon forget about what happened last night as long as you can help me." He paused, suddenly cautious about admitting his predicament or mentioning his stranded friends. "I can leave, right? I didn't ask to come here and, to tell you the truth, I don't even know where here is."

"Mister …?"

"Oh, sorry," Ridge said, standing up and holding out his hand. In the far right corner, he noticed the padlocked door that led to a second room.

Tarrant waved away the proffered handshake. The blazon of black tattoos along his arm loomed large for a moment. A twisty Quetzal-coatl extended from the spiralized Aztec calendar around his deltoid to the back of his hand. The mythical creature's tail ended in licks of flame behind each knuckle. A corresponding sun-shape in the form of a ceremonial mask adorned the left deltoid. From this figure depended a serpentine phoenix in the same abstract Mesoamerican style. The acidic tinge to these designs suggested a bleary and bracing otherworld.

Ridge managed a contrite smile and sat down again. "Ridge Dantley. I'm a journalist. I write for *The Atlanta Journal-Constitution*—politics." He added hurriedly: "I should tell you that my family has plenty of friends in government, so the Coast Guard or the Navy or whatever should be out looking for me."

Tarrant burst out laughing. The restless howl rolled around the room like a cannon shot.

Putting a hand to his temple, Ridge tried to formulate a measured response. But he couldn't think straight. His head had the consistency of damp wood.

"Forgive me Mr. Dantley." Tarrant pretended to dry his eyes. "You ain't been around long. You don't understand that positions and titles and all those sandfly distinctions outside don't mean a thumb smudge worth a damn here. See, in this place, a man ain't nothing but what he can kill or dig out of the ground and carry away."

Ridge couldn't help but be intimidated. Tousled shoulder-length hair. Heavy brow. A tautness around the base of the neck. Flaring shoulders and arms veined with muscle. Tarrant appeared the model for a bolder, livelier race of men. Whether that race belonged properly to the past or the future, Ridge couldn't say.

"How many are with you, Mr. Dantley?"

"No one but me," Ridge ventured.

"You weren't sailing by yourself now were you?"

"There was a friend—someone from college. He didn't make it." Telling a half-truth felt easier to Ridge, more persuasive.

"Do you really know your Bible?"

"Not especially. I mean, I was—I'm a lapsed Episcopalian, I guess is what you'd call me. The school I went to had an Episcopalian bias, but... I'm Unitarian now. Why do you ask?"

"Unitarian, huh? The religion of Isaac Newton, Thomas Jefferson and that phony mystic, Emerson. Why you're practically an atheist." He flung the Bible at Ridge. "Tell me, what does it say in John, chapter eight, verse 32?"

Ridge obediently riffled the pages in search of the passage. He had to get control of the conversation. The verse leapt out at him: "*And you shall know the truth and the truth shall make you free.*"

"Believe me, Mr. Dantley, those are true words." Tarrant said, pointing to the book. "That's the only fiction I got in here, but in respect to your situation, that passage there is entirely true."

Wishing he could match the masterful timbre of Tarrant's voice, Ridge said, "What is it you want from me?"

"The truth, Mr. Dantley. Admittedly, there are problems of meaning whenever the truth is involved, certain—how can I put it?—ambiguities. But I ain't talking 'bout those things. I'm talking 'bout plain speech where a person tells a story the same way twice. The way I heard it, you got friends on an atoll somewhere close by."

Ridge's heart collapsed. *Christ. What did I say last night?* He resisted the impulse to lower his eyes. He met Tarrant's harsh stare with a vacant look. "Who told you that? Gerrit?"

"Who told me is irrelevant. What you said is what matters. Perhaps they were confused with drink but several men reported that when you described the wreck, you said 'we' made it to shore. Correct me if I'm wrong. I am, after all, a self-taught primitive but that suggests there are more survivors than just you." Tarrant stepped behind the desk. The spare lamplight contoured his face in shadow. He reached into a hinged Cuesta-Rey cigar box. "Ask anyone here, I'm an honest man—relentlessly honest some would say. But I only deal truthfully with men who give me the same courtesy." A six-shot revolver flashed in his hand. Tarrant casually pointed the short-barreled gun at Ridge.

"See, that was Maslen's real problem," he continued. "He wasn't honest with me until the end. He had the blackest of hates for me for a long time. He stayed up nights, figuring out ways to do me in. But face-to-face, he was a smiling coward. He was a shadow of a man. Personally, I couldn't live that kind of lie." With a flick of the wrist, Tarrant tossed the revolver to Ridge.

Startled, Ridge fumbled and dropped the weapon. The Bible thunked to the floor. Ridge hurriedly retrieved the gun and, resuming his full height, aimed it squarely at Tarrant's chest. *Okay... Calmly now... Okay...* Tarrant went on as before: "After a while, Maslen finally tried it—tried to kill me. It was a pathetic attempt. That's why I put him out of his misery."

Ridge tried to determine if the weapon were loaded based on its weight. He didn't have enough experience with handguns to know.

"That there's a Astra Terminator, semi-automatic .44 magnum modeled on the Smith & Wesson 'N' frame," Tarrant said. "Go ahead, check the cylinder for rounds. There's a release button..."

Ridge managed to swing the cylinder out, confirmed the gun was fully loaded then snapped it back into place. "Okay."

"How many are there? Is your father with them?"

"All I want is for you to get me to the nearest inhabited island," Ridge said. "Or, if you can just loan me a boat—you must have one around here, so you can get supplies or whatever—and direct me to the closest shipping lane, that would be fine, too." He balanced the gun on his free arm as he'd seen movie heroes do.

"Where are your friends?" Tarrant asked, growing bored. "There ain't many atolls around here within swimming distance and the Marokatu got a way with canoes. If I really want to go out after them, I can." He raised an accusatory finger. "It's simple: If you don't trust me, pull the trigger."

Ridge considered the implications of shooting him. How would the miners react? *Would they want to keep me quiet too? Most of them are probably criminals after all. Christ, I've got to do something. I can't just walk away.* He tightened his grip on the gun. The steel threatened to slip from his fingers.

The situation assumed a paralyzing unreality. He couldn't pull the trigger. The gun numbed his fingers. Tarrant appeared so remote and untouchable … There was a brute dignity to him. Tarrant didn't feign goodwill. He didn't deny the ego. Ridge recalled a passage from *The Prince* about cruelty being better than mercy, fear stronger than love.

"I'm not doing this because I trust you," Ridge announced, laying the gun on the stool. "I'm just not prepared to kill you." He was colored with shame when he'd expected triumph. He thought sparing Tarrant would prove his righteousness, that he had his own equally powerful principles he wouldn't abandon for the sake of expediency. But he still felt helpless and humiliated. He just wanted out of the room. "You can find out for yourself if I'm telling the truth."

"That's the way it stands then," Tarrant said.

"Can I leave?"

"Leave? You mean, the camp?" Tarrant shook his head. "It may not look like much to you, but this operation is my motherlode, the end-all and be-all of my travails. You're young. What? Twenty-one? Twenty-two?"

"Twenty-six," Ridge said.

"I know you won't believe me—the arrogance of youth and everything—but you really haven't lived yet. You don't know the hardness of this life. For all my grown days, I've lived in these kinds of unmapped places—dangerous places most of them—always on the verge of some glory-find. Hell, it ain't even the gold I'm after. It's what it stands for, what it intimates about me, you, *us* as a species in geologic time. Because time—it comes at you in waves, turning and returning … Prob'ly ain't real to you yet at your age. Just a dark suggestion …"

"You don't know a damn thing about me," Ridge said, trembling with anger.

"We'll have some good talks, you and me, Mr. Dantley. Some spirited backchat. As you might suspect, ain't too many men here been educated. Why don't you get some rest? You're listing to port a bit. We can talk more later."

The seconds died away in Ridge' chest. There was nothing left to be said on his side. Without another word, he turned and walked out into the anxiety-warped light of morning, unsure if he'd saved or condemned the others.

Tarrant shadowed him to the door, caught it before it closed and called for his number one, a man they called Foucher. He would know the simple truth of Ridge's story and quickly.

CHAPTER 14

The Black Vines

Foucher leaned into the wind to breathe the fresh sea air rather than the stink of the half-dozen Marokatu paddling the dugout canoe. The wind whipped about his broad smiling face, fanning his dirty-blonde ponytail. The sharp lines around his mouth ended in dimples. He took a quiet pleasure in the freedom of the open sea. The far horizon unburdened him. Here, he could dispense with the wearisome niceties of communal life. He could go anywhere, do anything, without fear of judgment. He could hurt somebody and feel good about it. Stronger.

Ever since he could remember, Foucher had suffered from a constant pressure inside. He imagined it as a tangle of black vines suffocating his heart. His whole life, he hadn't found a way to exorcise this pressure. Even during his tenure as a dog soldier in the Chicago-based mystery cult, the Society of the Black Sun. But Tarrant had given him a chance to meet civilization halfway. Tarrant allowed Foucher instances of relief—the chance to beat a Marokatu thief or spear-hunt a wild pig. These episodes helped perpetuate his facade of self-mastery.

The effect of these liberties, however, was all-too-brief. The pressure to strike out, to kick and scream against the constraints of living always intensified again. At these junctures, he either vented his unspent anger on one of the natives, or Tarrant, sensing an impending outburst, gave him a task designed to lighten his heart for a while. Foucher sometimes chafed at Tarrant's unsparing authority but knew deep down he was a better person for the unwanted checks. In his most lucid moments, he understood that unbridled license was somehow beneath him.

The Marokatu paddled in a swift unvarying rhythm. The body of the canoe was a long deep well connected with an outrigger float parallel to the body. Fashioned from light materials, the canoe skimmed the surface of the water with gratifying speed. An identical canoe of Marokatu cut across the waves on a parallel course.

Foucher distrusted the natives even more than himself. He considered them slaves to a deadening sameness, every aspect of their lives, from sex to song, regulated by tradition. As the outside world encroached, he predicted a generational rebellion, ancestor worship or no.

Closing in on another atoll, Foucher traded his spectacles for a pair of battered binoculars. The atoll gradually assumed details as he adjusted the magnification. The green of the palms along the lagoon loomed large in his vision. The apparent closeness of the scene surprised him. Hurriedly, he scanned the white sand beach. It gleamed like a pearl under the sweltering sun. Then a lithesome shadow—a woman. He could make out the contours of her body but her features were as yet indistinct.

Foucher's chest pounded with anticipation. The black vines writhed against the shell of his chest. They were maddeningly close to freedom, to realizing their accumulated urges. The aborigines couldn't paddle fast enough to satisfy them. *Whatever higher powers may inhere in Man, he is first and foremost an animal,* says the psalm book. A sorely neglected truth in the squarejohn world of enfeebling social norms and legal niceties. Foucher yelled, "More you bastards! Give it more! That's it! That's the one!"

The Marokatu pulled their leaf-shaped paddles as before, steady and sure. The canoes sped across the ocean.

Foucher slipped his glasses into the front pocket of his untucked shirt then felt for the double-action pistol holstered at his thigh. The cold metal gave his sportive vigor an outlet. *Since Moloch was Moloch...* He unsnapped the holster, stretched his fingers around the .41 magnum Bren Ten and stroked the curve of the trigger, resisting the playful inspiration to fire the weapon at the sky. He wanted to preserve the element of surprise as long as possible. Not yet, he told himself. Not yet.

CHAPTER 15

The Prisoner

Ridge rested for a few hours on Maslen's old bunk before he was awakened by Gerrit and directed to the mining area for work detail. "Every able man gottta bust his own way," Gerrit said. Unprepared to resist, Ridge shrugged into a pair of loosely fitting overalls Gerrit provided then followed the overseer to the hillside he'd stumbled down the night before.

The handcuffs and length of bicycle chain Gerrit carried presented new sources of worry. The chain dangled from Gerrit's broad shoulder like a hanging rope. Ridge eyed its swings and jolts with dread; at the same time, a perverse thrill ran through him. Here at last was something from his own life worth writing. He might be able to turn everything around in the mere telling of it. The shipwreck would only set the stage for his singular adventure. The cause of the accident would be lost in the urgency of the aftermath.

The national press would be all over the story. They'd punch up the irony of the situation: son of a wealthy Southern businessman forced to endure archaic punishments at the hands of savage gold-seekers ... Oh, yeah, what potential! *Time, Newsweek, People, US,* the tabloids ... He'd get the "Drama in Real Life" section of *Reader's Digest*: FROM PRINCETON TO PRISONER Page 60 ... at the very least, a book deal and a national speaking tour ... network news, CNN, no problem, maybe even a talk-show appearance or a segment on one of those primetime news shows ... His fair cheeks turned pink. Christ almighty. What was he thinking? Who knew what was happening with Mira and the Senator and the others? He had to survive, to find a way out of here first. There were people—his fiancée for Chrissake—depending on him. *Got to stay focused ... look for an opening ...* In Hollywood movies, there was always a significant yet somehow overlooked breach of security in situations like this ... It was poor speculation but what else could he use as a guide?

The mining area, methodically stripped of the brush, trees and morning glory which adorned the rest of the hillside, stretched for about three hundred yards. Two outcrops of gray rock made a prominent dimple in the face of the hillside near its crest. A series of numbered wooden stakes marked a half-pyramid of sample holes. The bald contrast between the auburn-tinged mining area and the surrounding greenery gave the elongated barrenness an unearthly cast. It looked as if the trade cloud that hovered perpetually overhead had deprived it of nurturing sun.

Vaguely distinguishable men were scattered about the mining site engaged in measuring, drilling, digging, cleaning and amalgamating concentrate, panning, chopping and collecting firewood. In most cases, they labored without the aid of sophisticated tools. With little more than screwdrivers, crowbars, picks and shovels, they plied the hillside for its mineral treasure. Several natives helped with the exacting work, including the native boy Ridge recognized from the night before as the one who'd distributed the dueling spears.

Gerrit pointed out the portable rock drill sitting idle near the creek bank, remarking that it was the only piece of real mining equipment they had and, much to their dismay, its motor had been damaged beyond repair. Before Ridge could inquire further, Gerrit handed him a bent screwdriver and began to show him how to crevice mine along the stream. "Ain't no hippie chore wheel here. Every job's a ballbreaker," said Gerrit. "We found some nuggets in this area already, real smooth'n flat. That's why we got the diggin's up there." He tossed the handcuffs and rusty chain aside.

"Have you found anything on the hill?" Ridge asked. His true thoughts were with Mira. He simply wanted Gerrit to continue talking about the operation in hopes he'd inadvertently relay something that could figure into an escape plan.

"Yeah, a little. Jus' a couple a nuggets. Coulda been planted for all I know. That's what I think sometimes—to keep us busy, you know, thinkin' we gonna get rich," he said. "And we damn well better. I mean, that's why we're all here. That's sure as hell why I'm here. And we're doing better at this site already—found more gold it seems—than downstream. Yeah, that other camp … that place was stone cold broke. No motherlode there, I tell ya."

Ridge kneeled down next to Gerrit, who was investigating a fissure with squinty eyes. "How long have you been here?"

Without interrupting his work, Gerrit said, "At this camp, you mean? Not long. Three weeks comin' on a month."

"No, I meant the whole time you've been on this island altogether."

"I been here since the beginning—'bout five months. Hooked up with Tarrant in Bolivia a few years back. Talk about a fucked up operation. Man, every piss-poor peasant in the country was there in Guanay thinkin' they were gonna land a major pay streak. Nuthin' but dirt and disease, man. There were open sewers, we had mosquitos like you wouldn't believe, fuckin' yellow fever, TB, you name it. Goddamn cesspool, believe you me."

"So is this what you do—you and Tarrant—mine for gold?"

"Not always. We done some nighttime archeology—a few Olmec sites, a Mayan grave ... Not like I got some place in the outside world to be. Just as soon be here and doin' a livin' man's work than makin' dead time back in the States." Gerrit paused for a moment and looked Ridge in the eye. "Don't you be expectin' me to tell you what I done, neither. I might a got the pride of a dog but that's all I got left, you know? I went to college. I know how you educated sonsabitches think about guys like me."

"Where'd you go?"

"Played football for Mississippi Valley, you know, in the Southwestern Athletic Conference. Practically in my own backyard a Vicksburg—just 'bout 90 minutes up MS-7. Played wide receiver some. You follow college ball?"

"No, not really."

"What? You some faggoty art student?"

"Princeton," Ridge said. "Just don't follow sports." At least, sports with which Gerrit would be familiar. His fitful interest in athletics was limited to a handful of genteel pursuits: swimming, sailing, tennis and golf.

Grabbing the screwdriver from Ridge's hand, Gerrit said, "Boy, am I gonna fuckin' get ya in shape. This is hard work, some of the hardest you ask me and I been layin' block since the age a nine. Now, when ya dig out the crevice, you take everythin'. There's gonna be rocks and silt and roots and shit. Just take everythin' and put it in this here bucket." He pushed a battered aluminum pail toward Ridge. "The roots are important. Sometimes 'cause the gold sinks down in the earth, you find little flakes on the end a them."

Ridge picked up a length of copper. "What's the wire for?"

"Let me get to that," said Gerrit. "Once you dig out the crevice a bit, you know, using your screwdriver and your hand shovel or whatever, you take that and poke it down into the crevice to see how far it goes. Some a these things go halfway to hell."

"Looks like where I'm headed anyway."

"This place really ain't that bad," said Gerrit, rising to his feet. "Tarrant's a bastard know-it-all, yeah, and the work's hard, but if we hit the motherlode, you know, it's worth it. Anyway, don't be afraid to really dig into that crevice. When ya got the bucket full a dirt, just call to Waxman there." He pointed to the man with the prosthetic arm Ridge had met at the burial service. The hump-shouldered man was farther up the river, separating gold from gravel with a mini-rocker. The sunlight filtering through the sago palms gave his gray beard an eerie glow. "He'll test it for ya," Gerrit added. "Then, ya know, you can just keep goin' upstream."

"Great," Ridge said bitterly.

"Hey." Gerrit delivered a steel-toed kick to Ridge' backside. "I feel for ya and all that kid. You didn't ask for this shit. But don't give me no trouble. I don't wanna see no attitude, all right? I got Tarrant on me all the time and if'n I don't get some work outta you, he's gonna skin me like a mole rat. And that means I'm gonna do that to you. Understand, frat boy?"

Arching his back to take the sting out of the blow, Ridge said, "Yeah, sure."

"I gotta put this on you too," Gerrit said, holding the handcuffs in one hand and the chain in the other.

Ridge nodded. *Forced to endure archaic punishments...* He would suffer now for his ambitions.

Gerrit placed one cuff around his left foot and hooked the other through the chain. Then he wrapped the end of the chain around a nearby sago tree and secured it with a small padlock, leaving Ridge about 25 yards of leeway. Indicating the padlock, Gerrit said, "I don't gotta tell you not to mess with this, right?"

Without a word, Ridge turned away and started digging. He heard the steady crunch of Gerrit's footsteps along the creek bank. In a faint, almost apologetic voice, Gerrit told him there would be a lunch break in a couple of hours. Ridge closed his eyes for a minute or so, listening to the gentle music of the stream and breathing the pungent air. Christ almighty. His situation seemed so unfair.

Gradually, he expelled his darkest thoughts and began digging with drone-like alacrity. While he worked the bent metal into the bedrock, he surveyed the immediate area, looking for a crew chief or guard— someone with a gun—capable of preventing him from testing the strength of the padlock. Down on his knees, the forest circumscribing the mining area obscured his view of the area. He didn't stand or move upstream, however, to get a better look. He picked out the crevice as he'd been told, trusting images of Mira would dispel the pessimistic fog into which he'd descended: her roseate cheeks when embarrassed or irritated; the way she held her book bag over her breasts with crossed arms; her habit of fingering the strands of hair around her ears; the pom-pom socks she insisted on wearing to the bowling alley ... Here he was—back to the moony daze of remembrances that had sustained him through so many college nights alone. What kind of deal would he be willing to make with Tarrant or even with God, he wondered, to see her again and safe? How many good things in the future would he be willing to give up, never to know?

CHAPTER 16

The First Killing

Under the meager shade of a coconut palm, Mira half-dreamed of home. She tried to conjure up pleasant images of college life pre-Ridge: enjoying coffee at Teresa's Pizzetta Café; browsing Labyrinth Books; hanging out at Hoagie Haven or Zaffy's, the bowling alley and sometime concert venue in Piscataway. Despite vague recurrent worries about her future, she'd never been more carefree than during her years at Princeton. She'd always been attentive to herself and her needs. When was the last time she'd taken the time to enjoy a good meal or an impromptu hike? Between Ridge and her job as a counselor at the Gettinger Institute for Family Therapy, she'd lost all sense of herself as a person in time. The flywheel of days provoked a constant anxiety about the next thing and the next and the next after that … Her thoughts took an unwanted turn and she found herself recalling (again!) a troubling childhood conversation with her mother. Mira had been 12 years old when her father passed away, the luckless victim of a drunk driver. She remembered his death as a slow-motion funeral crowded with obscure black shapes, a bitterness that rendered her teenage years monotonous. The seriousness behind her easy charm was less a sign of fashionable intellectualism than of tightly suppressed gloom.

"What do you expect, *bubee*? You want the Shechinah to appear, maybe and explain things?" her mother had said, holding her arms out for an embrace.

Mira remained adamant, saying she didn't understand how anyone could think her father's death was right in the eyes of God. There was a terrible banality to his passing she couldn't move beyond. *Gevalt*, Lord, enough!

"You want you should turn against the faith of your parents and your parent's parents on top of all this *dreck*? *Chas vesholem*! Don't do this, Miriam. I know you're angry. I'm angry. Think of it: my husband of 21 years, your father, a Holocaust survivor … How can I not be? But you can't let it turn you against your faith, against your people," her mother said. "Our heritage, our entire history, is survival by the grace of God. Elohim hasn't forgotten you my child. And you must not forget Him."

Mira's stubborn refusal to break down at that moment, to even acknowledge her mother's pain with a hug, shamed her all over again. She lifted the black crepe from her face and sat up. When she drowsily opened her eyes, the sea blinded her with its reflections.

So much for the Shechinah... She recalled the old Jewish fable her mother had told her time and again as a child. According to this fable, Emperor Hadrian once asked a Rabbi to show him God. The Rabbi instructed the Emperor to stare into the sun. After a moment, the Emperor's eyes began to water and he averted his gaze, saying the sun was too bright. Then the Rabbi asked calmly, "If you are unable to look at the sun, which is only a servant of God, how can you possibly see the Shechinah, the glorious Presence of the Lord Himself?"

The radiance of the sea invited Mira to lose herself in its luminosity. The mirrored sunlight drew her into a comforting philosophical state away from concern for Ridge or memories of home. No worry crept into this realm of associations. There were only images of water: as the primordial source of life, swelling with embryonic animals; water poured lovingly over a fat infant's head at a christening or baptism; water coursing gently through the first garden on earth; water encircling the land, eroding it slowly, discretely, a patient elemental force.

The cascading images formed a veil through which the glistening Pacific appeared as a bridge of the gods into the distant blue. The true ocean appeared so faint to Mira that even though she looked in the right direction, she failed to recognize the two elongated shapes in the center of her vision as canoes until the crafts sailed into the lagoon. Thank the Lord! Rescued!

She shouted to the others, "Kenny! Paige! Ridge is here! A canoe's here!" Her heart pounded with anticipation.

The others were no less enthusiastic about the arrival of the boats. Paige greeted the prospect of rescue with whoops and cries of delight. She ran to the lagoon with long graceful strides. She skipped across the wet sand, playfully holding out the hem of her slip as though she were a Radio City showgirl. Mira took her hands and they danced an awkward circle in the surf.

Kenny followed closely behind Paige, grinning. The Senator was nowhere in sight.

With a hand on his holstered gun, the white man at the head of the first canoe jumped out and waded the last few yards to shore. He approached Kenny and said, "Hey, how you doin'? You friends with Ridge Dantley?"

"Yeah," Kenny said. "Is he okay?" He waved his thanks to the natives running the canoes ashore.

"Better than you." The man leveled his gun.

The crack of the weapon roared across the placid lagoon. Kenny tumbled to the sand like a scarecrow suddenly robbed of its supports. An irregular pool of crimson spread quickly from the hole in his chest.

The gunman's demeanor was suitably dour for a moment, as if he'd fired the pistol against his will. Then he broke into a toothy smile.

A few yards from the body, Mira leaned against Paige for balance. Her pulse surged hotly in her ears. She thought of herself as just another done-for animal.

The Melanesians flanked the gunman in support. He raised the weapon again.

Mira clutched Paige's hand for some small comfort, unsure if she'd have time to fit in a second thought before—

CHAPTER 17

Gold Scientifically Regarded

The ancient Greek philosopher Aristotle believed gold was the glittering residue of the sun's rays. His theory lasted for nearly 2,000 years and gave rise to various fantasies about the relationship between metals and celestial bodies. Modern geology holds exactly the opposite: gold rises from the depths of the earth, a rare precipitate of millions of years of geological change.

According to the theory of plate tectonics, the earth's crust and upper mantle consist of seven colossal moving plates and possibly, eighteen smaller ones. The plates shift, scrape and collide like pieces of an immense puzzle assembled by a frustrated child. At most, the plates move only a few inches per year; but over time their lethargic violence shapes the oceans, divides continents, births volcanoes and mountain ranges, and causes massive earthquakes.

Only the tumultuous collision of tectonic plates allows the luster of gold to come to light. Sometimes when plates collide, one plate slides under another. The leading edge of the heavier plate plunges into the depths of the earth. The plate's upper layers are sheared clean and partly melted as it careens toward the earth's core. The molten material, containing particles of gold, silver and other minerals, rises through cracks in the dominant continental plate. The partially solid mass ascends from buried earth closer to the surface, closer to God, usually accumulating in an underground magma chamber.

There, a hot mineral-rich solution separates from the magma and combines with cooler groundwater seeping down from above. With the fiery magma chamber providing the force, the hydrothermal solution circulates continuously, amassing gold from the chamber and the surrounding rock. This water rises, cools and solidifies, depositing gold, among other minerals, in existing fissures. The resultant deposits are first revealed by years of exposure to wind and rain then opened wide by backbreaking labor.

As might be expected, the most significant known metal deposits are clustered around the boundaries of the tectonic plates. The legendary Motherlode of California was the result of an epic clash between the American Plate and the Pacific Plate some 77 to 210 million years ago. The two roughly parallel chains of islands that comprise the Solomons describe part of the northeastern boundary of the Australian and Pacific plates. There are some notable exceptions to this pattern, specifically, large deposits in eastern Canada and Central Russia, but most of these deposits appear in areas where active plate boundaries existed long ago. Still others formed before the plates themselves came to be.

Gold may be associated with the sun and the greater heavens but it comes from the smashing intensity of terrestrial elements—the collision of immense land masses and the consequent release of hell-fired magma. It has its origin in naturally-occurring cataclysms. And sadly, its end is often determined by no less natural, though more tragic, events.

CHAPTER 18

Hard Lessons

"This native stuff ain't nuthin' compared to what the forty-niners had to go through, eatin'-wise," said Waxman, loading his wooden bowl with pasty sago dumplings. "Why, there were so many stampeders, whole towns would sprout up overnight, and where the hell were they gonna get food? Jaws, people forget that California's a desert. When I was readin' through some a the correspondence a the time, tryin' to get clues, you unnerstand, I ran across one 'bout these guys in Coloma. Why, food was so scarce, they paid a dollar apiece for pears still hangin' on the tree—hard green ones—and waited aroun' for 'em to ripen."

Waxman passed the dumplings to Ridge, who, seated at the end of the long wooden table, promptly set them aside. Ridge was numb. The conversation around him registered in the same faint spectrum as dialogue in a half-remembered dream. His right arm, pockmarked with mosquito bites, ached from his work along the stream. The rigorous labor, compounded by constant worrying and the unyielding humidity, had drained him. He stared down the table past Waxman and the other dozen or so miners eating in the shade of the mess tent toward the bright central clearing.

"Why do you insist on eating that shit, Waxman?" asked Beattie from behind his smoking grill. "I have perfectly good ham steaks and fresh bread. Taste buds gone, you old plonker?"

"Just bein' friendly with the natives."

"Think that'll save you if they get hacked off at us, eh? Breakin' bread and all that?"

"Maybe."

"Get away." The short barrel-chested cook waved goodbye to the idea. "If it happens, they'll off us all, regardless. You know what they think of us, the arrogant bastards. We're not even human to them. Think we're cannibals. Ain't that a gob-smacker? They think *we're* cannibals. Nanokwe was telling me the word Marokatu means 'the people.'

Like *the* people, like there's no one else."

"Nanokwe's the witch-doctor, shaman, holy head-shrinker, whatever they call 'em," Waxman informed Ridge. "He's the one speaks English— talks it like this Aussie rogue here on account a some Brit missionaries. Wait 'til you hear him. Unbelievable." Waxman ran his fingers through his long unkempt beard, fishing for errant dumplings. His silvery-gray mustache trailed over his top lip.

Gerrit took a seat across from Ridge. "Hey, how's the Tourist? Sorry we can't offer a split a champagne with your chow." Following Gerrit's lead, that's what everyone had taken to calling him: the Tourist. Some wit, the fucking animals.

"Oh, you know, laughing on the inside," Ridge said. He felt awkward and inadequate around these men. Their rank was determined by attributes foreign to him: rude physical strength, vulgarity, sexual prowess, thievery, a generous capacity for drink. The situation was a persistent assault on his manhood. So he tried to detach himself from it, adopt a firm reportorial perspective. If he couldn't play the action hero, he would play the stoic. Maybe his tough passivity would win them over.

Beattie returned to the clay oven just outside the mess tent where he was preparing another batch of dinner rolls.

Gerrit turned to Waxman. "Did he find anything?"

"'Bout a grandmother's thimbleful of dust."

Gerrit grunted. "You heard about the find on the hillside?"

"Yeah, a vein, right?"

"Just enough to call for blasting, I think. I want to get down to the fuckin' lode in a hurry."

"You and everybody else."

Ridge saw a three, maybe four year old, aborigine inadvertently knock down one of his smaller playmates while darting after a chicken. The smaller boy promptly burst into tears. The wailing brought out the boy's mother who jerked him to his feet and, shouting authoritatively, set him on his friend. With his arms outstretched and eyes half-closed, the smaller boy made a charge at his unsuspecting playmate, who had taken an interest in a discarded piece of sugar cane. The naked boys tumbled to the ground.

"'Avenge yourself'—that's what she told the kid," a gravelly voice sounded in Ridge's ear.

Ridge looked up to see a dark-skinned man with black swept-back hair and a thin goatee. He wore a string of elk vertebrae around his neck. "They teach 'em all to be badass warriors," the man said.

"Oh, shut the hell up, Tree," Gerrit said. "You don't know what you're talkin' 'bout." Eyeing Ridge, he added, "If you're smart, you won't listen to this junkie b.s. artist."

Tree held out his hand. The two smallest fingers were black and blue. "Lone Tree White Eagle. Full-blooded native American. Yakima tribe to be exact. Oregon country."

Ridge shook hands reluctantly. He narrowed his eyes, trying to look gruff. He suspected, however, that he came across as petulant.

"Don't mind the fingers. They ain't broken; just useless." He held up his hand and turned it from front to back. "See the puncture marks on either side? Little red circles?"

Ridge nodded even though the wounds eluded him.

"One time, I was so desperate to get high, I let a rattler bite me thinkin' the venom might have psychedelic properties. Damn near screwed up my hand permanent." Nodding toward the village square, Tree said, "I been learnin' their language for a while now. I figure we're in native territory, you know, we ought to be adoptin' their ways, learnin' to live with the land and everythin'. It's imperialism pure and simple to just come in here and take. We gotta respect 'em somehow. Seems I'm the only one around here 'sides Tarrant who understands that, you know, since my people were practically wiped out by white greed. Yeah, ain't that sweet irony? Whites started takin' over *our* land when gold was discovered on the Snake River."

Based on Tree's facial features, Ridge doubted he was a genuine native American. The ridge of bone above his eyes protruded too far, his eyebrows were too thick and close together and his nose too broad. If anything, he looked Hispanic.

"Hey, scoot over a sec, will you?" Tree asked, nudging Ridge.

Gerrit growled, "I ain't talkin' to you Tree."

"I ain't talkin' to you, neither. I'm talkin' to Waxman here." He looked past Ridge to the inveterate prospector. "Waxman, you gotta help me out on this. With all your knowledge of explorers and shit, you the only one can 'preciate, you know, pushing new frontiers—not just physical frontiers like the Old West, but the ones inside, too—the frontiers a perception, so to speak."

Waxman glared at Tree with his rheumy eyes. "Tree, everyone's already told you—jaws, Mayano's told you hisself—jus' 'cause he's from Peru don't mean he got any coke or whatever it is you're after. You know Tarrant wouldn't stand for it."

"Do as I say not as I do, right?"

"Hey, he's a seeker, Tree. His time in the lodge smokin' that *kava* shit—strictly spiritual hoogah-boogah."

"And I'm different how? I got my spiritual needs, too. I'm tryin'—I need, you know... There's Whee-me-me-ow-ah, the Great Chief Above, my animal spirit..."

"I never seen you with no peace pipe."

"Peace pipe," Tree snorted. "That's a white man's slur."

"Yeah, what're you people call it then?"

Tree screwed up his eyes in concentration. "That ain't for you to know. It's the kinda sacred word stays in the tribe..."

Ridge noticed that the village square was now crowded with natives. He could make out the two boys in the center of the throng. A broad-shouldered woman had an arm around the larger boy, apparently restraining him, while she launched a harsh verbal assault on his playmate's mother.

"Mayano's holdin'," Tree said. "Trust me. That group he was with—that Shinin' Path—they had control a the largest cocoa-growing region in the world, runnin' drugs all over the place and everything and you expect me to believe he ain't got shit? C'mon."

"Didn't you learn anything when you fucked yourself up shooting coffee grounds?" Gerrit asked. "Jus' leave it alone, will you?"

"I wouldn't be selfish with it. I'd share, make it a gift, partly. Think what Nanokwe would do... My guess is, he'd think it was a cool new way to commune with their sea god, get in touch with his ancestors, or whatever he does. I mean, don't you think he would be grateful for this? It would be like shit-hot manna from heaven. Maybe he'd help us out more. I don't know, but it's worth a shot, right?"

"And I take it you'd be the middleman on this deal?"

"I'm the only one who's taken a real interest in the Marokatu as a people. You can't deny me that."

Waxman interjected: "Tree, I lived around Indians for years and years in Alaska. I guarantee you bein' a native means you jus' got there first. They don't have any kinda special vision or moral edge or anythin.'"

The square was crowded with Marokatu now. Two distinct kinship groups claimed roughly half of the uneven ground in a suddenly tense standoff. Some of the men brandished large pine clubs. The clubs resembled oversized railroad ties.

Several miners got up from the table to watch the impending fight.

"Oh, they ain't gonna do it," Tree told the immediate group. "They can't go nowhere—the family been put down. They don't want to split the village now."

Slashing hastily with a stick, the larger boy's mother broadened the area between her kinship group and the other. Her palm frond skirt swished against her dark thighs.

The smaller boy's mother appealed to her husband in guttural shouts. When she'd exhausted herself, he waved his club menacingly at the rival clan, making similarly strident noises. Apparently unsatisfied, his wife slapped him on the chest then pushed him forward.

"See how those nigger women cajole their men?" Gerrit said to Ridge, standing to get a better view of the action. "Jus' bitch, bitch, bitch, bitch, bitch."

Too fatigued to stand, Ridge lost his view of the scene to the burgeoning crowd of miners. He held his head in his hands, feeling his face give off evanescent waves. With each feverish pulse, he imagined drifting farther and farther away, now above the camp, now above the island, now above the glassy ocean … Despite a furious moment when the larger boy's mother placed a stick in her son's hand and pulled him into a charge at his playmate, the squabble proved a disappointing spectacle. Tree translated the flurry of insults in a laconic tone, ad-libbing key phrases for effect: "'You want to leave, pigfucker? Go, then.'

"'If you strike my son, you will have to confront me in a club fight. Do you think I will let you insult my family without a fitting answer? You yourself, Waikrishi, you make a show of being *rico suave*, your skin is greasy like that of a warrior, but it is well known that you throw your spear like a faggot…'

"'Shut up, you ugly mouth twisted by evil thoughts. You talk of leaving, of separating yourselves from us; maybe I will go too so as not to hear you any longer…'"

The miners soon tired of this ritual banter and resumed their places at the table, glancing toward the square periodically in case true violence erupted. Gerrit, with an unwelcome Tree following him, left the table to join a poker game just outside one of the bunkhouses. Waxman remained with Ridge, playfully stabbing raw sago dumplings with his fork.

"You gonna make it, boy? Lookin' a bit jarred," Waxman said.

Rubbing his eyes, Ridge nodded. He liked Waxman. The mangy old miner was a harmless and accomplished talker.

"It ain't as bad as all that. Just stay clear a Tarrant and you'll come outta this like a waxed peach. He's always testin' himself—'gainst the elements, 'gainst himself, everybody. Ain't no accident his cabin don't got any winders. Better for meditation that way. I seen him once in a snow flurry up in the Andes. We was on another treasure hunt then. Meditatin', he got his temp so hot the snow melted around him. No lie." Lost in thought for a moment, he wet his cracked lips with his tongue. "Conditions here ain't anywhere near what other adventurin' types have suffered. Jaws, some a those guys…Columbus' father-in-law, for instance. You ever heard tell of him?"

Ridge shook his head.

"This is a funny story. I know I shouldn't say that up front 'cause you might not think so but…Anyway, Columbus' father-in-law was a 15th century explorer, too." Waxman took a cheap briar pipe and a rolled-up pouch of tobacco from his shirt pocket and proceeded to prep a smoke. Ridge was impressed with how deftly Waxman managed the process with the claw-end of his prosthetic. "His name was Perestrelo," Waxman said, "and he discovered this island called Madeira, which is Portuguese for 'wood,' I think. Anyway, from the shore, he saw this weird cloud, and he decided to sail into it, and it turned out to be an island—Madeira. As a reward for his discovery, he was made a captain of part of the island. But he had a problem: rabbits. There were thousands, maybe millions, of the furry beasts. So he set out to exterminate 'em." He gritted the pipe, showing small tobacco-stained teeth, and sparked the Missouri Meerschaum blend with a lighter flick. After a test draw, he continued: "Sadly, he had a poor constitution and all—he weren't really cut out for the work—and after killing an army a rabbits, he just up and died. Practically had an island to himself and what happens? Dies of exhaustion or whatever tryin' to kill a bunch a cottontails." Waxman laughed heartily at his own joke.

Ridge glared at him. "If it's not so bad—which everybody keeps telling me—why did you ask me about my boat then? At the burial, you asked me if my boat sunk."

"Yeah, well if you ain't noticed, we could use the parts 'round here." Waxman paused to tamp the tobacco with an acrylic tool and re-light the bowl. "Jaws, I ain't got any plans to escape. This here's my last chance. I got a daughter about your age. She's a hard surface welder in Washington State. Wants to be an artist—a sculptor—usin' her weldin' skills. I been jerkin' off most a my life, goin' after one thing or another, and I don't got much to leave her. Most a her trust fund's in my mouth." Waxman sighed out a drift of smoke and peeled his lips back to reveal a cluster of dirty-gold teeth. "I can try to make things easier for you. But I won't risk my neck, no sir. I can't be implicated in anything stupid."

Ridge leaned toward the hunched-over prospector and hissed, "The only thing you can do to 'make things easy' is to tell me how to get the fuck out of here." He sounded more desperate than menacing.

Waxman eyed Ridge through the sweet tobacco fume as if he were indulging a slow child. "That's what I'm tryin' s'plain: you gotta accept this, Johnny Newcome. For however long it lasts, you jus' gotta accept it. You ain't no ol' west desperader. Look at you, already dead tired 'n' done. And we gotta helluva lot more'n rabbits here."

CHAPTER 19

The Living & the Dead

Senator Neeland watched the outgoing tide swirl around Kenny's disheveled remains. The body cast a long shadow in the light of the dying sun. The Senator sat far enough away that he couldn't see the clumps of dried blood in Kenny's hair, the crimson webs across the face. He'd seen enough blood when he first came upon the body, panicked at the sight of the unbroken horizon. The Senator hoped the tide would drag the remains into the smooth gold-rimmed sea.

The Senator presumed Mira and Paige were also dead, their bodies in the surf or in the nearby underbrush. He didn't have the strength of heart to search. If he chanced upon them he knew their fetid remains would be shrunken like rotten apples. More than Kenny's body or even the likelihood of his own slow demise, this lingering unknown made him sick inside.

He wiped his sunken cheeks dry with the back of his hand. His throat was raw, his chest constricted. He had no more tears, only sad contemplative memories. Over the years, he'd come to regard Kenny as an errant son. Following the resignation of his long-time chief of staff Graham Wyse, Kenny had taken over his DC office with a vengeance, relishing the 'bad cop' role assigned to him—the role which allowed the Senator to perpetuate his image of philosophical detachment.

The Senator had cultivated this image from his earliest days as a House member to contravene the North's feudalistic notion of the South. Inspired by glowing histories of Thomas Jefferson, he'd wanted desperately to somehow remain above mere politics. The Senator had hoped to emulate Jefferson's shrewd synthesis of liberal and republican traditions in the Declaration, balancing the South's perennial concerns for both personal freedom and communal values.

As the everyday demands of life on the Hill confused his desire for philosophical purity, however, he took a greater interest in Jefferson's acute hypocrisies: his predatory affair with 14 year old slave Sally

Hemings; his unwillingness to free his slaves, even after his death; and his blind support for the bloody French Revolution. These things and more gave the Senator an increasingly powerful excuse to make his own no less baleful compromises.

As circumstances dictated, the Senator alternately abandoned and resumed the task of shaping himself after a purified version of Jefferson. He gave himself away in bits and pieces but successfully retained, even improved, his stature as a statesman. Political character had grown so thin in recent years, he was a giant in comparison to his periodic rivals and to most of his peers. Kenny had guarded this image as if it were his own.

The Senator recalled with fresh sorrow and hurt the night of his last campaign victory when he offered to make Kenny his chief of staff. It was in the small hours of the morning. Most everyone had left his stately Buckhead home. In a noticeably drunken euphoria, Kenny was smoking a pricey Davidoff Panatella—a gift from one of the Senator's affluent supporters. The Senator ushered him into his study, a steeply-roofed library with shiny blond-wood and brass appointments. He began the conversation with a brief catalog of Kenny's virtues—his dedication, his attention to detail, his keen intelligence.

Before he could make the offer, however, Kenny said he had a secular confession to make. "I admire you too much to let this go," he said, smiling. "I know what you're going to do and before you make a decision you regret, you have to know this: I got Graham fired."

The Senator tried to appear taciturn. He'd reluctantly asked Graham to resign after an Atlanta television station accused the Senator of mounting a "dirty tricks" effort against his opponent, state attorney general Alan Metzler. The campaign had leaked a story to the press involving Metzler's teenage daughter. During Metzler's tenure as attorney general, she'd been arrested for, but never charged with, possession of crystal meth. Graham had gone on the evening news apparently unprepared for questions about the story. His halting performance that night and later revelations about a team of private investigators hired by the campaign, had seemed to confirm the charges of dirty tricks. "How's that?"

"That team of PIs? Graham didn't know anything about 'em. I took care of it. I was worried Metzler's accusations on the crime issue were scoring. You know better than me how keyed up Georgians get about crime. Back when the state was a colony, you so much as pissed in the wind, you got branded or whipped or locked up in the stocks. Governor Arnall didn't abolish chain gangs until—what?—the 40s sometime? I agree with your principled stand against mandatory sentencing but Metzler had the emotional edge. I could feel our big mo' grinding down under his TV blitz." He took a long comfortable drag on his cigar.

The Senator had never seen Kenny smoke before but knew him to be an expert mimic. Kenny had buried his blue-collar upbringing under a barrage of clever banter, most of which he gleaned from staff-written summaries of popular novels and classic political tomes. He dressed purposely like a clerk at a chic East Coast bookstore. He wore a pair of non-prescription designer glasses and at parties occasionally tossed out that he was pursuing a PH.D. in political philosophy. At the same time, he nurtured an invidious hatred of the so-called elite.

"You better explain yourself better than that, Kenny," A couple of bourbons had given the Senator's voice a pleasing rasp.

Much to the Senator's surprise, rather than rationalizing his behavior, Kenny reveled in its amusing wickedness. He countered the Senator's earlier praise with a litany of self-aggrandizing faults. He inflated his failings to Olympian proportions as a way to shield himself from further, potentially more damaging charges. Coming from one of the most indulgent states in the South, where governors freely boasted about their gambling and loose women, he testified against himself with convincing fervor.

"I made some godawful mistakes and I'm truly sorry about Graham," he said. "I set him up, pure and simple. I hired the PIs and got the goods on Metzler's daughter. Then I leaked the information to the TV station just before Graham's interview. I knew the press would ask about the so-called 'dirty tricks' and I didn't tell Graham about it. I just let him die on the evening news. But I didn't do it just for myself. You needed me and Graham, he was competent, yeah, but he was burned out. I mean, he was comin' up on 50, right? It was an act of excessive devotion. That's all there was to it."

"But it was so unnecessary Kenny. We were far ahead in the polls.

I wasn't worried about what Metzler was saying. I was worried about a serious misstep on our part and the 'dirty tricks' charge just spilled us open like a bad melon." The Senator sipped his bourbon. The slow char burn in his chest soothed his nerves. "And you didn't just betray Graham, you betrayed me, too. I've relied on Graham for almost three terms and you forced me to cut him loose."

"I didn't have to tell you," Kenny said. "I could have play-acted my way through everything."

"Children are sometimes rewarded for honesty when they've done something wrong. But you're not a child, Kenny."

"I'm giving you everything here, Senator. I mean, there's other oppo research we used that you never knew about. Do you know why Metzler refused to release his wife's tax returns? Because he hid some stocks and other assets in his wife's name to keep his ex-wife from knowing about 'em and demanding more alimony. His wife's returns were legit. He just didn't want his ex-wife to see what was in 'em. I just told you to keep making it an issue and it worked beautifully. As attorney general, he had to be totally clean, *look* totally clean. You didn't know why the issue worked so well and it didn't matter." Kenny was showing off as though the Senator were a prom date. Smoke curled around his ruddy face.

As a veteran of nearly a dozen elections, the Senator was familiar with obscene election-year mechanics. Almost nothing Kenny could say would've shocked him. Years ago, he'd reconciled himself to a restful hypocrisy not unlike the one which sustained the idea of America itself. The way the Senator saw things, since the beginning of Reconstruction, the South had aspired to be what the North pretended to be—a place of common justice. The North, unburdened by the evils of slavery, had become all of America, inviolate; the South, the nation's fount of sin.

In his early years as a Representative, the Senator had failed to appreciate this need for a private darkness. He was full of youthful puritanism, determined like Jefferson before him to be principled in all things. Soon, however, he began to understand, even sympathize with, Jefferson's failings, the compromises that made an occasional small kindness possible.

"I know how it was with you and Graham, Senator. I understand the relationship," Kenny continued, putting out his cigar in his Tanqueray and tonic. "That's why you didn't know about any of this. If you want to know, if you want to make the decisions, I can do that, too. But with all due respect, sir, I think you should marshal your resources, concentrate on the big picture. You have more important things to worry about."

As much as the Senator disliked Kenny's juvenile bombast, he couldn't deny the force of his arguments. What had begun as a grudging recognition of political reality was now an established pattern: he operated on the grand level of ideas while his staff engaged in the necessary labors of the Beltway. Still, the Senator balked at conceding Kenny's point immediately. The impulsive youth had, after all, openly flouted his reputation as a statesman.

"When I was a boy, growing up on my daddy's cotton farm, I had this mangy dog, a mutt. Think he was some kinda lab," the Senator said, warming to the story. "I didn't know where he'd come from or what'd happened to him, but he had only three legs. Daddy called him Tripod. That's about as much of a joke as I heard my daddy tell my whole life. Anyway, the dog didn't know he was cripple. He acted like a regular dog, chasing the chickens and hogs, digging around the fence and whatnot. And to this day, I can't figure out if he was the smartest dog I ever seen or the dumbest. If he knew he was standing on three legs and he coped with it, that's one thing. But if he thought he had four legs all along, well, that's different.

"Now, I'm convinced you gotta helluva future in politics, Kenny, with or without me. What with your smarts and the way you talk, you could charm the lard off a hog. But you gotta know how many legs you're standin' on. Think about it for a while, and when you figure it out, come see me."

Kenny had visited the Senator at home about two weeks later, not exactly chastened, but with a deepened capacity for self-awareness. The Senator had taken Kenny's changed demeanor as a positive sign and, almost as an afterthought, offered him the job. In keeping with his new mien, Kenny accepted without even the hint of a smile.

Now more than ever, the Senator knew politics was the art of knowing what to remember and what to forget. As the sun dipped below the horizon, he got to his feet, breathed in the sharp ocean air. He could no longer watch the elements abuse Kenny's body. He waited a while for the sun to disappear and the water to go dark. Then, in the cold light of the moon, when everything was the same dead blue, he dragged his friend's remains out of the surf.

CHAPTER 20

The Empty Camp

After the anxious ocean crossing and urgent trek through the black half-seen jungle, Mira was relieved when they came to a clearing of several squat native huts. She was impatient with fate now; for good or ill, she wanted an end to the silent panic she shared with Paige. She wanted her fear to find a proper object.

"What now?" Mira asked, surveying the scene. The natives' flash-lights revealed the surrounding jungle in discrete hazy expanses. A dense fog obscured the landscape beyond the immediate range of the beams, heightening the surrealism of the moment.

Foucher turned to her and put a finger to the thin smile on his lips.

"I don't understand what you want with us," Mira said, tired of imploring him. "What's Ridge done? I just … For me anyway, I don't even care anymore. I don't give a damn what you do. If you're going to kill me, just get it over with." She shook with her own temerity. To say that … *Oh, Lord, give me a good excuse.*

"You done?" Foucher's voice was reedy, almost adolescent. "'Cause I'm tryin' to get things situated here."

Mira glanced at Paige, whose ethereal beauty had been emasculated by the hard journey. Paige had cried softly, persistently, in the dugout canoe. Her eyes were red and swollen from the unhurried flow of tears.

As Foucher huddled with a couple of natives, giving orders in broken English, Paige reached over and touched Mira's hand lightly. It was the first time they'd touched since Kenny's murder. They'd spoken little during the journey. Words had seemed either superfluous or woefully inadequate. Besides, they'd known each other only since the beginning of the trip five days ago. They were content to pursue similar but separate thoughts.

Paige evidently meant the touch as a parting gesture because she jerked away and bolted for the protection of the forest. She bounded over the pitted clearing like a dancer. Her close-cropped red hair flashed in the darkness.

Surprised, the two native escorts closest to her readied their spears.

"No!" Foucher commanded. "Just bring her back!"

"Run, Paige! Go!" Mira shouted. *Please Lord, let her make it.*

The blackness of the forest extinguished the plaited silk glow of Paige's undergarments. The natives sped after her, the beams from their flashlights strafing the trees and bushes.

Mira looked on, whispering a prayer for Paige. She felt hollow inside. A rip in her soiled evening gown revealed a deep abrasion on her right thigh where she'd scraped it on a jagged limestone outcropping. Her tender feet throbbed. Until now, only the violent unknown had kept her awake and alert.

With a gesture, Foucher sent another half-dozen aborigines into the forest. Others fanned out into the coconut leaf thatched huts.

"Even if she gets away," Foucher said, interrupting Mira's prayer, "I wouldn't get your hopes up. All kinds of things out there and I'm not just talkin' 'bout snakes and whatever else. The worst thing is mosquitoes. Dengue fever, yellow fever, malaria, you name it. Dengue fever's the new one. Got it from Australia, prob'ly. That's how I stayed alive so long out here, not just in the Solomons, but in the Philippines, Honduras, Peru, places like that—bein' paranoid 'bout disease."

Mira retreated a few steps, glancing expectantly toward the forest where Paige had vanished. Despite the humidity, as the heat from the hike began to fade, her skin goosepimpled.

Foucher adjusted his wire-rimmed glasses. "There's two kinds a dengue from what I understand: with the first, you get a fever, the chills, the shits, you vomit, all that crap. Then the headaches start and you feel like your bones are goin' weak, breakin' up one by one, like chicken bones too small for to support you." He shook a hand in her face. "The second kind is like a bonus package. You get the same shit as the first, but you also start hemorrhaging. Not a lot at the beginning. It starts out as red spots on your legs, little splotches of blood wellin' up inside. Then the hemorrhaging gets worse and pretty soon the blood's seepin' into your lungs, your stomach, even your brain, fillin' up your head. That's when you really hurt, coughin' up blood and all that, right before you go into shock and die. No, you really don't want her to make it."

"*Chas vesholem*," said Mira, turning away from him. She figured Foucher had probably been the type of teenage ruffian who mistook meanness for bravery. She couldn't discern any signs of struggle in the forest. The mist-enshrouded trees revealed only scattered flashes of light. The sound of underbrush trampled underfoot occasionally penetrated the now-familiar twitters and screeches but little else. The darkness prevailed.

CHAPTER 21

The Foot-Chase

The pressure in Paige's head began to ease the moment she started running. She'd first felt it the morning after the shipwreck. She'd blamed Kenny for the accident, figuring the group would've sailed back to the condo without incident if only he'd kept quiet about her birthday. She'd been angry with him also for casually dismissing her pained reaction to Honiara's oppressive poverty. Conditions in the capital city had overwhelmed her liberal sympathies: the extravagant blight of public housing, dilapidated and riddled with graffiti; homeless people sharing welfare tins of corned hash; incessant mobs of children begging for American dollars and Chiclets. Kenny had scoffed at her shame, saying she was "hypersensitive."

On the atoll, bound to the others only by a common disaster, she'd borne her irritation with him by keeping busy—mainly gathering coconuts and stockpiling underbrush on the beach to make a signal fire. After Kenny's callous murder, she'd sobbed uncontrollably in the dugout canoe, not for him but for herself. She counted the incident as merely another sign she'd made a mess of her life. Perhaps she'd even laid the spiritual groundwork for it with her black thoughts about him.

The forest was a ruin of shadowy spires under the pale moonlight. Searching beams of light raked over the tangle of ironwood and thick undergrowth. Aimless flickering played against the trees off to the left. Paige spun in the opposite direction and cut down a steep embankment, all arms and legs. Everything was an effort. She winced at each stride, her bare feet bruised and aching. Her path ended in an acute drop-off. She heard a profusion of guttural voices and considered finding a place to hide. But the lack of viable cover forced her to keep moving.

The ground leveled out and Paige found herself running parallel to the trail they'd taken from the beach. A peripheral light touched on her arm. Then another, fragmented by intervening tree limbs, followed by

a bright convergence that conjured a horde of fleeing shadows. Paige willed against reason for the light to set everything ablaze—the brush, the trees, even her. But the light refused her prayerful wish. There would be no easy release, no transcendent self-destruction. She would continue to suffer the world as it is and its consequences, all the backwoods horrors she'd temporarily banished from her thoughts. The patter of her feet was like a slackening countdown. She came to a pained stop at a skirt of underbrush and put a hand on her jolting heart. The natives came on all ablur, huffing and shouting. The triangulated light stabbed her blind.

CHAPTER 22

The Dead Recounted

A thin white dazzle of ocean, the cusp of life, advancing and retreating... retreating and advancing, infinitely... Laying on the beach several yards from Kenny's corpse, the Senator closed his milky gray eyes against the unforgiving sun... and an army took shape behind his lids... a multitude of dead... flesh... blackness... decay... the *first* body somewhere near the blue opaque of New Caledonia... The Senator was young then, just three weeks out of basic training. The dead man was a middle-aged Naval Reserve Officer, a stoic Italian who captained one of the cruiser's two seaplanes, a Curtiss SOC Seagull. The lightly armored bi-plane, launched from the deck of the cruiser with a massive catapult and a charge of powder, was carrying sleeves for gunnery practice.

With frightening speed, the plane hit the water full force. As the propeller shattered into a cloud of black fragments, the Senator envisioned the pilot bouncing up to meet the accordioned canopy then falling into the bloody embrace of the instrument panel, the cowled Pratt and Whitney engine smashing through the cockpit. The impact bent the low-cantilevered wings to a tortuous angle. Sections of the plane were stripped of its stressed-fabric skin to reveal a dull metal. A moment later, the aircraft's two 100-pound bombs exploded, sending up a terrific geyser of water and metal.

That first experience with death actually proved the easiest to stomach. The pilot's demise was sufficiently remote and occurred under such fantastic circumstances that he could summarily dismiss any dreadful portent in the accident. His initial, palpable disgust soon gave way to macabre curiosity. When the light cruiser pulled up alongside the wrecked aircraft to winch it aboard, he was tempted to sneak a look at the body to see if he could discern some vital secret in the position of the limbs, the way the body was crushed.

The horror of dying at sea quickly eviscerated this mild enthusiasm.

As a gunner, the Senator was confined in battle to a superheated turret. The turret covered an area about 15 square feet with a 6" gun in the center. In addition to the crew and the large caliber gun, the restricted space housed the loading apparatus, which handled shells weighing up to 135 lbs., radar, communications and fire-fighting equipment.

The blast from the 6" gun was powerful enough to rip the clothes off the back of a soldier. Sometimes when the turret turned, the men crouched behind the 40mm machine guns could look right into the barrels. More than once, he'd found a machine gunner knocked unconscious by the weapon's concussive charge. The 6" gun also generated unbearable heat. During battle, the air blowers were switched off, leaving him and his fellow crew members gasping for fresh air.

Even with the aid of radar, targeting the weapon was hectic guesswork. The platform moved in several directions at once. As the ship maneuvered for tactical advantage, it also pitched and rolled with the motion of the sea. Prospective targets did the same. Only a shell fired on a relatively level trajectory would inflict substantial damage on an armored ship, so he had to anticipate, not just adjust for conditions.

The *USS Denver*, popularly referred to as the 'Dirty D,' had a well-deserved reputation among the fleet for initiating and prosecuting attacks with overwhelming gunfire. During nighttime engagements, the barrage of star shells and tracers and 5" and 6" shells formed a fugitive galaxy. The Senator used to gauge the intensity of a battle by the brightness of the luminous cloud. He observed the blinding cluster of smoke and shells with apprehension, convinced the world would end in a sudden conflagration if the man-made galaxy collided with the earth.

This worry was fueled by scenes of men roasted alive, their skin charred a smoky black, their eyes jellied. There was no refuge at sea from a burning ship, only equally fatal choices: the flames, sharks, enemy fire or suicide. The open water left nothing to chance.

After each battle, the Senator used to imagine piling up the bloodied dead, allies and enemies alike. The accumulated compost of gray flesh was his private Valhalla, a primitive tribute to the warrior dead. The mountain of remains reached its apex on November 13th, 1943 when the *Denver* was disabled by a Japanese torpedo plane. The plane had emerged from the day's first light in a fateful arc.

When he spun the turret around, he caught a glimpse of the screeching torpedo before it slammed into the cruiser amidships on the starboard side. A violent quaking. The cruiser tilted abruptly. He fell to his knees... *Lord, no, please, no...* The screaming, a desperate human wail, his ear plugs no defense... The frantic cries clashed with his childhood memories of hurt, moments of small exaggerated fear. He felt claustrophobic. The turret appeared to close in on him... The air thinned... He couldn't breathe... Then the mount captain was in his face urging him to return fire. Mechanically, he got to his feet, surprised to still be alive... Without a glance at the radar, he fired the 6" gun toward the bright horizon. *Please, Lord, not here, please...* The remainder of the battle was a dimly remembered series of devastating noises. The regular blast of the 6" gun was overwhelmed by a shocking roar of flame and jagged metal. The shrapnel sounded against the turret like so many fateful coins. The platform on which the turret rested tilted crazily first one way then another.

When the Senator finally emerged from the turret, exhausted and slick with sweat, he found the deck shredded by the Japanese salvo. Blood and twisted debris everywhere. The initial torpedo had taken out the steering-engine room, followed by the after-fuel tanks and the 5" mount. Looking down the gaping hole on the starboard side, he could see a host of waxen bodies floating aimlessly in the flooded mess hall. The ashen faces swirling around in the dark water resembled so many primitive things viewed through a microscope. He recognized one of the staff sergeants, visible from the chest up. The corpse's eyes were wide with disbelief. Miraculously, the thin dead lips still held the sergeant's hand-made pipe. The dead remained in that watery pit for four days while the *Denver* was towed to drydock, their slow putrefaction a mortifying display... *Dear Christ...*

Fingers of ocean, oh, so fragile, grasping for more life... reaching and dissipating... dissipating and reaching... the multitude of dead... flesh... blackness... decay... The *worst* one in the cathode blue of the hospital, the air stale... The cold burnished machines, the tangle of ivs... Where was Sarah? *Oh, God.* Spittle collected at the corner of her round colorless mouth each time the respirator kicked in... About every thirty seconds now... The real Sarah was already gone, he knew.

Curled up and sleeping inside that blackened husk. Starting with her left breast, the cancer had spread through her body like some malignant wisteria. The mastectomy the year before hadn't stopped it.

The Senator had loved Sarah more than he'd loved anyone and had asked her to marry him several times. But each time, she would flash her crooked smile and dismiss the question as a joke. Her marriage to a broken down dairy farmer, which ended in abuse and alcoholism, had forever tainted the sanctity of marriage for her. She preferred their relationship of convenience, arguing that love, at all times freely given and received, was the truest test of fidelity.

She could be stubborn that way, as though she were daring him to dislike her, eager to give him some excuse to break up. She baited him on gun control, placing copies of *Guns and Ammo* conspicuously around her cedar-paneled living room and affixing a National Rifle Association sticker to the back of her '83 Dodge Ram pick-up. She would've made an exemplary Western pioneer: a decent big-boned woman who loved the open sky and her freedom. *Hang government!* she used to say, even though she was a government employee, the executive director of the Fulton County Agricultural Museum.

That was where he met her, during summer recess in 1979, seven years after his divorce from a rapacious debutante-turned-Holy Roller. He sometimes took afternoon bike rides to the museum, where he indulged in nostalgia for the farming life he knew as a boy. The museum housed farming implements going back as far as the 18th century: double-handled hay knives, planters hoes, silage choppers, fruit pomaces, loom-like grain cradles, hand tobacco setters, flax breaks, cotton gins, bridles, yokes and plows…

What struck the Senator first about Sarah was her fine prodigious hair. It was of Biblical proportions—a straight cascade of blonde mixed with gray down to the small of her back. She wore it either in a single glorious ponytail or less frequently, piled up like a crown. In bed, before her mastectomy, she used to drape her hair over her naked breasts. Later, when the cancer had further insinuated itself, corrupting her lungs and stomach, she refused chemotherapy, resigned to her fate and wanting to die with her hair brushed out across a hospital pillow…

The Senator sat up to take yet another inventory of his supplies. His

red-rimmed eyes and unshaven face gave him a grizzled, almost ma-
niacal, appearance. A tuft of thin gray hair stuck up on the back of his
head like tail feathers. He paused in his methodical work to glance at
Kenny's remains. His hands shook uncontrollably. From the war, he
knew the unflagging heat had accelerated the body's graceless ruin.
Under the palm fronds he'd placed on the corpse in a half-hearted attempt to discourage the inevitable plague of insects, he knew the end
was only just beginning.

The body was already infested with a swarm of flies, seeding Kenny's orifices with horrible new life. The Senator had always hated insects, especially after his tour of duty in the Solomons. At one time or
another virtually everyone aboard the *Denver*, most of whom slept on
deck because of the sweltering heat, had suffered an aggravating rash
or sore. One morning, the Senator had awakened to find a swath of
startling red skin around his beltline. What he'd assumed to be only a
nasty rash turned out to be an infestation of chiggers.

Arrayed in symmetrical rows in front of the Senator were a few
tools and the last of the rations from the yacht: a metal match; two
flashlights; several lengths of rope, including about ten feet of white
waxy rope from the ring buoy; a hatchet; a pair of scissors; an empty
sports bottle; a package of tampons; some spray-on deodorant; dental
tape and a tube of Crest mint gel (but no toothbrush); a 12-oz. jar of
Jiffy peanut butter; a stale box of Wheat Chex; a box of hard coffee-
flavored candy; a half-dozen onion bagels; an old bag of ridged potato
chips; two bottles of Evian; a half-liter of Coca-Cola; two bottles of
Heineken; a box of cookies for infants, labeled "baby biscuits"; three
chocolate chip granola bars; and a package of raspberry fruit roll-ups.
A few snack foods, notably the beverages, had been brought on board
by the Senator's party; most, however, had been left on the yacht by
whomever had taken it out before them.

The Senator surveyed his rations, trying to figure out how to make
the most efficient use of them. So far, he'd been eating mainly peanut
butter, granola bars, cheese (now gone) and the odd bit of coconut
meat. Neither the local authorities nor the US Coast Guard had apparently responded to the distress signal Aaron had sent. Maybe it would
be better to eat the peanut butter and the other energy foods a little at

a time, he thought. Just in case.

He couldn't recall how Robinson Crusoe had survived before the arrival of Friday or even if Friday were more than a delusion. There had to be fish of some kind in the lagoon. Tuna, maybe. But what to use for bait? The bagels? No. He opened the package of fruit roll-ups and peeled off a thin red strip with his thumb and forefinger. There was an unpleasant medicinal sweetness to it. Hardly appropriate for bait. He glanced over at the body, momentarily overwhelmed by the shivery glare of day. He could use a finger maybe or a toe. Or, instead of using the flesh for bait, maybe …? He could always hide the evidence—bury or burn or somehow sink the remains in the event he was rescued.

Picking up the hatchet, the Senator slowly got to his feet and walked toward the corpse. The trade wind had displaced most of the browning palm fronds with which he'd covered the remains last night. The stench compelled him to cover his nose and mouth with his free hand. He stood near Kenny's bare sun-burned feet. The flies massed around the body appeared undisturbed by his long shadow. *It's a shame that I'll remember him this way now.* He was thankful Aaron had perished in a way that didn't betray or corrupt his cheerful memories of the boy.

The Senator stood there for several minutes, transfixed. He tried to envision resting the cutting edge of the hatchet on Kenny's right thumb, just above the first joint, and leaning with his full weight until it popped off. The body's disgusting decay urged him to act. If he waited until he'd exhausted his supplies to make use of the body, it would be too late. The remains would have begun to ferment, the skin to mold. But even alone he retained the imprint of society. No, looking at the real Kenny beneath the death mask, he silently promised the Lord that he wouldn't disgrace himself that way. If it came down to it, he'd rather drown.

He turned away from the body and started back toward his cache of supplies feeling shapeless and lethargic, his limbs loosely connected weights. Since his discharge from the Navy, he'd set one fixed goal after another for himself. His initial run for Congress, while publicly a patriotic crusade, had been a decidedly selfish attempt to perpetuate the lush emotion he'd felt during the war. His vision for the New South, as genuine as it was, had come later when he realized the need for a lasting persona. Because he'd found the local politicians who called on his daddy unimpressive at best, he thought he could do better. The war, by imbuing in him a sense of mission, had cursed him with the need to prove it.

Without the usual daily checklist on which to focus his energies, the past three days had severely tested his resolve. He needed a task, something to relieve his incessant demand for results, or at least what passed for them in Washington. As long as he still had rations from the yacht, he knew a survival task like fishing wouldn't prove sufficient. Something so small and desperate would only reinforce the aching dread which had infected his thinking. He needed to do something that promised to restore his faith.

That was it. That's what was missing. The beliefs which had erased early doubts about his political decisions and sustained him throughout his travails on the Hill had been lost in the downward spiral of recent days. After 43 years in Congress, his senatorial routine had become a regular affirmation of Providence. The shock of events and the possibility of that kind of authority coming to an end had momentarily wrecked his faith. All these thoughts of disgrace, death, decay... The Senator gazed out over the shimmering blue Pacific. It was the first time he'd looked with any intensity beyond his transient supplies, beyond the surf. The sharp horizon appeared to give credence to the notion of a flat earth. The enormity of the sea and the sky, together, insisted on humility. Here was the true measure of Man to God's Creation. On a primitive level, the level of the body, which to this point had been his overriding concern, the relative size of things frightened him; but the vista also allowed for belief. What sublime beauty, however terrifying, was without the hand of God?

Maybe he would drown after all. He felt woefully unprepared for the task ahead. The hatchet and a few inadequate pieces of rope were his only tools. Nonetheless, he accepted the challenge: he would build a raft. And he hoped the Lord God, as his only companion now, would see him through. He had so much more to do. His mission couldn't end with him betraying his first, best principles. He would go forward unbowed.

CHAPTER 23

The Power of the One

Digging post-holes under the searing midmorning sun, Ridge wished for a cool breeze. The movements of the roughly arrow-shaped trade cloud and its wispy companions above suggested a moderate wind from the southeast. The westerly slope of the hillside, however, cut him off from it. He worked at a grim pace, parallel to the wooden sluicing flume, swallowing the heat and the spoiled garden smell of the forest. The naked hillside gave off shimmering waves, distorting his view of the camp below.

The Marlboro T-shirt Ridge wore was soaked through with sweat. He doffed his Panama hat and pressed the back of his hand against his forehead, feeling feverish. He looked doubtfully over the plague of mosquito bites on his arms for signs of infection. Then he resumed his work, leaning on the post-hole digger to penetrate the dense gray topsoil.

As much as he exercised, Ridge was fundamentally unsuited to this kind of work. He didn't have a feel for it. The pleasure of discrete physical chores eluded him. Had he been drinking with friends at The Colonnade, he would've freely admitted it, almost as point of pride, but here, the very suggestion he was unfit for hard labor made him flush with anger. College boy, Tourist, *enough!*

On the other hand, he couldn't join in with too much enthusiasm. That would mean he'd accepted his lowly condition, that he'd become, in Aristotle's words, an "animated tool"; instead, he would apply himself with a bleak steadiness. He wanted to come across as an inexhaustible but mean-spirited pack animal.

"Okay, okay." Gerrit's amplified voice echoed across the valley. "It's fireworks time, ladies. Off the mountain now."

Ridge tossed his rusty post-hole digger aside and leaned against the flume. His hands were raw, blistered. He wiped the stinging sweat from his face with the bottom of his T-shirt and called out to Tugger, the resident engineer. The squat black man, examining the angle of the flume farther down the hillside, waved in acknowledgment.

Ridge needed Tugger to unchain him. He'd formulated and summarily dismissed one escape plan after another as nothing better than a ludicrous TV movie scenario. Living in Atlanta, number three in the nation for violent crime, he had a ready catalogue of mental plans for getting the drop on muggers and carjackers and doped up murderers. The despairing truth of his situation revealed the vanity of these strategies.

The past three days had been like a narrative without infinitives. Nothing passed from one state to another, nothing came to be. The same tedious labor. The same forlorn thoughts. Under constant watch, chained up, outnumbered, weaker...He would just have to risk it. There was no other way. He would have to believe in some fortuitous event, in a possibility he couldn't quite name. But what if he merely succeeded in leading Tarrant to the others? He could never forgive himself for that. It was better to stay a little longer—until he was certain they were safe.

Tugger trudged up the hillside along the elevated flume. He was broad and flabby, like a rudimentary clay figurine. His eyes were hidden behind huge wraparound sunglasses. He was as austere as the poor East Kansas prairie where he grew up. He bobbed his shiny bald head gently to the R&B coming over his Sony headphones.

The flume sloped down the hillside and over the muddy river for over a hundred yards. The prospect of a viable hillside deposit had increased the pressure on Tugger to perfect it. The wooden rockers and long toms used so far couldn't possibly handle the anticipated volume of earth.

The flume consisted of a series of interconnected troughs. The bottom of the troughs were replete with cleats of auger-drilled boards lined with quicksilver. When the flume was completed, raw earth would be spaded into the hopper at the uppermost end and washed with stream water. The heavier rocks and gravel would remain in the hopper while the lighter gravel, gold and sandy water would wash through the flume, the gold collecting behind the cleats. For the flume to be effective, however, it had to be positioned correctly. Set at the wrong angle, the miners stood to lose a quarter to half the gold they grubbed out of the hillside.

From Ridge's elevated vantage point, the village of native huts and nearly colorless shacks resembled a squalid, misplaced nativity scene. He could make out a group of dusky red women hacking out baskets of pulp from a downed sago palm, children flitting about, teasing each other, troublesome pigs rooting in coconut husks, chickens and poi dogs, the ironwood statue that marked the spirit hut or men's lodge, the sizeable garden beyond, a patchwork of tobacco, bananas, sweet potatoes, rice, pineapples and mangos with a fringe of blackened earth, a fragile semblance of civilization, woefully wrong. Ridge felt the forest could somehow reclaim the village at any time. The towering unknown made the village strange, almost an insult to nature.

Breathing heavily out of his wide mouth, Tugger heaved his massive gut the last few yards to reach Ridge. He breathed like a storybook locomotive: chug-chug, chug-chug. He removed the key to the padlock from the breast pocket of his muddy overalls and briefly held it up to the sun.

Tapping his ear to indicate Tugger's headphones, Ridge asked, "What are you listening to?"

The stolid giant either ignored the question or didn't hear it. "Gather up the chain, will you? And don't strangle me with it now."

Ridge shook his bowed head and proceeded to collect the bicycle chain still connected to his right ankle by a pair of handcuffs. He made a hoop of the chain, wrapping it from elbow to palm. "What are you listening to?"

Tugger talked into his chest in his *basso profoundo* voice. "My man."

"The man?" *Christ, speak up.*

"No, *my* man, James." Chug-chug. "You know, his bad self, Mr. Dynamite, the Godfather of Soul. Ever hear *Live at the Apollo*?" Tugger asked, slipping off his headphones.

"Can't say I have." Ridge started down the denuded hillside. He carried the bicycle chain in his right hand, swinging it in time with the movement of his manacled foot.

"Thought you from Georgia?" Chug-chug.

"Yeah."

"Album was recorded right in Atlanta, GA," Tugger said. Chug-chug. "You missin' out on the One." Chug-chug.

"Pardon?"

Tugger broke into a braying laugh, a deep scowl on his face. "I ain't got no fly in my soup, Pierre. Pardon? *Shee-it.*" Chug-chug.

"All right. Forget about politeness."

"My man, he come up with the One," Tugger said, inhaling deeply. "That signature beat, that *hah*, du-da, du-da, du-da, *hah*, you know, that beat. See, regular rock 'n' roll, I'm talkin' Chuck Berry stuff here, is built on the four-four rhythm with the accent on the two and the four." He came up for air: chug-chug, chug-chug. "But my man, James, he gots the idea of the One, you know, puttin' the accent on the first beat, the first one, and then workin' around it, addin' flourishes and shit. The One get everything off to the right start. It ties everythin' together." Chug-chug. "Ever wonder how you know a James Brown song you hearin' even if you never heard it before? It the One. Always there, settin' the groove. James just fill in the spaces between." Chug-chug.

"Uh-huh," Ridge said. "Does your Walkman have a radio? Or is it just a tape player?"

"A radio? No. Tarrant only one got radio." Chug-chug. "I do work on it when it acts up—ol' shortwave set."

Ridge hadn't seen Tarrant since his miserable interview. He appeared to direct the mining operations from his cabin.

Gerrit's voice rumbled down the hillside again: "Let's go, ladies. Bust your balls. The other side a the river, yeah? Any closer 'n' we're gonna bury ya."

"How often does he use it?"

"Don't know." Chug-chug. "Not much, I s'pose. Just for weather reports and the supply ship."

"How often does that come?"

"Ain't no set schedule." Chug-chug. "Once a month seems like, sometimes more. Depends on what we need in way of equipment." Chug-chug.

The sun blazed on the back of Ridge's neck. "Where does it land?"

Tugger shook his head, flashing a patronizing smile. "Don't know where it comes—goes—whatever." Chug-chug. He wiped his forehead with a dirty handkerchief, sweating profusely now. "Tarrant send the Marokatu for everything."

Ridge coughed into his free hand, momentarily overwhelmed by the dust stirred up by the miners charging down the hillside, dragging picks, shovels and surveying equipment.

"Why? You lookin' to order somethin' from the Sears & Roebuck?" Tugger asked. He gave a muted, rumbling laugh. Chug-chug. "Pair a bolt cutters maybe? Speedboat?" His voice cracked with that last suggestion; he could hardly contain himself.

"Glad I can amuse you, Tugger."

"'Bout time is what I say. Black man been slaved and 'buked and poked fun of fo' so long…" Chug-chug. "'Bout time…"

"And here I thought you'd be more sympathetic."

"Get to be my age in a hard life… see if you got sympathy to spare."

CHAPTER 24

The Blasting

Ridge sat in the shade of a sago palm near the stream's edge, appraising the miners ranged along the bank and listening absently to Waxman describe the blasting preparations on the hillside.

"They usin' dynamite, though there's this new explosive, comes in two parts—a powder and a liquid. Or ammonium nitrate fertilizer and diesel fuel. That's the cheapest way. But dynamite—powder—that's what I grew up on..."

As Waxman droned on, Ridge slipped into a spell of sorts. The old man's voice became like a distant radio broadcast. The earth fell away, everything beyond the river sinking into a fathomless abyss, and he became a phantom observer. The miners appeared to be creatures from a lower hemisphere: their foreheads broad, their cheeks sunken, their burnished arms lanky and ill-proportioned. They wore body masks of fine dirt, the anglos turned to dusty savages with only their eyes and teeth showing white. Ridge wondered if they would even recognize themselves if they dropped their shovels or got up from their squat positions on the ground and found their murky reflections in the stream.

They jostled each other and joked and swore in low tones, the grit of the land in their mouths. Most just as soon smoked as breathed, turning their lungs into blackened stalactites. Ridge guessed they represented at least a dozen nations, brought together by greed, myth and an almost adolescent wanderlust. To a man, they were shell-backed, their features tight, their eyes deadened by punishing labor. Christ, what a rude growling tribe. The ages had apparently passed them by, leaving their vile ignorance unscathed.

The miners' attitude toward the world, their stubborn insistence that life was inherently cruel no matter where you lived it, reminded Ridge of the people he'd encountered on one of his first real assignments for *The Atlanta Journal-Constitution*: a profile of the Sweet Auburn area, the distressed site of Martin Luther King's birthplace and memorial.

The cover story was one in a series on prominent neighborhoods following Atlanta's successful bid to host the 1996 Summer Games. He'd walked Martin Luther King Boulevard and its adjacent streets for a few humid June nights, interviewing residents. Some, probably most, thought he was a police officer. "My friends can't see me talkin' to you," said a youth in a Hawks cap, eating pork noodles out of a styrofoam carton. He pointed to a group of kids across the street drinking forties out of paper bags. "They gon think I'mma snitch. No offense, man. These is jus' crazy times."

That was the answer Ridge had expected, the only one that really made sense. He was there for only a few picaresque nights, ready to step back into upper-class comfort at a moment's notice. What else could the people of that neighborhood think except that he was out to degrade them, to dramatize their failings, to fit them into smart clinical categories? And for what? A reputation? Money? Nothing they could get a piece of anyway.

"Been here 15 years and I'm dyin' to move on," a 21 year old mother on welfare told him. Where? "I don't know. I don't know. Everywhere you go is the same." She'd either resigned herself to a hardscrabble life no matter where she lived, or the madness of the neighborhood had conditioned her to believe the rest of the country looked the same, at least for people in her predicament.

The miners didn't give the world the benefit of the doubt, either. When, packed into the grimy refuge of their bunkhouses for the night, they bellowed "Oh Joe" one after the other like an otherworldly roll-call, there was something more than tradition at work. The strange lament was allegedly based on an incident in which a California prospector trapped in a hole called to his partner for help. It was a regular goodnight to things—defiant, comical and sad. "Oh Joe" ... Yes, today would be the same as the day before, would impose the same hardships, take the same strength ... *They should have known better.* Their callowness was an affront to the intellect of the times. They'd suffered, sure, but that was no excuse. They should've known better. And because they didn't, they sanctioned the natives' violent ideas about the larger world.

In spite of his liberal sympathies, Ridge found the Marokatu little

different than his worst preconceptions. They were coarse and belliger-
ent, habituated to war, associated manhood with battle scars, accorded
the highest standing to the rich. He'd heard ugly rumors of infanticide.
Because the natives practiced polygamy, which prevented some males
from acquiring wives, they apparently believed there was a shortage
of females on the island. This deficit encouraged them to raid neighboring isles to secure more women and, in an instance of damnable
circular thinking, favor male over female births in order to increase
the number of warriors to carry out these raids.

Sometimes then, Marokatu mothers would murder their newborn
daughters in the forest, strangling them with the baby's own blood-
slicked umbilical cord. Yes, they were fine upright savages, their pos-
ture made Victorian perfect by the routine of carrying loads of food,
water and supplies on bamboo poles across their shoulders.

Christ almighty. The unrepentant barbarism, the constant dalli-
ance with instinct ... Ridge wondered if he could preserve his civility
here. Would he haltingly adopt the rough mannerisms, the raw language, even the grim facial expressions, in order to better get along?
Up against Northern stereotypes and repeated ridicule at Choate he
had, after all, abandoned his Southern accent ... Maybe he wouldn't
write this story for a popular magazine or turn it into a celebratory
book. Maybe, with his rational powers degenerated, he would succeed
only in scratching out his name in the earth, just testify to his existence ... "Hey, Curious George! Get your ass up here, boy!"

Gerrit's command returned Ridge to the moment.

Waxman was saying: "... loop the wires of the fuse around the last
stick of dynamite so the cap won't come off if someone trips over 'em."

Ridge stood up and shielded his eyes with his hand to get a clear
view of the blasting area. The sun washed the granite blister white.
There was Gerrit, sheltered by the piddling shadow of a rock outcropping, the megaphone at his side. Foucher was with him, standing several yards away, consulting a book.

Curious George, the native boy Ridge recognized from the duel,
mounted the hill in response to Gerrit's call. His thin painted face
shone briefly in the sun before he turned toward the summit. Like all
Marokatu, the back of his head was startlingly flat—a consequence, the

natives believed, of babies cradled on their backs on sheets of bark-cloth. He moved with typical adolescent gawkiness, springing forward on large thick-soled feet.

Placing a cinnamon-flavored toothpick between his teeth, Waxman announced, "They're almost ready now."

"What's the boy doing up there?" Ridge asked.

"Oh, it's just some game."

"Are they fixing to let him set off the dynamite?"

"Somethin' like that." Waxman pointed to a crowbar in Gerrit's hand. "That rod there is for the boy so he can tamp the drill hole. You have to pack dirt in around the powder."

Ridge felt a hand on his shoulder. "Hey, Tourist, come to watch the show?" *Tree.*

The pseudo-Native American exhaled a sour gust of air. "Got a smoke I can bum off you?"

"No, afraid not."

"Don't smoke? Figgers. Don't know what you're missin'. That nicotine rush is real—right to your central nervous system. Not like speed or coke or anythin' but it sure-God wakes you up, keeps you going. Works for me at least." He jerked his head toward Waxman. "How 'bout you, old timer? How 'bout one a them cinnamon toothpicks at least? Used to make those in fuckin' grade school, man. Do 'em right, you can get a pretty good rush."

Waxman didn't even turn around. "Go away, Tree."

"Yeah, run me off, that's it. Fuckin' story a my life." He looked imploringly at Ridge. "My great-grandfather's head—his fuckin' head—is on display at the Army Medical Museum in Washington. He was a chief when the army wiped out the tribe, so they made a example of 'im. Hung 'im and sent his head back to headquarters. They wouldn't a done that to your great-grandfather, English, Irish, fuckin' ice-white Swedish or whatever he was."

Ridge glanced over at Waxman, whose gaze was concentrated on the hillside. Up above, George was making his way to the blast point with the steel rod. His abbreviated shadow bounced against the up-raised earth.

Gerrit barked into his megaphone: "Ladies and, well, uh, ladies, please direct your attention to the center ring. I give you, Curious George, the bravest and prob'ly dumbest forest nigger of 'em all. Let's give him a big hand."

There was a smattering of applause and a few hoots and catcalls. Tree issued a shrill whistle. Waxman stood motionless.

The native boy allowed himself a small self-satisfied grin.

"You might wanna cover your ears," Tree advised Ridge. "Just in case."

"Why?"

"Could be a spark, man, the rock's flinty enough."

"Usually," Waxman chimed in, "you use wood for tamping."

George squatted above the drill hole and raised the crowbar high, unmindful of the crowd, then smashed it to the ground, again and again.

"But Gerrit and George, they got this thing goin'. It's like a test a manhood a some kind. I told you, these fuckin' Marokatu are killers."

"George knows about this?" Ridge asked. He was so embarrassed by the nickname, he could barely wrap his mouth around it.

"Oh, yeah. They done this before, five-six times, with Gerrit teasin' the boy."

"Goddamn insane," muttered Ridge. They were so casual about it … *Christ.* He began to second-guess the fatal moment, the flash, like a firefly winking out, the precipitous burst of pulverizing rock, the veil of smoke and debris, the swirl of spindly smoldering flesh … His heart thumped wildly against his chest. He started forward a couple of steps then stopped, unsure of himself.

The native boy continued to flail the hillside. He arced the crowbar over one shoulder, then the other, beating the air in a severe V.

Ridge grimaced at every blow. He had to do *something.*

"Okay, George. That's enough," Gerrit shouted, a distinct note of disappointment in his voice. "Come on back and you can set off the charge." He waved the native over.

There was a collective sigh from the crowd. Another failed distraction … Ridge enjoyed a deep breath.

"They got you in cuffs, huh?" Tree asked Ridge as though seeing the chains for the first time. "Easy pickin's, man." He flexed his wrist to simulate a key opening a lock. "Learned how to pick locks in grade school."

"I'm sure you're a regular Houdini," Waxman said, his eyes flashing. The color gathered in Tree's face.

Waxman shook his head in disgust. "I'm tellin' you, Tree, your mouth's gonna get you killed 'fore everything's said 'n' done. Jaws."

"I ain't done nuthin' wrong, old timer. I was just sayin' how—"

Gerrit's voice boomed down the hillside: "All right, let's pack it in ladies. Don't just stand there holdin' yer peckers. Take cover."

Tree gave Waxman a final corrosive look then flanked Ridge behind the exposed roots of a sago palm.

Glancing over his shoulder, Ridge noticed a group of Marokatu observing the scene from the edge of the village. They were uniformly sticky with tobacco residue. A few of them wore eyeshades of plaited coconut leaf. Did they really know what was going on?

"Okay, ready?" asked Gerrit's disembodied voice. "Here goes, on the count a three..."

Ridge ducked his head a little to get a view of the target area unobscured by the tree's broad fern-like leaves. Despite his situation, a buoyant, Fourth of July feeling began to rise in him.

"One..."

He looked over at Waxman. The veteran prospector sat hunched over, facing the village, his good hand wrapped around his head.

"Two..."

Ridge wondered absently if he should close his eyes.

"Three! Do it, George! Do it!" Gerrit mimicked smashing the plunger.

Nothing... And now...? And now...? A scald of sun revealed every unchanged feature of the hillside.

Gerrit emerged from behind the rock outcropping. "Goddamnit. Waxman? Where are you, you ol' bastard?" he asked through the megaphone.

Waving his arms as though surrendering to police, Waxman stepped out from under the shade of the sago palm.

"Get up here, will you?"

"C'mon," Waxman sighed, motioning for Ridge to accompany him.

Ridge followed like a Dickensian ghost. His chains sounded sharply against the pine bridge over the stream. "What is it, you think?"

"Don't know." Waxman stroked his straggly beard. "Could be any number a things: bad connection, dead battery, cap on too tight, even old dynamite…" He paused for breath, leaned into the hillside. "Thought I was dead one time back in Alaska workin' a site on the edge a Denali Park. I was diggin' with a pick when I come across a bundle a old powder. Put my pick right through it. Jaws, I thought it was over right then and there. I could see little white crystals on the ends a the sticks—bubbles a nitro."

Ridge climbed with hunched shoulders to better attack the slope.

"My heart stopped dead when I saw what I done," Waxman said. "I was afraid to move and desperate to run at the same time. Finally, I laid my pick down real careful and backed up on tiptoe. Yeah, I was a regular tiptoe dancer, I was so quiet and graceful. Then I got me some lighter fluid, doused the pile and set off a cap to destroy it. You never know how old dynamite's gonna react. Best thing to do is just burn it up."

Gerrit stepped out of the sliver of shade provided by the rock outcropping as Ridge and Waxman approached. "Take a look at the box will you?" he asked Waxman. "I pushed the fuckin' plunger a dozen times already. Gotta be the fuse cap."

"You run a test with just the cap and fuse?"

"No, goddamn it."

Ridge eyed the matte black detonator box warily. The plunger was down. He surveyed the stretch of twin wires running from the back of the box to the charge. Foucher was crouched next to the box, riffling through the *Blaster's Handbook*. He glanced up from the manual with his unfeeling eyes and gave Ridge a contemptuous smirk. Behind him, the native boy sat idly smacking the ground with the crowbar.

Moving past Gerrit, Waxman kneeled to inspect the box. He examined the contacts where the wires terminated on the box, careful to raise the plunger with his prosthetic arm before touching them. "Contacts seem solid. You know how old the dynamite is?"

"Came on the supply ship, I don't know, four months ago. Same shit we used at the last site. It should work."

"Batteries give at least six volts?"

"Got it covered. I'm tellin' you, it's the fuse cap." He screwed up his reddening face.

"Jaws, if you knew what it was, what'd you call me up here for?"

"Fuck it," Gerrit grunted. "Let's just throw another couple a sticks in there with a fuse cap."

"I ain't walkin' out there with live powder," Waxman protested. "That charge could still go off."

"I know that. I didn't mean *you*. We have George for that." Gerrit snapped his fingers at the native boy. "George, c'mere."

"We should wait at least half an hour. Could be you just crimped the fuse too tight."

"You don't have Tarrant on your back, neither. We gotta be hittin' paydirt after lunch or I'm fucked." Frustration showed on his face and neck in red impressionistic bursts. He turned to Foucher. "Get a couple a sticks ready. And don't crimp with the pliers this time."

"Use tape instead." Waxman stepped forward to take the sticks of dynamite from Foucher. "Here, I'll show you."

Gerrit drew a silver cigarette lighter from the back pocket of his chinos and presented it to the Marokatu boy. "You're gonna use this to light the fuse." He sparked a weak flame with his thumb. "See? You just flick it." He demonstrated the action again. The boy stared dumbly at it.

Watching Gerrit with the native boy, Ridge felt a soft caving in his stomach. He breathed the foul, the fragile, together. The air was close, thick, like the air in a crowded elevator. He couldn't stand it—the unrealized possibilities, George's sensations, however lurid, brought to a pitiless end, remembered for *what* he was, not who, an unlucky joke, Gerrit as the ambassador from the outside world, like plague to a pilgrim, the whole shameful Western cycle again, this time without any philosophical facade… What else could the boy think about Westerners but hateful things? Ridge wanted to stop wishing fine thoughts were actions and risk making a glorious mistake. He stretched his free hand toward Gerrit. "Give me the lighter," he said. "I'll do it."

"Like hell you will."

"No, I'm serious."

"Serious or not, it ain't gonna happen, Tourist."

"He doesn't even understand how to use the lighter," Ridge said. The native was rubbing the smooth metal against his open palm, a curious smile on his face.

Foucher threw Ridge a pair of dynamite sticks wrapped with duct tape. "Here, tough guy. Go ahead."

Gerrit cursed Foucher for intervening. "You know what will happen to me if this kid gets killed?"

Here's my chance… In one swift motion, Ridge dropped the bicycle chain and snatched the lighter from the unsuspecting native. He turned and ran. The blue-gray granite suddenly rose up on him. Christ almighty. Holding fast to the lighter, he skidded on his knuckles. The skin on the top of his hands peeled back like the stringy pulp of an overripe mango. The dynamite was safe, *thank God*, cradled under his arm.

Fewer than ten yards away, Gerrit had a heavy boot on the chain and a hand on George's wrist. The native was pulling against Gerrit with all his might, trembling and whipping about.

Getting to his feet, Ridge knew this moment would be a vivid and embarrassing memory.

"Son of a bitch!" Gerrit's color was apoplectic now. "What the fuck you doin'?" He tugged on George to regain some ground. "Foucher, get George, will you?"

Foucher manhandled the native from behind. "No, you dumb fuck. Stop it," he muttered. The two tumbled over but Foucher maintained his choke hold. George gurgled, coughed up a stream of black saliva and pushed his heels into the dirt.

"Shit," Foucher said. He slipped his legs over the inside of George's thighs and pushed the native's wiry legs down with his own.

"Just stay away from me," Ridge warned, getting to his feet. He flicked the lighter open with his sore thumb. "Or I'll set it off right here."

"You're not gonna get away."

"I'm not fixing to. Just get ready. I'll set off the charge."

"You're a crazy motherfucker, you know that, Tourist? Goddamn it. Get yourself killed for all I care."

Foucher smiled broadly, shaking his head in disbelief. The native lowered his eyes in a fierce scowl, calmer now, no longer struggling. Foucher had enveloped him.

"Get clear once the fuse is lit," Waxman said. His face drooped like an old embroidered pillow.

With the wires for guidance, Ridge walked backwards, watching Gerrit cautiously. He resisted the impulse to grin. *Take that, you sons of bitches! Didn't expect that, did you?*

Gerrit raised up the megaphone: "Okay, ladies, here we go again. Take cover."

The sun felt close to Ridge. He was aware of the dry light catching up everything equally, the chiaroscuro of the naked hillside, the false sparkle to the stream, the golden crown of the forest... He waited for Gerrit and the others to ensconce themselves behind the rock before he turned his back to them and toward the drill hole. Ah, about forty yards to go... What were the odds the charge would detonate without warning? *Tick... tick... tick...* He moved forward—at last— with a stride more and more certain, putting the emptiness of recent days behind him. He surveyed the landscape as if he could divide the world like a heavy evening, stared down at the misbegotten shadows of men... *tick... tick... TICK...* The distance closed swiftly now. He arrived with every step.... *tick... TICK... TICK...* Was that his own heart beating or... TICK... TICK... TICK... He came within an arm's reach of the half-buried dynamite. Swallowed hard. The wires were there...

The fuse cap pointed toward the sky like a child's rocket. He swept forward. Pushed the supplemental charge into the cascade of loose dirt... The lighter slipped through his fingers... sparks... pale flame... like glitter from a grinder's wheel... *That's it, okay, Christ...*

He fled from the blast site. The chain rattlesnaked behind him, looped dangerously in front. He swung his foot wide to avoid tripping up, hobbling awkwardly. *Don't look back.* The ground beneath him seemed to give way. Would he vanish like Lot's wife? If he could only reach—

A man-made thunderclap shook the glassy blue sky. His blood jumped. The leveling blast flattened him as though he'd been cast from the clouds... *Aahh, aahh...* A rain of earth smarted him like bee stings... *Christ almighty...* How far had he gotten? He clung to the ground, his hands over the back of his head, trying to make himself small... *Aahh...* He breathed in the stale earth... *Christ.*

The infernal stings lingered for another moment like a curse...

Then nothing—a disbelieved silence as alarming as the explosion, a whispered awe like the rustle of leaves, a few unintelligible shouts...

He raised his head cautiously. The sunlight was dirty with smoke, ochre. A shadow? Gerrit? Yes, advancing purposefully, arms taut, the crowbar clenched tightly in his fist...

CHAPTER 25

Some Qualities of Gold

Gold is the first among noble metals, exquisite and nearly immortal. The luster of gold has bewitched poets and painters, adventurers and prophets. Gold is not simply a color, but the color of heaven. Even the chemical symbol for gold, *Au*, acknowledges its ethereal beauty. The symbol comes from *aurum*, Latin for *shining dawn*.

Like all genuinely beautiful things, gold is rare. It's estimated to comprise about 0.005 parts per million of the earth's crust. Only two metals—rhenium and iridium—are rarer in nature. Even uranium is at least 800 times more abundant.

The enduring nature of gold can be attributed to a unique combination of chemical inertness, density and adaptability. Because gold is chemically inert, it doesn't dissolve or corrode in simple acids (sulfuric acid) or simple bases (lime); it doesn't rust like iron; and it doesn't tarnish like silver. Gold is one of the few metals often found in its pure or native state, unmixed with other elements. Among the alchemists of the Middle Ages, gold's resistance to the corrosive forces of nature earned it the epithet, "the royal metal."

Gold is among the densest metals and, surprisingly, the softest. An ounce of gold can be hammered into 187 square feet of gold leaf or drawn into a thin wire about 50 miles long. Gold may be shaped but not destroyed by nature, taking the form of flakes, nuggets, angular gems or even attenuated tree-like shapes.

Gold is also a superb conductor of heat and electricity. Only copper and silver conduct heat and electricity better. So despite its history as an object of beauty, gold has commercially useful qualities prized by science and industry.

Together, these properties have made gold a popular metaphor for the ideal. Phrases like the golden age, the golden mean and the golden rule attest to its sublime essence. As the 13th century English philosopher and scientist Roger Bacon wrote, "Nature always intends and strives to the perfection of gold: but many accidents, coming between, change the metals."

CHAPTER 26

The Witchdoctor

Ridge wanted to pass out from the searing pain in his leg. He closed his eyes briefly against the men crowding over him: Tree, Mayano, Waxman and that bastard Gerrit, all with their careless hands on him. Ah, if only time would dissolve... He heard Foucher, who walked alongside the small procession, downgrade his leg wound: "I seen bug bites worse than this, easy... I worked with this guy one time out in the Australian outback, he found this tick in his leg, buried on his upper thigh, right above the knee. Big motherfucker. Tried to get it out with tweezers first, but it was in so deep, he left the goddamn head in..."

Opening his eyes to mere slits, Ridge focused on the meager comfort of the endless sky. He tried to distinguish distinct levels of ever-deepening blue. The levels came in and out of focus as his bearers jostled him. The opening lines from "Prufrock" tumbled across his consciousness: *The evening spread out across the sky, / Like a patient etherised upon a table... Anesthetic, Christ, probably no chance for that.*

Waxman leaned over Ridge, his mangy beard trailing into Ridge's face. "Almost there," he said.

Ridge could hear the elemental noises of the village distinctly now: children screaming as though suffering the lash; canine barks and yelps; guttural conversations, some undoubtedly about him; rude hog snorts. He didn't dare turn his head. He wanted to just go limp. Christ almighty. The pain shooting up from his right leg—his tibula, femur, whatever that bone was below his knee—coursing through him. It was is if he'd been struck by lightning and the excess current were still circulating, alighting every nerve. Was it the Senator who had told him recently that almost all aches and pains came from the feet? That the nerves were bundled down there?

He recalled the moment of his injury in discrete flickering images: the baleful sky as he turned on his back, his knees as he brought them to his chest, Gerrit's dour expression, the crowbar swinging like a pendulum, the black behind his eyes, a purplish rococo bloom then black again, darker, the bone smashed to bits... Probably crippled for life... *Crippled for life.*

"Nanokwe!" Gerrit called halfway across the central clearing. "Hey, you crazy shit witchdoctor! I gotta victim for ya!"

Through half-closed lids, Ridge glimpsed a string of tobacco leaves strung across the square like Christmas decorations curing in the muggy air.

"Nanokwe!"

"What is up?" came the reply in stilted Old World English.

"Got a man with a broke leg."

"Ah, Bob is your uncle, no? I fix him good. Inside he go."

Gerrit nodded to Waxman, who cradled Ridge's head in his knobby hands. "You go in first and then drag him through... Okay, let him down."

Ridge opened his winter-blue eyes wide as he was lowered to the hard earth. Damn the pain. He wanted to curl up in the dirt. But not now, not in front of Gerrit and the others. Arching his neck slightly, he could see the low square entrance to Nanokwe's thatched hut.

"Give me your hand," Waxman said.

Ridge reached back over his head for Waxman's grip.

"All right."

Aaahh. There was a sudden aching flash. The inner arc blazed from the wound to his head, leaving the rest of him empty and singed. He gritted his teeth as Gerrit slid out of view.

"Over here, if you please. Never the—what you say?—rugs," Nanokwe said, referring to three grimy, plaited coconut leaf mats. "Ancestors no like that."

Waxman maneuvered Ridge to the desired spot, near one of the wooden supports. Ridge caught a glimpse of the shaman's dark face, decorated with a blood-red mosaic of shapes and framed by luxuriant hair. "They part of a ceremony or somethin'?"

"No, no. That where ancestors buried. In house, um-mmm. Keep ancestors out bad weather."

"Sure."

Gerrit stuck his head into the shelter. He resembled a cartoon bulldog there on his hands and knees, his chest puffed out. "After he's done, Waxman, let me know. I'll be gettin' some chow."

"Jaws, don't the old folk get theirs? I can just come back for him."

"All right." Turning to Ridge, Gerrit said, "You're not gonna fuck with me now are ya sissy boy?" He let out a priggish grin. "You are one lucky sonuvabitch, that's all I gotta say. If it wasn't for Tarrant, you'd be a dead man."

Sissy. That's what Archer Beane had called him once during PE in Fifth Form because of the way he'd placed his hands on his hips, with his thumbs in front and his elbows bent forward like an angry mother; after Andy called him on it, he'd self-consciously changed his stance, hooking his thumbs around his waist or in his front belt loops. There was nothing worse at that age than to be considered a sissy, or expressed more virulently, a faggot, especially coming from the South, the last bastion of undiminished manhood.

Ridge gave Gerrit a curt parade wave good-bye. "Yeah. Whatever."

"C'mon, Waxman. Let the witchdoctor at him with his knives and poisons. Yessiree. Case a the cure bein' worse'n the disease."

Adjusting the shoulder strap on his prosthetic, Waxman issued a nasally sigh then followed Gerrit outside.

"How it happen?" asked the shaman. He shuffled over to a bookshelf comprised of bricks and two-by-fours, his several brightly colored cowry necklaces jangling. The shelf was weighed down with outdated medical texts as large as headstones; a number of plastic bottles and unlabeled fruit jars of cloudy liquid; and, on the top shelf, a variety of metal instruments resembling old blacksmith's cutters, of which Ridge could see just the forbidding edges. Nanokwe pawed the contents of the shelves with his untrimmed fingernails.

"An accident, that's all." Ridge said, hoping to speed the moment along.

"What you *Inglis* believe," scoffed the shaman, kneeling at Ridge's side with a murky bottle, a torn-up T-shirt for a rag and what looked like a hedge knife. He wore only a coarse bark-cloth girdle. His skin was fine and dark and as oily as a reflecting pool at midnight. His face was narrow like a collie's, his henna-colored eyes poking out from an ornate pattern of red. According to Tree, the Marokatu painted their faces because they believed their ancestor spirits desired beauty.

Oh, Christ no. Ridge sat up on his hands when he saw the serrated blade.

The shaman put a hand on Ridge's chest. "Lay down. You be all right. This," he said, waving the knife, "for cut you pant." He reeked of sweat, tobacco and the pungent berry juice the natives used for insect repellent.

Ridge pressed himself against the ground.

With a single ferocious stroke, the shaman slashed Ridge's jeans from cuff to knee.

Ridge raised his head to examine his wound. There it was ... *Christ*: a white-hot gash swelled to the color of rhubarb. This was fucked-up. He'd probably have to drag a cane around like a prematurely aged dandy. What would Mira think of that? When they made love, she would have to minister to him like a nurse, always delicate, cautious. He'd see the pity behind her eyes, hear the false urgency in her breathing, not like before, no, not at all ... Goddamn Gerrit. There just had to be a way to make things right. "You can fix it? I'm not crippled ..."

"How it happen? Mr. Tarrant mess you about?"

"No, not directly anyway," Ridge said between clenched teeth. "You wouldn't happen to have aspirin, would you? Tylenol or whatever?"

"Just the thing, mister." The shaman retrieved a fruit jar of golden brown liquid and a blue plastic bottle from the bookshelf. The apparently haphazard collection reminded Ridge of his childhood agate and insect collections, his accidental killing jars.

"Ridge. My name's Ridge."

"Yes, I know. From the far outside." He uncapped the fruit jar and tilted it in Ridge's direction. "The bottle say 'Early Times.'"

Ridge wetted his lips just to make sure, *goddamn right*, and then took the jar from Nanokwe for a long calming draw of Kentucky whiskey. "Where'd you learn to speak and read English?"

"Ah, I speak crooked *Ingles*. Oxford Divinity School student teach me. A missionary in—on?—the island. He bring me to England for some year. Like a prize. 'Ah, see the aborigine accept Jesus Christ into heart!' Want me come back, turn Marokatu to Christian. But I see too much Christian. Much wicked magic. God powerful, yes, but ancestor spirits, cannot forget. No. I have much strong ancestor in my chest."

The whiskey began to numb Ridge's insides. "Did you learn any medicine there?"

"Some: first aid, vaccines, yes, nothing so hard. I read, but ... trouble. So long a words."

"But you can fix my leg, can't you?"

"Bob is your uncle, no?"

"I'm afraid I don't know what that means."

The shaman furrowed his brow, confused. "Yes. Mean, yes. You no use such word?"

"You fixing to put a splint on it?"

"Yes, wrap with bandages, tight on ... um, box-paper? Alongside ..." He pointed uncertainly at a mess of cardboard boxes along the far wall, behind his mesh hammock. "Keep for six, eight week. No have x-ray, so must treat like broke."

So there it was. The desperate verve in him dissipated. There was no way out now: none, zero, zilch. He'd wasted his heart on this effort; even more, he'd deepened his shame. When Mira and the others were rescued, if they hadn't been already, they would explain his whereabouts to the US Coast Guard or whoever, and he'd be found by an exacting soldier about his age who would summarily consider him too frail or simple to have escaped. Mira's defense of his actions, albeit heartfelt and persuasive among polite company, would tear him apart from the inside.

Holding up the blue plastic bottle, the shaman said, "This pain medicine. Dur-a-ge-sic. Only use one time since."

"You know that for sure? Not to be rude, but it doesn't have a label on it. Nothing does," Ridge added, sweeping his hand over the room.

"That Mr. Tarrant order. No want trouble, stealing."

"Tree, I bet."

Nanokwe crouched over a cardboard box with Huggies Ultrathin Diapers stenciled on the side and began emptying it of bottles and odd scraps of metal. "How it happen? You still no tell me."

Ridge gulped down more whiskey. The phrase *wrap tight* had conjured up unsettling images. "It happened after the blast, you know, the dynamiting. Gerrit." He pointed toward the doorway. "I guess he plays this game with one of the Marokatu boys. Curious George they call him."

His arms outstretched like thin wings, the shaman struggled to tear a side panel from the cardboard box.

Ridge waited for the box to give way before continuing: "Anyway, I don't want to sound immodest, I mean, I was really just pissed off at Gerrit, at being here at all, and the way Gerrit treated the boy just got to me. I interfered in his little game, so he took a swipe at me with a prybar."

"There much bad feeling here," the shaman said, twisting the cardboard strip in two.

"Forgive me, Nanokwe, but I don't understand why you put up with it. Why would you let Tarrant do this to the tribe? Are you just outgunned?"

"The gun something, but no. It Mr. Tarrant. He like original Marokatu. Like the now dead—the spirit at beginning time, spirit in chest." The shaman measured the length of the cardboard against Ridge's shin. Apparently satisfied, he opened a bottle of Betadine cleansing solution at his side, which he applied in painterly strokes with the corner of the shredded T-shirt. Ridge ground his teeth. "Is a shame story. Marokatu make war on enemy, see? Much blood, bad spirit. Enemy spirit eat much souls. Mr. Tarrant, he keep enemy away for us to make village. Much generous. Food, tobacco, medicine." The shaman smiled, showing his sharply filed yellow teeth. "Poor in Marokatu mean 'no tobacco.' Much gifts he bring. In Marokatu, much gifts make headman—make number one."

"He made you rich?"

"Important, gift. When die, Kagoroa ask only how you die. Good death go to place under the sea like Christian heaven, bad death, place of fire. But we no afraid place of fire. Kagoroa stupid. We tell him good death, he send to deep water." He gave a short throaty laugh. "Back where we start, the first people."

"How long is this supposed to go on—the mining? Don't you feel, I don't know, used?"

"What you speak, I understand. There much bad spirit. Ancestor no like foreigner. No human. Marokatu say: 'To be friend good, but not cut throat for him.'"

"Any chance the chief or whatever you call him will drive Tarrant away?"

Nanokwe chuckled. "Headman no have such power. He Tarrant dog. One word from headman, each man do what he want."

No difference there. "Listen," Ridge said in a conspiratorial whisper, "I know it's dangerous, but can you help me get out of here? I would be grateful. I don't know what I can offer you. Maybe there's something I can trade. I don't know. But I have friends waiting, depending on me."

"You not only one they take."

"What do you mean? Before me?"

"Yesterday."

"How many? Here at the camp?"

The shaman shook his head and grabbed up a bottle of Skin Tite glue and an Ace bandage. "Other village—over mountain."

"Are they dead then?"

"Told they two walking women. Eyeglass take them."

"What's 'walking women'?"

"Um, what you say? Much fanny?"

"I'm afraid I still don't understand."

The shaman grasped his crotch. "Fanny."

"Whatever. What was it you said about *Inglis*?"

"No. *Eieee-glasss.*" Nanokwe put the circle of his thumb and index finger against his eye.

"You mean Foucher? The guy with the glasses and ponytail?"

"Yes, much bad spirit. Like the death root."

"When was this?"

"Yesterday, I hear."

Christ almighty. It had to be Mira and Paige. Ridge's loving memories of Mira dispersed like a leaf storm; a lurid ghost remained, taunting him. The blood in his temples counted out time. "Are they all right? Sick or hurt?"

"Eyeglass make a single stranded night with one."

"Are you saying he raped her?"

The shaman nodded. "*Maki-maki.*"

Oh, God, no. Let it be a lie. Please. Not Mira. Ridge's vision misted over as his eyes filled with water. "You have to send somebody... He has to let them go." He sat up on his elbows.

Nanokwe put a restraining hand on his chest. "Me have much power. Send much spirit to eat the soul of enemy." He shook his head. "But help you I cannot."

"Just tell me where they are then or I swear to God... Just ..."

"No need. Tell Mr. Tarrant what I know. He no like such thing. Give Eyeglass beating with the mouth." He started to swaddle Ridge's knee with the bandage.

"You've got to be fucking kidding me."

"Mr. Tarrant want be weather: everywhere, no place, at same time. No man do Mr. Tarrant bad and live. He no like such thing, I say."

An angry tear spilled down Ridge's reddened cheek. The shaman was right. There was no other way but through Tarrant. "Jesus Christ." The hot tears trailed down his face and gathered at his chin, at first, slow to fall.

CHAPTER 27

The Counselor's Story

The sky brightened mercilessly through the breaks in the palm thatch. Mira turned away from the scouring light toward the clammy shaded area of the hut. She heard the lazy music of the stream. If only it were the black waters of Lethe, the river of forgetfulness ... Even more for Paige than for herself. *Paige, gevalt, Lord, enough ...* With jagged nails, Mira scratched her shoulders and arms vigorously. Her skin itched something awful. She felt as though she were teeming with invisible mites.

There was a sound like the rustle of clothes. The trees? Paige? She crawled within a foot or two of the wall that bordered Paige's hut and leaned forward, listening. The coarse twine around her right ankle went taut. Mira was held fast to a newly carved post in the center of the dirt floor like an animal in an Elizabethan bear-baiting contest. Nothing. Not a whisper of life. Should she call out? She ran a tongue over lips thick with uneasy sleep. She still hadn't thought of anything to say. *God forbid, to suffer the way Paige had last night ...* Mira swallowed the bile that rose in her throat. She replayed in her mind the sequence of Paige's cries all over again: the fierce cursing and spit-muddled consonants, the throaty appeals, *please, God ...* Then, Foucher gone, the whimpering, soft, softer, *please,* the labored breathing lost in the noise of unfamiliar birds. She'd called after Paige, asking if she were badly hurt. *Of course ...* Paige had replied as if her voice were too large for her throat: "No ... no, I'm all right."

"I'm sorry," Mira had said. *If only ...* But no. She couldn't wish that suffering on herself. She was heartsick, stricken with self-loathing at the prospect. God, she couldn't even bring herself to say the word. Rape. Ape. An association of letters, primordial, degenerate, backwards ... The ape-ing of human relations ... And she was probably next, *chas vesholem!* There were several plantains, a few white bulbous tubers and a canteen of tepid water on a plaited thatch mat near the

entrance. Foucher and his native retinue had apparently left the supplies in the pre-dawn darkness. *The bastard means to keep us like pets.*
She wondered if Paige, conscious or not, had come to the same terrible
conclusion.

She closed her eyes and began to recite a traditional Jewish bedtime
prayer, seeking the protection of angels to the north, south, east and
west: Gabriel for strength; Raphael for healing; Uriel for cleansing; and
Michael for power. The Talmud says every blade of grass has its own
angel who leans over to whisper, "Grow, grow." Mira wondered if her
personal angel were near. She needed to feel the calming presence of
God. She believed with Buber that speaking with Him was closer to
speaking with someone else than speaking with yourself. She considered her angel a convenient, if only conceptual, intermediary. Despite
her thoughtful study of Rudolf Steiner and years of meditative prayer
(first learned in college at the Congregation Beth-El), she had never
actually seen the angel she'd felt so often; only nebulous shapes of light,
hints of sugar-spun beauty. She supposed that imagery was in keeping
with Jewish teaching. Judaism had no winged messengers of God.

Mira tended to associate her angel with half-imagined images of
childhood perfection: racing straw-filled containers with clothespin
babies, so-called Moses baskets, down flooded streets; sleeping late on
Saturdays in the thick covers of her four-poster bed, feeling with arched
feet for tantalizing "cold spots"; her mother winding her hair into exquisite waxen ringlets; a sleepover birthday party where she and some
gradeschool friends stayed up all night, effusive with tenderness, sharing their nascent desires, unburdened by adolescent realism... There
was no sense in feeling sorry for herself. Others had suffered more
and grander punishments. Her father for one. He'd *looked* ordinary
enough: balding, hook-nosed, a bit overweight, with dark-spotted skin
as wrinkled as an unpressed cotton shirt. But his eyes were electric
with hard-won hope. There was a numinous aura about him, "a survivor's spirit," her mother called it. He didn't like to talk about his time
in the Lodz ghetto, the first ghetto in the *Wartheland* and the last on
Polish territory until its liberation in the winter of 1945. Most of what
she knew about his life during the war she'd learned secondhand from
her mother. Her father had thought his story invariably came across

as a boast, as if he owed his survival to superior character. "Everything I have, I owe to God," he'd said on many occasions. Growing up, his reticence to discuss the Holocaust gave it the character of mythology.

What she knew was this: When the Germans took the city in 1939, her father, then ten years old, was living with his parents and older brother above the family's modest furniture store. Her grandfather, a strict, supremely dignified city elder, lost his store in the fuel riot of 1941 to a destructive mob. He exhausted his life savings less than a year afterwards bartering with Christians for food and died of tuberculosis brought on by starvation. Her uncle buried the body in the communal garden behind the apartment in order to collect his dead father's bread and food coupons. Within a few months, the suspicious German police discovered the corpse and sent her uncle to Radogoszcz or central prison, where he presumably wasted away.

Her father provided for his worn and aged mother by working in a woodwork factory which churned out small furniture. Though as a productive young worker, her father was relatively well-treated, he lived on an impossible diet: *kley* soup made from flour and groats; the leaves of radishes; thoroughly cooked young carrots; the outer leaves of cabbages (formally used only for cattle feed); potato peels; "workshop soup"—largely flour and water, with a few groats and peas; beets grown in recesses carved out of the sidewalk. Everyone in the ghetto, including her father, carried a spoon in case they received an unexpected gift of food, some manna from heaven.

Occasionally, her father and grandmother took in newcomers from around the country. One of them was a fetching young opera singer who performed sometimes at soup kitchens. The dour soprano, whom Mira's mother in a jealous fit once called a "simple gypsy," was the object of her father's first crush. She favored the arias of Verdi, Leoncavallo, Puccini, Meyerbeer and Greig. The likes of "Solveig's Song," which the woman had performed at the Budapest State Opera, carried her father through his appointed drudgery. For a few months at least. Until she was deported to the concentration camp at Chelmno, where she was likely asphyxiated by car exhaust fumes and covered over in a mass grave in the Rzuwowski Forest.

As the years dragged on rations grew increasingly scarce. The ghetto-dwellers prayed for the Eternal, Praised be His Name, to liberate the ghetto from cabbage soup, *mehayro veyomaynu*. Her grandmother helped cover the long wide roof of her apartment building's courtyard with soil and planted radishes and leeks. But she never had a chance to claim her part of the paltry harvest. She was sent to Auschwitz-Birkenau in August 1944. Mira's father was one of about 700 people spared from deportation to help with the clean-up. When the city was liberated in January 1945, he was among only 877 survivors out of a pre-war Jewish population of 65,000 to 85,000. What a frightening bone-thin figure he must have made.

With the help of a Christian import-export merchant who used to do business with her grandfather, her father made the long ocean voyage to Boston. He brought with him only the clothes on his back, his father's wedding ring and so as not to be entirely empty-handed, a battered leather valise. The two most prominent marks of his ordeal: the perpetual circles around his eyes and a stern prejudice against factory labor. The Christian merchant gave him an accounting job in a Boston warehouse. He made his life from numbers; "universals" he called them, following Plato. At the time of his fatal car accident, he was a distinguished antiques appraiser for a renowned San Francisco auction house.

Mira couldn't have possibly loved him more. His giving nature, his patient spiritual strength... His words used to wash over her like cleansing water. She had relied on him particularly during her early adolescence, when many girls start to turn away from their parents. She'd matured earlier than most of her peers and felt like an awkward, exotic bird. She'd sorted out her confusion with her father's help instead of her mother's. Because of his wartime experiences, he'd been unashamed of the body, its smells, excretions and urges; he'd enjoyed raw physical humor, occasional lewdness. Her mother, while affectionate, could never conceal her upper-middle-class disdain for the physical.

After her father's death, relations between Mira and her mother worsened. They lived alone together. Mira temporarily discarded Judaism as a fatuous excuse for suffering; her mother, a Hebrew teacher, joined an Orthodox synagogue and withdrew into religious convention. Her mother's fundamentalist turn was part of a larger effort to hold back time. She turned their large ranch-style house into a museum, adorning the furniture with knit-cloth covers, laying plastic on the carpet and cellophane over the lampshades. It was ironic then that a relic from the war ultimately softened Mira's attitude toward her mother. The object: a Torah from Poland.

The end of the war found hundreds, maybe thousands of Torahs scattered across Europe, some hidden by Jews, others discarded by the defeated Nazis. Her mother's synagogue lacked a Torah of its own, relying instead on a borrowed pair, until an anonymous benefactor came across a number of Torahs during a visit to his hometown in Poland. This benefactor, like Mira's father, had lost his home, parents and siblings in the Holocaust. When the Torah arrived at the synagogue, with an embroidered inscription memorializing the six million Jewish victims of the war, it was like a supernatural gift.

"To think that a community should come so close to annihilation should live again," the rabbi said at the installation service. "This Torah represents that continuous link from generation to generation, and for it to be re-rooted here to carry on that tradition—it's a miracle." The words seemed a plea from the grave for generational solidarity. Mira was mortified, as though the ghost of her father had visited only to shake his head sadly, disappointed, and turn away. The way she had treated her mother, *a koloshes*… She would try, no she *would*, treat her mother better.

Looking warily at the door, Mira thought she now understood her father's humility before life. *He must have felt the same temptation to give up. But he didn't. Even though there was reason enough.* She put a hand on her chest to slow her beating heart. *His doubt must have kept him going, the great 'what if'—if the next day or the next would deliver on the promise of a new life…* She would make sure his sacrifice was not in vain. She would face whatever horror awaited her with his stubborn dignity and a blessing on her lips. *Ah, the morning light… Baruch atah adonai…* "Praised are You, God …"

CHAPTER 28

The Accusation

From behind his clenched fist, Tarrant said, "Nanowkwe, send for Foucher."

"Yessir, Mr. Tarrant," said the native. He smiled gamely before shuffling out.

Tarrant pushed away from his makeshift desk. He looked as though he'd been clapped out of a dream, his eyes restless, flashing from out of skeletal pits. "What do you reckon I should do, Mr. Dantley? Assuming the accusation proves true, that is." He walked out from behind a desk strewn with books: Schopenhauer, Fichte, Nietzsche, Lessing, Klatzkin. An open notebook revealed his furious scrawl.

Ridge felt a tightness travel up his spine. He glanced away from Tarrant, looked down the length of his splinted leg. The Duragesic—those big blue horse pills—must have begun to work. The hot aching in his leg had subsided. "I don't know. I hadn't thought past the point of knowing."

"Come on, Mr. Dantley. Don't play dumb. In your heart of hearts, you know, don't you? It ain't a shameful thing. Really. It's natural what you're feeling."

"Are you going to kill him?"

"Is that what you want?"

"I don't know." Ridge reeled from the proposition. The idea of condemning a man was hard to settle in his head. "Would you do it?"

Tarrant leaned against the edge of the desk. His shadow loomed on the wall like a sorcerer's cape. "Maybe if you asked me. Go on ...."

The seconds advanced with unforgiving slowness. "I'm not sure I want to."

"You just want him gone but not the responsibility for it? That don't seem Christian honest. You consider yourself Christian, Mr. Dantley? I don't know if Unitarians do that, typically, seeing as how you don't believe Christ was divine."

Why all these theological questions? He keeps pushing, pushing… A light unexpected rain sounded on the corrugated tin roof. "If you mean following the words of Jesus, his philosophy, doing good works, yes."

"But you don't believe in the Resurrection?"

Ridge shook his head. The line of questioning was a series of pinpricks. He knew what he believed but he'd never worked out a cohesive *system*. For some perverse reason, Tarrant kept testing him for religious consistency.

"When you're dead, you're dead full stop. We agree on that at least." The totemic shapes on Tarrant's forearm bulged as he crossed his arms. "You might study on how the Marokatu approach these matters. 'Course they don't recognize religion per se. It's part of their ritualized life, ingrained to the bone. The idea of it as somethin' separate and apart would mystify 'em. What's more, morality never enters into it. There's no moral force 'cept their ancestor-ghosts and whatever they decide on their own, in council and whatnot. The gods—they don't got any moral purchase. That big-ass statue out front of the spirit house—Kagoroa, god of the sea and rose-colored dawn—he looms large in their cosmology but in everyday affairs, he's a triflin' shadow. There's no universal love, no divine justice, no moral or karmic weighing up at the end. They got pure godless freedom to make their own way."

"And that's an improvement?"

"Closer to the truth of things, I'd wager, than, say, the Pope in his gilded city. They don't gotta twist themselves up tryin' to explain away the problem of sufferin'. Their gods are as confused and impulsive as any drunken bully. Feared but not revered." Tarrant allowed himself a smirk. "What's your relationship with these women? You said they was on the boat."

The gut-worry Ridge had borne since the accident seized him with renewed force. There was no avoiding the truth now, though it meant Tarrant would have more power over him than ever. Mira, without knowing the danger, wouldn't think to lie. If only he could thin out his worry like oil on water … "All right. One of them is my fiancée—Miriam—goes by Mira." He ran a hand over his stubbled chin. His sandy-brown facial hair was soft now. "The other I just met—Paige. She's the girlfriend of someone who was on the boat. I have no idea where he is if it's just the girls there." He met Tarrant's dark eyes. "You won't hurt them, right? Because I'd rather die than see them harmed."

"Mr. Dantley, your notions of me are gravely confused. I ain't the malicious sort."

The wind spit warm rain into the cabin as Foucher stepped inside, slick from the light shower. His features were pinched with distress. He wiped his glasses clean on his rain-spattered Nike T-shirt. "What's this, Tarrant?"

"I heard there was a bit of trouble."

"From him?" Foucher said derisively, pointing to Ridge. "You would've killed him for what he pulled."

"No, not that. He got what he deserved," said Tarrant, straightening. "No, it's something else entirely. And I have to say first, Foucher, out of respect for all the years between us, I apologize for asking this in front of the faintheart here—a nobody, a nothing—but he does have a proprietary interest in this matter. The question, not to put too fine a point on it, is this: You holding out on me in some way?"

Foucher blinked several times. His face went as white as that of a child who's been rubbed too hard. "What do you mean, 'holdin' out'?"

Ridge couldn't bear to meet Foucher's eyes. He turned away, anxiety rising in his throat... "Is there something I should know about you ain't told me?" Tarrant pressed.

"'Bout what?"

"About the job you did for me. You think the Marokatu don't talk?"

"You trust those fuckin' monkeys?"

"Oh, brother-seeker... *'Thou most lying slave, / Whom stripes may move, not kindness! I have used thee, / Filth as thou art, with human care; and lodged thee / In mine own cell...'* You take advantage, my friend. You take advantage."

Foucher scarcely registered Tarrant's consuming rage. He was not unlike a prisoner, who, living among the most vicious convicts, is surprised to hear visitors remark on their evil. "I thought I had *carte blanche* to do whatever I had to."

"There was no strategy to this, Foucher. Only a gross lack a discipline. You know as well as I: Vice is just another example of the herd-mentality—a degenerate form of escapism." Turning to Ridge, Tarrant spoke in a deep sorrowful tone: "What you don't know is, Foucher and me, we been partners since '86, since before Honduras. He's done necessary work for me—unpleasant work, mostly—but he's learned to control his animal spirit better with me around. See, I don't believe you grow through doin' good. That's the Christian lamb philosophy. The way I see it, you grow through struggle—with others, yes, but mostly with your own wrongheaded instincts. Foucher, here, I thought he'd rose above his birthpatch o' anger."

"Tarrant, look," Foucher said. "Just let me take care of this. I done the others like you wanted. Those bitches don't know any better. I can just go back—"

"No, absolutely no. I've given you liberties. You earned them partly, true, but I indulged you. And now we're gettin' close to the motherlode and you know how things get around major finds. The blood running high. One betrayal after another like a goddamn virus. I can't have this lack of discipline worrying me, too."

Christ almighty. Kenny and the Senator, oh, please, Christ, Mira be all right... "Which one did you rape?" Ridge blurted. "You did—you raped them, didn't you? Are they hurt?"

Foucher averted Tarrant's gaze, weak now with a mortal fatigue. He knew he was finished. "The redhead, guess it was." He raised his chin toward Tarrant. "What the fuck does it matter anyway? They don't know anything."

Ridge felt as though he were undergoing a slow stinging thaw. Then, ashamed of his relief, turned to plotting a cruel revenge on Paige's behalf.

"That's not the point," Tarrant growled. "You know, with anyone else, I wouldn't hesitate... But I can't do that. You just have to go away, Foucher, into exile. I'll make sure you get your mercenary rewards. Don't worry 'bout that. But you can't stay here at camp. You'll have to make your way out there someplace, out in the real wilderness. And no gun, not even a knife. Don't want to find you at my throat some night. If you can't control your animal urges then you ought to live like one."

When Foucher tried to reply, he made a soft gurgling, like the sound a stone makes when it's sucked underwater. He cleared his throat and stared mutely at Tarrant.

"I want to look over your things after you pack," Tarrant continued. "Otherwise, I'll send the Marokatu."

Foucher's features were hardened in hateful concentration.

"Are you wise to me, Foucher?"

"I can't believe this."

"Answer the question."

"That's the way you want it, I'm wise o' king," Foucher said. He stood there a few awkward moments, apparently deciding whether to say something else then turned and stalked out.

Ridge avenged Paige in his imagination. But stabbed, hung or shot in his mind's eye, Foucher remained stubbornly defiant, eyes bright, lips pressed into a cruel line. Ridge kidney-punched him to blot out the last twitch of resistance and—the door slammed, ending this line of thought. "It wasn't my fiancée," he sighed. Tarrant raised a finger. Ridge ignored it. "I want to go with them—whoever goes to get Mira and Paige."

"In your condition? Be realistic, Mr. Dantley. Though, if you had an interest, I could teach you some techniques to get over the pain— ways to get back to the inner strength of our ancient ancestors." Tarrant forced a smile. "'Sides, I have a special task for you. I'm going to take you into my confidence, reveal the full scope of my endeavors here, let you test my thinkin'. That's the truest side of me for certain— the thinkin' side—and you're the only one among these pig-ignorants might 'preciate it. I need a devil's advocate, or whatever passes for the same in hell, dependin' on your perspective." He walked from around his desk. "You're my number one now, Mr. Dantley. I trust you won't fuck it up like Foucher. You'll never see me so merciful again."

CHAPTER 29

The Lobbyist's Story

Paige cradled herself in the cool shade of the hut, wishing she could wander off and die unnoticed. Her youth was gone. What youth meant, the physical pleasures of it, those were invariably tainted now. Sex as willful forgetfulness, as a way of moving beyond herself, was over. She couldn't imagine wanting it again. She was now confined to her own thoughts. The bestial horror of last night, the agony and shame, the image of her own contorted face (as she pictured it), could never be escaped.

She rocked gently on her haunches, her hands tight around her knees, careful not to make a sound. She didn't want to hear Mira's soft-spoken pieties. Where was God's mercy in this? The world was the world and there was nothing you could do about it, no excuses you could make, nothing. *The universe is against you.* There was scientific evidence for it. She'd recently read an article in a medical journal about the real-world statistics behind Murphy's Law. According to the article, probability theory, the mathematics of arrangements and simple physics conspire to make the worst of things. Gravity and surface friction, for instance, dictate that a dropped slice of buttered toast typically lands on the linoleum butter-side down.

But this time … This time it wasn't buttered toast or mismatched socks or choosing the wrong line at the grocery store … It wasn't even physical. It was her spirit. The world was the world … *Oh, who the fuck am I kidding? I'm the one who's really made a mess of things—Roger, my career* … She'd been rummaging through life as though it were a toy box, trying this and that, without ever settling on anything. There had always been more growing up: more time, more money. Like the communal laundry room in her childhood home in Brookline. Figuring out what to wear for school had never been a worry. She (and her younger sister, Grady) could always borrow from the communal laundry room, a large upstairs closet her mother had turned into a disorganized fashion bar. The room precluded the need to order things. She knew there was bound to be something she liked amid the heaps of garments.

The emptiness she felt now was reminiscent of those despairing mornings after her divorce. At a superficial level, she'd recovered from it quickly but the loss, the haunting sense of failure, endured. Roger, a CPA at Ernst & Young, had been easy to dismiss as a comic mistake. He was handsome, suave even, but what she'd loved about him most was his hands. They were large and strong and as smooth as a broken-in leather jacket. When he folded her delicate hands in his, she was gone. He was her necessary counterpart: stolid, focused, ambitious. If anyone could, Roger would hold her to the earth. His sloppy, repetitive cheating showed, however, that she'd mistaken banality for strength.

In hindsight, she wondered how she ever thought their marriage would work, with Roger pursuing an MBA at the University of Michigan while she finished her bachelor's at U. Mass. The distance allowed them to exaggerate their similarities, indulge in common fantasies belied by the way they lived. The very decor of their respective apartments evinced fundamental and, as it happened, irresolvable differences. Roger's studio space consisted of spare exacting pieces reminiscent of the 1930s: a black Montis armchair; a cherry veneered desk with a frosted glass shelf; a maroon calfskin sectional; a slim cherry Ikea bookcase; and a chalk-colored Ligne Roset sofabed. No pictures on the desk, the mantel or the walls. Not even a wedding photo. In a rare moment of self-consciousness, Roger had once referred to his place as a form of pre-work conditioning. The apartment helped him "get into a Frederick Taylor frame of mind," he said.

Meanwhile, adopting an animal motif, Paige turned her one-room walk-up into a cozily informal menagerie. Her wrought-iron bed, draped with opaque Indian Saris, was crammed with pillows decorated with needlepoint rabbits and ducks. A faux leather screen with a painted lion separated the bed from a living room replete with atavistic images: terra cotta Siamese cats; a mop-headed zebra; bronze vases with antelope, reindeer, emu and other game in *bas relief*; enamel butterflies on the walls; plates decorated with lions and elephants; and dozens of surreal, brightly painted wooden creatures from Oaxaca.

The animals circled a pair of lemon-colored club chairs and a 25" television—scrunchy romantic comfort amidst frozen nature.

She'd thought there was some Apollonian-Dionysian tension there, but Roger's taste was a lazy kind of trendiness. His affectionate behavior—behavior seemingly bound by antiquated but endearing traditions—was evidently just habit rather than the result of conscientious effort. During their courtship, he'd been respectful in his advances, cautious. He'd called when running late, kept his appointments, humored her parents' liberal idiosyncrasies, wrote achingly sincere, ill-parsed poems, endured her taste for bohemian fashions and folksy alternative music—all too consistently to be a ruse. But his sexual escapades proved he wasn't as predictable as she supposed. Relativity imposed itself, made things unfamiliar, contrived.

For the first year or so following the divorce, she'd suffered a galling sleeplessness. Morning was an intrusion. She wanted nothing more than to lay in bed, burrowing into her own skin. Funny how she'd never dreamed of Roger since … More proof he was mere dumb flesh, not the dream-stuff she initially took him for … *Oh, what the hell was I even thinking—coming here with Kenny?* She'd been circling her authentic self in ever-widening circles for years. Even before Roger, she'd abandoned her pre-med track, frustrated with her own perfectionism. Since the divorce, she'd consistently scaled back her ambitions until she could be assured of success: hospital administrator, state health department administrator, county health department administrator, lobbyist for health reform … She preferred to be top-rated amateur over a struggling pro.

There's nothing she admired more than brazen excellence, no matter the field. That was the nucleus of her bohemian rich-girl ethic: the notion that the authentic self was revealed in excellence. Roger, Kenny, a number of other boyfriends, all seemingly disparate personalities, were all superior at their jobs. Uncomfortable with whom she'd become, she'd tried to find herself in the perfection of others. She was embarrassed to even be thinking about herself primarily in relation to men. Now, especially now, she wanted to go home and be like a little girl again, to know herself as children do without explanation.

When she pictured home, she didn't recall her parents' gabled two-story house so much as summery impressions of Fenway. Her father, a teaching doctor at Boston College, was an inveterate Red Sox fan and took her to the occasional game (just her as "Princess" Grady despised sports). There was something reassuring about the quirky old park. Even sitting far from the action on the uncomfortable concrete centerfield bleachers was an early joy. The patchwork history of the place had always calmed her. The leveled-off Duffy's Cliff, an embankment in front of the leftfield wall where fans used to be allowed to sit, the screen set up in 1936 to protect the windows of Lansdowne street and of course, the "Green Monster," the 37-foot leftfield sheet metal wall, all this and more attested to a natural resilience. It was like the park was charmed.

It didn't hurt either that Fred Lynn had the prettiest swing she'd ever seen. She remembered him rubbing his bare hand up the barrel of the bat before taking on a pitch, completely unflustered. His swing described a perfect arc. The force behind it was like the whole of the wind. He was the object of her first crush. In the summer of 1975, Lynn had one of the best games in baseball history, racking up three home runs, a triple and a single against Detroit. At the end of the television broadcast, she'd cried happily, in awe of his easy athleticism. He was like the figure of a poem, not only in his grace and precision, but also in his essence; his performance evoked a rare, preadolescent moment of clarity—

Wait. She could have sworn she'd heard something...Some forest animal rooting around? The shifting remains of a campfire? *There it is.* She rose to her full height, straightening her soiled slip across her thighs. Footsteps? *Please God, no, not again.* The mere thought of another attack turned her blood cold. Paige retreated from the door to the hut as far as the rope around her ankle would allow. Then she kneeled down, fixed her hands around the braided rope and tugged on it, desperate to loose the wooden post that held her fast. Just as before: no movement. Her arms fell to her sides, slack and useless.

She tiptoed to the side of the room that bordered Mira's hut. Yes, definitely footsteps. Coming closer. She winced, afraid to even whisper to Mira. One whisper could release a torrent of fearful words. *Please, please...*

"Hey, anyone here?"

Who? The drawn-out vowels suggested a southerner: *hee-yah.* The footsteps were close now. Just outside Mira's hut?

"Paige, you awake? Are you there?" Mira sounded small, lost.

She heard the rustle of palm thatch. *Whoever's there is going in—*

"I'm here Mira," she said, finding her voice. "Are you okay? I'm right here." She closed her eyes tightly, dreading Mira's reply. Her throat constricted. What choices did Mira have? Did she herself have? Fight, weep, cry out? God, she couldn't bear to listen, to hear Mira scream in an unrecognizable voice...

CHAPTER 30

His Treatise

What is essential to animal well-being, to sheer human instinct, is desire. I defend the liberties of desire with an uncommon vigor, despising the herd-mentality of the moral fanatic, especially the Christian moral fanatic. The supremacy of the drives, of instincts over rationality and logic, this is the overpower. The overpower can be likened to a mitochondrion, the powerhouse of the neuron which exists solely to manufacture and expel energy. Except the overpower involves the discharge of spiritual energy, what the Kabbalists call the Tzelem *or divine spark.*

Life itself is overpower—a primal struggle against cultural pressures, the demands of institutions, the masses and traditional spirituality. The man who manifests overpower prizes the struggle for self-mastery, for self-posited values more than potential harmony. Consequently, equating harmony with epistemic desperation and decadence, he decries the Socratic equation (reason = virtue = happiness) for its fundamental assumption of an end to overcoming/becoming.

Question: Does the overpower, in praxi, *extinguish the possibility of a moral standard by which society might judge itself and perhaps, prosper? Answer: In order to be truly human, one must needs gain self-mastery— a self-mastery that results in a final end or thing-in-itself (else, suffer an infinite regress). This self-mastery is not an unnatural stoicism imposed from the outside; rather, it is a condition in which the senses—even fully-engaged—do not interfere with the process of achieving objectives in accordance with the overpower—*

Ridge raised his eyes from the hand-scrawled manuscript to the surrounding forest. He perspired under a soft, wide-brimmed hat that shaded his eyes from the oppressive sun. *How much of this shit is there?* He thumbed through the sheaf of yellow paper. On the final page, there was an ink-smeared note indicating the manuscript was continued elsewhere. *This is ridiculous.* He looked around as though expecting someone to be there to agree with him. From his hammock, the Marokatu village was about 40 yards distant through the puraos, ironwood and pandanus. The scene was hazy with bluish smoke from scattered family fires.

How could Tarrant expect him to edit this material? It was pernicious, wasteful—just more vulgar Darwinism. Ridge couldn't believe Tarrant had spent more than a decade on this solipsistic rambling. Sententiously titled *Destruction of the Destruction: A Philosophy of the Future*, the manuscript constituted an assault on commonly accepted notions of law and morality. Tarrant argued from a crude evolutionary standpoint, claiming morality was only political compromise. According to him, all of our moral feelings are vestiges of a peculiar and purely arbitrary evolutionary path. He argued for a return to a guiltless pre-history where unconstrained egotism rules: *The prerequisite for becoming a truly moral man—an aristocrat of first principles—means playing with what others consider good, holy, proper.*

Just as Nietzsche did, Tarrant reserved his greatest spite for Christianity. He considered it hostile to the world, with its emphasis on the rewards of humility. Christians, according to Tarrant, had a slave morality; their exaltation of the poor, the meek, ascetics generally, was a form of revenge fantasy. They banned power, pride—the chief qualities that come from strength—qualities that tend to promote or elevate life. In short: Christianity inverted what Tarrant construed as the truest values.

Ridge wondered what Mira would say to that. As he understood it, she believed in a personal transcendent God who both expresses Himself in and comprises the world. This notion was apparently suggested by her reading of Spinoza's *Ethics*, along with the works of various Jewish mystics and Kabbalists. Mira posited that matter pre-exists in God on the principle that a being can't be the cause of something and, at the same time, have nothing of that thing. To Mira, the notion of an infinite God depended on Him being indistinct from Nature; if He were apart from the world then there would be substances other than God and so He wouldn't be infinite. She considered a belief in God before all the evidence was in a singular mark of character. It compelled a personable humility, this belief in something larger than ourselves. When pressed for further justification, Mira maintained that, in the absence of definitive proof to the contrary, such belief couldn't—at the very least—be considered irrational.

They'd visited this topic several times in the spirit of understanding. Ridge proposed an impersonal God, an ineffable source that makes something akin to a Kantian moral law possible. That was the heart of his Unitarian Universalist belief: We are a people separate and apart but blessed with a rationality that allows us to recognize our moral duties to each other. Whatever first made human rationality a reality—God, the Unmoved Mover, whatever—is immaterial. Everyday affairs are governed by a combination of natural phenomena (in essence, physics) and human psychology. There are no supernatural interventions. On that, Ridge agreed with Tarrant. But where Tarrant viewed life as a chain, one link after another, defined by master-slave relationships, Ridge saw it as closer to a Cat's Cradle, with everything intertwined. Tarrant seemed to intuit this difference between them and accept it as a challenge. When he'd enjoined Ridge to edit his treatise and, in fact, weave his colorful biography into its intermittently fable-like narrative, he'd called Ridge his "necessary foil."

Ridge's heart leapt to his throat at the thought of seeing Mira navigating this terror of an island. For all their differences, she was the one fixed point in his life. If he died now, his time on earth would be easily undone. With his parents' influence at its weakest, his job a matter of convenience, no real attachments, no lasting obsession except to achieve some vague measure of success, everything was transitory. Imagining his own obituary, he figured he'd be remembered only as a footnote to his father's story. He wanted so desperately to reach some destined plateau where he could rest, at last, satisfied with his accomplishments. Ever since he'd been aware of his privileged upbringing, he'd been so worried about trading on his past, working, striving, reaching for more, that he'd forgotten to live in the present. It was always the next thing and the next … Mira was the boldest extension of his life so far. She filled in the present. Before Mira, the now was like a waiting room, the still, unsettling space between yesterday and tomorrow. She made this in-between space significant. She exhibited none of his persistent struggle for the next thing. She was, in a word, equable, as though always conscious of her own breathing. He couldn't bear the thought of Tarrant snuffing out that immanence.

He set Tarrant's manuscript flat against his chest, leaving the damp imprint of his thumbs on its edges, and rubbed his sunken blue eyes with his knuckles. The words scared him, not because of what they said but because of what they left unsaid. Behind every written word, Ridge knew, there were a host of terrible deeds and unarticulated thoughts, an awful secret history—a history that would catch up to him if he said the wrong thing. What would he tell Tarrant about these slanted truths? Tarrant considered the tract a necessary counterpart to his gold-mining operation; he wanted renown as a dreamer-doer, maybe even a kind of messiah, with an epic life story and words that would sustain his philosophy in perpetuity. Tarrant understood that words are one of the few things that carry forward in time and he wanted his, with their vile effervescence, to inspire revolution, law, judgment, war, an enlightened savagery. *The history of the world is the history of the word.* Christ Almighty. What did he expect? Whatever it was, Ridge knew there was no use in lying about his opinions. He'd only be found out. Perhaps as long as he wasn't dismissive, pointed out gaps in logic as a way of shoring up Tarrant's arguments...Oh, why now? With Mira and Paige coming? The wrong response would inexorably put them at risk, too.

The tract roused in Ridge his impatience for the high-minded academics he'd met at Princeton, the roving intelligentsia who encouraged others to suffer for their principles. That's one of the reasons why, for all his love of learning, he'd rejected the notion of an academic life. He despised the wan academia of his day and had imbibed enough of his father's devotion to practical affairs to bristle at the thought of researching arcane subjects for the sake of a tenure track position at some regional college and the occasional amusement of a few peers. No, he felt compelled to do something that had an immediate and tangible social impact, to live in and to shape events. Here was an opportunity to make good on his cherished ideals, much like the opportunity the North had realized in fits and starts following the passage of the Fugitive Slave Act and before the Civil War, when injustice was so rampant and egregious even the most passive citizen could no longer ignore the invidiousness of slavery. If his acquaintance with business had taught

Ridge anything, it was an admiration for hard-won success. That, combined with his Unitarian concern for social good, prejudiced him in favor of action over reflection. His belief that the rightness of things depended entirely on human hands demanded he do something. But what? How could he strike back and survive?

Tarrant's polemic suggested failure was due largely to a weakness of spirit. This reasoning was enumerated in a series of extended metaphors: *The varieties of spirit number three: the shark, the dog and the bird. The shark spirit is something fossilized. It is a resistant spirit, not from principle, but from deadened habit. Sharks have survived millions of years in roughly the same form. The nature of their survival, however, is nothing for the spirit to emulate. Evolution has passed them by. The shark spirit betokens an inability to become. It is a spirit forever frozen in time and, as such, incapable of change, it says nay to life in all its aspects.*

The dog spirit is one of acquiescence. Just as the dog was bred from the wolf—de-fanged if not deracinated in the process—this spirit goes along to get along. In other words, it is overly pliant. The changes the dog spirit experiences are outer-driven rather than natural effects of becoming. Christianity may be deemed the most successful dog spirit of the age. Its slave morality affords a comfort in numbers, though it leads to privileging destructive weaknesses like humility. It evolves ever downward, suppressing our natural inclination to strive for the overpower.

The essence of the bird spirit is protean and perfecting. This spirit knows no fear. It resists life when it must and acquiesces only to its own instincts. It affirms existence as it is and, at once, transcends it. Much as the first birds of this earth survived the Permian Extinction or Great Dying, which extirpated almost every other animal species. No distorting veil is necessary for the bird spirit. Like the animal for which it is named, this spirit is above delusion. It understands our world as a source of temporary succor and respite, nothing more. It captures life in a transmuting philosophy that is the highest formulation of the yea-saying attitude. Its every impulse is to release the overpower that connects Man to Creation and to the prospect of eternal becoming. That is the goal: to make Man like the sun. For the sun continually gives its light, never needing anything in return.

So says Anthropos, the Man-God.

Anthropos was Tarrant's name for the harbinger of his nuclear ideals. At this point in the manuscript, Ridge understood it as a Homeric giant imbued somehow with the spiritual authority to re-write civilization's governing values. Anthropos was the final arbiter of material and spiritual justice. *With Anthropos, I've given humanity another, better inspiration...* The idea was clearly caught up in Tarrant's own narcissism. The Man-God was Tarrant writ large. More importantly, the notion ran counter to everything Ridge believed, to justice and mercy, to the concept of small 'r' republican democracy. It denied that we can be claimed by ends we didn't choose—ends given by Nature or God, or by virtue of being part of a family, tradition or society. Democracy and its values can't be dependent on mere individual will. That would make the country a purely volunteer enterprise, Ridge thought, riven by competing self-interests. If—

A group of Marokatu children burst through the underbrush not far from his hammock. The four boys made their way toward him without any acknowledgement of his presence. Lacking much exposure to children, Ridge wasn't sure about their ages, but guessed they ranged from seven to nine years old. The tallest and presumably oldest boy carried a crude spear in one hand and some indeterminate bundle in the other. On reaching a small clearing, the child set the bundle down, revealing a bluish green lizard with a prehensile tail. A skink. Ridge had seen several since his arrival. They appeared to be popular pets, kept much like iguanas back in the States.

The skink was about a foot-and-a-half long, with a short, wide head and a blunt snout. It took a few languid steps away from the boy then abruptly spun sideways, clawing at the dark earth. A short length of rope stretched between the boy's right ankle and the lizard's tail. While his companions backed up, the boy with the spear haltingly jerked the skink in a circle by rotating his right foot. He jumped the rope on his left foot to complete the arc and build momentum. The skink made a complete circuit... once... twice... The skink was lifted from the ground, flailing its sharp claws. One of the boy's companions shouted to him. Advice? Encouragement? The boy readied his spear. The skink passed in front of him at a distance of two or three feet. He cocked his throwing arm and hucked the spear. It bounced harmlessly away.

Squint-eyed frustration hindered the boy's timing. The rope wrapped around his left ankle. The skink careened into the ground, catching dirt in its snout. A companion fetched the throwing stick.

Ridge turned away and slid his good leg off the hammock. He retrieved his wooden crutch and tested the ground with it before lowering his splinted leg. Even with its wrapped-blanket padding, the crutch dug painfully into his armpit. Grabbing Tarrant's manuscript with his free hand, Ridge shuffled off for the village, keeping the children on the periphery of his vision. He'd had enough of violence and threats of violence. Somehow, if nothing else, he'd prove to Tarrant he had the will to end things on his own terms.

CHAPTER 31

The Raft

In the surf up to his thighs, braced against the approaching combers, Senator Neeland regarded his raft with dark hope. The curved trunks of the native palms, lashed together by bits of rope and stringy bark, made for warped and ill-fitted planks. The crosspieces on one side skewed inward due to misaligned notches on either end. Also, there were sizeable cracks between the six deck planks owing to their un-evenness. Driving quartered pieces of palm tree into the spaces between the planks had failed to level it. Much to his father's chagrin, the Senator had never been able to think with his hands.

He applied a knee to the raft and, when it burbled under the surface, scrambled for the center where he'd tied the diving bag of supplies. His shoulders strained against the awkward bulk of his life jacket. The raft seesawed and sank still farther. The Senator settled on his hands and knees. The craft regained some buoyancy, though it calmed at a level below the waterline. The sea lapped against his elbows. Then the next sizeable wave jolted the craft toward shore and foundered it in about a foot of water. He clambered to the edge and into the surf, scraping a knuckle raw on the outside log. "Hellfire," he muttered and pressed the cut to his blistered lips. Various nicks on his hands and forearms from the construction process vexed him with salted stings. He pined for a jolt of Old Weller Antique. He could have counted the months immediately following Sarah's death in quarts of it. The sea sparkled like church-glass. The glare made his eye-sockets ache.

The raft bumped against his shins. He steadied it with a hand, one slitted eye on the drybag. What next? Give in or go on? He tried to take courage from his fears. But he couldn't put the most painful memories from the war out of his mind. He imagined himself drifting beneath the waves, undiscoverable but not alone, a sodden thing touching bottom among shipwrack and bones. What would happen to his legacy? Most of his congressional accomplishments would be abandoned in the natural tumult of events. The gossip that passed for history in Washington would be the last word on his character. At best, death would be an incomplete summing up; at worst, a damning misery.

The Senator chastised himself for recycling the same thoughts, the same arguments for and against trying. Talking to himself had become a habit ever since Sarah's death—mouthing whole conversations over breakfast grits, raising his eyebrows, biting his lip in feigned thought, setting his jaw for punctuation. Once, catching him at one of these pantomimes, Kenny had said, "No wonder there's no slack in your rope. You're always rehearsing." His younger self would never have tolerated this kind of dithery fear-gathering. *Fine. Let God decide—fate, meaning, the whole shebang.*

When he bent to push the raft against the surf, his knees and lower back popped in complaint. The raft floated free and he grabbed at a crosspiece knot for a firmer grip. The horizon was a hazy ribbon past the incoming waves. He lessened the serial pains in his arms by pulling the raft across the swells at an angle instead of taking them straight-on. The water scaled from thigh to waist to mid-torso. His clothes became drag weights. The pressure in his chest rose with the sea. He was slipping along the bottom now. He missed a step, went under and inhaled an ocean. He came up gasping and spitting. His nose burned. He clutched the outer log, closed his bleary eyes against the vastness and made one last push from the sand. It felt more like letting go than launching into a fight. He was adrift, rising and falling in wayward purpose, his anemic kicks barely enough to keep his head above water.

The raft crowded out the far horizon. The ocean was a cold peripheral expanse and the sun vehement in its brightness. The swells besetting his craft shuddered him to the bone. He had to hold on to it and, at once, push it away; otherwise, it might smash him in the mouth. The pool of sea between his cramping arms slapped against his grizzled chin. He didn't risk taking a full-hearted breath. His childhood fear of drowning had exhausted him before he'd begun. He'd never muster the strength to pull himself up.

His unshared memories, his ideals and ambitions, the deeds undone, all that is ephemeral was everything and it was heavy. Contrary to his humble public statements on the matter, he'd gone to war in a fatalistic frame of mind. Faith and desperation had come by turns. He recalled cursing that archetypal draft-dodger John Wayne for impersonating a Flying Tiger in the movies. Talk about phony do-gooding … Haw.

His arms throbbed and weakened from the tension. He would never make it. What had he really expected to happen? He hadn't mustered the strength to put his undershorts on from a standing position since the Reagan era. The rough sea dinned in his ears. The waves would sound out the remaining intervals of his life. He grew more and more listless. His heart labored in fear. How long could he possibly last? An hour? Less? Forever?

When the ocean finally claimed him, he was past all caring.

CHAPTER 32
The Reunion

Mira checked her hopes and feelings for Ridge out of fear Tarrant would use their relationship against him. Tarrant's promises of safety could be nothing more than a cruel trick. Paige, hair sun-frizzed about her face, looked dazed and unsteady. Cuts and bruises marred her naked limbs. Mira dragged a wooden chair toward her. In a defiant mood, Paige gripped the back of it instead of sitting. Her dirtied slip clung to her sweat-chilled lower back. The veins in the tops of her hands stood out. Though Mira was eager to relieve her pained feet, she stood with Paige as a gesture of solidarity.

"While Gerrit fetches Mr. Dantley," Tarrant said in the hissing glow of the lantern, "let me apologize again for your mistreatment. The business I'm in appeals to some rough sorts and out here—beyond the usual strictures of law and culture—they sometimes mistake liberty for license. The offending party's already been reprimanded."

His deep judging tone resonated in Mira's chest. She tightened her throat against it.

"Reprimanded?" Paige asked. She was tense in every fiber. "What is that—a stiff talking to?" A trembling accented each syllable.

Tarrant wrinkled his brows in annoyance. "Miss . . . ?"

"Clery."

"I've meted out a fit punishment—exile—which in this place is tantamount to a death sentence." The darkness in his voice intimated finality. "You're in no danger of crossing paths with him again."

"Who is he? What's his name? He not only . . . assaulted me, he killed one of our friends—no reason, no warning. I'm going to need more than your word." Paige shot Mira a distrustful look as if Mira might undermine her resolve. Since the attack, Mira had sensed a change in Paige's attitude, as though she was partially to blame for the attack.

"I'm afraid you got no say in the matter," Tarrant said in a level tone. "Here, my word is law. I say that, not as a point of pride, but as a point of fact. My word's all that keeps you from more abuse. You can thank me for keeping you alive." He drummed his fingers on a stamped leatherbound tome on his desk. Heavy and dark with age, the volume looked like it could have come from a medieval friary.

Mira tried to distance herself from Paige's stance without offending her. She didn't see the point in aggravating Tarrant before they fully understood what was going on. "What is this camp? We saw the digging, the … chutes? Is that what you call them?"

"We're prospectin' after placer and shallow deposits. Don't got the gear for anythin' else." He extended a large hand across the desk. "And you—you must be the future Mrs. Dantley?"

"Mira Kessler." She took his fingertips in her sweat-slick hand out of courtesy. His strapping frame and casual arrogance unnerved her. But what a face he had—rugged and tawny—what hair, what broad hands and liquid-black eyes. And his voice had the depth of a *shofet* or Biblical judge if ever she heard one.

"Pleasure." Tarrant broke into a thin unctuous smile. "Don't be alarmed at the sight of your fiancé now. The leg was sheer bad luck. But it's been treated and I've given him light duties in keeping with his background and erudition. I'll leave it to him to explain."

"Hold up," Paige said, almost choking on the words. "I don't get it. You're not letting us go?" In clearing her throat, she almost screeched.

"Until we're quit of this place, no. I can't risk any upset to my operation. Shouldn't be too much longer now—couple-three weeks perhaps."

Mira flashed on the possibility of turning her captivity into a curious Passover anecdote. Her mother would probably read some larger portent into it. Mira imagined her invoking *Ha'makom*, the name of God traditionally used to console the bereaved.

The door banged open and Ridge staggered into the cabin, breathless, a scowling Gerrit behind him. With his flushed face and oversized clothes, Ridge looked ill. She threw her arms around his neck to both comfort him and blot the image from her vision. The brim of his Panama hat caught her on the temple. She ducked under it and brushed his stubbled neck with her lips. "Ridge, *neshomeleh*," she whispered.

The surge of feelings he inspired was difficult to name, mixed as it was with anxiety about their situation and his weak embrace. He smelled of sweat and tropical air and citronella. She wanted to hold him until the order of their previous life together was restored: work and Buckhead happy hours nursing Long Islands and shopping and wedding plans and gym workouts and the Sunday crossword and indie movies at the Plaza Theater. But Paige's hurt expression suggested this was the wrong moment for flagrant emotions. Mira drew back, eyes shining from relief, and indicated Ridge's injury. "What happened?"

He blinked the question away. "You all right?" Ridge asked, recovering his voice. His free hand lingered on her hip.

Mira nodded, trying to avoid Paige's addled look. There was a palpable imbalance between them. Her future husband had returned to her while Kenny, at best, a simple boyfriend-of-convenience, had been murdered; she'd been spared from brutal assault; and Tarrant treated her as someone to be respected. Guilt and compassion moved her to quell her own happiness for Paige's sake. At the same time, she wanted to say: it's dispiriting I know, but please, for all of us, calm yourself, *a bi gezunt.*

Shaking his head in irritation, Gerrit skirted around the couple. "Found 'im with Nanokwe," he reported.

"Hold on here a moment," Tarrant said. "They'll need an escort."

Ridge shoulder-hugged Paige. The outline of her body was evident through her half-slip. A worried smile crossed her face. She made small noises with her lips but no words came out.

Tarrant cleared his throat. "I was just about to explain the livin' rules."

"Don't know if that hut's ready yet," Gerrit said.

"Use more men if you have to," Tarrant said then louder to the others: "There's a shelter goin' up across the way—other side a the square from the bunkhouses. Marokatu will guard you women nights. You," he said to Ridge, "you'll stay put. No tomcattin' around and incitin' the men."

The idea embarrassed Ridge. He glared at the floor.

"Given your habit a runnin'," Tarrant said, eyeing Paige, "I'm compelled to cuff you at the ankles. Only when you're not workin' though—mainly at dark. Days, you'll be occupied doin' woman's work with the Marokatu. New clothes, somewhat more suitable, will be provided."

"I'm—I know you've been through a lot already," Ridge said to Paige in an effort to head off an argument. "I won't pretend to understand how you feel." He raised his hand as if to gentle her on the shoulder then reconsidered and pinched the brim of his hat. "But please, just accept the restraints ... We're off the map here, okay?"

Mira sensed in Ridge an uncharacteristic fear and wondered what he knew that she and Paige didn't. In her uncertain state, she thought it best to let him take charge.

Tarrant said, "It's a sorry accident—your situation. Not fate." He caught up a pair of U-shaped leg irons from his desk and said to Paige, "I'm regardin' these as a precaution. I trust you won't abuse my lenity. You wouldn't be the only one to suffer." He handed the shackles and their key to Gerrit. "Now, why don't you go get settled? We got field showers, clothes as I said, toiletries ..."

"Whatever else happens," Paige said, "I'm going to find out who he is and where."

Gerrit interceded at this provocation and turned her at the shoulders toward the door. "C'mon. Enough a that." The chains on the leg irons *ker-chanked* in his grip. Paige's jaw continued to work in soundless curses as he escorted her out.

"I'd caution you 'bout that Miss Clery," Tarrant said to her back. His voice was even and rich with scorn. "As Mr. Dantley put it, we're off the map here. You know what that usually comes with, right?" He tapped on the book again. "The risk a dragons."

Mira's conscience held her there in front of Tarrant for a few awkward moments. She deliberated whether to say something—about her displeasure at their confinement generally or about his treatment of Paige. But the spiritual upset Tarrant provoked led her to take Ridge's halting departure as her cue. She followed Ridge, hands at her waist and positioned to catch him should he stumble backwards, resisting all the while the urge to glance over her shoulder.

CHAPTER 33

Days Behind & Ahead

Ridge ushered Mira into the cooling shade of the mess tent. She swatted absently at a spit black mosquito and took up a camp chair at one end of a sawbuck table. The flared collar of her black crepe dress was discolored and its tie-neck ribbon was missing. Her long black hair, too, was dusty. She'd delayed her shower, intent on first seeing to Paige's care and safety and had been visibly disturbed at the sight of Paige's scrubbed raw skin. Ridge couldn't take his eyes off her. The renewed fact of Mira brought every anxiety close to the surface: his keen affection, their inadequacies in this situation, the concentrated peril. "Are you all right?" he asked.

At the edge of the canvas tent, the cook popped his head over the top of his 55 gallon drum smoker. An agitated look from Ridge persuaded him to return his attention to the pork fat and cracklings on the grill. Ridge folded himself into a seat adjacent to his fiancée and swung his bum leg onto another chair to elevate it. Her eyes went dark and abstracted. His heart beat fitfully. "I mean—you hungry or anything?"

"No, I'm okay. You don't need to keep asking…" She said this last in a too bright tone.

"I'm sorry. I just—I was on edge the whole time, not knowing…" Every night separated from her had been a misery of imagined hurts. Worry upon worry had crowded out his usual stoicism. Now that she was here, beside him, weary but unscarred, he expected a calm that refused to come. Almost without him realizing it, he'd trusted her personality to elide time, to re-instate the balance that had existed prior to the wreck. She seemed both more solid and weaker now. He bent awkwardly at the waist in her direction. She curled a tangle of hair behind her ear and leaned to meet him, her heat-swollen knees pressed together. Their brief kiss was like taking a warm breeze into his mouth.

Mira broke away and put a palm to one of her reddened cheeks. The equatorial sun was a ruin to her pale skin. "My mouth is all gummy."

"I don't mind."

"I know *you* don't…" She turned away, a new blankness behind her eyes.

Her reticence pained Ridge with its doubt and withheld desire. He didn't expect much—just some recognition that he'd done everything that could be expected under the circumstances. This brooding Mira wasn't the one he'd longed for. *That* Mira would've been more appreciative of his efforts, accepted their circumstances with a trusting determination… He wanted her to be confident of his grasp on things. Rightly or wrongly, he wanted the Mira as beautiful and clear and blurred as the one from memory.

"It's unbelievable—the bald absurdity of this… *Chas vesholem.*" She waved toward the angle of village outside their shelter. It was peopled by a scattering of elders and raucous children. The unforgiving sun had leached all evidence of rain. The vast sky dwarfed everything.

Ridge tried to draw her back in. "How's Paige doing? Can you tell?" They'd escorted her through a bracing cold shower and afterward, to a tree-shaded hammock a short distance from the mess tent. When Paige had drifted to sleep, a water bottle in the crook of her wrist, they'd crept away to get some shade and talk in private.

"I clench up at the thought of the assault," Mira said without looking at him. "It was awful to be so close, to hear it and be so helpless. It made me feel all dizzy; it reminded me of getting caught in an undertow…"

Every detail Mira relayed—this, Kenny's murder, the Senator's abandonment—tightened the screws on Ridge' humiliation. "I'm sorry you had to go through that." He caressed the back of her hand. His fingernails were torn and dirty. "I hate to say this, but here, the way things are, she has to watch the anger. Can you talk to her? She could get us killed."

Mira's mouth pinched at the corners in a distressingly familiar way. "I'll try. It seems like she resents me for not having been attacked."

Ridge could feel them slipping into a cryptic exchange in which one or both of them was irritated but too polite to say by what. "Foucher, the fucking animal. That's his name. You can tell Paige if you think it would help."

She frowned at his vulgarity. They'd agreed early in their relationship that the f-word was an ugly expression. But he'd felt the need to shock her into engaging with him. The tactic worked to draw her eyes at least. Ridge went on: "They have no compunction, I tell you. First thing when I got here, there was a duel. Tarrant and one of his men had it out in a spear throwing contest." He tugged a loose fold of t-shirt. "These are the dead man's clothes."

"What about your leg? Does it hurt?"

"It's at that constant heat stage. Definitely not a 'remember when' moment." He wavered on the point of telling her the story, but thought it would only come across as so much useless self-aggrandizement. He'd accomplished nothing. Gerrit and the others didn't even understand the point he'd tried to make. "There's a sort of doctor here, a native trained by missionaries. He put the splint together. Otherwise, I would've gone with Gerrit to get you."

"This whole chain of events ..." She shook her head at something in a private middle-distance. A cascade of yellow dust surged from the hillside to fog the village. A flurry of miners were excavating the dynamited crater into a sizeable tunnel.

"That's not everything. Tarrant has me editing this treatise or whatever it is, a weird amalgam of philosophy and fable. He's cracked, Mira. It's all about this overpower—some spiritual force he believes can make us god-like. The protagonist is even called Anthropos, the Man-God. That's the level of subtlety." Ridge didn't mention that, as a way to punctuate his unvoiced disagreements as he read, he'd ginned up an adversary, Columbia, the goddess of democracy. "From what I gather, he spends most of his time studying in his cabin—did you see those books?—and toking up in the men's lodge for the purposes of 'meditation.'" He gestured toward the timbered statue at the entrance to the spirit hut. "No, there's something else going on here besides the mining."

Mira lapsed into inattentiveness again, ignoring the mosquitoes droning around her. Ridge craned his neck to examine her bruised and blood-clotted feet. "We should get those looked at. Nanokwe's got peroxide, rubbing alcohol, bandages. Then we can find some boots for you. We'll have to pack maize husks or something in the toes to make them fit."

She shrugged off the suggestion. "I'm just glad to rest them. They're throbbing." Then she curled toward him and asked in a conspiratorial whisper: "Are we really going to stay here? Like we're part of his crew?"

"I've been thinking about escape since I got here and haven't hit on a plan with any kind of odds. Especially now..." Her dimpled pout seemed a reproach. She must be going through something like the five stages of grief, he thought. They were reasonable people caught in unreasonable circumstances. If forced to guess, he'd say she was in the depressive leave-it-to-chance stage. When she recovered, he expected her to explain how everything feckless and iffy to this point had actually been providential. "Like I said, I'm even more worried what Tarrant would do if we tried and failed, or maybe worse, if one or two made it. Whoever was left behind... It's partly why I didn't make a break earlier. I was afraid of what he'd do to you and everyone else."

"What do you think our friends and family are thinking? We were supposed to be back—what?—two days ago? You think they've started looking?"

The implication that they would need outside help exacerbated the tightness in his chest. What would he have to do to regain her confidence? The utter soundness of her questions made things worse. "Someone has to be looking for the Senator at least... And my dad, I'm sure he's doing something. They just won't know where to look."

"My mom must be worried sick. You know how she gets..."

Though Ridge resented the compulsion to make another apology, he cupped her hand in his and said, "I'm sorry, Mira—sorry for everything."

"This isn't your fault."

Her level tone offered no surety. He prodded her to say more: "I was the one who insisted on making that swim..."

Mira sucked in her bottom lip and sighed. "You didn't know you'd find this..." In front of the nearest hut, a branch-boned old woman fed a gaunt poi dog an indeterminate paste from her hand. "In the diary I kept in junior high and high school," Mira said, "I left a few empty lines after each entry so the 'future me' had room to comment. If I was keeping it now, I'm sure I'd add something like 'Stay off the yacht,' but that doesn't mean—"

"Shelter in place," Ridge said, continuing his self-examination as if she hadn't spoken. "Isn't that the rule in disasters?"

"I don't think they have rules for this."

A nauseating shame overtook Ridge. It was terrible enough to have this unrequited need for validation. It was even more terrible to recognize it. They fell into a commiserating silence. The clamor of the village competed with their thoughts—yowling dogs, the chittering and frenzies of children at play, the sporadic *chunk-chunk* of pick and shovel from the hillside. Ridge imagined his next words and the next becoming so insubstantial they barely reached his own ears. "C'mon," he said, hobbling to his feet. "You'll feel better after you get cleaned up."

Mira pushed away from the table. A cry of fear or aggression went up in the village. Her hand fluttered to her mouth to cover a wince.

CHAPTER 34

King Solomon's Gold

When King Solomon built the Temple in Jerusalem, only gold suited his divine purpose; he considered silver too base a metal. Work on the Temple began in the fourth year of Solomon's reign, after the king had secured an important alliance with Hiram, the king of Tyre. The alliance gave Solomon access to the timber and precious metals necessary to erect his sacred monument. The Temple took seven years to complete with the aid of thousands of hapless Canaanite laborers.

Biblical descriptions of the Temple in the books of *Kings* and *Chronicles* are confusing, even contradictory. Neither account is contemporary; *Kings* was written sometime after the Babylonians razed the Temple in 586 BC, and *Chronicles* later still. Consequently, the dimensions and decor of the Temple as detailed in these books reflect an exaggerated view of the Temple's significance. If the Temple were as massive as Scripture indicates then the edifice and its courts would have covered nearly all of Jerusalem. In accord with the best archeological evidence, the Temple probably resembled the relatively modest Phoenician sanctuaries of the time. More than likely, the Temple was a low-roofed building similar to a tabernacle with three internal chambers: a porch, a nave (or Holy Place), and a Holy of Holies which housed the Ark of the Covenant.

Although the size of the Temple may have been unimposing and the design pedestrian, the supreme luxury of its appointments amply justify its fame. As noted in *Kings*, Solomon "surpassed all the kings of the earth in riches" and he devoted much, if not most, of his wealth to the construction of the Temple and his adjacent palace. He controlled two major trade routes, employed forced labor, exacted tribute from all the kings of Arabia and imposed burdensome taxes to realize his dream. He received 666 talents of gold annually, besides "great gifts of gold" from Hiram and the anonymous Queen of Sheba as well as monies from trade, tribute and taxes. He valued gold above all, and sent his navy every three years along with the navy of Hiram to Tarshish for "gold and silver, elephants' teeth and apes and peacocks."

The source of gold for the Temple has tortured the fevered imaginations of explorers for ages. An obsessive evangelical, Christopher Columbus sailed halfway around the world in hopes of finding the mines of King Solomon. He longed for "the place called Ophir which is now called Gold Country which is in India," as described in a revered medieval account of Solomon's reign. Columbus, who thought his name prophesied that he would be Christoferens, or the Christ-bearer, planned to use the gold to raise an army to conquer Jerusalem and to rebuild the Holy Temple. Legends have traced King Solomon's mines to Parvaim or contemporary Ceylon; to the fabulous Asian island, Cipango; and to the Solomon Islands, first visited by a gold-seeking European, Alvaro de Mendana de Neyra, in 1568.

Whatever the source, Solomon lavished gold on his epochal monument to God and to his own calamitous greed. The hewn stone walls faced with richly carved cedar; the fir-tree beams supporting the roof; the altar within the Temple; the table of shewbread; the sphinx-like cherubim guarding the Ark; in short, virtually the entire monument was overlaid with precious gold. The finest and purest gold was reserved for the Holy of Holies, the secret shrine admissable by the High-priest alone.

The ancient Hebrews paid a terrible price for Solomon's lust for gold. The injustices Solomon visited on his people to build the Temple, his extravagant ways, his pagan indulgences, and his neglect of the one true God, shattered the material and moral foundations of Jerusalem. When Solomon died, his kingdom was on the brink of ruin, his people vulnerable to both internal division and foreign invasion.

As St. Augustine recounts in *The City of God*, Solomon's construction of the Temple fulfilled the prophecy of an earthly house of God and "forefigured the heavenly Jerusalem." Gold, pearls, sapphires, and emeralds, among other riches, figure prominently in the brief glimpse of heaven afforded by *Revelation*. There, the new Jerusalem is a realm of material and spiritual splendor: its walls, jasper, adorned with precious jewels; its streets gold; and the rest of the city "pure gold, like clear glass." Even the angels, beings of air and light, wear crowns of gold.

This promise of a gilded heaven has likely inspired more messianic quests for gold than any other. During his third voyage in 1489, Columbus was convinced he would find an earthly paradise of gold in the form of a nipple raised on the swelling breast of an imperfectly round world.

CHAPTER 35

An Altercation

Paige dragged herself through the line under the mess tent, unable to control her thoughts. They veered from one risk to another: pregnancy, further abuse, a quiet, unremarked death, fever and disease, loneliness, another assault … It was something in the blood, this worry. It rushed through her unbidden, poisoning her sense of self. Where she had once been a sister, a daughter, a friend or companion, she no longer felt connected to others. Even her own name registered as foreign.

When she looked at Mira, she recoiled inside from the contrast. Mira was decent and reliable; Mira, the witness to her shame; Mira with a hand on her fiancé's elbow; Mira, who had everything figured out, who knew exactly where she'd be in three years, in five, ten; Mira with the therapist's calming lilt. Paige wanted to scream at her: *Stop the sorry looks and light touches. You didn't get raped because you're fat. That's why. You carry your head like a bird and you're fucking fat. In a choice between us, I didn't have a chance.*

Then Paige realized the unfairness of her thoughts and began to worry about them, to worry about her worrying. She detested the cliché of the traumatized woman and the idea she'd become one through such absurd circumstances. But her condition—present and absent both—hurt all the same. She preferred the absent part of herself and its innate promise to disappear. If she felt distanced from everyone else, why not give full vent to the feeling? Remove the points of comparison and the sadness and self-accusing voices might die away. *Poon. Slut. Loose bitch.* The denunciations bleared out the small, tentative arguments proffered by her critical self. She put a hand to the crease across her brow. She didn't know how much longer she could stand being half a ghost.

Tree grazed her shoulder and her surroundings twitched into greater focus. "People," he was saying, "well, us 'cause we ain't got no souls to them, we're nuthin' more'n pet-meat."

Leaning past him, Waxman said, "Don't go gettin' up their fear with your poor choice a words. The Marokatu—they ain't cannibals."

"Good to know," Mira said, minding her place in the queue. She was ten or twelve miners back from the source of the charcoal smoke drifting into the tent. Like Paige, she wore oversized men's clothes: a waffle knit pullover, gray chinos and a pair of waterproof leather uppers. An awl-punched hole in her belt cinched the pants tight around her hips.

Tree shrugged. "I wouldn't a said 'pet-meat' if they was."

Ridge looked past Mira and Paige to ask Waxman, "What's the latest on the dig?" He kept a sideways view of the old miner as he hitched forward in line.

"We might be onto somethin' now after that blast." Waxman clawed through his beard to itch his neck.

"Wooo-ee," came a catcall from a group of miners seated nearby. "When we get the hoes?"

"Maybe we died back in that shaft and gone to heaven," another miner said.

Paige jerked her head at this remark and half-listened for more. The lanterns at the rough-hewn tables threw Halloween shadows against the inside of the tent.

A third miner leered over his pork chops and cheesy mash. "*¡Hola, Hermosa!* Tss! Tss!"

Tree nudged Paige to regain her attention. "Lotsa drillin' and diggin' … Can't be too long now. The guys say—"

"All spruced-up and places-to-go …" "C'mon, baby, you forget how to smile?" "Things ain't that bad, honey."

Paige turned to face her harassers. There were about a dozen men hunched over their plates. She identified one of the culprits by his upturned chin and self-congratulatory smirk. He sat two tables away, his teeth flashing in his dirtied face. "What?" he asked. "You can't be nice?" A long-billed cap was pushed up on his shaved head. He pretended to consult his fellows, squinting his small sharp-edged eyes. "Must be one a them pantsuit nags, huh?" His exaggerated laughter rattled Paige like a recurrent shock.

"Guys, please," Ridge said, lurching out of the line. "She's had a rough time of it."

"I think he just showed us his bitch face," someone farther back said. The half-shouted gibe broadened the attention on Paige. Men lowered their cups and cocked their heads in her direction.

"There a difference?" the man in the flat cap asked. Low-throated laughter rippled out from his table.

Paige's breathing shallowed as if she'd been punched. She lacked the strength to speak; instead, she bent her body into an awkward sema-phore for Stop! Her extra-large forest green collared shirt billowed out from under her raised arms. The stink of DEET was in her flared nos-trils.

The man in the cap asked, "Hey, can I ask her a question?"

Ridge revolved on his crutch before finding the man's eyes. "I can't think of a reason why."

Some part of Paige relished Ridge's discomfort. It pierced the bubble of self-contained immutability around he and Mira. Since that scene in Tarrant's cabin, she'd felt unfairly isolated—dismissed—while they joined their strengths in silence.

"What you wanna make trouble for? Nuthin' wrong with bein' friendly, right?" the man in the cap asked, fixed on Paige. "I jus' wanna ask her: You know you gotta sexy style?"

Paige stiffened at his evident hostility. Her thoughts turned darker. She was sure he was a predator, desperate to feel her under him, hum-bled by pain, broken. Her habit of provoking whomever she regarded as smug or rude came back to her. She marshalled her bitterness and said, "Think I'd look better with my boot up your ass."

The tent roared with mirth and derision. "Shit, Hines! You flat on the canvas now." "Fuck, she a freak." "*Paftarite pazhalusta!*" "Nuthin' else, you know she gotta mouth on her."

"Come on, guys," Ridge said as the laughter died down. "That's enough."

He started to turn back to the chow line when the man in the cap got to his feet. "What're you gonna do, Tourist?" He advanced on Ridge in measured steps. "I seen you out there with your correctin' pencils. Gonna write me up in your burn book?" Something flickered in his face.

Everyone was tense. Waxman threw a protective arm across Ridge. "Back it up, Hines. This group's under Tarrant's special protection."

A Latino at a front row table puckered his lips and offered a smacking pout. "That's my meanin' 'xactly," added someone else.

"What about it, Tourist?" Hines asked. "You pimpin' special protections?" He messed Ridge over with his eyes. Coward. Weakling. Chicken heart.

Ridge couldn't get past the notable gaps between the man's top teeth. One eye tooth had a peculiar snag to it.

In a show of gorilla manliness, Hines gave his prodigious silver belt buckle a full-bodied yank.

Mira put a hand on Ridge' arm, either as a show of support or as a preliminary to escorting him away. His eyes flitted in search of a face-saving out. The tent quieted for his response. "Lay off, all right? I didn't ask for this."

"Now you know how things work for the rest of us." Hines put a finger to Ridge' chest and when his mark looked down, gave Ridge's chin a vicious finger-flick. Several men jumped to their feet. Tin cups and silverware clattered.

Ridge fluttered back and, in a blurred instant, Hines finger-flicked him again, this time *thwap* on the forehead. Ridge colored up in stunned anger. There was a rush of bodies. Paige instantly regretted the secret pleasure she'd taken in Ridge's humiliation. This was us versus them, the harried against the lynch mob. She reared back to slap Hines. Tree grabbed her slender wrist on the upswing, suspending her open hand in air. Her fears multiplied, swelling her lungs. She flailed against the cage of Tree's ribs—glancing blows against his bulk.

Then the throng abruptly staggered and broke, arrested in its surge by some intervening authority. Hines turned at the approaching boot heel strikes and caught Gerrit's suckerpunch just below the left ear. Without a word, Gerrit pressed on, clouting Hines on the neck, the jaw, the back of the head, huffing with each arc of his fist. Hines trampled Ridge in his retreat. Ridge lost his crutch and tumbled sideways, swiping at emptiness. Gerrit pursued Hines for one, two more steps, his last punches going wild, then, having cleared a space, drew Foucher's old sidearm. "The fuck! Back the fuck down!"

"Holster it, Southie," said Hines from the ground, defiant. "This ain't none a your worry."

"You made it mine, ya rank bastard." Gerrit rolled his shoulders in a lean swagger as he swept the .41 magnum around. "I don't got no patience for this slappity-slap shit," he said to the crowd. "And neither does Tarrant. Where you think Foucher disappeared to, huh? Think he's on some kinda earth-love retreat? The Tourist and these girls, they're untouchable, all right?" He kicked dirt in Hines' sour face. "And the word is Southerner, you ign'ant fuckwit. I ain't no breed a dog."

Paige massaged the soft part of her wrist where Tree had left a streaky thumbprint. She wasn't frightened so much as mad. A terrible monologue swirled in her head. Traces of other hands, visible or not, were an abomination.

Tree and Waxman hefted Ridge to his feet by the armpits and Mira handed him his crutch. Ridge's lower lip bled onto his graphic tee and trousers in quivering drops. Shock-numbed and embarrassed, he probed the wound with an index finger, his mouth half-open.

Tears welled in Mira's eyes. The skin across her cheeks was pulled so tight it verged on transparent.

Gerrit huffed through his nose at Hines. "You do more'n breathe when I turn my back I'll fuckin' stomp you into your grave right here, believe you me." Hines put a hand to the purpled orbit of his right eye and gave the barest nod.

The miners returned to their suppers or places in the queue. "Goddamn idjit." "More work for the rest a us Hines gets gone." "…seen bloodier playground fights."

"Better get these rashers before they get cold or go chewy on the grill," Beattie said from around the smoker.

Ridge tilted his head from side to side as if relieving a crick in his neck. Mira put a hand on his shoulder. "All right?" she asked. He answered by pulling his tee to his split lip, trying to look at her as little as possible, afraid she would read too much in his reddened face.

Gerrit returned the Bren Ten to its thigh-holster and drew close to Ridge. His breath was thick and beery. "You ever put me in a position like that again 'cause a your own fool weakness, I gonna do more'n your leg. Keep them bitches in line."

Bitches. The word rankled Paige. To survive here, she realized, was to be brazen and mean. "You know what a bitch is, don't you?" she asked. "A female Southie with all the fight of the biggest bastard Southerner."

A harsh noise gusted from the back of Gerrit's throat. But he moved on without rebuking her or striking out, apparently satisfied she'd endured enough for one evening, or perhaps, concerned about what Ridge might pass on to Tarrant. Paige considered his discretion a punishment deferred. Doubtless there would be plenty of opportunities for him to exact his due.

CHAPTER 36

The Night Visit

Mira lay in the slab hut with her eyes closed, conscious of Paige's restlessness in the adjacent cot. The smell of freshly-planed wood and carpenter's glue conjured up childhood memories of sleeping in her backyard *sukkah* as part of the Feast of Booths. The *sukkah* symbolized the temporary shelters used by the Israelites during their 40 years of wandering. Her father had constructed theirs from 4 × 4 poles and several connecting 2 × 4s attached with bolts. Its walls consisted of painter's drop cloth secured to the frame by shower curtain rings. Loose corn stalks, a few tree branches and trimmings from her mother's overgrown rose bushes covered the roof. Per tradition, the roofing materials were sparsely arranged to allow for dappled light in the day and stargazing at night. Mira also decorated the *sukkah* by hanging dried squash and corn from its supports and by taping crayon drawings of various nature scenes to the walls—Mount Diablo, the Pacific surf, the Muir Woods, smiling goats and other petting zoo animals.

The *sukkah* was supposed to be a reminder of humanity's need to protect the earth. But it was Mira who'd needed protection the first time she slept in the *sukkah* by herself. To her seven year old self, the unfiltered sounds of Fremont, California had presaged a world on the brink: shouts and shrieks, the metallic skirr of patrolling helicopters, recurrent dog yelps, mockingbirds at their most annoying, pitchy car engines, the *titch-titch-titch* of unseen critters scrabbling in the trash, and the sirens, God, the relentless sirens. Burrowing into her sleeping bag had failed to slow her imagination. Her precipitant fears had overwhelmed her. She'd lasted less than an hour of night before she ran for the house and the safety of her four-poster bed, all pleasant anticipation gone and the beckoning stars forgotten …

Paige's shackles clanked against her cot's metal frame. "Sorry," she whispered.

"I'm not sleeping," Mira said. There were no childhood comforts here. She turned toward Paige but couldn't make out her expression in the gloom. The hut's only light was the peripheral glow of the guards' campfire through the high mesh window. She adjusted the wadded-up sweatshirt under her head. She'd given Paige the lone pillow. "Do they hurt?"

"No, just uncomfortable. The bar—the backing part—cuts right across my Achilles' tendon if I don't twist my foot to one side."

"I'm sorry."

"It's okay." Paige let out a sigh of resignation. "We should really make a pact: No more saying 'sorry'—to each other, ourselves, whatever. We're all sorry."

"It's my first instinct—to empathize." Mira immediately regretted her choice of words. The term 'instinct' suggested an indiscriminate impulse. She decided to risk explaining herself: "I just want you to know you don't have to go through this alone. You may remember I'm a family therapist, so I've worked with a number of survivors of sexual assault. I've seen them struggle with alternating feelings of shame, rage, loneliness…" Sensing resistance from Paige, she lost enthusiasm for her own words. She'd suffered no personal horrors, could reveal no confidences worthy of comparison. Her suffering came secondhand, inherited from her father or disclosed by her clients.

"I really don't want to talk about it, Mira." The tears brimming in Paige's eyes caught the fugitive light. She wiped them down her cheeks then dried her palms on the nylon throw blanket draped across her chest and legs.

Mira regarded the Kabbalistic injunction to repair the world, *tikkun olam*, as both a personal and professional responsibility. She continued as a matter of duty, careful not to come across as sanctimonious or superior when she was only lucky. "Let me just say this: I understand your reluctance. I understand the impulse to get some distance from it. Clarity can be painful—it *is* painful. We don't know each other well and I was there—and maybe that disqualifies me. It's reasonable for you to harbor some anger about that. But when we get back, I encourage you to seek out a trusted therapist. I can make some reco—"

"You realize, don't you, that they're never going to let us go?" Paige said in a dead bleak tone. "I mean, why would they? We're witnesses, nothing more. I don't even know why they're keeping us around now."

Paige's hopelessness had the opposite effect on Mira—her waning optimism was renewed. "We'll be all right. Ridge is working on something for Tarrant. He won't want to upset that."

"You're kidding."

Mira ignored the critical edge to Paige's voice. She understood that grief didn't conform neatly to the Kübler-Ross Model. Everyone experienced it differently. It could just as easily induce paralysis, fantasy, guilt, hermetic impulses and nonsense. After prompting Ridge's humiliation at dinner, though, she hoped Paige would talk about him with more respect, if not apologize outright. "He's editing some strange philosophy book Tarrant wrote."

"A philosophy book?" Paige cocked her head in Mira's direction but avoided her gaze.

"That's how Ridge described it. I gather it's a mix of things: Gnostic religion, autobiography, fable … Actually, he told me he's less of an editor and more a 'counter-irritant.' I guess Tarrant likes to argue things out."

"Whatever it is, for our sake, we better hope it's as long as the PDR."

"The what?"

"*Physician's Desk Reference*."

"Oh, right." Mira recalled that Paige was a lobbyist for a DC-based non-profit advocating universal healthcare. "He's a piece of work isn't he—Tarrant?"

Paige's expression turned pinched and angry. "More like a dirty slave-master. He reminds me of this old movie I saw in college. I can't remember the name of it. I always fell asleep in that class. The professor was from South America somewhere and spoke with a heavy accent using all this critical studies jargon—Foucault, Derrida, Lacan, all these maddening French thinkers we had to read. She practically put me to sleep every class before they brought the lights down. She also had this strange way of laughing. It was more of a titter. There were breaks in her laugh like she had to pause and translate before letting it out. Is there a foreignness to laughing? I don't mean to be snide …"

Mira started to get the impression that, despite Paige's liberal politics, she wasn't above sorority sister snark. She must have inadvertently made a face at the thought because Paige shifted to a tone of dorm-room intimacy, making her flat R's more conspicuous. "Anyway," she said, "the movie was about this doctor on a hidden island somewhere who operates on animals to turn them into people. The makeup on the animal people was pretty creepy for the time—early-30s, I think. Tarrant reminds me of him—the doctor—not physically, because the actor was pear-shaped and had this ridiculous van Dyke—but just in the way he created his own little world. This is Tarrant's creation—this island. Except he'd do the opposite if he could and turn *us* into animals."

"This place is something else all right." The conversation prompted Mira to wonder how her clients were doing, whether they panicked when they heard she hadn't returned from vacation.

"What do you miss the most from home? Besides a decent shower and air conditioning, I mean. Oh, and face moisturizer."

"Let's not start that ..."

"You're probably going to think I'm a freak, but what I miss, laying here in this thrown-together shack, is the plush carpet in my bedroom. I have this upholstered panel bed in lilac with a ruffled white duvet. The carpet is beige and super soft on your bare feet. I love feeling the tufts between my toes. Most evenings I lounge in my pajamas, you know, after a warm shower. The knit is like cashmere with a brushed velvet lining." She paused at the indistinct sound of voices outside then, dismissing the noise as irrelevant, filled in the intervening silence. "Though I could do without the footprint sheen and vacuum streaks, the feel of that carpet just cozies me up ..."

The voices resumed, more insistent, accompanied by the ominous staccato pounding of throwing spears.

The noise kinked Mira's nerves. "Don't worry," she said, grabbing up her overlarge boots. "I'll stay just outside the hut."

"Mira!" The wavering cry rose above the coarse gibberish of the Marokatu. "Mira!"

The shackles clanked to the floor as Paige bolted upright. "Is that Ridge?" She made a grimace of anxiety and tightened the throw blanket around her lap.

"Sounds like it." Mira unlatched the door and stepped out. The Marokatu hefted their spears to their chests. "No, it's okay," she said, gesturing for them to relax. They remained alert but made no further moves. She approached a muzzy-eyed Ridge. His hair on one side was a haphazard wing. There was a jag of rust-red where his split lip had clotted. She was embarrassed for him all over again.

"I didn't wake you, did I?" he asked, enunciating carefully.

"No, we were just talking." His voice had a telltale tremble to it. She stayed at arm's length, wary of what the Marokatu might do. They hung back a few paces, spears at hip-level. "What's going on? Have you been drinking?"

"A little, yeah … Not like Cooter Brown," he said, shamefaced. Cooter Brown was an infamous Civil War-era character who lived on the Mason-Dixon Line and allegedly stayed drunk for the duration of the war to avoid having to choose sides. "Sorry to scare you."

"I thought you weren't supposed to be out here." His behavior was out of character. Where was the steadfast Ridge she'd known only days earlier?

"No, no." He indicated the void beyond the firelight with a back-handed wave. "There's a hurricane on the way—between one and two days out. Gerrit just let us know. They have to reinforce the mine tomorrow just in case."

"Does he know you're here?"

Ridge gave a derisive snort. "Thinks I'm goin' to the latrine."

"You should get back then." She was compelled by his frailty to embrace him. She pressed her head to his chest and put an ear to his ragged breathing. He was redolent of sickly-sweet coconut pulque.

"I can protect you, Mira—you and Paige," Ridge said. "I worked out a way…"

"I'm sure you have," she said, drawing back. "But now's not the time…" She saw something disturbing in his clouded gaze and put a tender finger to his brow. It was a different sort of detached look. There was none of his habitual thoughtfulness in it. No, he was confused and emotionally torn. He stood before her fully exposed.

"It's a stalemate," he mumbled.

"Ridge, please, the time … You should go back."

"All right, I'm going," he said. "I just—sometimes, I wish life could be scripted out—at least my parts. I know when I get into my bunk,

I'm going to replay this conversation and think of what I should have said." He seemed to drift in and out of himself. "I get tired of the smart afterthoughts."

"Just like a writer," she teased, though she was similarly prone to seeing life through a literary lens. They'd met at a bookshop stoop sale, after all, and much of her therapeutic technique involved finding the right situational metaphor. She might describe a disruptive child, for instance, as an inmate, unduly confined by parental rules, or alternately, as a prison attendant who forced the rest of the household to change to accommodate his disruptions. Metaphor, she found, often served as a useful bridge between the logical and the emotional.

"Good night then." Ridge started to crab away on his crutch then added: "I mean, good morning." It was a routine bedtime joke about the Jewish day beginning at sunset.

"*Laila Tov,*" she said with only a hint of smile.

CHAPTER 37

The Radio Transmission

Ridge adjusted the position of his injured leg on the stool opposite his chair then snapped the looseleaf manuscript back into focus. He resumed reading while, just outside his peripheral vision, Tarrant was busy at the desk researching a native mask. A passage characterizing Anthropos' effect on humanity as "sublime wonder" recalled Edmund Burke's 18th century essay on the topic. Tarrant attributed a similarly fearsome aspect to the sublime. Ridge had to admit to himself that his feelings for his captor had shifted in the same direction—toward a mix of awe and alarm. The man's intellect, however undisciplined, never lacked for scope or forcefulness. It pushed Ridge to make connections among disparate things. Tarrant let the evidence for his outlandish theories (such as it was) lead him where it may, no matter how unsettling the implications. Ridge could admire the audacity of Tarrant's thinking even as he rejected his judgments. *Sublime wonder sounds about right…*

Tarrant paused in his researches. He was comparing a ceremonial Marokatu mask to descriptions of like artifacts in a timeworn British monograph. The mask was made from ebony or blackened wood. The face was a ghastly hollow, giving the hook nose added prominence. Tarrant had affixed a leather strap to it with screw eyes. The mizzling rain against the roof and the low-volume weather reports from the radio set accompanied their separate tasks. "What part you at now?" Tarrant asked.

"The, uh, parable of the gold coin, I guess you call it," Ridge said. "Page 317 if that helps." Tarrant had given him two handfuls of paper so far with no indication of the manuscript's total length, or even its state of completion.

"It come from the gnostics, that tale—how the gold coin sinks in the dirt but retains its glorious properties, regardless."

"But only the Man-God knows where to find it," Ridge said. Additional reading had confirmed his initial impression that the manuscript exposed Tarrant's character in the same way an overturned cockroach displays a hidden and ghastly order. "The whole messianic attitude troubles me. It runs counter to the very idea of self-government. You offer up Anthropos as a model to be followed, not a choice to be made. It's anti-democratic. No one votes, no one approves of him as their leader … It's governance by *fiat*."

"And all the better for it." Tarrant rested his elbows on the desk and entwined his fingers. "Man alone—unenlightened—is a muddled creature."

Now that Ridge had pricked Tarrant's pride, he was careful to frame his next argument as a question to soften its edge. "And the alternative is some mountaintop mystic dividing believers from heretics?"

"If that mystic speaks the truth—transcendent and forever—who's to say otherwise? The problem with your democracy, what you can't bear to admit, is this: people ain't fitted for it. They live in shadowed valleys and mistake them for the world entire. Their very natures are contradicted. That's why your country's always in turmoil." The vehemence with which he uttered the words 'your country' suggested Tarrant considered himself without one. "It ain't the government that's somehow gone bad. The fact is: it's a faithful product of its people— wholly inefficient, conflicted, subject to passin' emotion, of no more use than a weather vane. See, I got no illusions about us *qua* people. I'm goin' 'bout this with my eyes wide to our brokenness. My strength is the ability to say yea to life as it is."

Ridge was tempted to introduce the goddess of liberty, Columbia, into the conversation. He'd adopted her as a conceptual foil for the absolutism of Anthropos. Columbia was first popularized in a poem for George Washington by a Massachusetts slave. In "His Excellency, George Washington," the slave-poet described Columbia as a divine guide to freedom from British oppression. Ridge's version was less idealistic and fixed in its purpose than the original but no less an embodiment of democratic principles. Like the Olympians, who often visited Earth in borrowed forms—ants, bulls, swans, golden sparks et cetera— his reimagined Columbia was a shapeshifter, a symbol befitting the contradictory impulses of the people. Given this variable nature, Ridge accorded the goddess a humbling self-consciousness. She was aware of her all-too-human limitations and so, unlike the dictatorial Anthropos, cautious in her counsel. "What you're likely to get when you cross a man with a god," Ridge said, "is human mistakes on a Biblical scale. Besides, you can't believe the truth is that simple."

"It might be—not simple in the getting, but in the substance. Modern life like you've known it don't allow for broad, clear views. You been ruined by too much false history and confutation." Tarrant pursed his lips in thought then added: "The only question what counts is whether God is already here or to come. Disagreement on that point has been the source of history's worst tragedies."

Ridge decided to test the limits of Tarrant's strange millenarian hope. "So which is it? Is God here or to come?"

"My agglomerated labors suggest a bit a both. There are remnants of God here. Or *gods* as the case seems to be. But their concentrated powers are elsewhere." Tarrant got to his feet to give his arms more gestural freedom. "The crux of the matter is that our minds don't contrive reality—they receive it. We're receivers as much as that radio set there. Living receivers. The overpower ain't nothing to do with the usual hippie rummage. It's what's left of the gods, their energy. You come with me to the spirit house, you'll know. The visions I seen: the deep past, the dead, the future or possible futures … What if I told you Nanokwe predicted the cyclone bearin' down on us? Not in its exactitude but he warned me of some future danger after havin' a vision of snakes and skinks sunnin' themselves on the same rock—them bein' mortal enemies…" His eyes narrowed for a moment to shadowy pits. "Right now, without the aid of *kava* or meditation or whatnot, you're confined to a narrow spectrum o' the totality. Your conscious mind filters out the primordial light so you can make-do in this gray realm—a realm a shade away from nothingness. Like how your eye filters out everythin' but what we call 'visible light.' That's how stunted your perception is. The natural state of things is a pure wash o' light, infinite in everything—you, me, that pen and those papers in your hand—it's all light made manifest. That's what I mean by the overpower—it's the light, the energy—we don't know from everyday experience."

"So the purpose of this treatise, polemic, whatever you want to call

it—is to found a new religion?" Ridge was genuinely intrigued by Tarrant's penchant for mixing philosophy, religion and cult science like an erstwhile alchemist.

"There's nothing new about it. The Mayans and Aztecs, the ancient Egyptians, they were privy to this knowledge. This is the oldest religion there is. Our inclinations toward the overpower are encoded in our cells—DNA, RNA, down to the gut bacteria for all I know."

"If this is what you're really after—this sacred knowing—I don't understand why you're here, why the mining…"

"I'm questing for something—a crystalline substance often found alongside gold strikes. Ever wonder why gold figures so prominently in the world religions? No doubt some of it's due to the idea of the overpower, though differently expressed—gold as the purest manifestation of primordial light and so on and so forth. But to my mind, there's something else involved—these crystals. They're the so-called lens for focusing that godawful light. Some modern-day mystery religions call them Parmatmar crystals. If the legends are true, they was named by Captain Nemo—not that weak fiction of a man but the historical Nemo, Prince Dakkar. I've seen important fragments of his sea journals." He approached the warped plank bookshelf behind Ridge and slowly ran an index finger along the spines of several volumes along the topmost row. "But these crystals, rare as they are, weren't unknown to others long dead. You heard tell of the crystal skull?"

Ridge shook his head, wondering how fantastic Tarrant's theories would get before the end of their time together. Gnosticism and Captain Nemo? Spiritual powers encoded in our genes? Crystal skulls? Every new element increased the salability of his story. There was no reason he shouldn't get a Hollywood movie out of it, or at the very least, a network TV special. What had that so-called 'Long Island Lolita,' Amy Fisher, really done to warrant three rival TV movies aired within a week of each other? Her story had been tawdry and sadly mundane while his was an exotic adventure without precedent. If he managed to escape, he figured on as much attention for his unasked-for travails as she'd garnered for her criminal selfishness.

"No reason you should have," Tarrant said, turning from his books to face him. His thoughts were clearly buzzing now. "It's an artifact in the British Museum, but not part of any reg'lar display. Looks like how it sounds—completely transparent, pools a reflected light. A Brit adventurer supposedly found it sometime in the 1920s at a Mayan dig in Lubaantun, Belize, though he didn't come forward with it for another 20 years or so. He marked it at 3,600 years old and said the High Priest of the Mayas used it in sundry and grisly rites. He further claimed that, with the skull's help, this priest could will death on whoever he chose. I mention this only by way of example."

"Gerrit—and Waxman, too—said something about South America—Bolivia, Peru, Honduras…"

"Belize was called British Honduras at the time the skull was supposedly found."

"Is that what you were doing? Looking for archeological finds?" Ridge felt he was slowly zeroing in on Tarrant's hidden intent.

"Some were diggings, yes. Others—"

There was a succession of urgent knocks on the door.

"Enter," Tarrant said, visibly annoyed.

Gerrit stepped inside, accompanied by a gust of rain-flecked wind, and yanked back the hood of his slicker. Noting Tarrant's stern look, he knuckled the water out of his eyes and said, "Sorry to interrupt… But we could use your help up on the hill, make sure we got those supports in the right spots."

Tarrant deliberated for a moment. Gerrit half-expected a rebuke when the boss-man said, "Very well," and snatched up an oilskin duster from a peg on the wall behind his desk. "Get the door to the radio room."

"You want me to leave it on?" Gerrit asked, a hand on the knob.

"For the weather, yes."

Gerrit slammed the door lock hasp into place and affixed the combination padlock, reducing the broadcast to a monotonous hush. He gave a derisive nod in Ridge's direction at barring him from the transmitter and possible rescue.

"Diminished as it is under the circumstances," Tarrant said to Ridge, "my library is yours. I recommend this if you want to know more about that theory of mind I started to describe." He tipped a clothbound book from the shelf into a waiting hand and extended it to Ridge. "It's a neurobiological view of Freudian psych. You can ignore most of that aspect—I tend to side with Jung myself—except for the concept of free-energy. That's the author's rough idea of the overpower, though unformed and with no inkling of its real origins."

Ridge turned the thick book over in his hands: *Free-Energy Thinking: New Science on an Old Mode of Cognition* by Ruth Evan-Moore, ph.d. The cover art was redolent of the early-70s. It featured a tessellating abstract in garish reds and oranges. "Sure," Ridge said, masking his skepticism behind a tight smile.

Tarrant motioned Gerrit out and ventured into the pattering rain, leaving Ridge alone in the cabin. The radio sounded a new cycle of warning tones followed by an updated forecast: "This is a special weather statement issued at 4:21 PM UTC. The Solomon Islands Meteorological Service in Honiara has issued a special marine warning for coastal waters from the capital to Nauru in the northeast, covering the 675 nautical miles of ocean and low-lying atolls in between ..." Ridge lowered his injured leg to the floor, got to his feet, and placed the manuscript pages, the book and his ballpoint pen on the stool.

He hobbled to the padlocked door and listened. The area of low pressure where the cyclone originated had first been mentioned only three days before and the cyclone itself had been assigned a high probability of striking land less than 24 hours ago. Given the weather system's reported speed and direction, Tarrant predicted it would hit the island with Category 3 winds of about 152 kilometers per hour sometime tonight. He expected the surrounding foothills to somewhat moderate the winds but not enough to avoid significant damage to the camp. As best Ridge could tell, the updated forecast seemed to confirm Tarrant's assumptions.

When the hollow-voiced message began to repeat, Ridge started toward his chair then froze, recalling the pistol Tarrant had shown him on their initial meeting. He remembered Tarrant first tucking it into a cigar box then into a desk drawer. The gun could've been moved since, of course; still ... He remained at the locked door, one hand on the casing for balance while he mulled whether to search Tarrant's desk. Was Tarrant leaving him alone in the cabin a test of loyalty? To see if he'd break into the radio room or swipe the gun, or both? And even if he discovered the revolver, was he prepared to murder Tarrant and live with the consequences? *Ah, back to the start...* He felt the pulse beat of his heart creep into his throat. Here was a true, live and momentous decision: to continue with his subtle and decidedly safer plot, or to risk bold defiance. He resisted the urge to choose based on which stratagem promised to make the better story. Defining moments like this revealed how dangerous his longing for notoriety could be, however he earned it. Though at an intellectual level he denied the existence of a personal God or an operative karmic cycle, he suspected this dilemma was a punishment for his vain fantasies.

Ridge was about to push away from the door when the weather service was superseded by a new voice: "Un-cle? Un-cle? *Yu long hap,* boss?" On impulse, Ridge pressed his face to the thin edge of the door and yelled, "Yes! Yes, I'm here!" Then he recollected the need to activate the transmitter's mic and panicked all over again at the prospect of breaking in. Tarrant would exact revenge no doubt, perhaps even by harming Mira or Paige. But what if this were his one chance to alert the outside world to their plight? There was no time to tally the pros and cons in the manner of Benjamin Franklin. A hot dread shivered through him. His chance was fading second by second.

Unintelligible pidgin English issued from the radio. More questions awaiting answers. Ridge swallowed his next breath and heaved himself against the door. It gave a protracted groan. He gasped for air, almost choking in desperation and tried a second time, one narrowed eye on the lock's hasp. The door jounced uselessly in its frame. "Wait!" he shouted, slipping on the wooden floor. He pushed up against the tropical timber with renewed force. A Sisyphean stress, his legs quivering, his face blenched and sweaty... The screws holding the hasp to the door's casing screeched. "Wait," Ridge repeated helplessly, shaking from the strain. The hasp popped free and the door swung inward, spilling him on the floor.

The multi-unit radio set was on a secretary desk to his right. It wasn't radically dissimilar to the equipment used on cruising boats. Ridge lunged for the handheld mic in front of the transceiver. He grabbed it up and thumbed the talk button: "This—this is Ridge Dantley. I'm an American..." He paused to catch his breath. The deadening sound of static dismayed him. Was he too late? Was the transmitter inoperative? He scanned the military surplus equipment in a rush: the control unit, the receiver, the transmitter control ... The system had its own power supply in huge olive green cases under the desk.

"*Westap* Un-cle?" came the delayed reply.

Ridge thrust the mic to his chin: "No, this is Ridge Dantley. I'm an American who's been—"

There was an impenetrable slew of words and some talkback squeal. Ridge tried to tamp down his frustration. "I'm sorry. I don't understand. Is there someone there who speaks English?"

The reply was slower, more deliberate than before, though still mostly incomprehensible: "Say *long* Ta-rrant *mitupela gat* man he-yeah *hausboi luluai.*"

"I don't understand." Ridge began to despair. He'd done something irreversible and for what?

"*Hausboi long* sen-a-ta."

This last word suspended the moment. Had Ridge heard it right? "Senator? Senator Neeland?"

"Ya."

"Is he there? Can I speak to him?" Ridge shook his head, incredulous, and flush with relief.

"Mistah Ta-rrant *tasol. No mani, mitupela katim i pundaun.*"

"Tarrant's not here. You'll have to radio back," Ridge said. "Is that clear? You'll have to radio back." He couldn't understand why the Senator didn't intercede. Surely he was listening, unless ...

"*Mitupela anka na wetim, orait?*"

Ridge tossed the mic on the table and stumbled back, horrified by a sudden thought. What if, far from being a potential rescuer, the man on the line was one of Tarrant's paid agents and a kidnapper? A fast-spreading nausea besieged him. Christ almighty. The radio squawked a few times, punctuating his distress. He fled to the desk in the other room and, as the call petered into dead air, seized the handgun from the cigar box in the top drawer.

CHAPTER 38

The Cabin Before the Storm

The afternoon sky was a subterranean blue-black as Gerrit escorted Mira and Paige from their makeshift hut to Tarrant's cabin. The women clutched folded-up camping cots in one hand and plastic bags of toiletries, blankets and borrowed clothes in the other. Gerrit used an industrial flashlight to direct them through the rainy gloom. He trudged through the mud blunt-eyed and unsmiling. Paige's shackles were looped around his left shoulder like a harness.

The Marokatu had allowed the steadily increasing drizzle to extinguish the cooking fires that usually smudged the village. Red-ringed fragments of coconut husk hissed in their fire pits. The natives were packing their belongings in mats of palm leaf sewn up into sacks, hollering, quarreling, and gathering their children and animals. Some youths made a game of apprehending the chickens. Paige wondered where the aborigines would shelter. Raindrops accumulating on her eyelashes blurred the scene. She didn't make any special effort to blink them away. A pair of goats somewhere in the distance baa'ed and whined their unhappiness. But then everything sounded melancholy to her: the blustered palm fronds, the squelch of her boots in the muck, the frisking poi dogs, each drawn-out breath.

Gerrit opened the cabin door without preamble and ushered the women inside. As she brushed past him, Paige recalled the horrific nickname her mom had given her—Baldwin Butt—because her bottom moved like "two apples in a sack" when she walked. She hurried into the room and quickly turned her backside toward an adjoining wall.

"Mira, hey, what's going on?" Ridge asked, dropping his splinted leg from the corner of Tarrant's desk.

"Time to stop pullin' your pud, Tourist," Gerrit said. "Gotta batten down the hatches." He shut the door and, relieving Paige of her cot, began setting it up in the middle of the room.

"What's that?" Ridge repeated.

"You followin' the weather ain't ya? Wind 'bout heady enough to pluck them seabirds naked in the air," Gerrit said. The cot folded out with a metallic screech. "Tarrant's ordered everyone to their bunks. I don't trust that hut we cobbled together for the ladies, so he said they could hold tight here with you."

Mira inclined toward Ridge and asked him with the quizzical arch of an eyebrow if he intended to help her with the cot. But he stayed put, one hand below the desktop. She swallowed her dismay and started to unfold her cot, afraid her glassy expression would give something away.

"Not that I'm arguing," Ridge said, "but where's he planning to be?"

"Outside. Yeah, no shit." Gerrit locked the cot's metal frame into place and spun it into a position parallel to Mira's. "He had me lash him to that pug-ugly bastard front of the men's lodge. Part of his trainin' I guess."

"What kind of training is this?" Mira asked.

"I don't really know. He does this sometimes—to test his … uh, what do you call it? Your heart and lungs 'n' shit that works without you thinkin' 'bout 'em?" Although Mira was having no difficulty assembling her cot, he interposed himself. "Here, let me get that."

"Autonomic," Paige said. "Autonomic functions." She tossed her plastic sack and child's pillow on her cot.

"Yeah. He told me once it was like tryin' to fight back a sneeze but on a higher level." Gerrit set the last metal joint. "Said that in the Andes, half-naked, meditated his body temp up high enough to melt the snow off 'im. That was some fuckin' magic."

"Waxman mentioned that to me," Ridge said.

"The fuck?" Gerrit stomped to the cracked-open door to the radio room. "The fuck you do? You better not a been messin' with the radio …"

"No, well, yes, but it's not what you think …"

Ignoring Ridge's stammered admission, Gerrit gave the door a tentative push. It swung free of the lock's hasp. The weather report infringed on the tense silence: "… Islands Meteorological Service in Honiara has issued a special marine warning for coastal waters from the capital to Nauru …" Gerrit glared at Ridge then ducked into the radio room for more evidence of mischief.

Ridge pivoted on his injured leg around the edge of the desk and leveled a handgun at the threshold. Mira squeaked in surprise. Gerrit rushed back at the sound and was brought up short by the gun barrel pointed at his chest. "The fuck you think you're doin'?" he asked.

"To be honest," Ridge said, "I'm not exactly sure. But I guess I'm committed. Mira, you're closest. Take his gun, will you?"

Mira hesitated at Gerrit's inflamed look. Paige grabbed the shackles from the floor and reared back, prepared to clout him on the jaw if he resisted. She felt herself drawing more and more from the forsaken teen-self who once burned the inside of her arm with a cigarette as a test of toughness. Mira unsnapped Gerrit's thigh-holster and relieved him of his weapon.

"Where you think you're gonna go in this weather?" Gerrit asked Ridge.

"Who said we were going anywhere? I just want a chance to explain myself to Tarrant, that's all." Ridge brought up his other hand to steady his aim. "I had to get to the radio. One of our friends was mentioned." He fixed on Mira and Paige and in a keyed-up voice said: "The Senator—I think he made it onto a ship." Turning back to Gerrit, he continued, "He got left behind on the atoll. I couldn't understand most of what he said—not the Senator, the captain or whoever I talked to. He spoke some kind of pidgin English."

"Prob'ly the supply crew. Pirates outta New Guinea." Gerrit shook his head at the damaged door. "Tarrant's gonna shit fire, believe you me."

"I had to do it," Ridge said.

Paige was grudgingly impressed by Ridge's firmness with Gerrit. Since their first meeting, she'd considered him brainy and earnest but innately bland. He was like a man with all the alluring edges rounded off.

Mira pointed the pistol at Gerrit with dubious conviction. He dismissed her with a smirk but kept an eye on Paige, who refused to lower her guard. "Ain't me you gotta convince … Fuck. What'd you say to him—the ship captain?"

"Just that Tarrant wasn't here. About the only thing I could make out from his side was the name of our friend. I don't even know if he could understand me."

"I wouldn't know. Foucher always handled everythin' regardin' the supply ship. Fuckin' A. You're really makin' it hard to take it easy on you. I don't know if you're cracked in the head or got balls the size a clementines..."

"You think the supply ship will be okay in this weather?"

"Depends on where they berthed. Gonna be a king-helluva storm." Gerrit turned to Paige. "Would you mind? I ain't gonna jump ya, two guns on me."

Paige retreated a couple of steps and dropped the shackles to the floor.

Ridge motioned Gerrit toward the exit with the gun. "Don't worry, we'll be here when the storm's over."

"How long's it supposed to last?" Mira asked.

"The fuck you askin' me for? You're one with the radio." Gerrit made his way to the cabin door without turning his back to them. "You know I could take you with a few men and some machetes, right?"

"But you won't," Ridge said. "I have something Tarrant values more than you, more than this whole operation, and if you try to hurt any of us, he'll never get it. I'll shoot my own damn self before that happens." Then, unable to resist, added Gerrit's habitual phrase: "Believe you me."

Gerrit adjusted the Velcro at the throat of his rain slicker and pulled the hood tight over his head. "It might just come to that."

"Wait," Paige said, stepping forward. "The key." She locked on Gerrit through a haze of red hate.

"What? Fixin' to lose it?" he balked.

"Give it to her," Ridge said.

Gerrit dug into his pocket with a disappointed sigh and flicked the key to Paige as though it were a betting coin.

Paige refused to be distracted like an animal. She kept her hardened eyes on Gerrit. The key to the shackles skittered on the plank flooring.

"Guess we'll see after the storm who got who." Gerrit flung the door open to the roiling elements, stamped his right foot once then slammed the door behind him.

"How much trouble are we in?" Mira asked.

"I don't really know. When I heard that radio call…" Ridge's face collapsed. "Christ, I'm sorry." He set the gun down on the desk.

Mira said, "We agreed not to say that anymore—at least to each other." She glanced at Paige for confirmation. "Might as well stop apologizing for the things we can't change."

"Isn't that part of the Serenity Prayer?" Ridge hobbled in her direction.

"If only drunkenness was our excuse to say it." Mira broke into a wry smile and put a hand on his shoulder. "You sure it was the Senator's voice?"

"I never heard it. I asked for him but the speaker either didn't understand me or refused to put him on. He said 'Senator' pretty clearly, though, enunciating it syllable by syllable."

"*Sababa*. At last, some good news."

"But can he do anything for us here?" Paige instantly regretted the question. It sounded petulant and selfish. But she couldn't help the impulse to pull others into her suffering.

"I would think—once he gets to Honiara," Ridge said.

"Well, we have plenty of reading material for the wait," Mira said, trying to lower the temperature of the room. "Look at this stuff: *The Chronology of Ancient Kingdoms Amended*—Isaac Newton, by the way—*Manna: A Disquisition of the Nature of Alchemy …*"

"Great," Paige said. "Now I know where to turn in the event I self-diagnose too much black bile." She faced Ridge and made a testy barb of her lips. "So what is it? What do you have on Tarrant?"

"I'm not sure I should tell you—either of you. That way Tarrant can't play us off each other. I wouldn't want him, for instance, threatening to harm Mira to coerce it from you."

Paige could barely contain her hurt. The conversation began to resemble the damaging thought-spiral she'd endured since her assault. "What makes you think I'd be the one to give in?"

"It was a hypothetical."

"But oh so specific. And what if something happens to you before this plan goes into action? How would we know how to carry on?"

"Go to Nanokwe."

"The shaman?"

Ridge nodded. "You don't seem convinced?"

Paige regarded candor as the first quality of a free woman. "I've already made up my mind so there's no point in arguing, but I'm telling you now: as soon as the village is cleared out, I'm leaving. I don't care about this hurricane."

"Just how do you think that's going to play out?" Ridge asked. "You do something foolish and the rest of us suffer."

Paige pointed out the broken door lock. "You mean like that?"

"It might've been our only chance to get rescued anytime soon. It was a calculated risk."

Mira gave his arm a squeeze as a signal to relent. He frowned without a glance at her.

"You have no idea how sick and weak this place makes me," Paige said. She'd begun to fear she'd have to pretend for the rest of her life. Even a crooked smile was a struggle. "The sight of these men, their stench … I'd just as soon run, fight, whatever—anything but sit and wait for them to hurt me again."

"Run where?" Ridge asked. "The natives will catch you in a DC-minute. And even if you made it to the beach, so what?"

"I'm not going to the beach—I mean, I might, but … I'm never going to have this chance again."

Ridge threw up his hands. Only a few feet separated him from Paige but their darkening moods made the distance seem vast.

"I'm not delusional," Paige continued. "I know the odds. I'm not running to escape—not permanently. More than likely, I'll just turn around and set fire to this place." Her mood was like suffering a long mysterious fever. Maybe feeding it, she thought, would burn it out faster than starving it.

"When I first arrived," Ridge said, "Tarrant offered me this gun straight-up. It was one of his intimidation tactics. Hell, I could walk out there now, what with him tied up and shoot him before he could blink. But where would that get us? Right now, he's the one person keeping us alive. You heard Gerrit's threat …"

Paige let loose the fears whirling in her head, wishing for the cyclone to end all consciousness. *No more doubts, no more mistakes or self-crippling tendencies, just so long as I don't have to face the next day or the next, to wake up and realize I have to deal with it again.* "What does it matter? Dead tomorrow, or in a few days, a week?"

"We have to hope that the longer we survive, the greater the chance someone will come along," Mira said. "If the Senator can get help..."

Her leveling reasonableness was another source of irritation for Paige. "I knew I'd be hot-boxed by the two of you," she said. The couple came across as so self-contained it was hard for Paige to feel a part of the same desperate circumstance. She almost went so far as wanting to see them die of naiveté before her own inexorable demise. To be right about their collective fate meant more to her in the moment—and easier to accept—than the idea of starting life over back home. "Never mind," she said, retrieving the key from the floor. "Just pretend I didn't say anything about it. Then I can disappear in the middle of the night and just like your plan—whatever it is—leave you with a clean conscience."

Here was life as an excruciating belly-crawl to a dark and thorny end. Paige was dead in every way but the one that mattered most, the one others would recognize by its ugliness and stink. No, this kind of death condemned her to go through the motions of living—waking and washing, dressing and eating and talking around the pain as if anyone else understood it—all the while, her future was already decided. Not much longer now, she thought. Soon, she would catch up to it.

CHAPTER 39

Landfall

*(The miners wait out the burgeoning storm. Those on the lower bunks
look blankly at the undersides of the berths above them; those on
the upper bunks stare at the ceiling as if to gauge the tempest's power
through the tarpapered planks.)*

MAYANO.

These hurricane—it never happen in Peru. Or all South America. The
water—it too cold for this kind weather.

TREE.

I beg to differ, *hombre*. What about, oh, what was that hurricane called,
the one in '73-'74, somewhere in there? Hit mainly in Honduras but
also Mexico... Anyway, the floods killed 10,000, maybe more. What
do you call that?

MAYANO.

Central America, *pinche idiota*.

RUSSIAN MINER.

In Russia, we have no hurricane. We have—what you say?—tornado.
Famous Moscow tornado in nineteen hundred four. Devil must have
sent. Church first in path, gone go roof and cross from dome. *Bog dal,
bog i vzyal.*

WAXMAN.

Technically, this here's a cyclone. Hurricanes are for the Atlantic
and northeast Pacific and typhoons for the northwest Pacific. I been
through one or t'other over these maundering years.

TREE.

You know the name 'hurricane' comes from the Caribbean god a storms, *huracán*?

WAXMAN.

Or the Mayan storm god gave fire to mankind, Hom- or Hun-raken, somethin' like that. Tarrant would know a course.

TREE.

Got that from those jaunts in Belize and Honduras, huh? Wish I coulda been there...

WAXMAN.

No you don't 'cause there weren't no lazin' on that venture. Every man jack had to carry his own load. Never been so dirty-tired in my life. Spent whole days hackin' through stands a heliconia and jungle brush from the dinosaur ages to gain maybe 50 yards afore dusk. Coulda easily slashed each other dead by accident. Had to mark our machetes with day-glo tape to make certain of our own blades. Chokin' heat, drug gangs, rebel *communistas*, flesh-eatin' disease and the skeeters, jaws, you never seen the like—it was the worst pick 'n' mix a horrors.

TREE.

I think you're forgettin' 'bout my native constitution. They got indigenous peoples there not much different—the Garifuna, the Lenca, the Miskito—

TUGGER.

The Orkin Man say Atlanta the number one skeeter city... in the US of A.

WAXMAN.

The night don't fall there neither so much as drop on your head when you least 'spect it. And if you're in a clearing, say, and got some moonlight, the ground shimmers like crystal with the eyes of a thousand man-killin' spiders, no foolin'.

(Enter: Gerrit, giving the others a glimpse of the low grayed-out sky and spitting wind.)

DUTCH MINER.

Daar is hij! Da new *bass.*

MAYANO.

How does it look like?

GERRIT.

What it looks like is: the goddamn Pacific has a black hate for us.

WAXMAN.

And Tarrant out there in it ...

TREE.

What is it with that? Some kinda *Iron John* thing?

GERRIT.

You mean that whiny howlin' therapy shit? Like to see you ask 'im.

TREE.

No, no, you got it all wrong. It's about gettin' back to nature—the ancient ways—bringin' out the inner wild man ...

GERRIT.

Guess I shoulda double-knotted 'im then.

WAXMAN.

Like he ain't already the peak a savageness.

GERRIT.

I don't even want to know. My plan's to do some drinkin', saw logs and say nuthin'.

TUGGER.

That there sound like a plan fo' life.

(Ridge, Mira and Paige lay in the semidarkness of Tarrant's cabin while the cyclone fumes around it, shaking the slat walls. Paige's pillowcase is heavy with supplies.)

MIRA.

Where's the tribe? Not in those patchy huts…

(Ridge marks his place in Free-Energy Thinking *with an index finger.)*

RIDGE.

I don't know. The spirit house? Of all the village structures, it seems the sturdiest, what with its terrace and reinforced stilt-platform.

PAIGE.

What about the women then? Would they let them in for safety's sake?

RIDGE.

I doubt it. They're not even allowed on the stair, much less the porch or the inside. I don't know. I've heard there are some limestone caves higher up in the foothills. Maybe they've gone there. Maybe they all went.

PAIGE.

The way they treat women… Did you know they can't sit around a cooking fire started by a man? That they can't eat pork?

RIDGE.

There's worse, you'd discover. Some say they practice infanticide, either to make sure they have enough male warriors for raids on neighboring islands or to keep their numbers down because of worries about famine. At the opposite extreme, if a child takes a dislike to a stranger, they can have the person killed on their word alone. It's a life of contradictions …

                              MIRA.

Is that why they're upset? Because they see Tarrant and his men breaking all these taboos?

                              RIDGE.

No, it's not that so much. We're exempt—whites, Westerners. They figure we're under more liberal gods. No, what's getting to them is their reliance on Tarrant for tobacco, supplies, the gradual loss of their ancestral ways. He's even supplanted their chief.

                              PAIGE.

They feel used then …

                              RIDGE.

Yeah, basically. They used to pride themselves on having resisted the outside world … Hell, they believe they were never even supposed to live on land, that it was a mistake on the part of the gods. They belong in their own underwater universe, according to Nanokwe. I guess Tarrant forced them to abandon a settlement on the beach to come here.

                              PAIGE.

Well, it's a good thing we're not there now. The waves would be wicked huge.

(The walls bulge and separate at the corners under the strain before collapsing back into place.)

                              MIRA.

I've never been in a major storm before. Do you think the cabin will hold up?

RIDGE.

A low-level tornado passed through my home county when I was around ten. Actually, I can't remember if it was a tornado or a water spout. Whatever it was, in the morning, our yard, the streets, everything was covered in dead grasshoppers. You couldn't go anywhere without crunching them under your feet. It was surreal.

MIRA.

Like a plague averted. The locusts from *Exodus* were supposedly swept into the Red Sea by a windstorm.

RIDGE.

But only after they devastated Egypt ...

MIRA.

It *was* divine punishment ...

PAIGE.

That sounds like an oxymoron.

MIRA.

I admit: these are the times that try my faith.

PAIGE.

(Twisting up under her throw blanket.)

But why? Why the need to test us? It doesn't make any sense. Not to pick on you, but if God is all-powerful, if He can intervene whenever He wants, why does He need constant proof from us? It's flat out cruel to put us in situations like this and ask us, no, have the gall to *demand* we love Him. And for what? For doing nothing while the worst happens?

MIRA.

I know the feeling. I grew up with it. My father was a Holocaust survivor. That's why I'm trying to look past all this to the future. I could also cite the *Book of Job*, I guess, or the wrestling match in *Genesis* between

Jacob and an angel or God, as the case may be. But I take it you're not really looking for a strictly theological answer ...

(Paige sits up and pulls a rain poncho over her head.)

PAIGE.
No. I don't know. If that's all I can get—if not satisfaction in this world, just some religious understanding ...

(Ridge resumes reading his book.)

MIRA.
Well, fast-forwarding to the end, the notion from these stories is that God redeems our self-destructive nature. We'll understand and inherit His wisdom only when we learn to accept our enemies as ourselves and not before. As my rabbi is fond of saying, 'What cannot be known through reason must be embraced in love.'

PAIGE.
Guess I still have a long way to go then. Your dad, he ever get over it?

MIRA.
I'm not sure he was meant to, frankly. He brought me up to believe that evil exists because God and His Creation are incomplete and, no matter what we suffer, no matter how long, it's up to us—through faith, good works, *mitzvot*—to help make everything whole.

PAIGE.
Does it help you? Before they joined EST, you know, that self-help cult, my parents took us to Old Cambridge Baptist a few times. But they weren't believers. They went for its liberal reputation—civil rights and anti-Vietnam protests. Not that I'm looking to convert or anything ... *(She laces up her boots.)*

MIRA.

Most people—*goyim*—make the mistake of thinking Judaism is a religion of persecution and continuous grief. That isn't it at all. It's about praise and trust and community: praise of God, trust that our lives are not in vain, and community both in the present and through the generations. These things come together in a prayer we often say to ourselves, the *berachah.*

PAIGE.

How does it go?

(She stands up and assembles her belongings then deliberates whether to take the child-sized pillow.)

MIRA.

It's a silent prayer, usually just a single sentence that starts '*Baruch atah adonai …*'—'Praised are you, God …'

PAIGE.

Ba-ruch …

MIRA.

… atah adonai …

PAIGE.

… atah adonai …

MIRA.

The rest is usually something memorized passed on from parent to child. At bedtime, for instance, we ask God to give us peace in our sleep.

(Paige slips the shackles over one shoulder and touches Mira on the arm in thanks.)

PAIGE.

That would be a start ... This place just makes you want to believe in every kind of bad luck.

(Mira gets to her feet and Ridge follows suit.)

MIRA.

You sure about this? Especially with the wind getting stronger ...

PAIGE.

Means there won't be anybody watching. And besides, I have this. (*She pats the shackles.*) I can always follow Tarrant's example and cuff myself to a tree.

(Paige embraces her companions, Ridge awkwardly, leading with her shoulders, then gathers up her supplies.)

MIRA.

Be safe. *Hazak.*

PAIGE.

You, too—both of you.

(Exeunt Paige.)

RIDGE.

We better hope I've done enough.

MIRA.

You've done all you can, right? (*She puts an arm around him.*) Whether it's enough is out of our hands.

CHAPTER 40

The Cyclone

(Tarrant, bound with braided nylon rope at wrists and ankles to the stat-ue of Kagoroa, lifts his face to the howling storm.)

What is this vortical chaos if not a call to arms? It challenges me and all mankind for substance. 'You are but froth on my oceans,' the mael-strom thunders. This vasty indifference burdens me day-in and day-out! Better to contend with some malevolent design. Then I could per-sonify my enemy and make a ritual of hate. As it is, my foe inheres in air and slashing rain and presents nothing to grasp or pierce, or by common science, scatter. Thus do the Outer Gods veil their truths, consigning the human creature to its own self-serving lies and slave religions *in saecula saeculorum.*

Ah, the gale increases, riffling the palms and pandanus in fierce gusts. Loose dirt and ash freewheel into the black and tumbled sky. I strain to keep my footing. The statue quakes from the crest of its con-cave helm to its base. The oversized battle helm that serves as its head is adorned with emergent, toad-like figures. I cannot see them, fixed in place as I am, but I know the shapes from memory. They have always struck me as impish rebels after lives free and independent of the god what birthed them. According to the tales, Kagoroa is grasping and imperious and aspires to rule the skies as well as the seas. The prospect of dying, fettered to this pagan icon, brings a sardonic smile to my lips.

The huts of the Marokatu fan up into odd distended shapes and fly apart before the cyclone maw. What powerful black magic, they will say in the aftermath, *buliembo.* Pandanus thatch, tropical timber, plaited floor and sleeping mats, all the trivial proof of their lives whirls into the leveling dark. In his most famous oration, "Hymn to King Helios," the last pagan Emperor of Rome, Julian ii, declares the visible sun symbolic of the absolute godhead: *Among the gods whom we can perceive, who revolve eternally in their most blessed path, he is leader and lord; since he bestows on their nature its generative power, and fills the whole heavens not only with visible rays of light but with countless other blessings that are invisible…* How then would the devout Mithraist have apprehended this angry and rapturous black? Absolute death? The anti-god? Regardless, its ambient madness renders me purblind, drowns out the clamor of panicked animals and at once, renews my will to defy, defy, defy.

Nothing—neither material nor mental horrors, nothing—can turn me from my self-appointed aim: to achieve the highest summit of thought and, from that lofty vantage, burn the so-called civilizing myths from human memory. These myths—Platonism, the world religions, democracy and its bastard economies, popular history, the very idea of linear time—demand the wrong things and not enough. They pervert the instincts. They privilege messengers over monarchs. As a species, we have vacillated in our purpose because of trivial modernities, distracting us one after the other. Science has become the mere proliferation of gadgets. The vertigo begun by Galileo has been too long forgot amid our lesser circles.

Buffet me as you will o' shrouding fury, batter me with your forest debris, twist the curses from out my lips. None of your ravages will buckle me under or divert me from my purpose. Somehow, I will expose the real blood red maw behind this facade and gut the world down to its immutable fate. Somehow, I will bash new thoughts into the human creature, not only to disabuse it of the lies it's told itself through the ages, but also to prove how few thoughts are worth preserving.

CHAPTER 41

In the Eye or Not

Rainwater mixed with soot trickled down the wall behind Tarrant's desk. Standing on rickety chairs at either corner, Ridge and Mira held a rolled-up bedspread between them. Ridge pressed his end of the Indian bedspread into the joint where the wall met the ceiling, stoppering a troublesome surge. The wind roared on the other side like a roused up monster. The slat wall tremored under the mounting pressure. Its tarred-over chinks popped and split. He cast a nervous glance at Mira. It felt as if the whole wall could spin away at any moment and the ceiling along with it.

Mira was wadding the bedspread into the opposite corner with her fingertips. She caught his worried look and mouthed something lost to the deafening wind.

"What was that?" Ridge braced his injured leg against the wall for better balance.

"I can't imagine Paige out there," Mira said at an outdoor volume. "The wind in every direction, all this water, the—" The tin roof resounded with flying debris. The clatter reverberated down the wall, triggering more leakage. Mira rose up on her toes to mash the dark blue bedspread into the gap. "*A broch!*"

"We tried ..."

"I know."

"This keeps up, we'll be out in it, too," Ridge said. The radio's 25-foot antenna whipcracked against the roof. "Sounds like we'll lose that antenna at least."

"How do you think Tarrant's going to react to her leaving?"

"No thinking necessary. We're down to fight or flight." Ridge brooded a few moments. "The question is: How much do we lay on the line? He calls my bluff, sends the Marokatu after Paige, do we threaten to die along with her? Because it could come to that." The cabin door rattled in its frame. *This place has got to hold together.* "We should bolster that

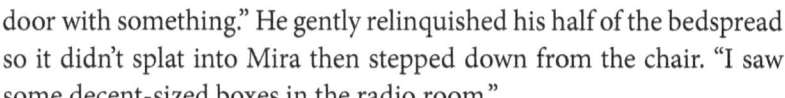

door with something." He gently relinquished his half of the bedspread so it didn't splat into Mira then stepped down from the chair. "I saw some decent-sized boxes in the radio room."

On entering the adjacent space, Ridge examined the wall behind the dead radio for leaks and, finding only a few veined cracks, turned his attention to the other side of the room. A crowded bookcase took up one wall. On the floor was a small air compressor, a standing safe and several wine boxes. The boxes overflowed with an eclectic variety of books. Ridge stepped past the air compressor and cradled the nearest box to his hip in labored stages. One leather-bound volume was hot stamped *Psychology from Beyond the Veil*. With his good leg bearing the brunt of the box's weight, he loped to the cabin door.

"Want help?" Mira asked. Though the noise outside persisted at the same high decibel, the wall no longer wavered so violently.

Ridge shrugged and quickly slid the box in place before his strength gave out. He issued a plosive sigh. "There's a few of these we can stack." He pulled up his shirt to mop the sweat from his brow. The air was thick and fusty. The cabin smelled like an old steamer trunk.

She gestured toward the gun belted against the small of his back. "You have that now if he threatens us ..."

Why does she keep revisiting this argument? Every mention of Tarrant compelled him to size up his own weaknesses. "So we kill him and take our chances with the others?"

"No, not necessarily. I was just trying to think of alternatives to, well, just giving in."

"He's going to ask for the gun back first thing, so if I'm going to do it, I won't have any time to deliberate." His tone was harsher than intended.

Mira turned fully around on the chair to face him and said in a clipped, admonishing voice: "Do you really think he's going to let us go in the end?" Anxiety showed in the tight set of her jaw.

"I don't know." Ridge wanted to believe their best chance of escape was also the least dangerous: keep their heads down and wait for Tarrant to lose interest. "It's possible. If he gets what he wants—whatever that is—we won't matter anymore."

The cacophony of wind-driven rain and refuse tapered to an eerie calm. Mira stepped from her chair, eyes on the ceiling, wary of the sudden quiet. She draped the sodden bedspread over the back of the chair. Her footsteps sounded overloud. Ridge reached for her hand. He needed to feel her warmth. The forceful pulsebeat in her palm joined with his. "What do you think?" she whispered. "Are we in the eye or is it over?"

"Let's open the door a crack and see."

She nodded in agreement and, when he bent to the wine box, scurried to help slide it away.

Ridge gave her a significant look and inched the door open. The dark gray sky was inchoate and formless as if the earth were new. A flaw of inky red shivered in the upper atmosphere. Ground lightning? Some kind of aurora? Palm fronds raked past the cabin. The trees in view had either been splintered apart or bowed at odd angles. "Christ, the devastation…" Where the village once stood was a mere scattering of tree branches and uprooted brush, blackened fire pit stones, assorted camping gear and smashed flumes. He could pick out the dim glint of metal tools here and there in the standing water. "Looks like the supply shed came down." Reluctant to open the door further to the ambient madness outside, he motioned for Mira to take his place.

She regarded the sight with deepening horror and disbelief. "It's like another world. Everything is blurred-out and gray except that scary bit of sky." She shut the door and turned to Ridge. Her mouth trembled at the corners. "Paige better have made it to those caves or wherever she was going because this—out in the open—she couldn't have survived it. *Chas vesholem*, did you see those trees? Like a jumble of kindling."

"Tarrant estimated we'd just get the outer rainbands so I'm thinking it's over. But I wouldn't go out just yet." The dilemma of what to do next lay hard on his heart. He pulled the gun from his waistband, careful not to touch the trigger. The safety was off to allow for quick firing. "Guess this is as good a place as any to confront Tarrant…"

"I couldn't see him, not even the lodge."

"The cabin's angled the wrong way. And even if we were facing the right direction, the air's so murky…" He consulted his watch. "Believe it or not, it's about a quarter to five."

"So it lasted—what?—about seven-eight hours?"

Ridge was seized by a jittery fatigue. Was the redness in the sky a distorted sign of dawn? Then in a voice that strained to come out of his throat, he said, "Maybe I should just blast him while he's still tied up."

"I keep thinking about my father, what he would do. For him, the war was sheer endurance." Mira pressed against Ridge. "Would he expect me to do the same? Or fight back? I don't know. But I can't stand the thought of losing Paige—not after what she's gone through already."

Did she want him to do it or not? Ridge was afraid to ask the question aloud. "It's terrible what happened—and it makes me feel guilty. But I'm not ready to give up our future because she's not thinking clearly. The situation's unfair, yes, we know that but ... It makes me angry that she's willing to sacrifice us, if need be, for her own peace of mind."

"Are you blaming her?" She pulled away, her mouth twisted in hurt.

"For putting us in this situation, yes." Ridge squared his shoulders. "Look, I understand her mindset and all, the trauma, I just can't condone what she's done."

"Maybe she's braver than us."

Ridge began to despise himself for arguing. Why was he doing this now when this could be one of their last moments together? But the quarrel had its own unavailing impetus. "No, she just has less to lose."

"Her life," Mira said. "There's not much more here for her to give up." Ridge heard a strange tetchiness to her voice. Despite the occasional scolding, he could usually rely on her to be reasonable. It was more an outward sign of her nature than a by-product of her therapist's training. The assault on Paige had apparently angered and horrified her past all intrinsic limits.

A scrape like a long birdscratch sounded against the wooden cladding. The wind swelled from silence into a dire moan. *Plip-plip-plip* came the rain again. The slat wall resumed its oscillations. The drizzle quickened into a torrent. "Goddamn it," Ridge said.

"Just a lull." Mira climbed back on her chair. "*A shaynem dank dir im pupik.*"

"Or the eye came closer than Tarrant thought." Ridge moved slowly, carrying the dread of what had gone unspoken. He couldn't shake the feeling that Mira's story so far was the story of his failure. He gripped the back of his chair for balance and stood on the seat with his good leg. "I know what you're thinking about Paige. Despite what you said earlier—about Judaism not being a religion of persecution—you can't help feeling that suffering somehow makes you special. It's obvious, the way you talk about your dad, your heritage..."

As a young girl, Mira had considered her father's tales of the Holocaust another, private branch of mythology—a branch that led to Kabbalism, the study of auras and angels and the notion of Job-like suffering as a spiritual mark. Her reflective eyes dimmed in the kerosene light. "I won't deny the idea, but it's not what you think. It's, well, it's not just any suffering, it's suffering on principle, not resigning yourself to the world as it is. I go back to the example of Masada: 'God can defend one against a thousand.'"

"I don't know it outside of the name," Ridge said. Though the escalating storm forced him to raise his voice, the earlier firmness was missing. "I mean, I know it was a battle between the Jews and the Romans but that's about it."

"The Jews had no hope of holding out against the Romans, outnumbered as they were, so they set fire to their own palace and all their treasures and killed themselves before the Romans arrived." Mira extended the bedspread to Ridge and he touched her outstretched hand briefly in accepting it. "Masada was also known as the Hill of Gold," she said, a strained smile on her mulberry lips.

That smile was an awful blow to his heart. Her face looked about to shatter. "And that's what you think we should do?" he asked. Whatever her answer, he decided, he would be bound to it. Every line and plane in the room took on a hyper-realistic sharpness.

Mira's mouth became small and thoughtful. "It's pretty close to what Paige said, isn't it? Coming back and burning down the camp? There's a strength in it, *koach* we call it—the ability to cope."

Dazed by her sullen resolve, he said blankly, "So how do we know for sure when we're facing the final battle, outnumbered? And what do we give up in the meantime? The gun? The Senator?" The illimitable future he seemed poised to inherit just days earlier continued to shrink around him.

The wall jolted free of the ceiling joint and back again. Mira sopped up the subsequent freshet of rainwater with rapid finger-presses. "I don't know. Let's get through this first." She scowled at the wall and the unseen forces outside, saying, "At some point the odds against us will be clear and, God willing, we'll have the chance to decide for ourselves what happens next." Her words were thin and remote.

Ridge tried to catch her eye. He saw that Mira had turned inward against the maelstrom. *Calling on her personal angel?* He ached to bring her close. The ups and downs of emotional life made him feel clumsy. He found his emotions more demanding than exhilarating, a burden that drove him to always seek compromise. But what did compromise mean in this absurd circumstance? Despite or perhaps because of this lingering question, he was compelled to reassure her somehow. "I just want you to know, if it comes to it, my last breath will be yours." He said this with restored determination though he wasn't exactly sure what it meant. Her hesitant smile suggested she didn't either. She tugged on the hem of her oversized T-shirt.

Then the urgency of surviving in the instant took over. Turbulence shook them from all directions and the drastic changes in air pressure made their ears pop. Wild convulsions followed breath-catching pauses. Each moment was like an impetuous wave, an upsurge in the dark fundament of things with no purpose other than its own vexing formation. They spent themselves in countless small defenses and, throughout it all, Ridge envied Mira her quiet resignation. He wouldn't trust himself to God, he suspected, even if it were true. Not out of misplaced pride but because he was too much of a rationalist. He yearned for a religion set on a logical foundation. Sometimes, as now, he found Mira's faith naïve instead of a steadying counterbalance. Like the magical thinking of children. The thought of it made him confused and anxious. Could it be that, after almost five years together, they remained mysteries to each other still?

But more than anything else, Ridge was tired. He was tired of being awake to peril: the yacht, the sea, the aborigines, Tarrant and his men and now this mindless squall. He was tired of the shame and guilt for inadvertently loosing these threats on his friends and companions. He was tired of the obligations that shame and guilt entailed, of failing to regain control of things, of losing people—Kenny, Aaron, most likely

Paige, maybe even Mira by slow degrees. And as the hours grew longer and longer with no hint of day, his fatigue seemed part of living out a continuous and uneasy dream.

CHAPTER 42

The Sea God

When the silence prompted Ridge to finally open the cabin door again, he wished time had stopped along with the wind. He could no longer avoid Tarrant; soon, he would have to make an irreparable choice. His heart gave a sick pulse. He fingered the gun belted against the small of his back. The quiet was appalling. "Ready?"

Mira said, "What's it look like?"

The landscape was a riot of mud and debris under a dirtied sky. It reminded Ridge of grainy newspaper photos of the Flint and Altahama Rivers during the heyday of Georgia logging, the shoreline rucked from heavy timber and littered with detritus. Beattie's oil drum smoker lay smashed against a tangle of swept-together trees. "Same as in the lull—just more ruin." He breathed in the stench from the overflowed latrine then pushed down the cleated ramp on his crutch.

At the bottom, he jerked to a halt and waved Mira back. *Christ, of all things to survive…* He swallowed the catch in his throat. The two-story statue of Kagoroa at the far end of the village loomed above the devastation. Ridge could make out Tarrant's thick-shouldered silhouette in the bleak afternoon light. Any lingering hope of escaping his wrath vanished.

He crutched forward through irregular stretches of cloudy water, fixed on the ironwood totem. The statue was a compacted mass topped by a head like a curled shield. The exaggerated head angled downward in a sullen or sagacious attitude. Its widely set eyes were hollow. Around them reposed a series of squatting, vaguely amphibious figures confected from knobs and bulges rather than complete and connected shapes. The arms, following the contours of the triangular torso, framed a fetish bundle inset with mother-of-pearl. Four additional figures embellished the totem's chest and belly. Though human in form, their legs scissored like those of frogs on the water.

The statue impressed Ridge with its coiled strength and suggestive ornamentation: *The emptiness in the eyes—what of it? Would the Ma-rokatu worship a blind god? No, no. We must be meant to see the body and the void around it as a whole. The eyes aren't empty; instead, they're full of the sun's light, the world, all-seeing. Kagoroa: the ultimate witness-bearer. There's some acknowledgement of the trickiness to that role, too. That's where the figures come in. Those shapes—they could represent the lives witnessed and recorded, the history of these islands in a few dashed-off lives. To an immortal the human span would seem fleeting, half-lived, hence, the unformed figures. Or no, maybe they symbolize the whole relationship between observer and observed. The observer takes in the observed as partially-imagined things. The figures in that case could be melting into the statue. You can then see it as the symbiosis of objective and subjective, outside and inside … Better that than the observer alone, marking down time, forever obsessed with just one-damn-thing-after-another and no chance of any totality …*

He cut a mazy path around shredded palms and drowned chickens and half-buried scrap wood and the remnants of the portable rock drill. Mira trailed him by some 20-odd yards amid a scourge of mosquitoes. Out of a sense of loyalty, she'd refused his entreaties to flee and seek out the supply ship. He'd insisted she hold back in the event Tarrant was armed or otherwise decided to turn on her. There was no sense in offering themselves like prey one by one. Though she'd given in to that logic, a disharmony remained, stemming, in part, from her insistence that the storm was part of some Biblical allegory and he just lacked the perspective to understand it.

The aftermath of the storm appeared to confirm the idea. The cyclone had changed every visible sign of life from the somber clouds on down into an augury of death: the Pacific black ducks and Old World vultures, the mosquitoes and blow flies, the little fire ants swarming over the downed trees and human wreckage. A number of ancestral graves formerly hidden by plaited mats were now flooded messes. The gurgling stream swelled high up the bank, edged in brown spume. Closer up, the grimed statue resembled a giant born of primeval sludge and Tarrant a prisoner about to be dragged into the bowels of the earth.

A dozen yards out, Ridge leaned his crutch against a heap of storm-wrack and took up the gun. Hawser-laid rope crisscrossed from torso to toe secured Tarrant to one of the statue's stunted legs. Tarrant had worn only a tank top and military drab chinos into the gale and was soaked to the marrow. His head lolled unmoving, chin against his chest.

"Is he even alive?" asked Mira.

Ridge stepped forward instead of answering. Then he heard the miners stirring from their bunkhouses. Their low-throated tones and trial investigations of the ruins resounded across the flattened distance and through the leafless trees. He motioned for Mira to hunker down out of sight then hurried to Tarrant's limp body.

Tarrant betrayed no sign of life. *Was he...?* Ridge was afraid to finish the thought. The ropes assured him he could assess Tarrant's condition at no risk to himself. What a trifling difference that separates the living and the dead—a missed breath, a dream gone rogue. He brushed away the snarled hair at the man's throat and put two fingers to his windpipe. At the first instant of warmth, he withdrew his hand like a gigged frog. The shock of this made him doubt his senses. He wondered if he'd mistaken his own emphatic finger-pulses for a positive reading.

"Motherfuckin' Tourist!" barked Gerrit at a bounding run. "You better not a killed him!" The claw-end of a crowbar jutted above his head with every other stride. He would close the gap in no time. Mayano and an untold number of other miners joined in the chase.

The pressure on Ridge's chest closed around his heart. He aimed the revolver at Tarrant in a sleepwalking gesture, unsure if he intended to take him hostage or fire point-blank. Tarrant's uncertain status was a torment. A natural demise would absolve him of the dizzying need to act; otherwise... Sweat worked its way down his back. Gerrit, the miners, Mira in their path—everything magnified the fact that time was running short.

Spooked by Gerrit's full pelt advance, Mira darted out from behind a heap of broken flumes. She scampered toward the mess tent area where deep-sunk posts protruded from a brackish pond. Gerrit slowed in surprise at her reveal and started after her. Until a menacing guncrack rent the air. He slued to a stop in the mire. Mayano and the others scurrying after him likewise paused in their charge. Mira seized a hand fork from the mud and turned to face her pursuer.

Ridge had fired before he'd determined what to do next. He cleared his throat and thrust the gun toward Gerrit, blustering to hide his fear: "I can't get everyone. But you—I'll be sure to get you at least." He snatched up his crutch but kept it in his left hand, unused, as he shuffled toward Mira. He cut his eyes at Gerrit. "You can have him. I didn't touch Tarrant other than to see if he was still alive."

"He better be." Gerrit resumed his advance, slowly this time, the crowbar at his side. When he passed within Ridge's orbit, he gave a wide grin and unsheathed the serrated fish knife looped to his belt. "Gonna take more'n a whisker-shot to scare me off ya permanent."

Ridge backed away, eyes rushing. Mira ambled to his side and together, silent and abashed, they watched Gerrit put an ear to Tarrant's lips. Gerrit nodded, lips pursed in cool relief, then slashed the ropes around Tarrant's ankles. The knife strokes were strong and sure and clean. Ridge shrunk from the sound. Tarrant sagged at the knees and Mayano braced him while Gerrit attacked the remaining bonds.

"I couldn't tell whether he was alive or not." Ridge dipped toward Mira's cheek. "I thought maybe... He felt warm." He sounded unconvincing even to himself. He organized a defense in his head, saying he never had enough time to decide, that there could never have been enough time. Nothing in his past had prepared him for the enormity of the situation. To shoot Tarrant in cold blood would've been a betrayal of principle. It wasn't in his character. Still, he'd come close to pulling the trigger. It would've taken no time at all. The accidental jerk of his finger would've been as good as a premeditated one. But what then? What kind of blowback would they have endured? There was no end of *ifs* and *buts* and noble excuses for his lack of resolve. Now, he had to trust that he could extort some reasonable assurance of safety.

Gerrit directed a sallow-faced Russian to take Tarrant's feet while he and Mayano hoisted him from the armpits. Ridge kept the gun raised chest-high in what he thought was a casual stance. The other miners, already focused on cleanup and recovery, took scarcely any notice of him. Somehow, just staying alive felt like defeat. Mira leaned into his shoulder and breathed in his overnight musk. Her bosom rose and fell against his back in low hitching sighs. There was no hiding in this place from the fact that life is a self-consuming thing.

The miners lugged Tarrant past the muck-spattered bunkhouses to the cabin Ridge and Mira had preserved in his stead. The sun sparked off the tin roof. The radio antenna pointed straight to the upraised heavens.

CHAPTER 43

In the Foothills

Paige edged out from under the protective bluff. The long period of suspension was over and the world had resumed its form. A colorless sun beamed through an upper layer of residual gray. Its light was of a different quality than before—dusty and subtle rather than the searing white that split everything into sunwash and hard shadow. The forest below was riven and confused. Downed trees and wind-tossed underbrush made for a snarl of muted colors.

Pins and needles ran through Paige's forearms from the long pressure of her elbows on the rock. She massaged each arm then shook out her tattered rain poncho before she decided it wasn't worth saving and stuffed it into a cleft in the rock. She rummaged in her pillowcase for a dry T-shirt and came up with a tribute to Oliver North. The graphic consisted of his pen and ink smirk framed by a garish American flag. A banner above the image asserted: *He told it like it was ... 1987*. Dry is dry, she thought.

The cyclone had been a crashing terror. She'd rushed through its preliminaries half-blind, the forest snagging at her poncho, telling herself she could somehow outrace the teeming destruction. The path into the hills had been a muddy slog but otherwise easy to follow and, for the first time since the assault, her senses had been fully alert and alive. The panic in her chest had given her some much-needed materiality.

After about forty minutes of racing through the storm, spot-sweating through her shirt, the bluff had presented itself as an expedient hide. She'd clambered across a slickened rockface to reach it, grateful for once for having short nails. The bluff gave way to a low-ceilinged alcove just deep enough to provide shelter. The spitefulness of the storm had somewhat eased her worries about venomous spiders or snakes as she'd snugged into the darkness. Lying flat against the rock, the storm had buffeted her face and upper-body with skirling winds and rain like birdshot. She'd cuffed herself to the sapling just in case. In her groggier moments, arms and knees numbing up, she'd imagined she was a pet-rifying memorial to failure.

Paige sipped from a thermos of tepid water and scanned the rump of hills. Her plan was simple: head for the coast and circle the island for the supply ship's berth. In the depths of the storm, she'd dismissed her earlier notion of setting fire to the camp. Escape would make for a better—more complete—kind of revenge. When she arrived in the capital, she'd wire the ship's captain his due, see the Senator to a hospi-tal or the US consular agent, inform the authorities of Tarrant's crimes then decide whether to return home or disappear for a while, maybe do some foreign charity work. A change of scene, she thought, might disrupt the misery cycle into which she'd fallen: the fogginess in her brain, the heart-spasms provoked by every word that recalled the at-tack, the sobbing fits, the despair of yet more shapeless days. One way or another, this exhausting routine had to stop.

She felt for Gerrit's gun through her pillowcase and unlocked her shackles. With the twist of her right hand, her old engagement ring caught her eye. It was the only sentimental token of her failed mar-riage. She resisted the melancholy thoughts the dulled ring brought on; instead, she pocketed the key to the shackles and rose up from her crouch. This was no time for fretful self-reflection. It was already late in the day.

CHAPTER 44

Resettlement

Mira added a soggy, mud-caked 1971 edition of the *British National Formulary* to the medical texts, surgical tools and medicines drying in the fading sun. She set the book on the small canvas tarp then collapsed next to it, tired and anxious and red in the face. The perspiration at the base of her neck trickled down her spine. A continuous swarm of mosquitoes discouraged the removal of her sweatshirt. Didn't all those televised appeals for flood relief cite standing water as a breeding ground for mosquito-borne disease? Thick mud circumscribed her carpenter's boots. The Marokatu would have to wait at least another day before the ponded water evaporated enough to permit them to rebuild their huts. Tonight, according to Nanokwe, the men would sleep in the spirit house and the women would retire to the limestone caves.

Several Marokatu were reinforcing the roof of the spirit house with salvaged thatch. Mira thought it a pagan miracle the structure had survived, along with Tarrant and the statue that served as colonnade and monument. She examined the statue in detail for the first time. Its wavelike head and the half-submerged figures that made up its facial features struck her as significant. *Those figures—they're caught in a deluge. Like Jonah, they can't escape God's Providence. They're fleeing His presence. Or, at least trying to. The Book of Jonah, as the Kabbalists would have it, is the story of our soul's lifetime journey. Just as Jonah must be roused from his sleep in the storm and his conscience revived, we—I—must be mindful of Him no matter the seeming distance between us. The wind, the kikayon plant, the sea, even the Leviathan are all extensions of His being. If only I knew what He meant by these signs. If only I knew the message that would deliver us like the people of Nineveh. There: that's the secret moral of the Mincha service during Yom Kippur: we can never be sure which message will save us. We can only let our human fears wash over us and pray we don't succumb before the right one comes unbidden.*

Embroiled in an argument with a weedy white-haired elder, the shaman acknowledged her with a flick of his eyes. The elder issued a guttural challenge, gesturing toward the nearby statue and spirit house. Chaw-black drool coursed down his chin and spidered onto his chest. Nanokwe countered in a strident but reedy voice. He rattled a bottle of antacids for emphasis. The elder seemed undeterred and jerked his body toward Kagoroa, flinging his arms around as if gathering in a knot of fishing line.

The dispute between the aborigines continued at a higher pitch. Mira felt the burden of decisions made and unmade. The strain had robbed her of sleep and appetite. Yesterday, she'd stolen a handkerchief from the clothesline to address some mid-cycle spotting. Around her, miners and Marokatu clustered in various tasks to restore the village. Time passed at a fateful drag.

The elder screeched his last words to Nanokwe then, worn out rather than defeated, gave a shake of his shoulders and quit, leaving the shaman nonplussed. "Sorry to you for hearing that argy-bargy, good miss," he said.

"No, no that's all right." Mira got to her feet. Despite herself, the native's outmoded Briticisms brought a compressed smile to her lips. "And you don't need to be so formal with me. Just Mira, please." She looked around for Ridge. For reasons she didn't fully understand, he'd been adamant about helping Nanokwe regain his belongings. She couldn't see Ridge in the tumult of busy reconstruction. A scrum of miners close by struggled to discharge a stormswept pandanus tree from the hardening mud. The root-end was a cumbersome weight. Expletives of doubt and frustration abounded.

Nanokwe said of the elder, "He got the monkey-mind. Want bone-pointing ceremony."

"What does that mean?"

"Marokatu after storm fine, yes. Lose much chicken, some goat, some pig. But Marokatu know storm. Kagoroa protect. Roof need repair. No lose peoples but Marokatu feel god, ancestor angry." Nanwoke's face elongated into an open-mouthed sigh that showed tobacco-stained teeth. "Some talk bone-pointing ceremony for find cause of storm-trouble; others, no."

"I'm afraid I don't understand."

"Some want shaman—me—fix guilt." Nanokwe swiveled his head to ensure he couldn't be overheard. "Much peoples say Tarrant sir out of nature," he murmured.

Mira staged an even tone in her throat but what emerged quivered with emotion. "I'm sorry, what? They blame Tarrant for the storm?"

"Need balance in nature. Land bleed for him. Bad feeling grow."

Nanokwe was clearly struggling with the ramifications of the storm. Mira pressed him to confirm her suspicions. "What would happen if you performed this bone-pointing?"

"Point Mr. Tarrant, he must leave."

The possibility shocked and assuaged her. She strained to keep the disappointment out of her voice when she asked, "But you don't want to do it?"

"Might divide the peoples, weaken us for bad nature and enemies." Flustered, Nanokwe turned his head to spit. "Also, Tarrant sick now. He got headache, migraine. Since younger age. Weather change cause it sometime, food, worry. He see things in pain—ghost, angel, maybe, like in *weikau*." He indicated the spirit house. "I take medicine bag to cave. Protect. Give Mi-drin for him."

Mira gathered Nanokwe was torn between his obligations as Tarrant's doctor and his duties as the tribe's spiritual leader. She suspected Tarrant of nurturing this conflict as an added precaution. *The mad schlenterer*...She was about to say something more when Ridge appeared toting a couple of medical texts and a Ziploc bag of cotton balls. "Got a few more. How many are we up to now?"

"Forty, no, forty-two." Mira relieved Ridge of his finds and deposited them on the tarp. He looked about done in. "Nanokwe was just telling me something interesting about Tarrant."

Either missing or expressly ignoring Mira's cue, the shaman said, "Much book wet, scatter about. Much mess."

"You know we have to find them, Nanokwe." Ridge shuffled closer to the shaman. "To protect myself and Mira, I'm going to have to tell Tarrant what I've done. You should take precautions yourself."

"Protect by spirit, *tabu*. Take you to *weikau*, some *kava*, you see how spirit go."

"Sure, we make it out of this ..." He touched Mira on the arm to draw her attention to Gerrit charging in their direction. The sight choked off any words of comfort or solidarity she might have offered him. She couldn't get over the radical change in her circumstances. The time between home and the island seemed a waste dark abyss. Her reunion with Ridge had done little to mitigate the growing sense of estrangement from her past. There'd been no time for them to be themselves, nothing that extended beyond mere survival. Circumstances hadn't allowed them to renew any of their former intimacies—talking over their workaday concerns, indulging in pop culture inanities, pleasuring each other on a warm lazy night—all the commonplaces that make up a complete life; instead, they'd been regularly staggered by incident.

Ridge plucked the handgun from his belt and trained it on Gerrit. When Gerrit got within an easy range, he signaled him to stop.

"I seen ya seize up when you notice me comin' on." Gerrit doffed his trucker's cap to better shade his face. "Ya got the revolver, yeah, but do ya got the sack for it? I think that's why ya hate on us lowdown scrappers. For all our lack a silver spoon refinement, ya know somethin' happens—a bigger, different kinda storm or whatever and the whole trammel a civilization turn to mudwater and pig shit—we the ones gonna make the most of it. Sure ain't gonna be no leetist beards in their fuckin' poplin shorts and wove leather sandals, believe you me." He gave a dismissive huff. "Don't worry, I ain't gonna knock ya back on yer haunches. Though ya deserve that and more, the bossman wants ya direct."

"Guess I'm lucky that way."

Something like a smile formed on Gerrit's lips. "Like a hog jostlin' his way into the butcherin' house."

Ridge motioned for him to lead the way.

The masculine posturing irritated Mira like a predictable bit of theater. She entwined an arm in Ridge's. How likely was it they'd see this sky, this sun, again? Tarrant, she supposed, would resolve things with a simple yea or nay. *Chas vesholem.* She wondered how many times her father, condemned to the Lodz ghetto, had thought the next moment or the next would be his last.

CHAPTER 45

Ransom

Crossing the threshold into the cabin, Ridge waggled the gun at Gerrit and said, "This is for you, not him, all right?"

Tarrant reclined in his corner hammock mantled in plaid camp blankets. A foam bench cushion propped up his head. Purple bruises ringed his dilated eyes. The diminished whites caught the faint lamplight. "Mr. Dantley, Miss Kessler ..." Even rough and depleted, his voice retained its brute authority.

"You're gonna have to get close in," Gerrit said.

Mira minced forward to stand within an arm's length of Tarrant while Ridge held back. Ridge's eyes flitted between Tarrant and Gerrit. He thumbed the gun's hammer in a rhythmic fidget. What would happen once he revealed his scheme? Would he be forced to use the pistol? He couldn't picture himself as a murderer. But the need to decide was plain and imminent.

"Not used to this layin' down," Tarrant said. "I normally sleep like the monks of Tibet—upright against the wall. More aware of your surroundings and easier to wake that way. Took me a while to stop lolling to one side, though, and gettin' a stiff neck in the bargain."

"How is it—your migraine?" Mira asked. "Nanokwe told me he gave you something for it."

"Down to tolerable." He pointed at Ridge. The kerosene lamp made chancy shadows from his naked, raw-muscled arm. Red striations cut across his forearm and wrist. "These migraines are what set me on my course of adventurin' after knowledge. As a child, I thought these migraine auras were a kinda second sight affordin' a glimpse into another, higher dimension. That was my telltale—that mix a pain and distorted light. Got the migraine shakes so bad growin' up I took to hangin' a sweatsock on the back of a chair at the end of my bed. That way I knew if the sock wasn't shakin' it was only me."

Ridge couldn't stand waiting any longer for the inevitable confrontation. "If this is about the radio," he said, "I already explained to Gerrit. I heard one of my friends mentioned. I just wanted to make sure he was safe."

"The radio, the gun, Paige wanderin' off… you can understand why I'd be a mite dismayed?"

"We're just surviving the best way we can. Wouldn't you do the same if our positions were reversed?"

Tarrant's voice gained some of its former strength: "Let's dispense with the hypotheticals."

"Okay." Ridge couldn't seem to find the right pitch for Tarrant. His words sounded desperate and weak. He suspected it wouldn't matter either way in this case. Tarrant saw no substantive difference between the lie of our confused realities and personal betrayals. It was just a matter of scope. Every setback in his private pursuits fed his existential rage at the shrouding forces around him.

"First, the radio… What happened there?"

"I heard my friend's name over the mic." Ridge took a deep breath and began again. "Well, not his name but his title—he's a US senator. That's about the only word I could understand besides your name at the end. I busted the clasp from the door and tried to talk. Not much more to tell than that. The ship captain—if that's who it was—didn't speak much English. Said he'd try again. After the storm I suppose."

"Another undisclosed friend?"

"I thought he was lost and dying. Or already dead."

"Might be now for all we know. How 'bout we raise 'im?" Tarrant turned out of the hammock dressed only in a pair of baggy trousers. Dark-blooded traces of rope showed against his tanned chest. He closed his eyes to steady himself against a migraine tremor then cloaked a blanket around his shoulders.

Ridge followed Gerrit with the gun as the miner bumped open the door to the radio room for Tarrant. Gerrit ignored the weapon as if to say, *You could never surprise me.*

The transmitter buzzed to life. Tarrant took the only chair and shunted it close to the set. Ridge and Mira remained in the doorway. How far was he prepared to go to extend their youthful promise, if only for another moment? Their greeting card romance had depended on mutual good sense and wishful thinking. How much of their animal selves could they reveal and remain unchanged? What if he were to murder Tarrant now, unprovoked? Would she still love him? He couldn't begin to guess her thoughts.

"Lagi, Lagi," Tarrant said into the mic. "This is Uncle, repeat, *dispela stap* Uncle, over." He issued the call signs in pidgin English again.

The ensuing interval teemed with claustrophobia. Ridge resisted the urge to kick like a horse in its stall to rid himself of the feeling.

Then the answering sign broke the silence: "*Distela stap*, Lagi. *Yu long hap*, boss?"

Tarrant pitched into an extended dialogue in the ship captain's makeshift trade language, growing more and more disgruntled. Ridge struggled to grasp the gist of it. Their speech was soft and nasally and seemed to vibrate on the tip of the tongue. Tarrant broke off the conversation, muttering a curse, then thrust the mic at Ridge. "He's going to put your friend on for proof."

Ridge deliberated for a moment about what to do with the gun. Keep it in his free hand? Give it to Mira? He belted it to the small of his back and clutched the mic. Mira put a precautionary hand on his waist, eyeing Gerrit.

The voice that came through was a complete and wrenching shock: "Ridge? Is that you? Over."

Ridge's heart misgave. He looked doubtfully at Mira. Could he have possibly heard it wrong? "Aaron? Aaron, Christ, is that you? What happened? Are you all right? Over." The questions carried on in his head in a disorderly rush.

"Man, it's good to hear your voice. I thought I'd lost you. Over."

Ridge's voice spiked in excitement. "Copy that. We thought the same. Mira's here. And Paige, somewhere close ..." He flashed Mira an apologetic look. "Over."

"I'm sorry I worried you. I got off-course in the lop and swell and floated to shore after—I don't know—two days? I'll say my kindergarten swim teacher steered me wrong—making motorboat sounds didn't help at all."

They were momentarily boys again swapping stories. With his insouciant attitude, Aaron, the lovable bluffer, could've been describing how he recently got McCoshed (sent to Princeton's on-campus clinic for alcohol poisoning). Ridge said, "We thought they had the Senator, over."

"Did he get separated, too?"

The question reminded Ridge of how much was still outside his purview, unknown. "Long story on that, over."

"I said I worked for him. Must be the only word they got. You know this bossman they keep talking about?"

"Yeah, he's right—"

Tarrant closed his hand over Ridge's and relieved him of the mic. "Put the captain back on."

Ridge took Mira's hand, pulsing with relief. "It's unbelievable—Aaron alive." His breathing halted and raced and paused again.

Tarrant resumed his heated exchange over the radio.

Conscious of Gerrit's watchful presence, Mira gave Ridge a brisk shoulder hug. "*A shtik naches.*"

"Wilco damn ye." Tarrant slid the mic aside and turned to Gerrit with a pinched expression. "Naturally, Lagi wants payment for him along with the rest of the supplies. The drop is set for tomorrow, 11 in the A.M. You'll be leadin' the Marokatu in Foucher's absence."

"Yessir," Gerrit said.

"What's that?" Ridge asked. "Payment as in ransom?"

"That's right, Mr. Dantley." Tarrant locked on his eyes and spoke in a scowling murmur, "You wouldn't think it to look at you—all diffident and cautious—but I have to say: you're a singular source of trouble."

"How much?" Ridge felt his personality dwindle under Tarrant's scrutiny. "Whatever it is, I'll pay it. I can get the money to you somehow—wire it to some offshore account. We need him back." Christ almighty. When would the day come when he didn't have to negotiate away some awful consequence?

"And you'll get him, I assure you. But not for ransom, no."

Mira's face was patient in a flat, clinical way. Ridge asked Tarrant, "You won't put him in danger, will you?"

"Whatever do you mean?" Tarrant shot Gerrit a conspiratorial grin. "He's in the custody of pirates. We'll be doin' the rescuin'."

Ridge freed the gun in an effort to regain a sense of balance. He concentrated hard on not looking at Tarrant. That seemed to help. "He has to come back."

"We got that much."

"You're listening all right but I need to know you hear me." Ridge puffed himself up with nightmares: Mira stripped and bleeding, eyes wide; Aaron drowned in crucial inches of surf; Paige lost to the night. With an in-suck of breath, he said, "I have your manuscript—a good sheaf of it, anyway. I've hidden it where you'll never find it." He tried for a kind of knockabout bravado. "Never. Anything happens to me, my friends, including Aaron, it's gone."

Tarrant wet his lips in jeering amusement. "As in ransom? Seems a sharp good business these days." Then his demeanor turned serious and dark. He flexed his right hand until the veins popped along his tattooed forearm. "After this, I need more'n your word you'll act on good faith. How much of it have you hid away?"

"Almost everything to this point—well over 200 pages."

"Ten pages a day then," he pronounced, brooking no further argument. "To prove you can actually get them back. You'll read the rest here under my supervision. That's your bounden responsibility."

"Ten pages then."

"And the gun," Tarrant added. "Gerrit will need it for tomorrow's meet." His stillness checked a compacted anger.

"If I do this—"

Tarrant tensed under the blanket. "Just to be clear: the deal includes you, Miss Kessler, this friend on the supply ship and no more. I'm afraid that dotty redhead's beyond your help now."

"We tried to talk her out of it," Ridge gave out weakly.

Mira said, "She's grieving and troubled and acting out." Her eyes were shining wet. "You can't expect her to heal on your timeline."

"The gun?" Tarrant asked Ridge as if Mira hadn't spoken.

Ridge pendelumed between two futures: one meant opposing Tarrant in all things, constant vigilance and sleepless nights; the other an awkward truce but Tarrant's continued protection and more time for escape. Withhold the gun or turn it over? Mira regarded him expectantly. The dark wisps at the edges of her upper lip pulled taut in a grimace. For her, he told himself, and tendered the gun by the barrel.

Tarrant rose to accept it and in the same motion walloped Ridge in the chest. The pain came in one vitiating jolt, spangle white and overpowering. Ridge splayed on his backside. His expression, he knew, exposed him as nothing more than a boy.

"Ever touch that radio again," said Tarrant, "ever threaten me again, manuscript or no, I'll string you up one after the other. The order of the hangings ain't even a question."

Gerrit vented a harsh syllable of laughter. "C'mon, milktooth, ya didn't really expect this to go any other way did ya?"

Ridge swallowed the slurry of humbling and hate in his throat. Mira grasped him by the elbow to help him up and he brushed her off, unthinking, impatient to get out and past his own fogged vision. The cabin was like an irradiated disaster site. Leaving his crutch, Ridge banged through the door and down the ramp, face burning. His story was unfolding pell-mell. Mira followed a few paces behind. Ridge wished again for the foresight to know at any given moment which decision was right and which wrong. Had his gambit earned Tarrant's grudging respect and the chance to live? Or only hastened their ruin?

The hut built for Mira and Paige remained standing but veered off its footings. *She has to know all this anger comes from nerves—from worry about her.* Ridge's stride went from swervy to smart, decisive. The gravity-fed shower stalls were gone, the hardware buried somewhere in the clouds. Sporadic fires and the glow of cigarettes deepened the convergent night. The statue of Kagoroa edged the horizon, promising inhuman vistas to come.

Unready to turn around and apologize, Ridge said in a cracked whisper to the sky, "We need to find Nanokwe. It's time he decide: us or them."

CHAPTER 46

A Private Wilderness

Wielding a Marokatu war club, Foucher thrashed the lower branches of a wild hibiscus tree, scattering leaves and storm-brittled limbs. The slumbering opossum or *cuscus* lodged in the boughs roiled its spine without waking. Foucher snarled and bawled and leapt and whacked the tree repeatedly. He could be playful at moments like this, losing himself in predatory ritual. The ruckus gradually worked a bother into the dirty-brown creature. The *cuscus* blinked out of its torpor. More antic drubbing started the opossum from its hide toward the tree's thin extremities. The *cuscus* coiled its tail around its unsteady perch. The limb bent toward the foliage of the adjacent tree. To finish the animal was only a matter of timing. Foucher jumped for a two-handed *coup de grace* but was a little too early.

The *cuscus* flipped its bulk to the adjoining tree and proceeded to scrabble and tail-spring to the ground. Exactly where Foucher wanted it. The creature waddled through the mud and duff on stubby legs. Foucher strafed it at a run, clobbering it on the hindparts. He was in sync with the blood and misrule of this earth. Crippled, the *cuscus* twisted around and let out a guttural screech. Foucher howled then brained the animal to the limit of his wiry strength. *Thwack, thwack.* Blood gushed from the opossum's snub nose and toothy rictus of a mouth. *Thwack.* An eye convulsed into a viscous red blotch. *Thwack, thwack, thwack.* The beating persisted until the creature's rasping ire died in the back of its throat.

Foucher toed the *cuscus* onto its back. Though its muddied belly was still and breathless, its foreclaws grabbled the air in residual defense. To be human is to be shunned by every animal, even the lame and dying. Foucher exchanged the war club for a tent peg, sagged to his knees and punched the metal stake through the creature's kidney. The spew of warm blood was a consecration. The body curled inward reflexively then relaxed into a sodden weight. Foucher withdrew the tent peg and wiped his hands on his chinos. It would be tough going to skin and dress the animal using sharpened tent pegs. He held the *cuscus* by the tail to drain the wound before rolling it up into a plastic tent cover. Blood fouled the forest floor in painterly drizzles.

The cyclone had forced him inland and away from his favored cove where archer fish loitered among the mangroves. He'd return to the beachfront refuge tomorrow, a blue emptiness in one direction, a green emptiness in the other. The storm water should have fully drained back into the sea by then. Primitive living had exerted a calming effect on his psyche, lessening the fervor of his violent compunctions. He now thought himself an avatar of eerie, prehistoric nature, translating its ancient rhythms into human action. His growing sense of balance gave credence to Tarrant's opinion that Foucher's superiors in the Society of the Black Sun had misread him as a mere sociopath.

According to Tarrant, Foucher wasn't a mental deviant so much as a man "born for the worst the wilderness could offer." Evolution must have selected Foucher's outsized instincts for a reason, Tarrant argued, else they would have been long bred out of humanity. Ergo: there must be a place, either already in existence or in the world to come, where those instincts would confer some advantage. It was fortuitous that the Apocalypse, *Frasokereti, Ragnarok, al-Qlyamah*, what have you, had become an increasingly mainstream goal. Foucher would no doubt flourish in a world scabbed over in scarlet-tracked badlands. *And the earth will be despoiled unto an unshadowed desert and become as home to the Celestial Pantheon and their terrible servants*, affirms the psalm book.

The Society of the Black Sun had mobilized toward this end, vying with rival cults and a resurgent Integrand General for the means; yet Tarrant, working from limited knowledge and hopelessly underfunded, appeared closest to achieving it. That's what pained Foucher the most about his exile: not disappointing his mentor and friend, not his gross lack of discipline, but missing the moment of Tarrant's transcendence. Despite lacking any talent for dreamtime magick himself, Foucher's years in the Society had prepared him to recognize it. He ranked Tarrant the first among the dreamtime adepts he'd known, though to be sure, helped more by *kava* and a generous intuition than the rum intellect the adventurer prized so much. Tarrant's mastery of the dreamtime came across in the astral journeys he recounted and in his stern and sometimes unwonted wisdom. If anyone was prepared to rise above the taint of humanity it was him. Foucher pictured Tarrant in his transcendent state as a colossus not unlike the statue of Kagoroa: abstracted from the earth, bereft of the mind's protections, completely open to the cosmos and its emanations.

The blood draining from the opossum began to crust along the lip of its pouch. Foucher secured the carcass inside the rolled-up tent cover with a length of twine and headed back to his inland camp. His shirt collar was damp with sweat and chill against his neck. Shadows were lengthening apace. Night fell sooner in the forest than on the beach. Already, faint stars were visible in the gaps between the trees. Foucher knew their distance obscured a universal chaos. Like everything else, how long the stars survived and why was a matter of banal chance.

CHAPTER 47

The Spirit House

When the morning's disputations over the manuscript began to test Tarrant's patience, Ridge pulled back from arguing further and, to regain a measure of comity, agreed to join him in the spirit house. Mira had stayed in bed this morning, exhausted and nauseous. Her depleted state compounded Ridge's anxieties and made him question his worth again. What good would he be if he failed to bring her home safely? How could he ever face his family and friends again? Her mother? No matter the somewhat antique honor at stake, he'd never forgive himself.

He coped by projecting himself into the future, safe and at ease in the apartment he shared with Mira, the present dangers no more than grist for celebrity. Who knows? he asked himself. This trip to the spirit house alone could make for a breathless Tom Wolfe-style diary piece or screwball interview in *Rolling Stone*. Regardless, he needed the distraction to take his mind off Aaron and the precarious deal he'd struck with Nanokwe. His luxury wristwatch, guaranteed to be precise over the next 1,000 years, showed 11:52 A.M. Aaron's fate had been decided—and Ridge's along with it. Word of that decision couldn't arrive soon enough.

Using his crutch for leverage, Ridge gimped up the timber stairs to the spirit house while Tarrant charged ahead. The noises of reconstruction sounded at his back. All but the largest ponds of standing water had evaporated in the oppressive heat. The Marokatu approached the rebuilding with affectless industry. Scarcely a word passed between them as they swept their ancestral graves clear of debris, gathered and assembled bamboo, spread thatch, hauled rocks for their cooking fires and attended to spoiled gardens. Their animals had been returned from the foothills en masse, the pigs funneled into a makeshift sty and the chickens corralled onto a patch of dryness seeded with pigeon peas and monitored by several children, who, of course, made a game of penning them in. Most of the miners had gone back to laboring on the hillside or on the banks of the stream, though a few were busy raising the mess tent. Beattie's shouted directives, intermixed with insults of Bolshie and Sook, rose above the general tumult.

The portico framed by the statue of Kagoroa gave way to a thatch-covered foyer notable for its decorative painted columns and the array of masks depending from the exposed joists. The clamor from outside diminished to a hush. Waiting at the threshold to the sanctuary, Tarrant said, "You've heard of *kava-kava*?" His tone suggested a statement more than a question. He'd evidently recovered from the cyclone and his follow-on migraine with no lasting effects. His manner was as brusque and presumptuous as ever.

"A few of them have mentioned it—Nanokwe, Tree. Some kind of psychedelic, right?"

"Not to any great extent, no. Standard issue *kava* has mainly narcotic effects. Puts you into a pleasant dreamstate but without the euphoric feeling of most opiates." Tarrant held up a shaving kit bag. "This—the Marokatu variety—however, is something different. I'm convinced the *kava* root here, in fact, the whole of the island's mycoflora, is tinged with Parmatmar crystals. It allows for a deeper, more intense experience of reality. Much closer to the higher order strangeness induced by the famed Black Lotus." He said this last in a whisper and stepped into the sanctuary.

The room was about fifty feet in length and stately in its bareness: a plain, shadowed chamber lit by small votive candles at fixed points around the perimeter. Plaited mats checkered the plank flooring. Ridge could hardly breathe the fusty air. "Is this really necessary? I'm not a smoker—not even cigarettes. Some of my college buddies were into clove cigarettes but I've never seen the appeal of filling my lungs with hot gas."

"You could drink it or place it under your tongue, but smoking's the Goldilocks optimum for novices." Tarrant hung the wax canvas bag from a nail and began prepping a glass pipe. "I know you're a fervid materialist. But indulge me here. After this—after feeling the truth of my philosophy—I'm confident you won't be so dismissive of its fabulist turns." From a repurposed bottle of wood glue, he squeezed a viscous brown paste into the bowl of the pipe then fitted a screen to it. "Every line of my manuscript could be underscored: *I have lived it.*"

"And just what am I supposed to experience?"

"The overpower—at least a low-energy aspect of it. The *kava* only ensures a receptive state of mind. The true stimulus, well, I don't know for certain. Something from the far outside—a frequency of thought, both signal and signifier ..." Tarrant extended the pipe to Ridge, who, afraid he might drop it, took the pipe into his palm rather than pinching it by the stem. "My best clue to the source comes from an old Irish story from the mid-19th century. An itinerant doctor—a specialist in sight and hearing—stumbled upon this coastal village where he detected weird phenomena presumably caused by the crashing waves. Of a scientific bent, he thought the nearby cay produced what's called infrasound—a sound what operates below the level of conscious hearing—and that this sound was prompting daylight hallucinations and disturbing dreams alike." He removed a clamshell case from his bag the size of a woman's compact and unscrewed the lid. "But the villagers clearly took it all serious, even blinding hapless babes ever so often to increase their sensitivity to these signals and raise them up as spiritual go-betweens. They fashioned their own provincial religion— a dark paganism not unlike that of the Marokatu here: worshipped a seaborne god, considered their ancestors living confidants, pined for an afterlife underwater ..."

Ridge grasped the pipe and held it close to his mouth. "We sit on the mats?"

"Spread out as you'd like." Tarrant passed him a lighter. "When you're ready, just light the bowl."

"All right." Ridge sat crosslegged on the nearest mat. The *kava* goo was opaque in the dim candlelight. He placed the pipe in his mouth and readied the lighter. Though it wasn't his idea, the prospect of getting high while Mira was sick struck him as insensitive at best and hazardous at worst. The *kava* would likely just put him to sleep. His nerves had been agitating him since the yacht accident. He'd slept only in restless bursts of one or two hours. One dose of this narcotic and he'd surely go under.

Tarrant eyed him with growing impatience. The implicit challenge quashed the last of Ridge's scruples. Besides, he reasoned, simple bad luck might end things at any moment: food poisoning, infection, malarial fever, a mistaken word or misperception ... When that happened, this decision will have meant exactly nothing. Ridge thumbed the lighter—*ffft*—*ffft*—*ffft*—until it caught and ran the flame under the pipe.

"Gotta warn you: the smoke's none too pleasant." Tarrant situated himself on the adjacent mat. "Reminiscent a burnt rubber. And it's gonna taste a mite harsh at first, but after a couple a tokes, your mouth'll numb and it won't hardly taste no more."

Ridge pursed his lips but stopped short of taking a drag. The first whiff of vaporized *kava* stung his nostrils.

"Just a easy pull, that's it," Tarrant coaxed.

In a fit of paranoia, Ridge considered the possibility that Nanokwe had informed on him and even now, as Tarrant urged him on, the Marokatu were erecting the gallows from which Mira would hang. He gave the pipe a slow pull. His lungs seized and he coughed acrid smoke. "Christ, it's awful." The taste was like bitter tree bark.

"Remember what I said about the numbness."

"Yeah, not fast enough."

"Another drag or two is all. The high will come on then."

Ridge applied his lips to the heat again, if nothing else, to jolt time forward. His tongue seemed thicker already. He eased the smoke down his throat then to the tips of his lungs and breathed an endless, cooling breath. The textured shadows above began to oscillate and cross. "How long's it last?"

"Steady on and it should do you a good couple of hours. You'll learn time is a highly subjective thing in a heightened state of awareness." Tarrant swiped a fingerful of *kava* goo from the case and rubbed it across his gums, upper then lower. "Don't worry, though. As a novice, the time dilation effects will be relatively minor. You won't find yourself among centuries-dead ancestors or shot into the deep future. It'll likely play out like an extended dream—your natural thoughts twisted up and transmuted. By what, again, I don't rightly know ... some sympathetic force. Just resist the urge to close yourself off like you do. This ain't no moment for journalistic detachment. Gotta open up to the possibilities you have any chance to sense the overpower. Manifests as a light—that background light I told you of—the kind makes up this plane of existence. Only here in this dimension is light and matter separate."

The *kava* deadened the inside of Ridge's mouth. Each successive toke from the pipe registered on his tongue like a dot of cayenne. "My tongue…" The words came out thick and barely intelligible to his own ears.

"The Marokatu—they believe the source of their visions is a dead sun under the sea—the one what lights their watery heaven."

"There is a yellowy cast to things…" Given his distended tongue, Ridge wasn't sure if he could be understood anymore. The competing candle-shadows suddenly demanded his attention. The sway and spin of the earth accelerated. He felt a light sweat on his face and his thoughts raced ahead of his perceptions, clear in themselves but too swift for him to assimilate.

"That's the start afore your head joins the sky and becomes its own sun." Tarrant's voice buzzed in Ridge's ears as if it came from inside his own head. "Kava will help separate your ethereal or astral self from your body so you can experience the backdrop light hidden around us. That's the simple reason for my constant self-seeking: to see and master this invisible energy."

"The overpower," Ridge said as if encountering the term for the first time. The dimensions of the room vanished, the distance between him and the walls deepened. He set the pipe aside and stretched out on the mat. The shadows undulating on the conical ceiling assumed vaguely recognizable shapes. The pain that usually materialized in the small of his back when he attempted to lay flat was of no concern. He'd been anesthetized. He could sense the structure of his shipwreck story forming around him.

"If you start to lose yourself in the visions, just remember: you are a man, alive." This time Tarrant's voice boomed across a great distance. "That's what the Marokatu mean by the word. To them, a man is someone among the living, not a ghost. They got no false distinctions between men and beasts, only warm flesh and the spirit. That's 'cause they know the dangers a the dreamtime, the astral realm—somethin' they both aspire to and got a deathly fear of…"

The shapes came at Ridge from everywhere in languid rolling motions like a dream-sea of shadow, waves spilling from the sky, the earth its basin and him at the bottom, witness to some new aspect of Creation, deluged yet somehow entirely at peace.

CHAPTER 48
The Drop

The pandemonium on deck bore down on Aaron like a whirlwind, now distant, now close, now distant again. A crash of bodies might be followed by a shout or whanging gun-clap. Each new noise prompted him to shift the disposition of forces in his head. He closed his eyes under the blackout hood and breathed his own sour panic. There was a sudden crescendo of gunfire from starboard. He started from the driver's seat in the forklift as much as his trussed hands and feet would allow. The zip ties binding his wrists to the steering wheel scored his flesh purple. His heartbeat pounded low in his throat. Down in the cargo hold there was no way to tell which side was gaining ground or how much time remained for him. He alternately dreaded and anticipated the clang of the pallet elevator settling on this level. Assuming Ridge wasn't part of the negotiating party, he wasn't even sure which side he wanted to win. Both appeared about as likely to kill him as let him go.

He owed his survival to unearned luck and no more. By the time the sea had swept him toward the pirates' hidden port, he was parched and exhausted. The atoll had first appeared as a thin slip of sand and palms. Flutter-kicking closer, Aaron grasped it more completely as a larger, crescent-shaped mass comprised of strung together coral islets or *motu*. He plied a narrow gap in the reef to discover a hidden lagoon. The encircling *motu* allowed him a merciful respite from the swells of the open ocean. He clung to the ring buoy and kicked only as necessary to stay on course. The small general cargo ship appeared as a mirage-like find. Anchored on the lee side of a palm-covered islet, the ship's bridge and deck crane made for an unreal dazzle of sun. Gusting trade winds helped push him in the right direction.

The aboriginal pirates were friendly and gave him a canned lager, pointing and poking fun at his clumsy guzzling. The laughter didn't last long. As soon as Aaron explained his circumstances, they grew quiet, which made him figure they'd been alerted to the incident or had their own protocols for handling castaways. They used zip ties to secure him and forced a hood over his head. They made him sleep in the forklift slumped over the wheel. His lower back was killing him and the lack of circulation rendered his legs a tingly misery.

What sustained him was thoughts of his childhood home in Fernandina, Florida, of his parents and sick younger brother, Henry. He thought about old pleasures like surf fishing for "whities" and golfing at Ponte Vedra Beach and sitting knee-to-knee with some girl he just met. His ambitions were modest and wholly conventional. He was more of a feeler than a thinker. Marrying a fun gal, being a good husband and father, making decent money, giving back as he was able and, in the end, leaving behind a small history would be enough. Provided, of course, he was granted the time. The possibility that everything might end, here, in moments, stuck in his heart like a sharp bone.

At the sound of the pallet elevator starting down, Aaron was afraid all over again. The deck seemed preternaturally quiet. Had he missed something? He strained to catch the slightest noise above the elevator grind. The service door clanged open. Footsteps. Three, maybe four people. They came to a halt around the forklift. The lull was menacing. Aaron's eyes watered from the effort to control his breathing. Was this the decisive pause before…? He thought it better to die without prelude; then dying would only be a further muffling under the hood, a deeper blankness. "Who?" The question was a hitch in his throat. He jerked from his seat.

"Too late to matter, kid." It was a tired southern drawl.

Aaron tensed. *Fuck the odds of this—murdered here by a fellow southerner…* "Wait, wait—" Then a succession of noises: a bonecrack; an echoey clatter; a foot scuffle; another bonecrack and another, an unforgiving barrage; a downed body; and still more beatings; a few throaty sounds; a heartpounding stillness. A set of hands on his head ripped off the hood and he saw a Marokatu crowned with a monkey tail. The dingy fluorescents in the cargo hold hurt Aaron's eyes. Everything was ringed with an unnatural brightness. His face was hot and sweaty and he was almost panting. The man Aaron presumed to be the southerner lay on the floor, head battered purplish, gawping mouth pulped. His gun was on the floor several feet out of reach. Aaron rolled a shoulder toward his cheek in a wasted effort to dry his tears. *God, the blood, the smashed-in teeth…* He wondered what was happening inside the body, if the man's heart was pumping its last, circulating blood and oxygen to no purpose.

The Marokatu dropped the hood and took up a skinning knife from the dead man's belt to cut Aaron's hands loose from the steering wheel. "Thank you." Aaron's chest heaved in relief. He wiped his cheeks dry with the heel of his hand. "Thank you," he repeated more forcefully. He extended his legs so the native could free his feet. Then he clambered down, shaking in wondrous disbelief. He could see three more natives now bearing bloodied war clubs and throwing spears. The halos around them began to dissipate and he had a sense of time resuming its normal flow. "Are you—is Ridge with you?"

The man distinguished by a monkey tail around his head offered a tightly rolled-up bit of notebook paper. "You mah *pleni*," he said.

Aaron bowed slightly to acknowledge the statement (whatever it meant) and accepted the paper. He recognized Ridge's small and precise script in an instant. Among other things, the message instructed him to pilot the supply ship to Honiara and alert the Royal Solomon Islands Police Force to Ridge's whereabouts. A crude drawing identified the spot, along with the atoll where the Senator had been abandoned. Aaron suffered a pang of guilt for the comparative ease of his captivity. Ridge crippled, Paige raped, "every day a fresh hell" … Here was a chance for him to help and more, to make amends for the shipwreck, the life raft, his worrying disappearance. His history with Ridge was a history of unpaid debts.

Uncertain of how much the aborigines knew about the message, Aaron nodded to the group and motioned for them to follow. He was anxious to get to the bridge, weigh anchor, cool his face in the breeze. He'd already let too many things just happen to him. He retrieved the dropped handgun and got into the elevator. The natives formed around him. Above was the whole of the Pacific, Honiara, more islands and vaster lands beyond. I can do this, he told himself. Home was somewhere on the horizon, at once faraway and close.

CHAPTER 49

The Outcast

Paige zigzagged the coast at a steady clip, keeping to the patchy edge of the tree line. The open beach presented unnecessary risks and no easy escape routes. She'd be compelled to either hazard the ocean or shoot through her pursuers. Under other circumstances she would've enjoyed the forest's summery isolation, even at the risk of getting lost. The ancient terrain and trace of brine in the air invited a primitive clarity. As it was, the pressure building in her chest stoppered up her thinking. There was only the next inlet or bay, surveilling, moving, anticipating. Who knew how much time remained? She had to find the supply ship before it departed or Tarrant's Marokatu agents invariably tracked her down. Perhaps it was already too late. Perhaps she'd been marked for a rotten end regardless of what she did. In her worst moments, she wondered if some immutable darkness had settled in her bones.

She followed the sun's arc through the trees with increasing despair. After three or four crooked miles she had yet to come across a likely harbor, much less the supply ship. The tree line dipped from a mild slope to a finger of beach. She cut a path through the ferny undergrowth by swinging her weighted pillow case. The air was sluggish amid the riot of plant life. The humidity soaked her hair and clothes. She negotiated the woodslope with her shoulders braced, ready to freeze or turn at the first hint of intrusion. Sweat greased her face and arms and the small of her back bristled with it.

The trees maintained their density right up until the shoreline. The tang of salt was sharp in Paige's nose when she got her first unobstructed view of the white sand. She hunkered down and ventured into the shade of the outermost palm, thinking she might cool herself in the ocean before resuming her search.

Peering over a rock slab at the base of the palm, she could make out the full stretch of beach. It extended for about three hundred yards and culminated in a gently curved inlet. A swatch of mangrove trees bordered the cove. Absorbed by all the emptiness, she didn't notice the man emerging from the surf until he was almost entirely out of the water. Her throat constricted at the sight. She eased onto her stomach and rested her head in her hands. It was him—the man, the man-monster, Foucher—clothed only in a pair of gray boxers. His body was as lank as a hungry dog's. His shoulder blades jutted out on either side of his ponytail. He joined his shadow on the shore and grabbed up a towel, oblivious and damnably free.

Paige's anger overwhelmed her caution. She rummaged in the pillow case for the handgun. The weight of it alone was some relief. She extended the weapon, bracing it against the rock, and tried sighting down the barrel, closing one eye then the other. She settled on the left but wasn't sure whether to focus on the front sight, the rear sight or the target. Foucher came in and out of focus. Her equilibrium faltered. Over the years she'd struggled to define herself and let choice overwhelm her and now, circumstances beyond her control had made a victim of her. Would killing her attacker restore her sense of agency? Or just fracture her into another haunted self? *This—revenge, murder, call it what you will—would follow me everywhere: Brookline, DC, Acapulco, Paris, the most remote getaway*... She raised her eyes to the wisps of cloud dissipating over the sea.

The toe of her boot brushed something unexpected. The sand at her feet quickened into motion. There was a crazed lashing out and a pronged sting high on her calf. She bit her tongue to keep from crying out: snake, snake, *snake*. Her pant snagged on the creature's fangs as it disengaged. She twisted in panic, desperate to note its markings. The snake slithered between an extrusion of rock and vanished in the brush. Beige with white bands. She was afraid to exhale for fear of bawling. *Holy fuck, it hurts.* She lowered her face into the sand, allowed the pain to eke out her throat then gulped for air.

The wound was like a penetrating scald. She imagined the misery racing up her body, blackening her skin, reducing her to picked-clean bones. How would she know if she'd been poisoned? Would the area around the bite turn blue? Would her joints seize up? And what's more, how soon would the venom take effect?

Foucher was a distant blur through her silent tears. He shifted his weight to put on a pair of baggy trousers. She huddled behind the rock, mumbling in grief and anger.

The pistol was still in her hand. It was no longer a comforting weight; now, it was like a sounding lead that threatened to drag her under. She felt herself sinking in time—her parents, her sister and friends, her job, everything she'd known, left farther and farther behind. The prayer Mira taught her came back as a last-gasp mantra: *"Baruch atah adonai...Baruch atah adonai..."*

CHAPTER 50

At Sunset

Ridge woke from a long dream that defied recall. His chest vibrated with the sensation of a straight-down drop into the moment. The sanctuary was darker now or the votive candles dimmer. Tarrant and his paraphernalia were gone. Ridge sat up, putting a hand to the base of his neck to bolster his unsteady head. Sweat pooled in the crack of his ass. He felt nauseous, out of balance. How long…? The room's everyday dimensions ran from stunted and plain to cracked Cubist distraction. He ran his tongue across gums tacky from *kava* and delirious sleep. A slight numbness persisted.

He hung his head and focused on breathing, holding in the air then letting it out slowly, down, down. With each conscious breath, the feeling in his body returned to a semblance of normal. The room levelled out, assumed solidity. He swallowed the vile mud drip in the back of his throat and got to his feet. *Water then Mira, make sure she's all right, and Aaron, too…* His thoughts resounded like screechy loudspeaker announcements so he tried to keep them short.

When he reached the terrace, he was stupefied by the soft, warm streak of low sun visible under the arched legs of Kagoroa. The reddish-gold light transformed the revived village into a gauzy pastoral. Ridge felt himself on the brink between his lost history and the present working itself out. The scene reminded him of the rustic lands he'd imagined as a boy gazing out from the third-floor balcony over his family's manicured acreage—faraway lands where he could be wholly himself, unknown, even unnamed, and not his father's son.

Then the focal point of his vision shifted and the statue came to the fore as a kind of frame, smoldering at the edges. The position of the large stumpy legs relative to the terrace suggested a pyramid of forms, one god perched atop another, the deities above and below hidden only by Ridge's limited vantage point. A few flickering impressions from his *kava*-induced slumber came back to him: a surge of underwater shadows, a chasm, the bottom dropping out, a debilitating insignificance. This feeling of cosmic smallness goaded him on. He spit off the side of the terrace then thrust his crutch onto the first warped stair. Forget the water, he thought, and took the rest of the steps at a charge.

CHAPTER 51

Milkhemet Mitzvah

The insistent knocking started Mira out of a light, anxious sleep.

"Mira?" Ridge barged into the slab hut before she could answer. He looked sicker than she felt. Sweat stained his T-shirt in dark whorls. His color reminded her of a Yukon potato going green in the kitchen window.

Ridge's appearance made her self-conscious about her own. She'd never enjoyed the process of beautifying herself, preferring to spend time on substantive pursuits, but she had some base requirements to feel comfortable in her own skin. Her long fine hair needed a thickening shampoo, her ivory skin needed moisturizing cream to minimize redness and acne, and her curvy shape demanded shift skirts or longer line tops that fell over her hips. God forbid she should catch herself in a mirror here. "I went looking for you a couple of hours ago." She arranged the Indian blanket at the end of the cot to cover her bare feet, careful not to overturn a bundle of newly-washed clothes. The heat had swollen her thick ankles.

"Sorry." Ridge plopped on the adjacent cot side on, letting his crutch clatter to the floor. His face was slack and the blue of his eyes dull in the lamplight. "I was in the spirit house with Tarrant. What's happened? Did you hear from Nanokwe?"

The shaman had been so eager to deliver the good news from the Marokatu warriors she'd had to ask him to slow down—twice—before she could make out what he was saying. "Aaron's fine, *a shtik naches*, safe and on his way to Honiara." She straightened her back against the wall in order to talk more comfortably.

Ridge ran a hand across his forehead and breathed out in relief. "And Gerrit?" he asked without looking up.

"His body was thrown overboard." She abjured from the details—the gang beating, the skull broken and bleeding out. There was no getting around it: she'd crossed a red line. She'd joined Ridge in asking

Nanokwe to arrange Gerrit's killing. She was a murderess. A week ago, the idea would've been absurd, impossible.

Ridge sought her eyes. "There was no other way."

"I know." Mira managed the flat and logical tone she'd rehearsed. Jewish law considers killing a sin—an offense before God. Even soldiers are expected to bring a sin offering to the temple. But she rationalized Gerrit's murder as part of a *milkhemet mitzvah* or obligatory war. She hadn't brought the surrounding atmosphere of violence down on herself. What was done to Gerrit was done in self-defense. It was as justifiable as the bloody climax to the Biblical Megillat Esther. She finger-combed a limp strand of hair away from her ear.

"So it worked then." His smile was uneven, verging on grim. But the sure set of his jaw indicated he was pleased with himself. He'd outsmarted Tarrant on at least one critical turn and rescued a childhood friend in the bargain. He expected to have the last word. If everything continued to plan, he'd return home the man of the hour. Mira knew she should acknowledge his part—his perceptiveness in figuring Nanokwe's stresses, his insights into the Marokatu power structure, his negotiating skills. The deal Ridge made would presumably save her life. She couldn't help thinking, however, that it was, at core, a cheat. It bolstered his naïve belief that ideas were tantamount to action. Like his use of the democratic goddess Columbia against Tarrant's Man-God, the deal was a means to make war by proxy instead of braving the enemy straight-on. She affected a trifling 'thank you' smile. Anything more struck her as unseemly—a case of exulting over an unsuspecting victim.

"We probably have three-four days before somebody shows up." Ridge put his face to the coolness of the empty cot.

She thought he might lapse into a sulk because she hadn't clutched him to her bosom in gratitude, lips against his temple. He might pretend otherwise, but deep down, she knew, he wanted the approval he never got at home except from servants and suck-ups. He wanted to hear that special musical lift in her voice.

"Feeling any better?" he asked, trying politeness to coax her admiration.

Mira dismissed the question with a wave of her hand. "I think it was just a bad combination of things going back to the cyclone: tiredness, the heat, Paige, a lack of appetite, my period…" She mentioned Paige as a not-so-subtle reminder. Her part in the plan was still undecided and Ridge seemed determined to forget it. "I'm fine, really. I've slept it off for the most part."

Ridge reached across the gap between the cots to put a hand on her Botticelli thigh. She gave his hand a tender squeeze. They remained like that in silence for a few moments. Then huzzahs and braying congratulations sounded from the hillside. There could be no lingering in hope or pride.

"I saw the crowd on the way here," Ridge said.

"They've made a big discovery. Nanokwe told me."

"Gold?"

"What else would it be?"

"Some kind of rare crystal." Ridge sat up and rubbed his bristly cheeks. The corners of his narrowed eyes showed red. "Tarrant's more interested in that than any gold."

"Why is that?"

"I can't say for sure. But it has something to do with this overpower energy." He'd described the concept to her earlier, tagging it "mulched Nietzche." Mira, on the other hand, regarded it as a Kabbalistic idea worth deliberating. "The crystal is supposed to magnify it—like a piece of glass held to the sun."

"To do what?"

"Don't ask me. I don't even know what's possible."

Mira struggled with a rising quarrel of dread and outright fear. She fully expected to be punished for Gerrit's murder, whether or not Tarrant discovered her role in it. Divine Providence would exact expiation. "We should leave now."

"But help won't be here for days."

"We can survive until then on the beach somewhere. It will give us time to find Paige. The Marokatu won't look for us now. Or they'll just pretend to. Wouldn't that fall under our deal with Nanokwe?" The shaman had agreed to help them as part of a larger effort to drive Tarrant and his crew from the island. The tribe was apparently split in its attitude toward Tarrant. For some time, Nanokwe had been looking for a way to reclaim the tribe's autonomy without risking a permanent divide. Ridge's plan to turn on Gerrit and draw the authorities promised to accomplish just that.

"Sure." Ridge leaned closer, careful not to upset the cot. "But what if Tarrant catches on, sends some of the miners? Or comes after us himself? I think it's safer to stay for now."

"What were you doing in the spirit house?"

He colored up and his eyes flicked around the room, anywhere but in contact with hers. "Tarrant asked me to try *kava-kava*. Said it would prove out his book of fables."

"You did drugs? *Oych a bashefenish.*" She'd spent most of the day in a cocoon of nervous exhaustion waiting for Nanokwe. His confirmation of their plan's success and her status as a killer had offered small comfort. After he'd gone she'd speculated about what it might be like on returning home, what casual traumas awaited her, how a local TV news story or even a stagey soap opera death might induce some heightened anxiety. She could never break down in front of Ridge because of Gerrit's murder. The deal was the best he—or anyone—could've done. How would he feel if she resented him for it? Not so much for the killing itself but how it was achieved—impersonally, at a distance. And all that time, Ridge was high, baffled from the pain of knowing.

"I was at a loss at what to do." His voice was thin and unconvincing. "We were arguing about his treatise and I thought he'd begun to suspect something in my resistance. I had to placate him somehow."

"That explains the look."

"What?"

"The color of your skin, the glazed-over eyes…"

Ridge limped to the door, shamefaced. "I'm—I'm sorry. I didn't think the effects would last so long. I fell asleep."

"And that's all?"

He leaned against the door jamb. "There were some hallucinations—mild ones, waves of onrushing shadows. I can barely remember them. More than anything, it left me with the hint of a presence, maybe even more than one. Which, I suppose, was the purpose."

"A presence?" The mention of anything remotely spiritual surprised her. Ridge always saw things in terms of sensory facts, organization, *systems*, ignoring the possibilities of the spirit. "In the Martin Buber sense? 'The one thing that matters is the full acceptance of presence.'"

"I guess. Something outside of normal experience anyway. But I could just as easily have been projecting. Tarrant led me to expect it."

That's more like it—reducing the spiritual to the psychological. She smiled at the way he walked back his initial, unexamined feelings. "And here I've just been praying and waiting for my personal angel to show … Maybe she's waiting for me to crack. Maybe I need to suffer like Sarah from the Hebrew Bible, clear-sighted throughout until I die of shock and sorrow." Praying was a source of private satisfaction to Mira even when it didn't produce any obvious results. It offered a continuous, felt connection to her parents and grandparents and the generations before them. She felt sorry for Ridge in this respect. Without a steady faith, he lacked a larger kinship to the world and its history except as ideas and political fodder. He couldn't pray with emotion but only observe the words and perhaps, admire them for their epochal poetry. She considered every prayer a burst of emotion that wafted around the globe on divine winds. Someday, she thought, one of those self-identifying bursts would rouse her personal angel. Nothing so gauche as a figure outfitted in a halo and wings but a quality of light radiant with serenity.

"The taste of it, the smoke was horrible," Ridge said. "Plus, it left me with a godawful headache."

"What about we leave tomorrow then?" She felt implicated by recent events, not just what happened on the supply ship, but the storm, the natives' dour mood, the escalating greed-fever among the miners, Ridge's motile shadows.

"Why be rash about it?" Ridge mustered up a more forthright set to his shoulders. It was clear he wanted to end the conversation. He was simply at a loss for how to do it. "Don't you think it will raise suspicion? Besides, we told Nanokwe we'd see this through. He might think we're running out on him, putting him in danger."

Mira sighed into her chest. "Even here it's politics and lies."

"That was the basis for Plato's supposed utopia—the noble lie—the notion that there was a natural hierarchy of men, from gold on down to iron and brass."

"So what do we do about Paige?" Mira couldn't help thinking that any lingering trauma that might surface for her in Georgia would be a breeze-like annoyance to Paige. For all Ridge's liberal sympathies, she doubted he could understand—emotionally, viscerally—the confounding horror Paige had suffered. Home would be a crash site visible to Paige alone, the pieces of her life just vaguely-recognizable debris. Mira felt obliged to represent her *in absentia*, to account, in part, for the intractable sense of having failed her. "Is she just another footnote to Plato, along with western philosophy?"

Ridge shied from the door, downcast and irritated at the thought of having to make yet another hard choice.

There was a glum undercurrent to the ensuing silence. Mira fixed on the bundle of men's clothes at her feet. The handgun Gerrit had carried on the supply ship was hidden in the folds of an extra-large sweatshirt. Nanokwe had delivered it in the event their plan went awry. Her willingness to make a dramatic gesture with the weapon—for Paige or otherwise—belied her shyness and ambient guilt. She imagined herself now as someone capable of taking high risks, even committing violence, to preserve her dignity as a woman and a Jew. She imagined doing this in the open, humbly, with a shrugging grace, letting her actions speak for themselves. As her people did against the seven nations that divided Israel at the time of Joshua, against the Amalek and the mad Caligula and in countless wars of self-defense. As she was convinced her father would've done against his Nazis oppressors had he been more than a castoff starveling.

CHAPTER 52

In Irons

Paige rippled up the beach like a caterpillar, dragging the gun in one hand and her pillowcase of supplies in the other. The snake-bitten leg was stiff and sore and God knows how livid with poison. She hadn't been in a position to examine it for several hours. A moonless, dead-black night had claimed the island, flattening the world, and she'd judged the flashlight a bad risk. In the one-dimensional darkness on the beach, the merest dartle would've given her away. Whenever she tried to picture the wound, she recalled the bloodied underside of her old bob-tailed cat, its liver torn free in a single taloned arc by some raccoon or territorial opossum. *A little farther and a little more...*

She humped forward on the strength of her good leg. The other was a limp and painful burden. She couldn't say what it was inside her that wanted to go on living. Perhaps it was the galling unfairness of dying, alone and by accident, while her attacker continued on, indulging boyhood fantasies of roughing it in wait of some reward. He *owed* her more life... Sand spilled over her waistband with each slow-motion push. It rasped the inside of her thighs and prickled her knees.

After more than an hour of intermittent progress across the strand, the beach seemingly expanding in front of her, Foucher's camp was now in full view. A dying fire revealed the shapes of a trail chair, a low rounded tent and a fishing rod propped against a large piece of driftwood. The mangroves behind the camp flickered in and out of existence. But where was Foucher? Her chest seized up in panic. She trained the gun on the tent, both hands on the grip, fingers tight, clocking her head around for him. There were no suggestive shadows inside the nylon tent, sheer hanging night on either side and nothing at her back except the rolling hiss and spit of the ocean.

She sensed the throwing spear more than saw it—a shearing zip across the gloom. It shivered the air around her upper back and scudded uselessly into the sand. Without thinking, she spindled to her left—toward the spear's general origin-point—churning up an obscuring haze. Another spear overshot her. The snake-bitten leg shuddered in fresh pain with each movement. She came to rest on her stomach and sighted into the darkness. Blinking through the dusted-up sand, she made out a naked arm, elbow bent, moving toward a weak outline of trees. She fingered the trigger, finally firing. The gunshot sent a shiver down her spine. There was a racket of bird-chatter from the woodslope. White skin flashed among the brush, prompting her to fire a second shot and a third. She tracked him by gunflash—flit, flit—aiming low, meaning to disable, not kill. How many rounds left? Six? Five? The beach hushed his urgent footfalls. She had the sense of him dashing from her vision altogether. *The goddamn poison...* She fired again, compounding the hurtful ringing in her ears. A thin vapor of white sand caught the scattered starlight. *Down? Down.* The noise in her head reached a crescendo then began to dwindle in distinct waves.

Should I...? Before she finished asking herself the question, she gritted her teeth and levered herself to her feet. The blood surged into her lower-half, making her so lightheaded she almost keeled over. Neither movement nor sound could be detected from Foucher's direction. The tent was a faint liquid glow in the dying firelight. She brushed the sand from her waistline, tucked the ten-shot pistol in her belt and advanced, wary, testing. *No, no, no...* The slightest pressure set her bad leg to throbbing from calf to sole. With an eye toward the opposing dark, she backtracked to the closest throwing spear and took it up as a walking stick. She then retrieved her supplies, removed the flashlight and knotted the pillowcase to the spear. Her chest was near to collapsing from the tension. *Where? Was he...?* She clutched the flashlight, a feeble beam across the sand, yes, there: crumpled like a thrown doll at the base of a palm tree. "Got you," she breathed. Pain and anxiety, however, eclipsed her sense of triumph.

She held the body in the center of the light as she trudged toward it, cautious of what might happen next. Would he snap back to life? Would she put him down for good? Would there be antivenom among his supplies? The possibilities haunted her one by one. She whispered a medley of curses and jumbled speculations. Her eyes narrowed as she drew closer to him: several yards, a few feet, an arm's length. He was flat on his back, unconscious or dead. She scanned him for injuries. His face was a terrible jolt to her memory but she refused to flinch. His glasses, twisted and broken, gleamed in the sand. There were no bullet wounds; in fact, no wounds whatsoever except for a darkening lump on his forehead and a grazed cheek. His chest rose and fell, the dreg of muscle at his core still pumping life. The positions of the body and the glasses, the facial abrasions, everything suggested he'd run smack into the cappala palm, knocking himself out. Laughter clotted in her throat. *Of all the crazy things...*

It was too easy, Paige knew, to see him purely as a mental case or his violence as the result of a deviant *idée fixe*. But she was only a damaged human, muddling through, wanting a kind of karmic balance. Here was the man who'd ruined her life—at least her sense of it, here, now—defenseless at her feet.

She flashed on his rough hands on either side of her fragile jaw, thumbs digging in, stretching her mouth to a taut parody of a smile, eyes watering until she closed them, tighter, tighter, the sparks behind the lids shifting, serpentine, teeth clenched to stifle the urge to scream... To think of his future all set and decided, a fortune in gold, or even a bucolic life in the wild, while she continued to drag herself around, to question her worth, each day a hopeless effort, stoked her fury. Why should she be the one to bear the cost of *his* sin? She released her hold on the spear and yanked out the gun. Who would dare question her if...?

She checked the ammo: five shots. She expended them into the night sky, exciting treetop shrieks and the slap of wings. When she'd emptied the weapon, she hurled it into the surf then, before she changed her mind, rummaged in the pillowcase for the key to the shackles. She'd come to fear too much clarity. She'd tried consigning the assault to the unreal, splitting body from spirit. She'd pursued a sort of everyday deadness, compelled to carry on by the passage of time but not much else. All in vain. She tossed the key away too and yoked herself to Foucher ankle to ankle. It felt as if wings on her back tilted her to the ground beside him. She would prove herself wholly alive, however long the pain lasted. Because whatever else it is—chaotic, grasping, oblique and more—grief is for the living.

CHAPTER 53

The Motherlode

(The miners celebrate the day's find under the restored mess tent, drinking pulque and playing poker. Ridge is leafing through Free-Energy Thinking *when Waxman and Tree take seats at his table. Waxman talks around the pipe in his mouth. Tree smokes a filterless cigarette.)*

WAXMAN.

—tellin' you I ain't never seen the like. Notice the liquid or whatever it was suspended in 'em? Like the floaty blobs inside a them hippie lamps—

TREE.

Lava lamps, you mean?

WAXMAN.

Yeah, yeah. *(to Ridge)* We're talkin' today's find...

RIDGE.

Didn't sound like gold...

WAXMAN.

Wasn't. Not all of it, leastways. Tarrant was more innerested in these shards a crystal.

TREE.

Clouded-up chunks with this weird liquid inside...

WAXMAN.

Got a soft glow to it...

RIDGE.

Where's he now?

WAXMAN.

Holed up in his cabin. Prob'ly got that crystal under jeweler's glass or sumthin'. Sure you figured by now he's put-near to mad.

TREE.

Heard you was with him when he got word? In the sanctum house?

RIDGE.

Yeah, he was trying to prove a point…

TREE.

With *kava-kava*? I can see it in your eyes—bit dilated there.

RIDGE.

I still have a dull, underlying headache and this strange lightness around the eyes.

TREE.

Smoked it, did you? Yeah, it's gotta few aftereffects. Do that, I'm blowin' brown snot for a coupla days. He tell you? Get a better high you jus' rub it on the gums, take it under the tongue. I sneak a root or two when I can, powder it good. Makes a paste like earwax.

WAXMAN.

Blasted drug fiend…

TREE.

Better than some sorry bucket loser.

WAXMAN.

Some sorry what?

TREE.

Bucket loser, you know, a dope ain't never checked nuthin' off his bucket list.

WAXMAN.

And this *kava* stuff was on your list?

TREE.

Under the circumstances seemed sensible to add it ...

WAXMAN.

I don't even wanna know what else qualified.

MAYANO.
(from the poker table)
Waxman, hey, we need spray poison tomorrow?

WAXMAN.

Cyanide, you mean? Yeah, you know how to do it. That new vein should get us somethin' worth leachin'. We recover the drums for it? Because it works best you put the rock in them drums then spray, keep it all contained.

MAYANO.

Drums? I think so, yes.

WAXMAN.

I'll go over the solution with you, make sure it's diluted proper.

MAYANO.

Todo bien.

TREE.
(to Ridge)
He tell you? Tarrant tapped ol' stumpy here to run the crew now Gerrit's out.

RIDGE.
(to Waxman)
I know you can't be happy about the circumstances but congrats.

WAXMAN.
Ain't nuthin'. Jus' gotta keep duffers like Tree here in line. Gets me a slight bigger percentage, anyways. *(beat)* Heard you lost somebody too. Somebody close?

RIDGE.
Yeah, a friend from childhood. To tell the truth, up until yesterday morning, I'd assumed he was already dead. This is worse—having to live through it twice...

WAXMAN.
I know it's polite to say sorry for things like that—for Gerrit, too—but it's like sayin' sorry for that cyclone or a earthquake or what have you. Gray hair like me don't got no truck with that kinda sorry. I seen people deserved the worst prosper all outta proportion and vicer versa. Don't drive yourself crazy thinkin' there's something godly in it. Things a this earth gotta way a turnin' on their own.

(Hunched over his newly-cleared desk, Tarrant shapes bits of vice-clamped Parmatmar crystal with a modified dental drill. The tungsten drill is powered by a small gas-powered air compressor.)

My spirit soars at this, the first inkling of true, exalted freedom. After all these years, oppressed by the sense our highest desires are incompatible with this scraggèd earth, here I am, at last, on the cusp of revelation. No longer a shadow of the real—some compromised wisdom little more than the filmy desire for truth—but its sublime, light-giving core. I know not what these next hours will bring. Bodily and spiritual pain, perhaps even death. But I'm assured of a place in the history of thought withal. To the masses, philosophy is the province of ivory tower types—professional cloud-minders. Its most critical discoveries, however, have ever been the doing of outsiders: Socrates, who calls himself 'most out of place' in the *Theaetetus*; the itinerant heckler Diogenes the Cynic; the heretical Marcion of Sinope and his rival gods; Descartes and Leibniz, both mathematicians by training; the hunchback encyclopedist Giacomo Leopardi; Nietzsche, who levelled the field with his damning psychologisms; C.G. Jung, particularly owing to his theories on the origins of dreams and his notion of the alchemical quaternity; and above all, L.M. Nicastro, the father of anti-enlightenment. With the construction of this ritual mask and the dreamtime journey to follow, I'll do better than join their storied ranks; I'll tower above them, whether alive or dead. Because I alone among human creatures will have dared the ramparts of the Outer Gods to behold them as they see themselves.

CHAPTER 54

The Harrowing

Ridge rapped on the door to the slab hut and waited, shifting his stance in the dirt, wondering how Mira would receive him after last night's dispute about Paige. He'd let his irritation with Paige's complicating selfishness spill into his tone and had finally quit the argument in wordless dissent, leaving the matter unresolved. Out of a need to settle things with minimal fuss, he was prepared to apologize for his behavior (again) and even, if necessary, for slighting Mira's opinion. Though it still irked him, he wouldn't even argue her claim that—as a man—he could never understand the full psychological consequences of the assault on Paige. He was, after all, a skillful journalist—observant, sympathetic. How could he *not* at least grasp the gist of it?

Hearing no movement inside, Ridge knocked a second time, louder. Still nothing. *Maybe she's gone to breakfast already...* Just to be sure she wasn't suffering a paralyzing fever-sleep or worse, he thrust his head inside. "Mira?" With the exception of the cot, the hut was empty. *Christ.* He stepped into the gloom, disbelieving. His footsteps resounded in his ears. Wait fullstop, there, at the head of the cot: a scrap of paper. He snatched it up. It was a note penciled on a signature page torn from *Free-Energy Thinking*. Her miniature, though precise, script compassed the page from top to bottom. *Dear Ridge, It is with much regret...* The message was gutting to read, polite and apologetic to a fault, intimating an essential weakness in him or a lack of conviction or both. A few sentences in, disheartened by its tone, he found it impossible to focus. He skimmed the rest as if looking for how phrases sat together rather than for their meaning. Mira had gone in search of Paige, alone but armed—*armed.*

His heart spasmed into an angry judder. The fact that she'd kept the gun a secret spoke to her feelings more clearly than the note. Whatever ease had existed between them, whatever security, was gone. It was plain she didn't trust him to safeguard her in this situation. After everything he'd done, the humiliations he'd endured for fear of endangering her, the risks he'd taken in managing Aaron's release and assuring their own, she'd chosen to lie and run and put him at risk all over again. What kind of retribution would Tarrant exact when he discovered her gone, regardless of the manuscript? Ridge recalled the Mira he'd known at Princeton: reserved, quick to blush, loving and thankful for his affections, each pause a dimpled pout... *How could she for Chrissake?* His memories of her seemed no truer than a childhood dream; still, he ached to revive them, to feel her again. He had to think seeing her would turn the situation sane. He should just go, now, follow her, or more practically, flee to the beach and wait for her and Paige to join him. There's no way he could outrun Tarrant or his crew. But would they even bother chasing him after yesterday's discovery? They didn't know how close he was to rescue. He might well—

A palpitating cry went up from the village, giving way to an incredible uproar. Ridge's thoughts went straight to Mira: *What if they've caught her? The gallows...* He crushed the note into his front pocket and bolted out the door, gritting his teeth with each jarring stab of the crutch. *Please, please, not her.* He rounded the hut and lurched to a stop, astonished. *Christ, he's really done it—the overpower...*

Tarrant, recognizable only from his shirtless physique, marched through the central clearing, scattering people and animals before him. He'd undergone a mystifying transformation in the night. His body radiated a sick, unseemly glow and his head shimmered with a brightness crowned by flaring plumes. Occasional energies crackled out from him like a whip with multiple thongs. He was an impossible glimpse of what Man might be. A spindly-legged aborigine in his path shrieked at the sparking air, overturned her basket of water and scampered away. Poi dogs bounded through the village, yowling in distress. A scurry of natives closed on Tarrant with their spears raised but lowered them from confusion or fear before making good on their threat. Others trailed behind him making small, jittery bows and suing for mercy. Most of the miners were on the far side of the clearing, drawn from the mess tent. Ridge couldn't see them due to the interposing huts. But he could hear their shouts of awe and befuddlement amid the growing bedlam.

Shaman! Tarrant called in a new omnipresent voice. The word had the ring of hammered iron in it.

Nature was gravely out of synch and Ridge had to set it right somehow. He shot forward to catch Tarrant, raising dust with each hobbled stride. The boars in their corral darted back and forth. Their squeals shifted into maddening screams. Ridge galumphed across the clearing, the crutch jabbing him until his arm began to weaken and tingle. It was all in doubt, he thought. The plan, his survival, the very laws of nature. The thickening crowd turned aside for him as he approached the first row of spectators, panting and riddled with sweat. Tarrant stood outside Nanokwe's hut wreathed in phosphorus-fire. The dense tattoos along his arms shone like ingots straight from the smelter. His features were hidden behind a large ceremonial mask. The eyeholes blazed with white-hot emptiness.

Tarrant called for the shaman again, broadcasting into everyone's head and the directive froze Ridge in his tracks. What, Ridge wondered, could he really do? Yell for Tarrant to stop and accept his blame? Threaten to discard the manuscript? That hardly seemed enough; in fact, it would be a pathetic joke. Tarrant was a mythical force made real—an Ajax in armor of gleaming bronze. Ridge leaned on his crutch, stunned.

Nanokwe crawled from the refashioned hut and, assuming his full height, shielded his eyes from Tarrant's unnatural florescence. He appeared nonplussed. Ridge wondered if the shaman had received a prophecy of this moment. Several miners—Waxman and Tree among them—eased closer from the opposite side. The crowd quieted, expectant, forgetting all else but the miracle unfolding in front of them.

Turning his eerie, gaze on Nanokwe, Tarrant recited: For I have sworn thee fair, / and thought thee bright, / who art as black as hell, / as dark as night.

The shaman refused to be cowed and replied as if he were in daily consort with daimons of Tarrant's sort. "You the one be the devil Bee-elza-bub. Look what you has become."

What I am, Tarrant said, addressing the multitude, is the first true Marokatu. I've seen Kagoroa in his underwater heaven. I know the meaning of the visions he sends—the glimpses of the past, the dead, the orphic hints of things to come.

"I should have seen." Nanokwe shook a crooked finger at Tarrant. "The warning—the snakes and skinks—not for storm, no, for you, what Christian say: abomination."

Raise not that slave superstition against me, Tarrant said. I am pagan truth incarnate. With a flourish of splintered light, he levitated the shaman in the air high above the throng. An awful gasp of stupefaction broke from the crowd. Some natives swooned with religious fervor. The whites of Nanokwe's eyes widened as he tipped into a near-fetal position. Then he was righted and suspended on level with the helm of Kagoroa.

A mutual fear of embarrassment helped the miners control their emotions. "Just tell me I've gone doolally! Just tell me—" "This is god-damn crazy!" "*Délo drjan'.*" "Un-fucking-believable..." "*¡Mierda!*" "...get the fuck out of here, yes?"

Ridge felt the blood pulsing in his neck and under his jaw. He feared Tarrant had divined his plot and planned to execute the shaman for his role in it. Why else expend his powers in this way? Ridge wanted nothing more than to rush Tarrant, strip the mask from him and dash it to the ground. Feel the flesh yield to his fists. See those haughty eyes blacken and close, the nose crack, the jaw sag, unhinged. *That's how the story should end.*

Tarrant spoke directly into the heads of everyone assembled: Truth, Nanokwe? Do you know it?

Though Nanokwe's face turned a muddy gray at these questions, he made no attempt to disguise his guilt. "I try save Marokatu tradition, turn back in time, keep ourself to ourself again." He found Ridge's desperate gaze as he added: "Before the Christian man, the trader, before the gun and government. Before you and here was here."

A phalanx of spear carriers jostled through the press of bodies and formed a semicircle around Tarrant.

He ignored them, saying to Nanokwe, You set yourself at naught, old friend. There's no going back. Only through.

The warrior with the monkey tail laurel spit a gobby curse as he released his spear. His fellows joined in the attack, desperate to throw sure and true. The energy around Tarrant's head lightninged out to vanish the aggressors and their weapons in a cold kaleidoscopic flash. The confusion of light left the crowd blinded. Ridge shut his eyes to quell the painful afterimages. When he opened them again, squinting, all that remained where the warriors had stood was a dissipating vapor. The vacuum separating him from Tarrant seemed its own in-between world.

This unearthly madness was becoming too much for him. None of his ideas made sense anymore and the strength of will he wanted to have in the face of their collapse, the strength he *should* have, was nothing more than a lost wish. He was bereft of hope for himself and this earth. Despondent. Alone. What could possibly prevent Tarrant from becoming the man-god he aspired to be? A child close by buckled and fell hard on his knees. Ridge recognized him belatedly as Curious George. Other natives adopted a peculiar crouch or cringed, hands clasped above their heads. A few whisked into the forest.

The miners were likewise shaken but stayed their ground, afraid of appearing lesser-than. "Fuck me!" "Jayzus, what—!" "Talk 'bout hell's bug zapper…" "Sick motherfucker!" "*¡Asu mare!*" "Jaws alive! Not even any blood…" "*Kakógo chërta!*"

Tarrant appeared to notice his men for the first time, saying, Ah, my complement and crew: see to yourselves. Your labors have been undone. The Royal Police will put ashore soon and the mine seized. You can meet them on the beach or risk the open sea in native craft. It matters not. Man's time on earth grows cursèd short. Already, you are as fugitive shades in mine eyes.

"The fuck kinda crazy is this?" "Talkin' like some god a heavy metal." "*Chërt voz'mí!* So who is to get our gold? Pushkin?" "He gotta stump up, right?" "Don't know 'bout ya'll but I'm takin' what's mine." "We got more in the tunnel. There's time…" "*Bacán.*"

I care not how you divide the spoils, paltry as they are, Tarrant said. I have no use for gold. You can't out-Mammon Mammon.

Waving his arms in an incantatory fashion, Nanokwe said, "You spirit no good for Makokatu. You spirit mark short, ugly, *bas-ucklan.*"

As for you, Tarrant said, raising his eyes to the shaman, your reward is death—god-damned and god-exalted. The stormy penumbra around his head seethed into a miniature sun. Its rays lashed and curled around Nanokwe—wrists and ankles, waist and neck. Air whistled in the native's throat and his lungs cracked and popped until, in one pinprick instant, the frenzied light burst and bled into the air. The heat blasted the assembly like a breakneck wave, staggering some to the dirt.

When Ridge recovered his sight, he was horrified to find a black-edged petroglyph of Nanokwe burned into the statue's wave-like head. The Marokatu around him dropped to the ground in obeisance, murmuring and moaning. A few steps away, a sweat-slicked warrior offered up his warclub, eyes downcast. The horizon was now at a level with Tarrant's feet, the sky commensurate with his crown.

"That cuts it!" "You see his bones smoke?" "Ain't no sleepin' easy after that, I tell you." "Fuck this! Whatever it is…" "*Nu kak?* How we leave?" "Yeah, he's one sick motherfucker all right." "…this kinda glory hallelujah hell!"

Exposed and shaking in his skin, Ridge felt as if he might implode. Everything seemed fated to end in blind fatality. A fine moral compunction had guided him throughout but to no advantage. The moment seemed infinite, the seconds falling away without effect. What to do? What to do? Now a muted possibility, now an accusation. *Ecce homo.* Of what possible use was he? Knowing the answer, he decided he had nothing to lose and met Tarrant's uncanny stare.

I know, Mister Dantley, Tarrant proclaimed in his head. Believe me, I know. And without so much as a gesture, he tumbled Ridge into the pale and shivering sky.

CHAPTER 55

Free-Energy Thinking

… Many important clinical studies in the fields of psychology and neurobiology are only now starting to inform our understanding of human potential. A recent time series study led by Dr. R.S. Delgado of the Torvis Research Center, for instance, offers indisputable proof of our capacity for self-transformation. In exploring a key relationship between Freud's tripartite division of the psyche and the physical structure of the human brain, Delgado establishes the scientific premises behind our inborn connection to the Divine Light.

What follows is a summary of these premises intended for laypeople interested in the growing material evidence for free-energy thinking.

FIRST premise. In *An Outline of Psychoanalysis* (1940), Freud posits two fundamentally different modes of cognition: 1) an animistic mode prevalent in non-ordinary states like dreaming and psychosis; and 2) a bounded mode prevalent in our ordinary waking state. Freud conjectures that, in the animistic mode, the exchange of energy generated by our neurons is free. The term 'free' in this context means neuronal energy is unconstrained and flows in accordance with the id or unconscious desire.

The second, bounded mode serves as a flow control valve for the neuronal energy available in the animistic mode. This mode minimizes free-energy by directing it in accordance with the ego or conscious desire. As the dominate mode in waking life, it has an inordinate influence in shaping our perceptions and worldly concepts. It's also safe to say that the bounded mode's hyperactive suppression of free-energy invariably results in a mundane life-orientation, evidenced partly by continued mainstream resistance to the human potential movement.

SECOND premise. Modern neurobiology shows that Freud's modes of cognition mirror the biology of the human brain. The brain's hierarchical structure includes the thalamic nuclei and the primary sensory cortex at the lowest level to the paralimbic cortex at the highest, e.g., from sensations, through perceptions to concepts. Neuroimaging suggests the medial prefrontal cortex has a distinctive limbic-suppressive function. In other words, this part of the brain, involved in memory, our sense of time and decision-making, suppresses neuronal activity in lower systems. (Not coincidentally, Freud considered timelessness a major characteristic of the id and time perception a function of the ego.)

THIRD premise. The suppressive function of the medial prefrontal cortex is overdeveloped, tamping down or directing neuronal energy into ordinary channels of thought as a matter of routine. The key implication here is that, by re-routing the free-energy flowing through the limbic system to the spiritual center of the brain, the pineal gland, we can achieve new heights of consciousness. The pineal gland, a pea-sized organ known also as the pineal body, epiphysis or 'third eye,' is situated in the middle of the brain's hemispheres. It works in conjunction with the hypothalamus to control our bio-rhythms. More importantly, the pineal body acts as the receiver-attenuator for the Divine Light.

Advanced neuroimaging reveals that the pineal gland is embedded in what's known as pineal sand, essentially thousands and thousands of crystals. If the pineal gland is the antenna for our dreamstate or astral form, then pineal sand is its oscillator and tuned circuit, allowing us to resonate at the proper frequency. A curious aside: pineal sand is also the reason some believe our natural psychic abilities can be amplified by so-called Parmatmar crystals, a rare mineral thought to operate on similar principles of resonance. Common New Age practices around crystal-enhanced energy centers or Chakras, the color spectrum, Reiki and even 'pyramid power' are likely faint echoes of ancient rites involving Parmatmar crystals.

The spiritual significance of the pineal body has been known for centuries. The ancient Zoroastrians considered this organ of central importance and adopted the practice of wearing turbans to protect it from damage by cosmic rays and psychic attack. Turbans were also used as a form of compress or bandage. A fully awakened pineal gland often creates a pressure behind the eyes and at the base of the brain. Nowadays, these aftereffects of intense free-energy thinking are sometimes mistaken for common migraines, a misdiagnosis emblematic of Western medicine's ignorant groupthink.

CONCLUSION. The evidence is overwhelming: Freud's modes of cognition are not only conceptually useful but scientifically accurate in describing how intrinsic brain networks function. This synthesis of psychology and neurobiology points out an underutilized reserve of free-energy. Taking advantage of this discovery for the purpose of self-transformation requires adopting effective techniques for weakening the ego's hold over the id (or put another way, the medial prefrontal cortex's hold over the limbic system) and learning how to redirect this free-energy to the pineal gland. The following chapters focus on the best—most efficacious—of these techniques based on ancient wisdom, namely, yoga, tantric meditation, lucid dreaming, astral projection and the judicious use of hallucinogens. Recent, little-known research affirms these practices can be mastered by any well-intentioned and disciplined person. So read on, fellow seeker, the secrets of the Divine Light await.

CHAPTER 56

The Search

The dense woodslope held in the hot breath of day. Perspiration ran from Mira's scalp into her eyes. She paused to knuckle the sting out of them and flutter the hem of her graphic tee to cool her skin a little. The next beach wasn't much farther. She could make out the ocean's faint weft through the trees. Though overheated and weary, she was determined to reach the shoreline before resting again. She tightened her ponytail, slung the supplies folded into the Indian blanket over her shoulder and started down. The short-barreled gun bulged from a front pocket. Her craftsman trousers, with their long pockets and many loops, seemed made for it.

She passed from slashes of light into shadowed recesses and back again. In her muggy-headedness, she was straying in and out of God's line of sight, in, out, in, out. She imagined God's vision was like R.M. Rilke's idea of *einsehen* or 'inseeing'—the process of seeing from the surface of a thing to its spiritual nub. Unlike ordinary sight, *einsehen* entails not only observing an object but empathizing with it—even if it's inanimate. Mira tried to adopt an *einsehen* state-of-mind as much as possible. She considered it part and parcel of her Kabbalistic commitment to fix our unfinished Earth.

Even as a child she couldn't escape feeling she was in the service of something larger than herself. She was lonely at times with this feeling, knowing Ridge would dismiss it as loose, unsystematic, akin to fantasy. He was too respectful to tell her outright, but she knew he largely humored her beliefs as an affectation or character quirk. His attitude was frustrating all the more because she knew his heart was in the right place. He shared much of her faith-based ethos and, in his way, he also wanted to repair the world, only on the grand scale of politics rather than at the level of families, one small kindness at a time.

For all his decency and reportorial acumen, though, she faulted him for failing to see life as a great mystery—one that carried an irrepressible spiritual charge. His Kantian attachment to reason blinded him to it, and he substituted the tenets of liberalism for scripture and the mechanics of governance for religious observance. Politics, however, struck her mainly as an uncountable number of dismal facts: the precipitous thinning of the ozone layer, rampant poverty, drug-fueled gang violence, the AIDS epidemic, children dying from treatable diseases, dozens since she'd started her trek through the forest... She admired Ridge for wanting to try but felt his efforts would be better spent working with small groups or individuals. There was always the chance to see into the heart of things then. You'd have to be God for *einsehen* to be possible in relation to an entire city, much less a state or a country.

Was being reasonable and accommodating enough for her to marry him? That was the real question she'd tried to answer—for herself if not for him—in the note. She loved him, of course, but love couldn't excuse inaction in the face of wrongdoing. He could be accommodating to a fault. If nothing else, this desperate situation had exposed his limitations. The right ideas alone can't protect you. They don't gain value on their own like a smart stock pick. No, you have to defend them. She was sorry for putting Ridge in a bad spot and, at the same time, hoped her leaving would spur him to act for himself now that neither she nor Paige could be used against him. Maybe, she thought, he just needed this push to show some resolve. Everything came down to the Talmudic maxim: *Talking is not the main thing; action is.*

Mira thought about their relationship as if it were one of her cases at the Institute. What would be the central metaphor for it? She worried over that still. The note had turned out more aloof because of this uncertainty. Was that a sign or symptom of her feelings? When you couldn't work up the energy to get past clichés? She'd forfeited emotion for clarity, thinking—

Beyond the last staggered swatch of palms, she spied the crest of a tent. Garish orange. Unmistakable in the fiery sun. *Chas vesholem.* It could only be Foucher's camp. She lowered the blanket to the ground and drew the gun. Her quavering pulse radiated from her heart into the hand around the grip. She widened her stance under the trees, mulling her choices. She could backtrack or... There was a voice, a man, no, two voices, the other soft and easily lost in the surf's dreamy hush. She crept behind the nearest palm then tip-toed to the next. The voices came from the mangroves—a confusion of shadows and floating patches of light. The second speaker was definitely a woman: Paige. How ...? Mira's throat closed up; still, she slipped closer, gun level, into the soft sand behind the tent.

They were seated side by side, silhouetted against the sun-glare on the water. Paige slumped on a gnarl of roots, one foot in the stream. Foucher reclined on the bank, legs outstretched, a fishing pole in the crook of his arm. He murmured what sounded like an old hymn. "Early ... our song ... Thee ... Which wert and ... shalt be ..."

Mira steadied the revolver by resting it in the palm of her other hand and closed in. A dry-mouthed fear threatened to arrest her breathing. She wondered what *einsehen* would mean for the bullet. What would it feel? Would it yield one long clap of vengeance? Or, once released, drop to a whisper in its course? She placed each footfall with care. Fewer than 20 yards separated her from the back of Foucher's partially obscured head.

She sidled over until a gap in the mangroves opened up. The trajectory was clear. *Milkhemet mitzvah.* She braced the gun against a knobby trunk and canted toward the barrel. His silhouette wavered in the pronged sights, in, out, in, out. She felt alive to a secret sense of things. It would take so little effort. A finger pull like a nervous tic. Just a fraction of an inch. Her pulse against the grip was insistent.

Foucher dropped the fishing pole and craned his neck to face her, lips raveling in surprise.

The main thing, she assured herself, is action.

CHAPTER 57

Opsis

A smeary whiteness disgorged Ridge into the surf. He pitched from the ethereal rift in space to his knees. His vision sparked and pained him. Why he wasn't dead was inexplicable. Doubled over and gasping, he put hand on his aching chest. The beating of his heart was a series of staccato shocks. The low tide compassed him in its cool indifference. His vision began to clear, the sky to become a striking blue. He could be on the spare edge of everything. The stark horizon somehow brought to mind the death-urge of sick animals to wander away and die alone.

You're no sicker than the rest. The voice boomed through the clefts and runnels of his mind. Tarrant floated into view, the air igniting before him. Or perhaps the floating was only an effect of his gently swirling glow, which revealed unguessed-at layers the longer Ridge stared at it, mesmerized. You just got a skittish heart.

Ridge refused to stay on his knees. He pushed himself up and onto his feet without benefit of his crutch (now lost), still dizzied, trying to quiet his thoughts. Contempt seemed the easiest way to disguise them. He had no shortage of it where Tarrant was concerned. "So this is it—the overpower?"

One manifestation of it. Tarrant took several strides toward him. The water purled away from his bare feet without touching them. What? No incredulous spit curse.

Even this close, Ridge felt no heat from Tarrant. He had the impression the preternatural glow was closer to frostbite than fire. "This is *your* idea of it then? The lightning mask? You stumble and the ground quakes?" The unfairness of Tarrant's advantage overcame his genuine awe. What made Tarrant deserving of these suprahuman powers? *Telepathy, telekinesis, teleportation—talents for a devil.* It was insufferable, this anti-apotheosis.

Everything is only one version of reality, Tarrant said. Another wave jigged around him.

"Well, I have to live in this one so ..."

The eyes are the nakedest of organs—scoops of viscous jelly and snarled nerve strings. Imagine your body thus naked, your spirit raw and exposed.

"The messiah's burden ..."

Don't confuse me with history's pigeon gods. This messenger won't be so easily broken.

Ridge gestured toward the line of the horizon. "Do you even know what you can do? What you *want* to do?"

I have occasional thoughts I don't recognize as my own. What I called the sea god—its voice is a persistent undersong. But I retain enough of my faculties to know. The Christian God done beget the night from the darkness of the sea. I aim to hale it back.

"Literally?" Ridge tried annoying him with random thoughts: *in when down night...*

Tarrant appeared unperturbed. I alone know our true relation to things. I've seen the distant, unrecorded past and the deep future both. What you call civilization doesn't suit our inmost nature. The greatest cities are just elaborate mausoleums that turn its peoples dead alive.

Ridge decided to keep his thoughts short, pointed, as if he were on assignment for the paper. *Get the essentials...* "How do you know this?"

The master crystals prismed and multiplied my dreamtime powers I don't know how much. I burned in the light of our eternal origins, lapsing and resurrecting, afeared to stop the change... No darkness can douse me now. I have a quantum sun in my head and a body luminous with its excesses... It is cosmic awareness, this light, a knowledge exalting and sublime. With it, I can penetrate your thoughts and the incipient consciousness of everything around me. I can reorder things down to the bare atoms. I can scud through dreams as on a cat's paw wind, gandering at the past, the future, at the dead in their astral habitat. They have no life of their own, the dead, merely traces of personality, imprints on the collective unconscious and like memories, deranged by egoistic fancy.

The grandeur of Tarrant's speech pushed Ridge over the edge. "I guess you've done it then," he said. "Tarrant, the Man-God..." The crash-hush of the ocean mixed with the din of heated blood in his ears. Impossible and anarchic forces had won out. There would be no rescue, no story, televised or otherwise—at least not for him. He balled his fists in angry resignation.

Tarrant's distorting radiance waned and flared. He definitely hung a few inches above the gentle waves. Perhaps further out than I previsioned …

"But not now?"

I'm no shepherd for the herd-minded. You studied business, right? You remember the Pareto power law?

Despite the circumstances, Ridge slipped into the familiar and comfortable role of student without pause. It helped him to be dispassionate in his hopelessness and separate from what was happening. "It explains the pyramid-like structure of societies, income distribution, the evolution of stock prices, city sizes, a whole host of things. The 80-20 rule— 20% of the people owning 80% of the wealth—came from it."

The principle never struck you as a counterfactual to the working creeds of democracy, Christianity, every value system promoting a shared mediocrity? You, reluctant member of the omnivorous elite …

"It's a series of equations that describes mass phenomena. It doesn't dictate how things ought to be."

That's part of what I meant when I said my strength lies in saying yea to the world as it is. You continue to live in a veiled reality … All your vaunted philosophies are mere delusion. I know the true, unerring instincts civilization's leached from us. I know what we were meant to be: spiritual warriors. Christianity—and here I throw Islam and all the other major religions into the same sorry midden heap—was one embattled god's way of establishing dominion over us, pacifying Man, turning us away from the destiny in our blood. We are a race of sleeping warriors, our access to the overpower purposely diminished.

"The world religions are a conspiracy?" Ridge had never allowed his skepticism of conventional religion to shade into contempt, much less scapegoating.

Organized religion, democracy, socialism, all of it, are just elaborate ploys for a niggling measure of control. And over what? So much of Man is nothing—trifling as frogspit. See, we're at the base of the Pareto pyramid, struggling amongst ourselves, ignorant to what's greater. Modern civilization has no use at all except one: to promote genius. Little men sans the great do not suffice. Genius is the only thing that can rewrite the human fable and redeem existence.

Ridge felt Tarrant's energy as an eerie prickling inside. The sensation moved from his brain to his chest and back again, a pulsing at the core of him like a fresh wound before you know the seriousness of it. "Now we're back to Anthropos dictating who lives and who dies…"

And your Columbia is the superior example? Democracy, characterized by Rousseau's general will, is the most insidious of levelers. Democracy despises genius, slurs it as unreasonable, beats it down and jails or institutionalizes it and invariably destroys it. That's why only an outsider like me can save civilization from itself. I am come to strip the world of its swaddlings of velvet and velour and knock it back to its hard beginnings.

"Still, you don't intend to lead us into this new age, whatever it is…" There was a tinge of vindication in these words.

Only because that future's been foretold. However misguided, your democratic virtues still hold sway in this moment in time. I could compel the masses to accept me as their god… But I refuse to be subject to their disreadings and jealousies and die in a soft putter somewhere, mid-thought, a dash upon the void. Here, I'm reminded of the 12th century Byzantine Doge who, returning from a successful campaign against the Greeks, giant columns in tow as evidence, was soon after torn apart by the mob from fear of despotism. No, my aim is not to save civilization by leading or preserving it—even in a radically different form. My aim is to smash the precepts on which it was built and free us—the survivors, that is—to live into our original promise…

"How? You haven't said. By seeding the clouds with your judgment?" The mask and the lurid glow, together, made Tarrant as faceless and unaccountable as any ancient icon.

Did you feel anything in the spirit house? The presence?

"I felt… something. I'd be lying if I gave it a personality."

I've been calling it Kagoroa. But I know now it's nothing like a god. It's a device—a beacon—sunk to the dead-bottom of the Pacific. There must be dozens of them scattered around the world's oceans. These beacons send out signals of mixed frequencies to one or more Out-er Gods. They vibrate all through us, these signals, crossing realities. We're so close to a beacon here, it's no wonder the Marokatu have a fierce quiet to them. They tend dreamward all the day long. The bea-cons even transmute the ocean life sometimes, give them bodies fit only for nightmares. Maybe it was one of those misbegotten creatures that sunk your boat?

"That begs the question of who set these beacons."

I can't say. But I plan to give this one here a boost and see if I can't get some errant god's attention.

Tarrant had buried the lede again. Here was the motive that under-lay all his globe-spanning travails: to prove a whole new cosmogony. Ridge trembled at the idea he might succeed; after all, he'd become a living miracle. "I'm still trying to take all this in," Ridge said. "Who are these gods?"

They're called by various names: the Outer Gods, the Celestial Pan-theon, the Universals. One a them or its creations are responsible for this plane of existence, for us poor misguided souls. And they're at war—a war for supremacy across dimensions.

"And you're going to bring us into it?" The scope of his protean cru-elties seemed limitless.

Not me alone. I previsioned others, one not more than a lank boy already ascended, another a homeless scholar, a motley bunch. I don't know if I'll come to meet them on this earth or not but I do know this: nothing can stop me from cutting through all the philosophy and reli-gion and poetry of the unknown until I get to the hardpan truth.

Ridge's mouth was tacky with foreboding. "What else have you previsioned? What can I expect? Not me, personally, but the world at-large."

Why attest to it when I can show you just as easily? Tarrant raised a shining hand and misted Ridge with light.

Ridge gave a brief insuck of surprise before a Kinetoscope-like flicker of disasters played out in his head—

—hellish root-veins fracturing the earth—wracked to bursting into smoke and ash—

—a pickup truck on a backcountry road steeped in ragged bodies—

a child's arm, boy, girl, who knows? wriggles out from under the desic-
cating mass, grasping at air—

—the unmistakable candescence of a nuclear bomb roils the horizon—

—an endless list of dead is recited over an old battery-powered radio—

—featureless sand and white stretches of salt, blinding in the open
sun—a half-rubbled temple—opposing bands of turbaned soldiers—a
superfluity of gunfire—Iraq? Afghanistan? somewhere in the Middle
East—an Assyrian winged-bull statue—centuries old limestone de-
faced by artillery—then everything overtaken by a lurid green gas—it
cascades over the fighters, toppling each in turn, pocking and graying
their skin—as the chemical fog disperses, they jerk to their feet, eyes
milky, all emotion gone—brothers in the same cause now, the men
cease their battle, collect themselves and their weapons and caravan
away—

—shadowed blocks of city—there, the Chrysler Building—Manhat-
tan then—choked through with spiked, bulbous flowers (not unlike
the low-mounding Campion)—the streets echoey in their lifelessness—

—a lustrous blonde, her face an alabaster blank with a long, prehensile appendage—

—Antarctic glaciers roseate with frozen blood—the sun occluded by
a giant white-shrouded figure—

—dozens of dead fish crows along the bank of a putrid-yellow creek—

—a wizened man on an urban rooftop bows the length of a worn
prayer mat—a military drone screams toward him—he is unwavering,
entranced, more dreaming than awake—the drone prepares to release
its deadly payload—he mouths a secret Dua—*ka-chunka-chunka-
chunk*—the drone falters in its rigid velocity, plummets, the missile
unlaunched—

—hunting hounds bay for their masters—future primitives in animal masks—the leader a hairy brute helmeted in ram's horn—

—a shimmery youth in glasses says, "Not all mysteries are tombed
in Latin"—

—a rubbish-strewn avenue burnished in oil—gutter rainbows awaiting a match—

—more abandoned cities—Tokyo, London, Sao Paulo, Berlin, Seoul, Osaka, Mexico City, Paris, Lagos, Madrid, Los Angeles, Timbuktu, Buenos Aires, Jakarta, Cairo, Beijing—a random itinerary of strange jungle-rot destruction—and amid the alien fauna, glimpses of ghastly life—a carapaced insect buzzes over corpse-laden boulevards on iridescent wings—tusked rodent-like creatures the size of Dachshunds snarfle the dead—

—slim fingers plink out a minor key melody on a warehouse piano—

—a rabblement of dirty children scurry around the town dump searching for weapons—garden spades, broken drill bits, lengths of chicken wire—

—spiraling, elliptic leaves along a central stalk—jointed, lance-shaped tendrils throughout its length—topped by a breathing foil and inside that gather of petals—

—stars ray out like in a child's drawing, swelling and subsiding as if just below the surface of a rippling pond—

The sky jolted into place. Ridge found himself sprawled on the sand, chest clenched and bile rising in his throat. He sat up shaking and spit out the hot acid taste. With a gesture, Tarrant lifted him to his feet. Ridge tightened his jaw against the queasiness. The prophetic horrors lingered—the devastation and violence, the countless dead. "Christ," he croaked. "It's a full-bore apocalypse." He felt like a young child again, wary of the ordinary world his parents discussed in disappointed tones and grateful for the moveable sanctuary their wealth afforded. He shook his head in disbelief. "And all of that will happen because of what you're going to do now?"

I am the willing catalyst for it—the early 21st century of the Dorum Sprawl, of zombified terrorists and god-monsters, the dead beside the dead across the latitudes, all nihilism, carnality and mercenary faith.

"Don't, you can't, you…" Ridge shut his eyes in order to focus on gathering himself up. He could no longer contain his fear and exasperation. "I know I can't stop you. But if we've really been cosmic outcasts from the start, you have to respect the best of what we've done, the ideals we've espoused, even if delusional or unachieved…" He was compelled to go on, to eschew the too-easy acrimony that sometimes tainted his journalism and to risk sounding hokey or old-fashioned in defense of his values. He knew Tarrant would remain unmoved. But he wanted to voice a last affirmation: "There's a good reason behind the prophecy of your defeat. Only gods and heroes who inspire us to be better—kinder, wiser—can win our permanent loyalty. The Golden Rule abides—even in this age of increasing division. The misrule of fear would only force us to hide our real selves. What you propose isn't liberation but a new kind of slavery."

You're naïve and finical, Mr. Dantley. Those sentiments bespeak the bloom of youth and of unfounded hope and nothing more. What would you sacrifice to sway me otherwise? On our first meeting, I offered you the chance to put me down like a diseased cur. Have you come to regret your choice? Would you make another now? Suppose I offered you this mask and its attendant powers?

Ridge looked inland as if expecting an answer to emerge from the forested verge. The vision Tarrant shared had unsettled him. The prospect of an extended awareness of it—the world warped around him, his intellect shrunk to a conscious pinhead—made his stomach churn. The mask would no doubt plunge him into some unfathomable *Inferno*. He'd never find his way back to reason. Even now, he wondered if Tarrant was still propping him up. "Without your level of training, what would happen to me? Would it even work?"

Imagine yourself a body of glass, whatever's precious about you a calm against the outside weather, shattered of a sudden by a brilliant disparity in pressure … The overpower, this light—the source of all— withers you in its radiant coursing, blinding you to everything but a dream without a morning, the truest there ever was and the more awful for it, you, a newborn godhead, desperate to gather up the shards of your being … There was a moment, I admit, when I yielded to animal fear.

The brightness around Tarrant's mask thinned to a slight deforming film. He gripped the mask by its protruding chin and lifted it from his face. His eyes were charred hollows, seething like embers in a light wind. I can still feel the snags on my brain as I clawed them out. What would happen to you? What happened to Phaethon when he stole Apollo's chariot? he asked, re-affixing the mask.

The need to maintain a façade of defiance prompted Ridge to ask,

"Could I even stop you then?"

Depends on your strength of will. My powers, of course, are not dependent on the mask. With its Parmatmar crystals for eyes, it just helps to amplify them. I don't need the mask to turn your heart to meteor iron.

Ridge lowered his eyes, expecting an interval of cringing pain.

But Tarrant did nothing except adopt a sharper, more swaggering tone. Well, Mr. Dantley, what shall it be? You're loath to believe the revelations I've shared but still, you have the moral urge to try me...

The collapse of everything against his sanity... Ridge avoided thinking too intently about what Mira would want of him. "If there's some truth to what you say, the vision you touched off..."

If, yes, that's the Pascal's wager here...

"This—the vision—it can't be right. I can't believe that's the future. It's too horrible." Ridge thought about snatching the mask in the narrowing space between heartbeats. Perhaps if he was quick about it...

Don't or can't? Tarrant turned his back on Ridge and toward the vast Pacific. You've been thinking in the wasteland without knowing it. I'm about to make its horizon plain, yea, as in the first inklings of dawn, enough to steer by.

Even more than failing to stop Tarrant, Ridge feared failing to live up to his own sense of self. What if the weakling child—chronically sick, passive in his reason—was the true Ridge? He couldn't endure that knowledge. "I can't, I mean, I can't take the mask. But you already knew that, didn't you?" He had the uncomfortable feeling he was speaking lines dictated from the future, that he was now living Tarrant's story.

Tarrant stretched his hands to the sky and bolts of etheric energy forked into the water, exciting flashes near and far under the surface. The answering flashes faded, gravity gave way and the sea showered into the air, first a few yards out then farther, deeper, until the swells formed spitting, spinning walls curled inward at their edges above the exposed sand and reef. The suspended waves reeled up and up into the far distance, their crests a jeweled green in the unclouded sunlight. The sight would've been storybook wondrous in a dream or a painting but not here, like this, a fact impossible to deny. Nature had been subverted on a whim and for what? As prelude to an unthinkable cataclysm.

Tarrant burned too fiercely for Ridge to gaze upon. Ridge turned away and blinked patchy whiteness.

Some will say of this shore, Here stood once the prophet of null and void. Because of you, Mr. Dantley…

Ridge watched intermittently between splayed fingers as Tarrant walked into the divided sea, untouched and untouchable. His emotions were too confused to name. He was neither the person he was when he woke this morning nor the future self he aspired to become. A kind of death had occurred. Tarrant had left him without youth, without God or even His possibility, without damnation or redemption, without the reason necessary to sustain the rest of his days.

The weight of his wretchedness brought him to his knees. He kept his eyes on the drying sand, numb, empty, until he heard the sea close in on itself and resolve into a mirroring flatness, as if the world were the same as it had ever been.

CHAPTER 58

Unchained

Foucher twitched at the bullet through his jawbone. The second round shattered his Adam's apple. He toppled sideways, wrenching on the shackles. The heft of him yanked Paige from her perch. The air went out of her in a panic. She stepped in time with his twisting to keep upright. The hand Foucher threw up in spastic self-defense fell across his chest. A glottal tic sounded in his burst throat for a few beats then gurgled into silence. Paige came to a halt braced against his knee and facing the inlet. She ducked and turned to spy her attacker, breathless and heated.

"Paige!" Mira bawled, poking her head through the trees. "Paige, I'm so sorry. I didn't mean to scare you. I just—I saw him, I thought, I didn't know you were…" Her voice was pinched tight. She gestured to indicate the leg irons. "*Chas vosholem.*"

Fuck, fuck, fuck… Paige reminded herself to inhale. "It's all right. It's okay." She dropped to the ground next to the body, every inch of her trembling in anguish. Circumstances had conspired to expose her nature. She couldn't begin to explain to Mira why she'd bound herself to Foucher. In her delirium over the snakebite, she'd thought it a canny maneuver. Help me, you bastard or drag my corpse around, she'd told him. Her motives were both vague and mixed: to save herself; to taunt and torment him; to commit suicide by proxy. Finding the right words for her pain had become a metaphysical problem. Shackling herself to him was a way to get beyond language. She'd made a metaphor of her body, she thought, even if she didn't know what that metaphor meant. How could she have known the snake wasn't poisonous (or, as Foucher had corrected her, venomous)?

Mira crouched next to Paige and looked askance at her knife-torn pant leg. "He didn't—Did he hurt you?"

Paige looked to the horizon as if unseeing. "No, not this time." Foucher had been brusque but wary. He'd considered her one of Tarrant's agents, a test to determine his worthiness.

"Do you know where the key is? Is it—"

"In the sand—at the edge of the ocean." She staggered to her feet. Foucher was heaped in a bramble of roots. She half-expected him to lunge and snarl. His death offered no relief. She was still an exile, misunderstood, her thoughts sweaty, careening, each breath an invitation to scream. "Here," she said, concentrating hard on the moment, "why don't we drag him out?" His eyes looked started from their sockets in astonishment.

"I can find it if you can tell me where he was standing, the direction …" Mira was flushed from the excitement but altogether in control. Typical Mira. Paige could scarcely look her in the eye.

"I'm just glad you're all right," Mira said. "I came looking for you because we expect a ship—the Royal Police—from Honiara. Should be here in a few days. I don't know where they'll land but they're bound to come looking. I thought we'd try the main beach—the one down from the path through the hills."

"You come by yourself?"

Mira nodded coyly.

Tears gathered behind Paige's eyes. Intentionally or not, Mira had taken on a share of her darkness. She wouldn't confuse or diminish the gesture by making explanations. Words of gratitude lodged in her throat. She was overcome by a feeling of sympathetic distance—standing outside herself, *ex stasis*—and broke into racking sobs. She cried, slump-shouldered and unabashed, and Mira embraced her. She was a species apart, alone and unknowable but *recognized*. With eyes closed, she breathed in Mira, the ocean. The sound of water lapping against the bank, she hoped, would echo into her dreams and give her peace. Tears coursed down her cheeks. The salt sting was a pleasant reminder of something real.

For the first time since the assault, she thought of Brookline as a possibility. Her mom had preserved her room and its college-era trappings as if it were a museum diorama. *Home is still there, still home…* She knew she would never fully put the trauma behind her but there was a chance she'd learn to absorb it, adjust. There was a chance her feelings of shame and guilt would fade with time. There was a chance she would die decades from now, settled, in the middle of things, collapsed by a stroke at the kitchen table, in familiar surroundings with family nearby. What more could she ask for *baruch atah adonai*?

CHAPTER 59

The Gathering

The longer the evening wore on without Ridge, the more anxious Mira became. The ache crowding her insides threatened to spread more weakness. She worried that she'd goaded him into a suicidal confrontation. As Waxman and the other displaced miners had described it, Tarrant's taunting had hinted at some terrible Old Testament punishment. *Oy gevalt!* What an outrageous return on her prayers! Where were the angels that constellated her life? "He was friends with Nanokwe," she told Waxman and Tree. "Can we use that to get a canoe? Or ask them to make a circuit along the coast?" She felt guilty, too, for warming herself beside a campfire, for raising a tin of black coffee to her lips, figuring that, best case, Ridge was wandering the island, alone, no crutch and no supplies.

"I'm tellin' you, sweets, he could be anywhere," Waxman said through teeth clenched around his pipe. "Anywhere in this world or the next." He fished a Bic from his front shirt pocket. "'Bout due for a simple pipeful."

Tree waggled his blunt at Waxman in agreement. His eyes were red and bleary.

"I'm sorry if I'm repeating myself here," Mira said, "but I just want to make sure I understand … He disappeared—literally?"

Waxman took a tentative puff. Light notes of chocolate and nuts sweetened the otherwise straight burley tang. "Ain't nuthin' to unnerstand. Tarrant, he—I ain't religious or nuthin' but if I had to say, I'd say he like to've stole the fires from hell."

All this time Mira had been praying to her personal angel to show another had apparently interposed itself. Could be, she thought. Doesn't rabbinic folklore describe the angel of death as a nomad like Cain, a "fugitive and wanderer?" She turned to Paige, who was seated on a driftwood log, swaddled in a blanket against the chill coastal air. "I feel like I'm abandoning him."

Paige's eyes flickered up from the firelight. "He's made it through a lot already," she said matter-of-factly.

Mira nodded and gazed over Foucher's tent into the blackness. From high up on the beach, she could make out a few indistinct huddles around the neighboring campfires. The rest of the beach might as well have been an abyss under the bare sliver of moon. The Pacific churned on and on, unseen. As she understood it, once Tarrant vanished, the Marokatu had turned violent and driven the miners away at the tips of their poisoned spears. Most of the men had settled in this provisional camp of tents and palm thatch lean-tos. Without Tarrant to keep them in check, Mira was concerned about what they might do to her and Paige. She kept the revolver in her trouser pocket with the safety off.

Tree clapped a hand on Waxman's shoulder. "You goin' back to the stateside grind, old-timer?"

"This beard don't mean I come to the afterpiece a life yet. Figure I got one more crazy venture in me. Not crazy like this, mind…" He took a satisfying pull on his pipe. "What about some breed injun like you?"

"Just gonna say, Beattie was mentionin' some jobs with Newcrest…"

"Oh, yeah. Don't they got operations in Jakarta now?"

"He was talkin' a exploratory vein somewhere near the Telfer Mine. Maybe it wasn't Newcrest directly but a smaller crew after gold and copper both."

"This crew legit?"

"Would it matter?" Tree asked. "'Sides, I heard they got this toad out there, kinda like the Sonora Desert variety… You stroke its neck until it squirts this venom out its glands. Let that dry on a hard surface, say, a Popsicle stick and you got yourself some damn fine medicine—15% s-MLD-DMT they estimate." He slurred the abbreviation so badly it sounded like *smell-dee-dee-emptee.* "Give you the outta body experience a your life."

"Jaws, haven't you had enough psychedelic weirdness after…?" Waxman declined to say more out of respect for Mira.

"Enough?" Tree blustered. "Why Tarrant just proved what I been tryna tell you from the start: This shit is a no-joke counterblast to reality. I gotta mind to go back and get me some *kava-kava* to-go no matter what those Marokatu pull. The police—"

A reedy, hailing shout from down the beach cut through the susurrus of tired conversation. The shout excited a muddle of answering calls from the men closest to the surfline. Beams of light dashed over the sand this way and that, searching for the source, settling in moments on a scraggly figure near the tidal edge—a man drooping from a walking stick. *Ridge! It has to be...* Mira started for him, following the flashlights of the advance scrum. The ache girdling her relaxed its hold. He'd come through alive. *A brocheh!* She surged across the beach as fast as she was able, frustrated by the ungainliness of her boots in the loose sand. Tree smiled in passing.

By the time Mira reached him, Ridge was already facing a barrage of questions: "Where'd ya end up?" "Got *some* luck, right? 'Cause a reg'lar man wouldn't be worth a whiskey dreg 'gainst that devil-magic he showed." "¡*Venga!* He let him go. How else this one escape?" "That it? He let you go?" "What happened to Tarrant then?" His face was fixed and bewildered and beaded in sweat.

She brushed through the ring of miners and wrapped her arms around him. The miners guffawed and complained at the delay in getting their answers. His hold on her was unsteady. "*Deigeh nisht,*" she whispered. "I've got you." He didn't reply. But she could hear his throat working as if he were getting up the strength to say something. She clasped him tighter until the pistol became an uncomfortable pressure between them.

Ridge gave her a dry kiss then stood her aside. "He's gone," he told the crowd. "Where, I don't know. But it's somewhere we can't follow."

"What he tell you? Anything?" Mayano asked.

"Nothing worth repeating. A lot of nonsense about dark gods and the coming apocalypse. Whatever the source of his powers, it drove him mad. He clawed out his own eyes."

The miners pressed Ridge for a few more details but when the answers proved of little interest or importance, they dispersed, assured of his uselessness. "Looks brain-fried to me." "And you'd a done better, bein' a half-wit to start?" "...luck ain't never run to flush anyway." "*Da nu!* The same luck is all of us here."

"Thirsty?" Mira took Ridge's arm and started to escort him toward her tent. He was more haggard than she'd ever seen him, almost limy. His appearance evoked more pity than love. "We have some food—mostly jerked meat, breadfruit and berries."

"You found Paige all right?"

"She was fine. I mean, not fine-fine, but... She's safe now."

"And you?"

"Hmm-mm." For a moment, she considered telling him about Foucher. But why compound his suffering by pointing out how wrong he'd been about Paige's safety? Besides, she'd made peace with what she'd done. Unlike in Gerrit's case, she'd taken on the risk directly. She would make her sin offering in compensation, sure, but without regret for raising a hand in her own salvation. Tarrant had fostered a contest of animal moralities and, given the environs, she'd chosen hunter over quarry. She counted the killing a *mitzvot*.

"When I read your letter, I didn't know what to think..."

"I know. I'm sorry for that. I just couldn't stand the thought of Paige on her own." The mention of the note surfaced emotions she would figure out later. She promised herself to think more on the matter tonight or tomorrow morning. But she already suspected the sad truth and no amount of deliberation would likely change it. "Is it true—what they're saying about Tarrant—about his powers?"

"Probably."

The sage-mystics of the Talmud, Mira knew, have long said that humanity was on the brink of a new era in consciousness, the *Eretz hattayyim*, the Land of the (true) Living. It was possible that, for all his flaws, Tarrant was part of some spiritual vanguard. She could be a witness to the next great spiritual revolution. The thought sent a thrill through her body. "Where did he send you?"

"The beach somewhere... Not too far for someone with a busted leg."

"You don't need to talk about it now if you don't want."

"Actually," he said, stopping and turning to face her. "I have to go back to the village. It can wait until morning. But I have to get the manuscript."

"Even now—with him gone?"

"There could be important clues."

"Clues to what? His transformation?"

"To the future—*our* future."

Mira balked at the direction Ridge's mind seemed to be tending. "You're not thinking of getting it published are you?"

"No, no." He brushed a stray tangle of hair behind her ear. "I'd never give that bastard the satisfaction."

Leaning into him, Mira said, "This—the absurdity of it all . . . We'll look back on it with different eyes when we're home again." Maybe that was the problem, she thought, not Ridge himself but the sheer stress of this place, the need to live in the moment at all times. Maybe it had skewed her feelings for him. A few days of peace might clarify things. She told herself she wouldn't make any decisions until they were returned to civilization.

She would reenter the States, however, with a greater sense of her capacity for change. The differences between who she was before and who she was after their ordeal called for a reassessment—of her career, of her home and impending marriage. Why deny herself other possibilities? With Tarrant as her example, she could take Kabbalah more seriously. She could move to Israel and apprentice herself to a Chassidic master. What was the secret of Kabbalah, after all, but metaphor and will rightly applied?

There was no telling how much change she had left in her.

CHAPTER 60

The Manuscript

Ridge left for the native village in the company of Tree before Mira emerged from her tent. He was afraid even a cursory goodbye might give him away. She knew when he was trying to disguise his emotions. He had a habit of tightening up, becoming solemn and self-conscious. As it was, more than a half-mile from the beach, his hiking gait was as stiff as a hinged puppet's.

Sometime in the dark of the morning he'd resolved to break his engagement. His chest seized up at the thought of Mira's response, the high forehead gathering in concern and consternation, the big eyes going soft, the warm tears and bitterness... But it seemed a hopeless surety. He couldn't imagine ever telling Mira about Tarrant's offer, about the mask and how he'd shrunk into a cowardly stupor. She expected and deserved better. She'd once said that failure allowed people to see themselves as God does and, from that perspective, he'd failed eternally and without any but the most selfish of excuses. Knowing that, he couldn't possibly sustain his feelings for her. He would only be a continual disappointment.

Maybe he'd fallen in love with her before he'd known what love was and, in the heat of youth, proposed before he'd known who they were, together and apart. He supposed it didn't matter now that he'd broken faith with himself—at least the future, idealized version. Put to extremes, he'd been found wanting and his good intentions worthless. He should've taken the mask, he thought, even if it had corrupted or destroyed him outright. His refusal cast doubt on his potential for anything of consequence. Mira's tentativeness and carefully chosen words last night suggested she was already close to intuiting as much. Better a firm break soon than a slow, arduous disintegration ending in divorce. His maternal grandmother would never forgive him in that instance. She was so committed to the old Episcopalian canon, she changed the TV channel if a divorced actor came onscreen.

"I told ya they looted Tarrant's cabin," Tree said. "Sure it's still there?" He put his lips to a cheap, smelly cigarette.

"They take the books?" Ridge adopted a false cheeriness. He was grateful to Tree for making the trip with him in case he needed a translator. He didn't want to put him out further by acting morose.

"What the hell'd they do with those 'cept maybe treat 'em as kindling?"

"Then yes. I pasted the pages behind the endpapers." In the tropical heat, it had been a simple task to separate the endpapers from their backing with one of Nanokwe's scalpels, insert two or three folded-up manuscript pages then apply a dollop of skin glue to reseal them.

Tree gave him a knowing wink. "You don't look it but you got some thief in you, Tourist." He took another drag.

Ridge was too distracted to do more than answer with a thin, polite smile. His so-called sleep in the lean-to had been fitful and punishing. The first nightmare had been a simple childhood vignette—something about him losing an expensive toy in the garden—but successive episodes had dragged him through the mistakes, reproaches and failures of a lifetime. Each new horror had raised a different question about his character or purpose. In the last one he could remember, the statue of Kagoroa had demanded he set himself aflame for not defending Nanokwe.

And despite what he'd promised Mira, he was undecided about how to dispose of the manuscript. Originally, he'd thought to collect it as a kind of *momento mori* for his broken heart. Then, considering its possible historical significance, he'd leaned toward publication, not straightaway but eventually, maybe under a pseudonym or stamped with the arch-insult, 'Anonymous.' He wasn't entirely set on doing that now. The idea of propagating Tarrant's pernicious philosophy got his blood up. The sheer injustice of it... But suppose he made serious alterations, included a few Socratic dialogues presenting Columbia as the superior thinker...

If only he could revise that dire prophetic vision so easily. The tragedies of ordinary life—fatal traffic accidents, summer picnic drownings, missing children, terminal illnesses without warning—offer glimpses of the humbling end. But we're compelled to forget or ignore them in order to carry on. The vision Tarrant shared was another order of dread altogether. As much as Ridge tried to dismiss it as a berserk form of wish-fulfillment, it persisted at the margins of every thought. The image-cycle swirled around him, a story unfinished, untold and probably untellable. It was the kind of fantastical story, he'd decided, that had to be lived through to the end rather than known. All he could do was observe things with a heightened double vision, trying to connect the ever-shifting present to the bedeviled future. He had to admit a grudging respect for Tarrant on one level: the man was willing to burn for his beliefs rather than endure a slow decay.

Ridge leaned on his driftwood walking stick as if decades older. He felt like he'd given up all of his years at once: his comforting romance with Mira; the personal triumph that could've launched a long and exceptional political career; his very sense of himself. Tarrant may have released him from the void but he remained lost and in despair, anticipating the time when the world in its billions would be compelled to join him.

FINIS

NIGHTSCAPE
THE DREAMS OF DEVILS

His Nightmares Corrupt
the Waking world…

Sixteen-year-old math prodigy Case Tannahill has suffered chronic nightmares ever since he can remember. They're so bound up with who he is that he calls them 'threaded dreams.' But the meaning of these night terrors seems forever lost to him.

Until one October morning when Case and fellow high school seniors Kat and Troy are drawn into a neighbor's corn patch by a scarecrow come to life. Investigating further, they're plunged into a shared, life-altering nightmare that threatens to collapse all of reality.

Available at Amazon and other fine retailers